BLOOD AND STONE

SUZANNE DOWNES

ASHRIDGE PRESS/COUNTRY BOOKS

Published and distributed by
Ashridge Press/Country Books
Courtyard Cottage, Little Longstone, Bakewell, Derbyshire DE45 1NN
Tel/Fax: 01629 640670

ISBN 1 901214 26 2

British Library Cataloguing in Publication Data.
A catalogue record for this book is available from the British Library.

This book is a work of fiction.
Names, characters, places and incidents
are either products of the Author's imagination
or are used fictitiously.
Any resemblance to actual events,
locations or persons living or dead,
is entirely coincidental.

Printed and bound by:
Antony Rowe Ltd, Eastbourne

AUTHOR'S NOTE

All the titles to each chapter are taken from the Celtic Myths and Legends and were chosen to (vaguely!) reflect the happenings in each chapter.

By the same author
The Devil Drives A Jaguar

For Zoë,
with Love,
Suzanne Downes.

15th October, 2005.

CHAPTER ONE

"The Lady of the Fountain – a shining vision in gold appeared to young Owain as the fairest, noblest, most chaste, most generous woman in the world."

"Where the hell are my walking boots?"

Fliss sat two year old Megan on the bed and walked to the door, which stood open, "In the hall cupboard," she called back.

"We don't have a hall cupboard!"

She took a deep breath and counted to five, "Yes, we do. It's under the stairs."

"That's the under-stairs cupboard."

"Since when have we called it that?" she muttered irritably, before adding aloud,

"It's also in the hall. Do you want me to come and get them for you?"

"No, don't bother. I'll do it."

There ensued a series and bangs, thumps and crashes that made her wince.

"They're not here!"

She went back to the bed, picked up her daughter and went reluctantly down the stairs.

The hall looked as though a whirlwind had blown through. She made a mental note to throw away at least half the crap that now lay at her feet.

"Come out of it. I'll find them."

Bryn emerged looking dishevelled and bad-tempered, "They are not bloody there! I'm not an idiot."

"Not an idiot, just a man."

5

She put Megan down, reached into the cupboard and withdrew a plastic bag, which she proceeded to upturn so that the disputed walking boots fell out with a satisfactory thud.

"Well how was I supposed to know you'd put them in a bag?"

"Because I told you I had. They were covered in mud and you refused to clean them, so I told you I'd put them in a poly bag."

"That was months ago."

"Yes, it was – and they still haven't been cleaned."

"Not to worry. They'll soon be muddied up again anyway." He gave what he liked to think was a disarming grin. Once it had been. Not any more. After five years he was going to have to think of something a bit more original than that.

"Is that it? Have you finished packing?"

"More or less."

"Do you want something to eat before you go?"

"Nah, I'll grab a bite on the way."

Megan had toddled off into the dining room and was sat playing with her box full of colourful toys. Seeing that she wasn't around, Bryn took the opportunity to grab his wife around the waist and nuzzle up against her neck, "Going to miss me, baby?"

Fliss stiffened slightly; her rigid body did not physically remove itself from his embrace but it might just as well have done, for he felt the tacit rejection even before she said quietly, "About as much as you'll miss me."

"I don't know what the hell your problem is," he whispered savagely.

"No you don't, do you? Perhaps that's part of the problem."

"Oh, for Christ's sake, don't start talking in riddles again. I haven't got time for your angst right now."

"You never have time for it. But don't let a little thing like our disintegrating marriage hold you up."

"Here we go again. Why don't you give it a rest, love? You know it's only the time of the month. Another couple of days and you'll be back to your old self."

She knew he was deliberately saying the one thing most calculated to make her hit the roof, so she chose to ignore him.

"Whatever. Are you planning to make it home for weekends or do I show Megan pictures to remind her who her daddy is?"

"Let's play it by ear, shall we?"

"In other words you want to see how much fun this gang is going to be before you commit yourself to missing out on drunken rampages every Friday night."

He grinned, "Come off it, kiddo. We are talking about a bunch of archaeologists – just how much of a rampage do you really think they're capable of?"

"With you to lead them astray, I dread to think."

"You flatter me."

"Do I? I was trying to insult you."

He laughed and gave her another quick hug, "You know you'll miss me, really. Well, that seems to be everything. I'll ring you."

He hoisted his bag over the pile of junk he had spread across the hall and headed for the front door.

"Aren't you going to say goodbye to your daughter?" Fliss said quietly. He glanced back towards the little girl, sitting, preoccupied on the floor of the dining room,

"Don't disturb her while she's quiet."

Fliss shrugged. She had given up trying to make him take an interest. She followed him to the door and stood on the step as he heaved his bag into the boot, along with all the other paraphernalia he had already packed. He gave her a cheery wave as he drove away, far too fast as always.

She shut the door and leaned against it, her eyes closed.

Should she be upset that he was leaving her alone, possibly for a couple of months? She couldn't remember ever feeling anything but relief when he went away. She must have pined for him once. She dreaded the moment when the silence descended on the house. They had only been married for five years, been together for six. Surely she shouldn't be feeling like this now? How did people manage to stay married for forty, fifty, sixty years, if the caring was dead and gone after only six?

Perhaps it was just her. Perhaps Bryn was right. She was a cold-hearted bitch, who did not have the depth to stay in love beyond the first few blissful months of a relationship. It's just that none of it had been what she had expected.

Bryn was not a new man. He thought his contribution ended with the production of his pay packet at the end of the month. Real men didn't wash dishes or change nappies and anyone who thought differently had been brainwashed by feminist claptrap.

Why had she let herself be swept away by the power of his personality? Why had it seemed like a scene from an old movie when he had come over all Clark Gable? Hot kisses and midnight rides on a Harley motorbike were no substitute for a bit of help around the house. She just wished she had realised it before bringing a child into the equation.

Megan chose this moment to come running down the hall and fling herself at Fliss's legs, "Park, mummy," she said imperiously.

Fliss looked down and smiled at the snub-nosed, pink-cheeked cherub grinning up at her.

"Why not," she said, "Daddy's gone so we can have the afternoon off."

She enjoyed the park. There were a couple of other mums there that she knew by sight and she felt relaxed enough to have a chat with them. Usually she was in a hurry to get home before Bryn began to grow impatient at her absence. He could moan to a World Championship degree. Hadn't she anything better to do than hang about gossiping with women who ought to be at home cooking and cleaning for their hard-working men?

She wished he worked away more often. In between contracts he could be rattling around the house for days or even weeks and on those occasions she felt her every movement was being monitored and found wanting.

She had thought he resented her giving up work to look after Megan, so she offered to go back, even though it was the last thing she wanted to do. He wouldn't hear of it. The very suggestion sent him off on one long rant about how she was trying to undermine his manhood, thinking that he wasn't man enough to earn the money required to keep his own wife and child.

She had had to admit to herself long ago that there were just some arguments she could never win. If she didn't work, she was a lazy, sponging bitch who had no conscience about how hard he had to work to make up for her shortcomings. If she offered to get a job she was not only unmanning him in the most callous way a woman can, she was also an unfeeling cow with not a maternal bone in her body. To even think of leaving her child with a stranger made her cruel beyond words.

She never mentioned it again, even when he was whining about how much she was spending on the housekeeping.

She let Megan have chips for her tea. Bryn didn't allow her to eat what he called 'rubbish', even though he rarely ate anything else. She had to make two different meals every night.

Even while she cooked, she couldn't quite believe that she had let herself fall to this level of submission. Why didn't she just tell him to take a running jump? That she would feed her child anything she chose and if he didn't like it, he could lump it.

She was tired. That was the real reason. She was sick and tired of every single thing becoming an issue to be fought over. It was so disheartening to quarrel and so much easier to just give in. She knew she shouldn't, but it wasn't easy to dredge up the will-power to fight on. Occasionally she would still find the energy to fight on Megan's behalf, but she had long since ceased to bother for herself.

Megan dipped chips in tomato sauce and smiled happily at her across the table, her face smeared red, her fingers dripping.

Small things please small minds, she thought, filled with contentment at the sight of her baby's happy face – and she didn't mean Megan, she meant herself. She was getting a real buzz from knowing that if Bryn were here he would be appalled at the mess his daughter was making.

When the door-bell rang, Fliss froze for a moment, the horrid thought that it might be Bryn back for some forgotten item filling her with dismay. Then she mentally shook herself. Don't be ridiculous. He wouldn't ring the bell. He had a key.

She left Megan in her high-chair – she was safely strapped in – and went to answer the door.

As soon as she opened it she found herself thrown backwards

9

by the violent entry of the two men on the step. She was smashed back against the wall, all the breath forced from her lungs and could only watch in helpless horror as they strolled in and slammed the door behind them.

She opened her lips, intending to scream, but the taller of the two men simply placed his hand over her mouth and said casually, "Don't waste your breath, love, there's no one to hear you."

The shorter man reached into his coat pocket and Fliss thought she would pass out with utter terror. She imagined he was reaching for a gun and her relief was palpable when he simply drew out a packet of cigarettes and a lighter.

"Are you Mrs Elmsworth?"

She nodded, her eyes wide.

"Good. I hate it when we get given a dud address. Now, are you going to be a sensible girl?"

She nodded again. She didn't really have a great deal of choice in the matter. The big man removed his hand from her face.

"We're looking for your husband. Would you like to tell us where we can find him?"

"I don't exactly know," she whispered.

The expression of the second man changed in a moment from impassive to twisted and cruel, "Wrong answer, sweetheart." He nodded to his companion who took something from his inner coat which he held directly under Fliss's nose. At the press of a catch a flick knife blade shot out, missing her face by a fraction of an inch. Startled she shied her head away and cracked it against the wall behind her.

"No, really..." she stuttered frantically, "I'm telling the truth. He's gone on a dig. Somewhere up North. I don't know the exact location..."

Megan chose that moment to call imperiously, "Mumma, want ice-cream!"

Both men looked towards the door, then they exchanged a glance, grinning delightedly.

"Let's see if the baby can refresh your memory, shall we love?"

"No..." Fliss found herself being bundled into the dining room.

As soon as she saw Megan she tried to break free and run to her child, but the big man held her arm in a grip that made her wince.

"Please," she whispered desperately, "Don't hurt my baby! What do you want?"

"Your husband owes us a lot of money, love, and we don't appreciate being let down."

Her surprise took over from her fear for a few seconds, "Bryn owes money?" she asked incredulously, "What the hell for?"

"Look, love," said the shorter man impatiently, "we're not a bank. We don't ask you to fill in a form telling us the purpose of the loan. We just hand over the money and expect you to be sensible enough to keep up with the repayments."

The taller man spoke unexpectedly, "He wanted the latest computer."

"What?" Fliss and the other man spoke together.

"He said he needed a new computer for his work. State of the art – and it cost a pretty penny, if he was to be believed."

"I can't believe this," said Fliss with barely concealed fury, "What the hell was he thinking? Why not just go to our bloody bank manager, if it was for a new computer?"

"I suggest you ask him that. In the meantime, he owes his first payment of three hundred and fifty quid."

"Three … I haven't got that sort of money!"

"You'd better find it – or tell us where we can find your man," said Shorty, as Fliss had begun mentally to call him, flicking his cigarette butt across the room so that it flew past Megan's face and landed, still smoking, on the carpet by the French window.

Fliss gasped in shock and tried once more to break free, but he still held her and merely grinned at her struggles, "I thought we'd agreed you were going to show a bit of sense?"

"Look," she said furiously, " I don't know where the hell he is. Do you really think I would protect the jerk who has put me and my baby in danger from ugly gangsters like you two?"

Shorty roared with laughter, and Long-shanks joined him, "Don't the middle classes have a quaint way with words, Chris? Gangsters, eh?"

Fliss blushed to the roots of her hair, "Whatever you are, gangsters, drug-dealers, loan-sharks, I don't really give a toss, just leave my baby alone and get out of my house."

"Not without an address or a wad," said Shorty, his face sliding into its habitually threatening expression, all trace of laughter wiped away.

"Then take the computer. It's upstairs – and as far as I'm concerned, you're welcome to it."

"What the fuck do I want with a computer? Get real, love."

"Can't you sell it?"

"Yeah, for about a third of what it cost. Stop playing silly buggers. Just ring your man and tell him to get his arse back here unless he wants to see his pretty wife and daughter as patients of the local plastic surgeon."

"Please don't do anything to her," begged Fliss, panic setting in and making her voice quiver on the edge of tears, "I can't ring him. He doesn't have a mobile – state of the art computer, yes, mobile phone, no! Just give me twenty four hours. In the morning I can ring the University and find out the exact location of the dig."

Shorty hesitated for a moment, looking at her, as though trying to read just how trustworthy she was. He seemed to decide she was harmless, because he shrugged and conceded, "You've got 'til tomorrow at noon – we'll be back and you had better have something for us – or your husband will be attending another sort of dig – he won't be looking for bones, he'll be making them."

"I promise I'll get hold of him and he'll pay you."

"He better had."

He had the nerve to ruffle Megan's hair before he made for the door. Fliss rushed to her baby's side, sobbing with shock, horror and fury. Long-shanks grinned at her, "Bye, love – and take some friendly advice. The faintest whiff of the rozzers around here tomorrow, and you'll be watching your back for the rest of your life, understand?"

Fliss nodded, her tears dripping onto Megan's head as she pressed her close against her breast, "Just go away!"

She heard the front door slam and she ran out into the hall to make sure they really had gone. Pulling the curtain aside she peered through the side window and watched as they drove away in a large silver car.

She ran to the telephone. Her hands were shaking so much that she could barely press the buttons, but after a couple of false starts she managed to reach the number she required.

"Mum? Hi, it's Fliss. Listen, I can't talk now, something urgent has come up and I really need to borrow your car for a couple of days."

"Really, Felicity, you know I don't like you to borrow."

"Yes, I know, and I wouldn't ask if it wasn't important."

"You sound upset. Is everything all right?"

"No, that's why I need to borrow the car," Fliss couldn't keep the edge of impatience and near-hysteria out of her voice any longer.

"Very well, dear. Come and get it as soon as you're ready."

"You'll have to bring it here. I'll drop you back at home on my way out."

"That's not very convenient, dear."

"Just do it, mum. I haven't time to argue." She replaced the receiver.

She was going to drive to the Peak District and find Bryn Elmsworth – and then she was going to strangle him with her own two hands.

CHAPTER TWO

"Ethne; a gentle maiden who was lost to the Otherworld when she mislaid her cloak of Invisibility."

Her mother arrived about half an hour later, during which time she had fallen apart, then pulled herself back together again. She couldn't believe Bryn had been such an idiot. How could he have risked getting involved with those dodgy characters — and all for a bloody computer?

Mrs Cottrell was, not surprisingly, astounded when Fliss responded to her ringing of the doorbell by securing the chain on the door and peering suspiciously through a gap about two inches wide.

"Oh, it is you. Good. Come in."

For once her mother was rendered almost speechless. She walked into the house, an expression of complete incredulity adorning her features.

Sadly for her, nothing became any clearer when she entered the sitting room and found that Fliss had packed a holdall and was endeavouring to close its zip over its bulging contents.

"What on earth is going on?" she asked, curiosity being the key to restoring her tongue, "I thought Bryn said you weren't going with him."

"I wasn't. There has been a change of plan. I need to go away for a few days."

"Why?"

Fliss looked up from her task, "I'm sorry. I can't tell you. Just please understand that I really need to get to Bryn."

"I think," said her mother firmly, "That since you are expecting me to manage without my car that the very least I deserve is to know the reason why."

The last thing she wanted was to allow her mother enough ammunition to fire for the next five years. Hearing that Bryn had fallen into the hands of moneylenders of a less than salubrious sort would provide fruit for endless lectures — because, no matter how Fliss tried to convince her, it would all be Fliss's fault. Her mother would know, beyond any shadow of doubt that Fliss had been over-spending and forcing "poor" Bryn to these extremes.

"If it was my affair, mum, I promise, I would tell you. But this concerns someone else and I really can't break a confidence."

That seemed to do the trick. With a pained sigh, her mother held out the keys to her daughter.

"No, I need you to drive back to yours, mum. And we'll have to wait for it to go dark, so that I can pack the car."

"Now you're just being silly!"

"No, take my word, I'm not. I'll explain everything when I get back. Could you do me a huge favour and keep an eye on Megan whilst I finish packing and then lock everywhere up?"

With very bad grace, her mother did as she was asked. Within half an hour, the sky had darkened enough to satisfy Fliss that she could pack the car without attracting too much attention.

Her mother watched impatiently from the front step as Fliss sidled down the path, crouching below the line of the hedge.

"Your silly mummy thinks she's training to be a spy," she said huffily to the bemused Megan, "If she was a few years younger, I'd put her over my knee."

"Knee," said Megan intelligently, pointing to her own chubby limb. For the first time since her arrival Fliss's mother smiled, "Yes, knee, sweetheart, you're such a clever girl."

"Clever girl."

Conversation on the road to Fliss's childhood home was stilted to say the least. Though her mother tried hard to draw Fliss into spilling her secrets, she had no luck. Fliss confined herself to one word answers and besides, she was lying across the back seat, her head below the windows, whilst Megan was occupying the front seat next to her grandma, safely strapped into her car seat.

Fliss refused to go into the house, merely clambering out of the back seat, pecking her mother dutifully on the cheek, and driving off, but not before peering suspiciously around to see if she was being followed. Satisfied that for the moment she was safe and unobserved, she gave her mother a distracted wave and headed for the motorway.

After an hour she was exhausted. The rush hour traffic, with a fractious three-year old, and a rumbling stomach were not ideal driving conditions. At the first opportunity she pulled off into a service area and took Megan in search of food and entertainment.

They managed to kill a mind-numbingly boring hour with an indifferent meal and endless games of "round and round the garden" until Fliss decided that the traffic had probably died down sufficiently to allow a less stressful journey.

It was after nine o'clock when she finally reached the Peak district and she suddenly realised that her brilliant plan of finding Bryn and making him either go home with her or pay up the money he owed had certain flaws. For a start, though she knew in theory where he was, in reality she had no idea. She had the address of the farm, but that was all. No directions and no clear notion of where exactly it lay in relation to where she now found herself.

Obviously there was no other choice than to find a B and B, get some sleep and start fresh in the morning.

She stopped at the first little dangling sign she saw which bore the welcoming legend, "Vacancies". The greeting she received, however, was less than she had hoped for, being the sight of a sour-faced individual who upon spying the sleepy Megan in her arms, tried to close the door saying, "Oh no. No children or animals!"

Fliss didn't know where she found the courage, but she was tired, scared and hungry. She pulled the age-old stunt of firmly putting her foot in the door and began to cajole, "Oh come on, don't be so miserable! You can see for yourself that she's a good kid. It's long after her bedtime and she'll be asleep in no time."

She never knew whether it was Megan's angelic expression, her own determination or the fact that the woman had no other guests, but the door reluctantly opened a fraction more and she was allowed to cross the threshold.

"Very well, but I'm warning you, if she starts kicking off, screaming and crying, you're out — middle of the night or not!"

"Fine, but we both need something to eat."

The frosty look returned, "I think you'll find that the sign outside clearly states "Bed and Breakfast" – no mention of evening meal, and certainly not at this time of the night."

"Fine, we'll have our breakfast now – and you can have a lie-in in the morning. Either that or we'll have a few sandwiches now and you can add a little extra to the bill."

"Bloody cheek! I knew I shouldn't have let you in."

"Congratulate yourself that you've secured your place in Heaven, taking pity on a child in need. If you show us to our room, we'll freshen up while you make the sandwiches."

When the woman had gone, leaving her unwanted guests in a tiny room, two floors up, under the eaves, Fliss sank onto the edge of the bed, hugging her daughter close and fighting back the tears. Bryn wasn't going to hear the end of this for a very long time.

It was only when Megan's plump little arms crept around her neck and she felt the tiny hands comfortingly patting her back that she began to cheer up a little. So long as she had Megan, she had everything in life that she needed.

A knock at the door made her sit up hastily and wipe away any trace of tears. She wouldn't give the horrible landlady the satisfaction of seeing her weep.

"Come in," she called.

She hadn't thought the woman could have looked any more sour than she had before, but now she looked like she been sucking lemons, "I only had cheese and I only brought it up so the child doesn't have to sit in the dining room at this time of night," she said frostily, determined that Fliss should know how many concessions were being made.

"That's fine, thank you — and I want to apologise. I know I was rude earlier, but I've had one heck of a day and I'm tired and hungry. I really do appreciate your taking us in like this." Fliss had decided in the intervening minutes to get some information and to that end she was prepared to be conciliatory.

The stiff expression relaxed a little, "Yes, well, you've got to understand my point of view. I've other guests to think about and they don't want their peace disturbed with screaming kids."

"Megan will behave, I promise. Listen, perhaps you could help me. In the morning I'm headed for a village called Broadbarrow Loe, do you know it?"

"I do. It's about five miles away, but I wouldn't expect a warm welcome if I were you. They're a miserable lot up there – comes of living so high up on the moors that you spend half your time shrouded in mist and the other half battling against wind and rain!"

"It's really that bad?"

"Oh, aye. It's always two cardigans colder than down here!"

Fliss smiled at the quaint turn of phrase. It said it all really. She just hoped Bryn would freeze his extremities off up there, once she had the money to pay the thugs.

Megan eyed the tray and began tugging at her mother's sleeve. Fliss absent-mindedly handed her a small plate with a sandwich on it. Megan tucked in with relish, happily unaware of the landlady's hawk-eyes upon her for the least sign of a stray crumb.

"I have to find Barrow Loe farm."

"If you find Broadbarrow, then you've found the farm. It all used to be one huge estate, but the family fell on hard times – oh, way back in the eighteen nineties, I think. A lot of the land was sold off. It's ended up a big, half-derelict manor house, with hardly any land still being farmed, surrounded by workmen's cottages, built for the now defunct mine. You only live in Broadbarrow nowadays if you can't afford to live anywhere else, or you have a thing about all this New Age harking back to the Celts stuff."

"So there really is a barrow up there – it's not just a name?"

"Barrow?"

"Ancient burial site."

"Oh, is that what it means? When you grow up with these names, you never think to find out where they come from. Yes, there's said to be a burial ground – but most of the nutters go up

18

there for the stone circle. It drives Ted Armitage mad! He hates trespassers and has been known to fire off his gun at them. He'll get himself into trouble over it one of these days," she added reflectively.

"Is Ted Armitage the farmer?"

"If you can call it that," the woman sniffed derisively, "I've told you, there's hardly any land left and what remains has a bloody great stone circle slap bang in the middle of it! I don't know how he's kept body and soul together all these years. He won't even do what the rest of us have had to do and start up a B and B. He'll only let the select few on his land, I can tell you."

"He's letting strangers on now. My husband is on an archaeological dig up there, That's why I'm going."

"Bloody hell, that's a first. Ted must really be running short if he's letting them dig up his precious stone circle."

Fliss made no reply to this, but it gave her several things to think about. It didn't look as though Bryn was going to have his usual rip-roaring time if the man upon whom their work depended was going to be as unaccommodating as this Ted person.

Fliss began to almost look forward to seeing her husband. She would certainly enjoy watching him being glowered at by a disgruntled yokel.

"Well thanks for the food – and thanks for letting us stay. I really do appreciate it."

Slightly mollified, the landlady took herself off and for the first time that day, Fliss realised that she was starving. She joined Megan on the bed and they ate their meagre repast as though they hadn't eaten for days.

✳

Much to Fliss's relief, Megan kept her promise for her. She slept the night through without a sound – and thankfully without any little accidents in the water-works department. She was usually dry day and night, but after the excitements of the day, Fliss couldn't be sure.

19

It didn't take long to pack their few belongings back into the car and set off once more, though thankfully only a short – though immensely steep – journey on this occasion.

In what seemed like only minutes they were passing signs which announced their arrival in Broadbarrow and thence on to Barrow Loe Farm. The landlady had been right, there was barely any distinction between the village ending and the farm beginning, just two huge stone gateposts, without gates, at the far end of the street. Evidently there was nowhere beyond Broadbarrow, for the road ended at the farm. Once you were here you didn't go anywhere else.

It was, however, a very long drive indeed. Except for the fact that on either side of the track there were only ditches and a straggly hedgerow, with acres of unhealthy looking fields beyond, Fliss felt she might almost have been on that epic journey from the road to the house "Manderley" in the Du Maurier classic "Rebecca". She thought she was never going to reach the farm. She could see its chimneys thrust skyward between stark, bare branches of a group of sickly-looking trees that evidently surrounded it, but the house itself never seemed to get any nearer, until suddenly there was a dip and a twist in the road and she found herself amongst the trees.

It was a larger area of wood than she had been expecting and it was another five minutes of driving through the gloom before she was plunged once more into daylight.

Bright spring sunlight bounced off the now dirty windscreen, temporarily blinding her, and automatically she stepped on the brake, blinking and wincing to clear her vision.

The sight that met her eyes was unprepossessing, to say the least. What had once been a magnificent, possibly Tudor, manor house, stone-lintled, stone-tiled and set square against the prevailing winds, was now a neglected wreck of a place, one side of which was literally falling down. The crumbling wall had been shored up with untidy brick-work that also looked as though it was about to fall. The windows on that side of the house were boarded up, but the section of house that was still in use might just as well

20

have been treated in the same manner, so grubby and over-grown with ivy were the windows.

As Fliss stared, open-mouthed, at the half-ruin, a man came out of the front door and began to cross the muddy yard towards her.

Aware that until she explained her presence, she was technically trespassing, Fliss climbed hastily out of the car to greet him.

"Mr Armitage, I presume?" she asked, then almost giggled at the connotations such an expression possessed, though this was hardly the African jungle and she was no Stanley.

Fliss had real difficulty stifling her laughter when she saw the appalled expression that crossed the man's face, "Good God, no!" he exclaimed, then hastily back-tracked when he realized just how rude he had sounded.

"I do beg your pardon! No, I'm not Armitage," – she could almost hear the unspoken, *"Thank God"* – "I'm afraid I don't know his whereabouts just now, but if you want me to deliver a message..."

"Well, no, not really. I wasn't actually looking for Mr Armitage himself. I'm more interested in the dig..."

"Then you have found the right man. My name is Fergus Ripley – I'm one of the archaeologists."

He held out his hand and Fliss took it, remembering as she did so that she had just been giving chocolate biscuits to Megan and was likely to be sticky. This made her flustered and she stumbled over her introduction, "I'm Fliss ... Felicity and this is my daughter Megan." She gestured towards the car and he lowered his head in order to be able to see into the interior and smile at the dirty-faced urchin, who cheerfully waved a soggy biscuit in his direction.

"Well, Felicity, I'd love to be able to show you around the dig," he said, straightening up, "Normally we welcome visitors – especially if they are likely to offer to help with the initial donkey work, but I'm afraid on this occasion we are under restrictions of a most unusual sort. The owner of the property, Mr Armitage, is, shall we say, a mildly eccentric man who has allowed this excavation only under duress. He has made it quite clear that no-one but a small group of selected persons can, as he puts it, go tramping across his fields. I'm so sorry."

He waited, obviously expecting her to get back into the car and drive obediently away. Fliss laughed nervously, "Oh no, you have me quite wrong. I'm not here as an archaeology junkie! I'm married to Bryn Elmsworth and I need to see him urgently."

"I beg your pardon. I didn't realise. Of course, if you want to see Bryn, then there's no problem. I'll take you to where he's working."

"Thank you." Fliss skirted the car in order to unstrap Megan from her car seat, then hoisted the child up onto her hip, "After you," she said. He eyed her uneasily for a moment, "It's pretty rough terrain – and very muddy. Do you think I ought to bring Bryn to you?"

She met his eyes squarely. "I hate to be a bother, but it might be just as well. I have some straight talking to do, and I suspect Bryn would not be particularly happy to have his colleagues hear it!"

His eyes widened slightly. It wasn't often one heard a comment so bald from a complete stranger. It made him look at her with what appeared to be new interest. She supposed he had just seen her as a young wife and mother, dark-haired and dark-eyed. Now he saw the furious set of her jaw and realized that perhaps his friend Bryn might be in for a rough ride.

He smiled – she thought, slightly wickedly – as though he was enjoying the prospect of witnessing her subdued anger, "Oh dear, ought I to have covered for Bryn and told you that he's not here?"

"It might have been a relief to him – but it's too late now!" she said grimly.

"I'll go and find him. Do you want to go inside the house while you wait?"

"Won't Mr Armitage object?"

"I'll deal with Armitage. I gather you and Bryn need a little privacy."

He showed her into the house, which, surprisingly, was rather tidier and more homely than the outside had led her to believe. The ruined half had been quite effectively blocked off and though the rest was rather dim and dusty, it was warm and furnished, albeit with shabby chairs, thick with dog hairs, and scuffed wooden tables and dressers. Most of it looked contemporary with the fabric of the building and she guessed that some of it would have been worth a small fortune had it been properly cared for and maintained.

Fergus showed her into what must once have been an elegant drawing room, but was now lighted only by the small amount of light that could fight its way past the dirty, ivy-clad window. She sat on the edge of the sofa, Megan perched on her lap, and took the few minutes she was left alone to look around. It was amazing how grotty a room could look when it was crammed too full and not cleaned often enough. Taken individually some of the furniture was gorgeous and Fliss would have given her eye teeth to possess it, but as it stood in that room, she would have been hard pressed to even touch it let alone own it. A roll top desk in particular caught her eye, but it was full to over-flowing with bits of paper, receipts, newspaper cuttings, broken pens, and dog-eared ledgers adorned with cup-rings and spills. She shuddered with distaste. What were the chances that Mr Armitage was a single man?

Bryn came in at that moment with his usual affectionate greeting, "What the bloody hell is going on? What are you doing here?"

Fliss – unusually for her, admittedly – was ready to answer him in similar phraseology, but she saw Fergus had entered the room behind her husband and she bit back the riposte.

"May I assist by taking the little one off your hands for a few minutes Mrs Elmsworth? Will she come with me to see the lambs?" asked Fergus hastily, before Bryn could say anything more.

Bryn's already sallow skin darkened furiously at being so neatly caught out by his employer and Fliss could barely hide a malicious grin, "Are you sure you wouldn't mind, Mr Ripley?" she asked politely. It was Bryn's turn to gloat, "That's Professor Ripley, Fliss – and I wouldn't dream of troubling you, Fergie. My wife won't be staying long, I assure you."

"No trouble at all, Bryn. Take your time. I'll be in the yard or the barn with Megan, showing her the livestock – such as it is."

He held out his hand and Megan trustingly took it. The door had barely closed upon them when Bryn turned on his wife, speaking in a vicious whisper, "What the hell are you thinking? Bursting in here and asking the Professor to baby-sit for you?"

"I didn't ask, he offered," she countered calmly. Inside she was quaking, but was determined not to let him know it.

"Don't get smart with me. What do you want?"

"You've got a bloody nerve! Where do you get off throwing questions at me when you have some explaining of your own to do?"

He looked so startled at this reaction that it crossed her mind to wonder what other secrets he had besides the one she had now uncovered. "What do you mean?" he asked uneasily.

"I had a couple of visitors just after you left, Bryn! Real charmers, who threatened to rearrange mine and Megan's features with a flick-knife unless you came up with the money you owe them."

Was it her imagination or did he actually look quite relieved?

"Is that all? For God's sake, Fliss, grow up! Those are standard methods of extracting payments. No one ever really gets hurt. It's a stupid game. They threaten, you pretend you don't have the money, they threaten more and you pay up. Nothing to get hot up about I assure you."

"Good, then you won't mind giving me the money to pay them and I can sleep easy in my bed, knowing my baby is safe!"

He shifted his feet like a school-boy caught smoking by his headmaster and refused to meet her eyes, "It will have to wait until I've been paid at the end of next month."

Fliss stared at him open-mouthed. She had suspected from the moment the two men had burst in that Bryn didn't have the money to pay them, but part of her had been hoping that she was just being cynical and that he wouldn't really dream of plunging her and Megan into this horrifying situation.

She was silent for so long that he did eventually raise his eyes and look at her, if only to check that she hadn't walked quietly out of the room whilst his gaze had been directed at the dusty floor.

Her expression was such that he could read every one of the various emotions she was experiencing and to see them laid bare made him furiously angry. He did not want to see that she despised him, that she was utterly disgusted that he could do this to his wife and child, that she was afraid and heartsick and appalled.

He was angry with himself, but he directed his spleen at her of course, "Oh for crying out loud, stop looking so bloody tragic. If it means that much to you, borrow the money off your mother. I'll pay her back."

"Oh that's a good idea, Bryn! Give me the choice between a knife handled by a thug at my throat, or one twisting in my back for the rest of my life! Do you really think I would crawl to my mother and admit that despite all her warnings I've married a blithering idiot who thinks nothing of putting his wife and daughter in mortal danger just so that he can have the latest computer?"

"Listen, you stupid bint, I bought that computer for us! How do you think I can earn my living if I don't have the most up-to date technology?"

"Are you telling me that these people," she gestured towards the door and encompassed Professor Ripley and his team in a sweep of her arm, "don't have their own equipment?"

"Well, yes, of course they do, but it gives me an edge when I'm tendering for a job if I can show I have even better stuff than them."

She gave him one last look of withering contempt, "You are so full of it, Bryn! And if you think I'm going home to fend off your two friends, you are very sadly mistaken. I'm not leaving here until you come home with me and sort out this mess yourself."

"I can't possibly leave before next week end. I have acres of moor-land to survey."

"Where are you staying?"

'There are a couple of caravans around the back of the farm

25

house, and a huge old barn with a wood-burning stove and camp beds."

"Then you had better find a couple of beds for me and Megan, and get our sleeping bags out of the car, because I'm not leaving without you and I can see that affording a B and B is now very much out of the question."

"You can't just invite yourself to stay here. Hasn't Fergus explained about Armitage?"

"He has, and I don't give a toss. Mr Armitage is your problem, love!"

She crossed the room and wrenched open the door. Out in the hallway, it took her a moment to remember which way she had come in, but as she could feel Bryn coming up behind her, she took a risk and plunged in what she hoped was the right direction.

CHAPTER THREE

"Donn, God of the dead, who gathered souls around him as they assembled on his stormy island before setting out on their journey to the otherworld."

As he had promised, Fergus was in the farm yard, holding Megan safe as she perched on a five bar gate and squealed with delight at the sight of an exceptionally muddy pig. He turned with a smile as he heard Fliss squelch towards him, "She likes pigs," he said.

"She should – she has one for a father!" Fliss muttered, then blushed to the roots of her hair, "I'm so sorry, I shouldn't involve anyone else in my domestics. Please forget I said that, it was unforgivable."

"Unforgivable to say it – or unforgivable to say it aloud? Don't answer that, I'm just being ... what's the word?"

"Male?" she asked wryly and they both laughed.

"Whatever Bryn's done, I'm sure you'll forgive him. Young love was ever a rocky path to travel."

"Yeah, yeah. I'll bet you win your wife round with that one every time."

"Not me, I was never lucky enough to catch Miss Right in a weak moment."

"I find that hard to believe."

She meant it too. He was a good-looking man, about thirty, she would guess, noting his strapping shoulders and tanned skin, as men who work outdoors often possess. He grinned wickedly at her, well aware of her admiring glance and she couldn't resist returning the smile, even though her run-in with Bryn had left her seething. It was so long since she had been alone in a strange man's company, she had forgotten how easy it was to say things with a double meaning, or that could be misinterpreted as flirting. What on earth would he think of her if he imagined she was one of those dreadful married women who ran around behind their husband's backs, panting after anything in trousers?

In an attempt to deflect attention from her bad manners and the gaffe, she added, "I suppose I ought to ask your permission – even though it will have no effect on the outcome – but I've told Bryn that I'm not going home unless he comes with me. He insists he must stay until next week-end at least, so I'm afraid I'll be sticking around. I hope that's not too much of an imposition?"

"Are you asking for permission or telling me?" His amiable grin took the sting out of the words and she smiled back, "I suppose I'm just telling you, aren't I? But things are always better tied up in a pretty pink bow."

"I'll take your word for that. As it happens I'm not the real boss, just one of the troops, but Professor Norton isn't here right now, so we'll just have to take his agreement for granted, won't we?"

"Looks like it."

"Well, if you are here for the duration, would you like me to show you around? I've just seen Bryn storm out of the house with a face like thunder, so I don't think he'll be offering you a guided tour."

"I'd love it, thanks." She was about to follow him when a sudden thought struck her and she gave an involuntary exclamation, "Oh hell!"

"Something wrong?"

"Too right there is! I borrowed my mother's car to get here and I was so intent on confronting Bryn that I completely forgot that I ought to phone her and let her know we'll be staying. She's not going to be happy. I don't suppose you know where the nearest phone-box is, do you?"

"I imagine there's one in the village, but don't worry about that. You can use my mobile."

"Oh no, I wouldn't dream of it. It'll cost a fortune."

"Nonsense. Be my guest."

28

"You must let me pay for the call, then."

"Look, just use it will you?" He took the phone out of his pocket and showed her how to work it, then discreetly took himself and Megan off a few yards to afford her a little privacy.

It hadn't taken much imagination to guess that her mother was livid on hearing her news. Of course she didn't actually tell her daughter to bring her car back, she just whined for ten minutes about how inconvenient it would be without it. Fliss wasn't particularly impressed. She could always use her husband's car – she just didn't want to. It was much more fun to make Fliss feel a thorough heel. In the end she just lost her temper – something she tried very hard not to do with her mother, but her nerves were shredded and Fliss just wanted to be left alone.

"Look, if you really need it that much, get dad or Daniel to run you up here and pick it up – but I'm not leaving without Bryn and that's final."

Her mother hung up on her.

Fliss ended the call and walked over to give Fergus his phone back, "All done?" he asked. She merely nodded and followed him as he crossed the farmyard and skirted around the old house, through what had obviously once been a rather nice little kitchen garden, where shrubs and tatty herbs grew wild and unkempt and tried their best to fight off the constant and unremitting invasion by lesser species. Being late March, none of the plants was doing particularly well, not even the weeds, but the remnants of the battle lay, temporarily defeated, united in death and decay, until the onset of spring and a whole new phase of the war.

Fliss liked gardening and she quickly spotted one or two little gems amongst the debris, but with a mental shrug she tore her gaze away. Not much point in hoping for leave to wage a rescue mission. If Armitage couldn't even be bothered to maintain the roof over his head, then there was not much likelihood that he would care about his garden.

They trod an ancient brick path down the centre of the devastation, then exited the garden through a gateway in the high stone wall, where the remains of a broken wooden gate hung

29

askew, a gathering of the most spectacularly coloured fungi, lichen, mould and moss clinging precariously to it. The sound of dripping water made Fliss turn back as they walked through the arched opening. Set at the base of the wall, almost obscured by browned ferns and a tangle of brambles was a stone trough, full to overflowing with black water and aged sludge, its use as a water trough obviously long-since abandoned, yet still a corroded pipe fed it with a constant dribble of rust-stained water. She could see tall, knobbly sticks which spoke of a summer of foxgloves and thought that though over-grown and neglected, the trough had probably looked remarkably pretty just a few months before.

She opened her mouth to say as much to Fergus, but he had forged on ahead and she was obliged to hitch Megan onto her hip and hurry after him.

There was a short walk across a field then they were once more amongst the trees which surrounded the farm. This time the path led upwards and as they progressed, so the way became quite considerably steeper. It was no surprise that the house was more or less invisible from the road, for it lay in the bottom of a hollow the rising sides of which were covered with a wood which even to Fliss's unpractised eyes seemed to be of a considerable age. Not for Armitage the money-spinning planting of ugly pines. He had evidently maintained a tiny portion of ancient forest – and maintained it rather better than he had his home. She spotted beech, oak and hazel before her sketchy knowledge gave out. The fact that few of them yet bore any foliage didn't make recognition any easier.

The path was clear and obviously well-used; the trees strong and disease free. There were occasional neat piles of sawn logs, and fallen branches had been pulled clear to prevent them becoming rotten and thus infecting nearby trees. But amongst all this care, there was a distinctly unpleasant atmosphere. The trees seemed – and Fliss felt stupid even thinking it, but it was nevertheless her opinion – oddly threatening and secretive. The only time she had ever felt this way before was when she had been in places where bad things had happened. It was the sort of thing her mother had chastised her for saying when she was small and which she had, as a consequence, ceased to allow herself to indulge in. For no reason she could fathom, she didn't like this wood.

When Megan nestled her face into her mother's neck and gave a tiny whimper, Fliss realised with a slight shock that her little girl didn't like being there either.

They climbed on for about ten minutes more, too breathless for conversation, then the trees began to thin out and almost before she knew it she was stepping from the confining shadows into brilliant early spring sunlight and a vast expanse of moor. Her first impression was of flatness, almost like calm water spreading out before her eyes, but as with the ocean, the picture was a false one. Of course the terrain was level when compared to the hill they had just climbed, but it was no more flat than the surface of the sea. She learned that as soon as they began to walk upon it. Undulations gave way to cracks in the peaty soil; whole chunks of earth had fallen away, leaving livid reddish black scars amongst the green tussocks. Bilberry and bracken grew in abundance, with odd little pathways winding their way to nowhere, the result of years and years of wandering sheep. Here and there rocks were strewn, grey and dull, scabrous with crusty patches of lichen.

Just ahead were more stones and as they crested another slight hill, she saw them more clearly and realised that this was no natural outcrop, but a deliberate placing of huge upright rocks in a rough circle.

It was neither as neat nor large as Stonehenge, but it was nevertheless a man-made circle. Directly behind it, so perfectly smooth that it was almost frighteningly symmetrical, was a small hill.

She gave a small gasp of shock and Fergus, who had been watching her face for a reaction, grinned and said, "Impressive, isn't it? Can you wonder that John Norton and I have been trying for the past fifteen years – ever since, in fact, we discovered its existence – to persuade Armitage to allow us access."

"It's amazing. One would never guess that anything so incredible is hidden up here. I thought stone circles were always on vast plains like Salisbury."

"Well, I suppose one would have to make use of whatever open ground was nearest, if one felt the need to build something so vast. Of course, Stonehenge will always hold sway because of sheer size, but there are many little spots like this all over Europe."

She was still staring in fascination, questions running through her mind so fast that she could barely marshal her thoughts to voice them, "The hill in the background; that must surely be man-made too? It can't possibly be natural."

"No, that's the barrow for which this area was named. Naturally we are hoping to find a burial of some importance within it. Another Sutton Hoo would be too much to hope for, but of course that is precisely why I'm here!"

Fliss wrenched her eyes away from the stones and looked at him, "I know it is your job, but it seems very wrong to me to disturb the dead – no matter how many eons have gone by."

"I suppose that is the eternal quandary for the archaeologist. When viewed in the cold light of day, it does smack of grave robbing, doesn't it?"

"A bit, I'm afraid," she admitted with a wry smile, well aware that her husband shared in Fergus Ripley's career choice and that she, by association, lived off the proceeds of that "grave robbery".

They began to walk – or in Fliss's case, stumble – across the rippled and corrugated ground towards the stones. Fergus realised she was having trouble carrying her daughter and keeping her feet, so he silently took Megan into his arms. Fliss managed a breathless "Thank you," but could say nothing more.

It was almost a shock to find the place a hive of activity when they finally reached it, for the sheltering stones had given off an air of inviolate peace and solitude. Fliss could have sworn there was no-one there when they had crested the hill, but various groups of people were diligently attending to tasks which looked both messy and mysterious to the newcomer.

She caught sight of Bryn, several hundred yards away, walking his geo-probe thing – as she thought of it – across the vast emptiness of the moor and she nodded towards him as she asked

Fergus, "What's Bryn up to?"

"Testing the area for signs of habitations. We're not sure if this place was purely ceremonial or if there was a community living up here. His contraption should be able to pinpoint any possible foundations of long-demolished dwellings."

"Oh. No-one seems to be doing any digging."

"It'll be some considerable time before we dive in with the spades and trowels. The whole area has to be carefully examined and logged first. We don't only have the circle and the barrow to contend with. A few hundred metres over to the right there is also a peat bog. The fact that the three things form a triangle suggests that the bog may also have ceremonial importance."

Fliss recalled a couple of programmes she had caught on the Discovery channel – Bryn never really talked about his work thinking, she supposed, that she was far too stupid to understand his jargon, "Do you think you might find a bog-body?" she asked incredulously.

"It would be too much to hope for – but yes, I hope we'll find another 'Pete Marsh'!"

"I'm surprised you can contain yourself! I think I would have to jump straight in with a shovel and hope for the best."

"Well, all men are boys at heart and of course I'd love to cut the red tape and get my hands dirty, but as a respectable professor of archaeology, I have to pretend to be clinical and emotionless!"

She laughed, "Now you're just teasing me," she said, looking sideways at him.

"I promise you I'm not." He made a sweeping gesture with his arm, as though escorting her into a ball room, "Let me show you the rest." She went ahead of him between a gap in the stones and into the centre of the circle.

CHAPTER FOUR

*"Ogma – God of eloquence who invented the Ogham script
which was carved on stone, or inscribed on bark or wands of
hazel or aspen"*

It was peculiar to be amongst the stones – very oddly claustro-
phobic. Fliss had never experienced anything quite like it. They
were set closer together than she had been expecting and suddenly
she felt caged in and rather sick. She had perhaps been expecting
stones like those at Salisbury plain, huge and widespread. These
were jagged, ill-matched and with narrow gaps between. And yet
they were still awe-inspiring. There was a curious dignity about the
fact that they had stood for so long, defying wind and weather for
generations. They had stood inviolate when Roman armies
marched across Britain, when Henry VIII had been bumping off
his wives. Wars against Napoleon, The Kaiser and Hitler had not
moved them one inch.

Fergus led her across to the tallest standing stone and pointed
out the barely discernible circular carvings. Hands that had been
dead for perhaps three thousand years or more had etched those
snake-like shapes. Fliss felt humbled and proud in the same
moment. It seemed like a rare privilege to be here witnessing the
strength of a belief that had lasted hundreds of generations of
human life.

Perhaps it was because she hadn't eaten for hours, or the stress
of the night drive, followed by the clash with the land-lady and
Bryn being such a callous jerk, but as she reached out her hand to
touch the carvings, she felt suddenly overcome with giddiness.
There was the loud buzzing in her ears which usually herald a faint

and the feeling of nausea gripped her so that she could hardly stand upright. She realised that she must have gone pale, because Fergus reached out and grabbed her arm, "Steady on! Don't faint on me. I can't hold you and the kid!"

She was dimly aware that Megan was gripping her face and saying, "Mummy, mummy!" over and over again, and it was the sound of her voice that made her focus on fighting off the waves of dizziness that threatened to overwhelm her. She took the child back into her arms, if only to prove she was quickly recovering her equanimity.

"I'm sorry. I'll be okay, it's just that Megan and I haven't eaten since early this morning." She felt the need to explain her extraordinary behaviour, though Fergus had said nothing about it.

He looked relieved to hear her speaking quite normally again. "That's all right, you can eat with us. The gang will be ready to break for lunch soon anyway. Come this way, and I'll find you somewhere to sit until you feel better."

"If you are sure, I'd be very grateful." He led her out of the circle and towards a large flat stone which was just a convenient height to sit on. She put Megan down on it, then slumped down herself and put her head down to her knees, though in truth she'd begun to feel better the moment she left the stone circle. She just thought she had better be sure she wasn't going to pass out and really humiliate herself in front of Fergus and the others.

When she raised her head, Fergus evidently thought she looked better because he said briskly, "We're due to have sandwiches delivered in about half an hour at the farm. Do you want to wend your own way back down or do you need me to show the way?"

He was still quite friendly, but Fliss had the distinct impression that he'd had enough of playing the nursemaid and wanted to get back to work.

"No, I think I can manage. I'll wait in the car, shall I?"

"Either that, or go into the big barn, where we've set up the field lab. You can't miss it."

"Okay. I'll see you in a little while then."

He hovered around for a few more seconds, until she said,

"Really, I'm fine now, and I've kept you long enough," and turned her attention to her daughter. She felt rather than saw him wander away and she gave herself a few more minutes before taking Megan by the hand and leading her back across the springy, sheep-cropped turf towards the wood.

Once back amongst the trees, she rather regretted not accepting Fergus's offer of company. She felt the familiar creeping sensation of the hairs on the nape of her neck rising.

It was the exact feeling she had when she knew someone was looking at her, even though she couldn't see them. Everyone has those sorts of moment, she told herself severely, when the weirdo is watching you on the late-night bus; or the frosty-faced cow in the pub who fancies your boyfriend and hates you for having him. Fliss gave an involuntary shudder. Someone walking on her grave.

She tried to stop herself, but in the end she couldn't help but look behind her, knowing there was nothing to see, but still unable to resist the urge. Even though she was only yards into the copse, the moor was lost to sight, almost as though the trees had closed ranks behind her, trapping her and Megan amongst the trunks.

Stupid, she chastised herself. It was broad daylight and there were half a dozen people within calling distance. It didn't matter how spooked she let herself get, nothing could happen to her.

It was Megan who brought her out of her reverie, by pulling excitedly on her hand and pointing into the undergrowth, "Mummy, look! Pig! Ickle pig!"

Fliss very much doubted her daughter could see a pig, but still she looked to where the child was indicating, her chubby hand still dimpled and baby-like.

There was nothing. The brown and decaying winter under-growth stirred as though something had passed by, but that was merely the wind.

"There's nothing there, sweetheart," she said, after a moment of intense scrutiny.

"Is," insisted Megan, a frown descending onto her brow, "Hairy pig with big teeth."

Fliss recalled the enormous pink porker down in the farm-yard.

No way could it be described as either hairy or toothy. She wondered what Megan thought she had seen. Whatever it was, it wasn't a standard British pig – probably a badger or something.

The sun slipped behind a cloud and a stiff little breeze suddenly blew up from nowhere causing her to shiver again.

"Never mind. Let's go and get some lunch."

Fliss suddenly wanted to be out of those trees – fast.

✳

Now that she had more time to look about her, Fliss noticed several things about the farmyard that she had not seen in her hurry to confront Bryn. There was the usual rusty pile of dead cars and out-moded farm equipment which most farmers seem to think are essential to create an atmosphere of rural bliss, along with a steaming pile of manure, a couple of corrugated iron sheds and cobbles that could be barely discerned beneath a layer of thick, drying, crusty mud, but more interestingly, behind the house and hidden from view unless you knew it was there, stood an old – very old – stone-built barn. Even with her restricted knowledge of agriculture – ancient and modern – Fliss could see that it probably predated the house. The fact that the tiles on the roof were trimmed stone and not slate told her that it was old, and the weight of those same tiles which had caused the roof to sink in the middle in a most alarming manner made the conclusion obvious. Initially she was in two minds whether to enter the building just in case today should be the day that the roof timbers finally gave up trying to support the weight – but common sense told her that if the oak had lasted several hundred years, then it wasn't going to collapse in a hurry and anyway, if Fergus had chosen the place to house his precious finds, he was sure to have checked it over thoroughly first.

Very bravely – Fliss thought so anyway – she led Megan across the field and entered the barn.

It was larger and brighter inside than she had been imagining. She had expected a dark, dusty and mysterious interior, and whilst it was indeed dusty – and festooned with cobwebs that looked a hundred years old – it was shadowy rather than dark. The roof – with its ancient, blackened oak beams – was higher than she had thought, and the large double doors through which she had made her entrance meant that sunlight filtered in, quite adequately illuminating the place.

As she looked around, she realised that the doors didn't provide the only light. At various spots along each wall there were tiny windows, some of which were open and others bearing small wooden shutters, through the gaps and knotholes of which the sun shone. Dust motes danced on these tiny beams and she found the effect quite enchanting; now this was rural beauty at its best! Why on earth did farmers tear down these magical buildings only to replace them with metal sheds which would not look out of place on an inner-city industrial estate? Why would anyone want steel girders when one could look up and see timber beams held together with wooden pegs, the marks and scars left by the adze and the axe still visible after hundreds of years? Frankly she couldn't understand it.

Further investigation showed that Fergus had indeed been very business-like in his approach. The far end of the barn had been swept and de-webbed, and now contained several rows of metal-framed camp-beds, for the moment empty of occupants but bearing folded bedding, ready for the evening.

A vague attempt at ensuring privacy for boys from girls came in the form of canvas partitions strung between the old oak uprights which in their turn supported the roof. It looked surprising clean and cosy and Fliss told herself that sleeping in here for a few nights would be no real hardship – as long as the giant spiders from the front end, who were obviously responsible for the huge webs, didn't decide to stroll down to the far end.

About mid way along the floor, pushed to the walls, were several trestle tables, which held various piles of paper, boxes, bubble-wrap, cotton wool, tape, pencils and assorted brushes and trowels. This was evidently the "field lab" Fergus had mentioned, ready and waiting for the hoped-for finds.

Just in front of the doors stood another table, this one

surrounded by several ill-matched chairs, some obviously old kitchen chairs, others of the fold down type used by sunbathers and fishermen. Fliss imagined this was where the food was to be served and almost as if the thought had prompted the action, she heard the sound of an approach from behind her and a youngish female voice called, "Hi, there. Do you want the food set out the same as yesterday?"

She turned to see who had spoken and was faced by an extremely well-built woman, slightly older than her voice had indicated – she was probably in her thirties rather than her twenties – with red hair that fell in corkscrew curls down to her shoulders, the greenest eyes Fliss had ever seen, and with a plastic bread tray full of sandwiches held out before her, its edge resting on the waistband of her jeans.

"Oh, hello," Fliss responded promptly, realising that the new-comer wouldn't want to stand around for too long bearing the weight of the lunch, "I wasn't here yesterday, but I imagine they'll want everything the same. Can I give you a hand?"

"If you're sure you don't mind, that'd be great. It's a real bummer having to carry everything over from the car. Pity old Ted can't be a bit more friendly and let you lot use the house instead of pushing you all over here."

Fliss followed her back out into the sunshine, Megan trailing behind, too busy looking around to protest she was too tired to walk anymore. "Yes, I had heard he's not the most out-going of characters."

She laughed, "You could say that. Mind you, he's not the recluse everyone takes him for. The rumour is that he'd shoot you as soon as look at you – but it's not quite true."

"Really? In what way?"

"Well, if you are one of these New-Age nutters who show the proper respect for his precious stone-circle, he'll let you tramp up there to your heart's content."

"Oh, that's the secret is it? You have to be a nutter?"

She laughed again, "Oh hell, I've not put my foot in it again, have I? You're not New Age, are you?"

Fliss smiled, "God no! I like my creature comforts too much. Sleeping under the stars and eating lentils cooked on an open fire has limited appeal for me – I barely know what star-sign I am – we Virgos don't believe in all that clap-trap you know!"

She laughed in appreciation of the little joke and held out her hand, "Very good. I'm Pauline, by the way – Polly from the pub."

"Fliss, and this is my daughter Megan."

She glanced down at Megan as if she had only just noticed her, "Forgive me for saying so, but is a dig really a good place to have a kid running around? Aren't you afraid she'll fall in a hole or be spooked by skulls or something?"

"Oh no, you've got the wrong end of the stick – I'm not really with the dig as such. My husband is – I'm just here for a visit." Fliss used the word "visit" for want of a better one. She hadn't been overwhelmed with feelings of welcome so far from her furious husband.

"Oh, I see. Sorry if I sounded rude."

"Think nothing of it – you did have a point, after all."

Fliss had been about to ask her the name of her pub, but as they approached the farmyard her little mini-van stood there, the name emblazoned on the side for all to see, "The Weary Sportsman".

"What a great name for a pub."

She smiled, "Do you think so? It's pretty old. Originally the sign was a picture of a huntsman resting on his gun, before that a Robin Hood type with his bow and arrow. Nowadays it's a cricketer leaning on his bat. Hunting scenes don't go down too well with the New Age-Love-Every-Living-Creature crowds."

"I can imagine."

She opened the back doors of the van and handed Fliss another bread tray, whilst she grabbed a crate of bottles, "This should keep 'em going for a bit."

They carried their burdens back to the barn and then Fliss helped her unpack and set the table out with trays of cling-film covered sandwiches and pies. The crate didn't just hold bottles of beer, as she had been expecting, but also soft drinks. The second bread tray had contained paper plates, plastic cutlery and two large flasks, one holding tea, the other coffee.

"Do they have this sort of spread every day?" Fliss asked, rather surprised.

"Yeah – I reckon there's someone with quite a lot of money behind this dig. They've not stinted on anything. They all eat in the pub every evening too – though they have to pay for their own drinks!"

"Bryn never said anything about a backer. I imagined it was just a University dig – something to keep the students occupied during the holidays."

"I don't think so. From what I've heard, they're having portaloos, JCBs, all sorts of stuff and still more diggers once the ground has been surveyed. I've been told to expect to cater for at least twice as many come the summer."

No wonder Bryn had felt he could risk taking out a huge loan – it seemed his living expenses were going to be negligible if what Polly was saying was true, and his fees for professional services were going to be far more than his wife had been led to believe. What other explanation was there? And what else wasn't he telling her?

Fliss decided to change the subject – she was getting close to losing her temper again and saying things she would later regret. She didn't particularly want this woman, nice as she seemed to be, to be her confidante in her marriage problems.

"Tell me about the village. It's a quaint little place, from what I saw when I drove through. Have you always lived here?"

"Oh aye, born and bred. I did go to London for a few years – doesn't everyone? – and that's where I met my husband. We both soon got sick of the rat race and it was back here – of course it helped that my dad had died and I inherited the pub!"

Fliss thought this was a curious way of phrasing this remark, but it seemed politic not to mention it.

"It must have been nice to come home – same old places, same people. When I married my husband, he tried to move me as far away from my roots as he could manage – though unfortunately for him having a baby meant he failed miserably. It was one of the few things I put my foot down about."

"Good for you. Show 'em their place, that's my motto. Well, there were a few familiar faces – like Ted Armitage – not that I'd ever been his bosom buddy, though we were at school together – but quite a lot of the old villagers had moved out and sold at a huge profit to incomers wanting to find the "good life" in the country-side. There's no jobs round here, you see. Farming's dying on its arse and we're too far away from any towns or cities to comfortably commute, especially in the winter. Broadbarrow Loe is a miniature theme park these days, haven to the New Age crowd wanting to "chill out", computer nerds who can afford to work from home, or the millionaires who've made their pile and want to pretend to be Lord of the Manor. You wouldn't believe the cut-glass accents we hear in the pub of a night! Still, I'm not com-plaining. Chardonnay earns me a crust just as cider used to."

"What happened to the people who used to live here?"

"One or two hang on, but most moved to town, took up an offer of Council housing and put the profit they made from their cottages into an ISA for their old age. The ones I feel sorry for are those who had tied cottages belonging to Douglas Merrington. He managed to get away with giving them a few hundred quid each to move out, then he sold the property on to his old school friends or property developers. His Stately Home of England is now a posh health farm, with a swimming pool in the orangery and "fresh country produce" on the menu – but which country? That's the question."

"Typical," Fliss said cynically, but added, "Though, to be fair, I suppose he had to survive somehow."

"Yeah, well there's ways of doing it without hurting people, don't you think?"

"I'd like to think so."

Further conversation was curtailed by the arrival of the first "diggers" coming down off the moor, Fliss's husband included. Trust him to be first at the feeding trough, she thought unkindly, though accurately.

Polly said goodbye, "Are you coming down to the pub

tonight?" she asked.

"Don't think so. No baby-sitter."

"Bring her down with you, early doors. If not, I'll see you tomorrow when I bring the lunches up again."

"Actually I could do with finding a shop and buying a few bits this afternoon. Would you have time to show me where everything is later?"

"Sure, no problem. See ya."

Soon Fliss was surrounded by Bryn's colleagues, who all smiled in a friendly way, before grabbing what food they could. Bryn of course made no attempt to introduce her to anyone, so she sat herself next to the quietest-looking girl and struck up a conversation with her. If Bryn thought he was going to drive her away by getting everyone to ignore her, he had another think coming.

CHAPTER FIVE

"Lleu had to turn into an eagle to escape his murderous wife."

Bryn walked past her, his face stiff and unsmiling. She decided to try and break the ice – after all, she was going to be here for a few days so they might as well try to be civil with each other.

"Found anything interesting yet?" she asked. He threw her the most cursory of glances,

"What's it to you?"

Fliss noticed that Fergus had walked up behind Bryn and when she caught his eye, he raised a brow. Utterly humiliated, she tried to make light of the situation, "Now you see why I don't come away with him more often," she remarked lightly, but redness stained her cheeks and she could cheerfully have strangled her husband. Bad enough that they were at loggerheads, but that was no reason for allowing everyone around them to enjoy a free soap-opera.

She turned back to the three girls nearest to her and forced a grin, "Men!"

They all dutifully smiled back, but they were obviously rather stunned. Pride forced her to continue the conversation, though she would much rather have slunk off to lick her wounds, "As you will have gathered I'm Bryn's wife, Fliss – let's face it, he wouldn't speak to anyone else like that, would he?"

"Oh, I don't know. He's had his moments," it was the one with long blond hair who spoke, "I'm Angela, this is Helen and Anne-Marie."

Fliss made a quick mental note of their appearance to help her remember them later. Helen, short dark hair, little round glasses. Anne-Marie tall, auburn and evidently shy, since she didn't meet

Fliss's eyes and merely grunted a greeting.

"I take it you all know Bryn of old, then?"

"We've worked with him before."

"Lucky you."

"Quite!"

"I sometimes think he's only happy when he's on his bloody motor-bike." Fliss commented.

"Does he have one?" asked Angela in surprise, "We've never seen him on it."

"You wouldn't. He had to get rid when the baby came along."

"That's probably why he's such a miserable sod, then," interjected Anne-Marie without lifting her head and continuing to eat her lunch.

Fliss supposed she should have been offended by that, but quite honestly it was a bit of a relief to find out that her husband was every bit as much of a pain with everyone else as he was with her. It sort of spread the blame, somehow. Their marriage had been hurtling towards the rocks for some time and it was nice to know that even though she was on board, he was in charge of the outboard motor. He had made it so obvious that he thought the fault lay with her that she was even beginning to believe it herself.

Luckily she was saved from having to reply to this stunner by Fergus tapping on the table to get everyone's attention.

"Ladies and gents, if I could interrupt your lunch for a moment. I've had a call on my mobile. As with all the best-laid plans, things have suddenly gone awry. Instead of coming next week, as requested, along with the rest of the gang, the mechanical digger and the portaloos are being delivered this afternoon. I'm going to need all the men up by the Circle to help unload and position the damn things."

"How are they getting them up top, Fergus?" asked a youngish man, with the obligatory pony-tail and unkempt beard, "we can't possibly man-handle them through the woods."

"No problem. There is a dirt track across the moors, leading off a narrow lane. The farmers around and about use it to get food and stuff up to the sheep during thin periods. It's tough going, but I understand perfectly passable with a four-wheel drive or caterpillar tracks. Luckily we've not had much rain in recent weeks."

He sat down again and some general chatter started up as people digested this information. Fliss turned her attention to Megan, thus avoiding further discussion with her companions without actually seeming to ignore them.

Just as peace was restored, the insistent jingle of a mobile phone broke in. Fergus answered it, then leaned forward and looked down the table towards Fliss. He caught her attention with a tiny wave of his hand, "Fliss, it's for you," he said.

She was stunned. How could it be? "For me?"

"Yep. Someone who says he's your brother."

The phone was passed down the table, hand to hand, until it came to her. She was bright pink and felt as though every eye in the place was on her. She took the phone as though it had been infected with the plague and spoke hesitantly into it, "Hello."

"What the bloody hell do you think you are playing at, Fliss? Stop messing about and get mum's car back here, now!"

She should have known. It was indeed her brother Daniel – known to her as Denial since that was his chief character trait. As was his wont, he was speaking to her as though she was still three and half years old and a half-wit. She wished someone would manage to get it through his thick skull that once adulthood was attained, the fact that he was older had very little bearing on how he ought to treat her. Not that it would ever make any difference. She was his kid-sister and that was that. She could be ninety and he'd still be condescending to her.

She could only hope that he hadn't spoken to Fergus in the same tone. She hastily left the table and went outside, "What the hell has it to do with you?" she hissed back, once out of earshot of the gathered archaeologists, "And how did you get hold of this number?"

"Never heard of last number recall?" he asked smoothly, obviously delighted to have made his sister lose her temper, "Anyway, it's got everything to do with me. Mum promised me the

46

car this week. Sandy wants mine." Sandy was his fourth wife – or was it the fifth. She'd lost count.

"Sandy always wants yours – usually in order to leave you and run home to her mother. Well, I'm sorry, but I can't bring it back. I'm stuck here for the moment. If you want it that badly, get Sandy to run you here and collect it."

"She's already gone."

"Well, I know they are a mystery to you, Dan, but there are things called buses and trains – they take you places. Sadly you have to pay for the privilege. I know that is an alien concept to you, but sometimes in life, you do have to pay your way."

"Ha, bloody ha! If it comes to that, why couldn't you have used public transport instead of pinching mum's car when I needed it?"

"Because I had an emergency and a child to think about."

"Oh, here we go. The classic excuse trotted out again. Anyone would think you were the only woman in the world to have a kid."

"At least I know where my daughter is. When was the last time you saw your two boys?" That wasn't nice, but he brought out the worst in her.

"Bitch!"

Fliss didn't have the time or the inclination for this. Every time she spoke to her brother and sister recently it had descended into verbal abuse and she hated herself for it.

"Don't use this number again, Dan, I'm warning you. I'll be back next week. If mum really needs her car between now and then, tell her to hire one and send Bryn the bill."

With that she pressed the "end" button and took the phone back to Fergus.

"I'm so sorry about that. I've told him not to ring your phone again."

"It's really not a problem. There was nothing serious he wanted you for, was there? You look a bit fraught."

"No, that's just the effect he has on me. He wanted to know when mother could have her car back, that's all."

"I see. Well, if you are all sorted out, I'll leave you to it. I'm going to have to get up to the site. Professor Norton is going to be livid when he finds out about this mess."

Despite his kindness, she went back to her seat feeling about two inches tall.

✳

Fliss began to realise what Polly had meant when she called the village a "theme park" as she drove back down the long drive after lunch was over. The road she had used to enter the farm sort of by-passed the edge of the village. The main road turned off it and suddenly she was in the heart of things. At the far end was the church, square-towered, grey-stone and looking as though it had stood there forever. Opposite was the village green, behind which was the pub, "The Weary Sportsman" she assumed, though she couldn't see the sign from this angle. The rest were houses and shops. Ordinary at first sight, then on closer inspection, obviously belonging to the "new age" incomers. It was the décor that gave it away. Doors and window frames were painted in colours that ranged from twee to downright bizarre. Cerise, purple, lime green. Admittedly there was the occasional black or white one, but they were few and far between.

She noticed then that though most of the houses had squeaky little swinging signs by the gate, they did not hold the usual "B & B Vacancies" message, but things like "Clairvoyant", "Crystals for sale" and "Herbal Remedies".

Somehow she didn't think she was going to find it easy to purchase kiddie toothpaste and environmentally unfriendly sanitary products, both of which she needed, along with several other non-pc objects.

She decided to head for the pub. Polly had seemed relatively down to earth, as opposed to being a friend of it. She would know where Fliss could buy her few simple items.

She parked the car and released Megan from her restraints, "Come on, kid, let's see what useful information we can get from Polly-at-the-pub."

"Polly-at-de-pub," echoed Megan gleefully. Fliss had a feeling

Polly might get sick of that nickname very quickly.

The door was open and she stepped into the dark interior some-what hesitantly. She had always hated going into pubs on her own. She wished she was a "ladette" and not phased by these things, but she was an old-fashioned girl.

The place seemed at first glance to be deserted, so Fliss had a good look around. It was a typical country pub, dimly-lit and smoky. Half the walls were exposed stone the other half mahogany-panelled. Low yellow ceilings, even lower beams. Various doorways led off into other rooms, some doors closed and forbidding, others open and welcoming. Along with horse-brasses, sepia photographs, horse paintings and pewter tankards, the picture was complete. She thought it was a bit sad that her surroundings had become such a cliché. This pub had probably been like this for over a hundred years, but modern "designer" theme pubs had copied the look and done it to death. Still, she supposed it was what people wanted.

As she ventured further in, she found the pub had one more cliché waiting for her. There was a tweed-clad old fellow sat in the inglenook, reading the Farmer's Weekly, puffing on a pipe and drinking a pint. Actually she didn't know for sure if it was the Farmer's Weekly, she couldn't see the title, but it was bound to have been. Either that or he was doing the Times Crossword.

"Good afternoon," he said, looking at her over the top of half-moon spectacles. Here was one of the "cut-glass" accents Polly had mentioned, and not the country drawl she had been expecting.

"Hello there," she answered shyly, "I don't suppose Polly is about, is she?"

"In the back. I'll call her for you."

He proceeded to do just that, without moving from his seat, issuing a roar that made Fliss's ears ring and Megan squeal with fright.

"Oops, sorry! Didn't mean to startle the little one."

"Bloody hell, Josh," came Polly's voice from somewhere behind the bar, "I'm only in the next room, not the next county."

"Visitor for you, Poll," he replied, scarcely less noisily.

She came through a doorway, hidden from Fliss's view by the optics and shelves of glasses.

"Hello, you," she said in the kind of hearty tone that told Fliss that she had forgotten her name.

"Fliss and Megan here as promised," she said brightly, to save her the embarrassment of having to ask, "Hope you're not too busy to tell me where everything is."

"'Course not. Come on over here and I'll fix us a drink."

"Would it be too much trouble to ask for a cup of tea?" Fliss asked, "I'm gasping for a decent brew."

"Sure, no problem. What will the little 'un have?"

"Anything still – orange, blackcurrant, thanks."

Megan and Fliss sat on a couple of high bar stools while she prepared the drinks and presently Fliss was sipping tea and Megan had a purple gash where her mouth ended and a blackcurrant smile began.

"Now, what did you want to know?" asked Polly, sipping a large gin and tonic and leaning on the bar.

"Just somewhere I can buy life's essentials – toothpaste, jaffa cakes, milk that's never seen a soya bean."

Polly laughed, "They can be found if you look hard enough. Believe it or not, there's a Spar shop down on the left past the church, but I can understand why you thought we all live on tofu. It's a bit "heavy duty" when you first drive into the village. Blame Ted Armitage and Douglas Merrington for it all."

"Why those two? What do you mean?"

"There's a long-standing feud going on between the two of them. Doug knows how much the stone circle means to Ted, so he came up with the idea of filling the village with all this New Age stuff, hoping that the constant trekking across his land would drive Ted mad. If he can sell or rent a cottage or a shop to someone who will infuriate Ted, he'll do it. Ted got his own back by welcoming them all with open arms and making the place a Mecca for the weird and wonderful. Now Doug is stuck with his tenants and is beginning to regret the whole thing."

"I didn't realize Mr Merrington had so much influence – and if it means so much to him, why is Mr Armitage's own house half-derelict?"

"That's all part of the plot. You see, about ninety-five years ago Douglas's great Grandfather lost the family manor house to one of his loyal retainers in a drunken card-game."

"An Armitage?" I guessed.

"Yep. Great Granddad Armitage. The Armitages suddenly moved up in the world. From being servants they were elevated to Lords of the Manor – of course they didn't have the money to back it all up, so a sober and chastened Merrington offered to buy it all back. Nothing he offered would sway old man Armitage. He had what he always wanted and there was no going back. Of course the accusation of cheating didn't take long to rear its ugly head and there followed years and years of court cases and litigation. It rumbled on until the First World War, when Merrington's oldest son was killed. That seemed to knock all the fight out of him. He built Merrington Hall and told Armitage he could rot in his old manor house."

"And the two descendants still carry on the quarrel?" Fliss asked.

"With a vengeance! They hate each other's guts. If one can do the other a bad turn, he will, with relish. I have to make sure neither of them meet up in here, or there's hell to pay."

"It's hard to believe they don't just leave it in the past where it belongs."

"If you stay here any length of time, Fliss, you'll learn that the past encroaches a great deal on the present. Yesterday or a hundred years ago – it makes very little difference in Broadbarrow Loe."

CHAPTER SIX

"Cailte – A Fenian warrior and bard, renowned for his songs and legends"

After she had finished her tea, Fliss and Megan set out to find the shop, which they did without too much trouble, then they made their way back to the car, loaded down with all sorts of goodies that Fliss had not intended to buy. Well, she excused herself, if she was going to be living in a barn for the next few days; she felt she needed some treats to help her through it.

Once she had filled the boot, she decided to have a quick look at some of the other shops on offer in Broadbarrow. Some of them had delightful names and intriguing window displays. One entire shop was devoted to fairies, named, not very imaginatively, she felt, "The Fairy Palace". There were incredibly expensive statues, of china, wood, bronze and crystal; relatively cheap ones made of resin and plaster. There were fairies for the garden, for the car and for the house. There were books of spells, magic charms and talismans of all sorts. Megan was enchanted.

Next door one could buy a crystal ball, a statue of Buddha, joss sticks and dream-catchers. Other shops had clothing of crushed velvet or raw cotton, silk or gauze, floaty and romantic or dark and mysterious. Jewellery was ethnic, large and overpowering, set with stones like amber and jade rather than emeralds and rubies. Not much of it was to Fliss's taste, but she was an old-fashioned girl who liked her diamonds (when she could get them!) The art gallery window was another revelation. One or two of the pictures were prettily pastel, ethereal fairies and elves danced under bright moonlight; but the rest were darkly forbidding, evil faces hidden in tree trunks and rocks, eyes with wicked glints followed one's progress and a generally macabre ambiance flowed from them all. Fliss felt that living with such art work in her house would ensure continuous nightmares, both when waking and sleeping. She shuddered slightly and moved on.

She found it quite odd to have all these shops in the one place. Usually there might perhaps be an occasional one in any town, hidden down a side street, as though landlords were almost ashamed to let such tenants rent a property, afraid the eccentricity of both sellers and buyers might rub off on the "normal" public. It was with the same almost behind-the-hand whisper that a doctor might suggest one could try reflexology or hypnotism to solve a problem that has stumped medical science.

Fliss liked to think of herself as open-minded about all these things – no, let's tell the truth here. She knew she was superstitious, gullible, and naïve. She felt she would quite like a crystal to ward off evil spirits, a tiny "safety" fairy dangling next to her St Christopher in the car and she wouldn't say no to a magic spell that would solve her marital problems and return her husband to the guy she thought she had married. She saw nothing at all incongruous in having the trappings of Christianity alongside the ancient symbols of paganism, being quite happy to go along with whatever religion might work best in her favour at any given time.

She settled for a crystal.

The woman behind the counter barely glanced up when she walked in to the musical jangle of brass bells hung on the back of the door. As she drew nearer she realized the shop assistant was occupied in scrutinising a spread of Tarot cards in front of her whilst consulting a book held in her hand.

"Sorry, be with you in a minute. I'm just at a crucial moment," she said breathlessly. She was a large lady and obviously excited, her panting breaths and red cheeks told Fliss as much. Fliss nodded and began to browse, but not before noticing that she was wearing – to no one's surprise – a deep purple velvet top, ruched with bright embroidery and bearing long, pointed, medieval style sleeves.

"Ah, now I get it!" she said in a triumphant undertone after a few minutes, then addressed her. "Can I help you?"

"I was looking for a crystal."

"For what purpose?"

Now she had Fliss over a barrel. Was this really the place and time to admit she was nervous about sleeping in an ancient barn and wanted something to ward off evil spirits? She thought perhaps not.

"Oh you know, general safety, good health, that sort of thing.

"Do you want one to wear, or a velvet bag full of different sorts to keep under your pillow?"

"Oh, just the one, thanks," Fliss said hastily. A bagful was getting a little too involved.

"They're in that basket there," she said, pointing.

Fliss was confronted with a choice of at least twenty, all different shapes and sizes and even a few different colours.

"How do I choose one?"

"Pick them up one at a time. Your crystal will choose you."

Frankly Fliss thought she was either having her on or was seriously deranged, but funnily enough when she started to handle the stones, she began to see what she meant. Some felt more comfortable in her hand than others, and when she finally found one that felt pleasantly heavy, with facets that were smooth to her fingers, it began, perceptibly, to warm up in her hand.

"I'll have this one." She handed it over and the woman shot her a swift look, part curiosity, part surprise.

"You are psychic, aren't you?"

Fliss laughed, "If I had been, I'd have known you were going to ask me that!" she joked, but the woman didn't smile back.

"I'm serious."

Fliss felt she had been duly chastised for levity, "Sorry. No, as far as I'm aware I'm no more psychic than the next person."

"What do you mean by that?"

She was beginning to get distinctly spooked by the woman's attitude and she almost grabbed Megan's hand and ran for it.

"I don't know. I suppose I sometimes know when the phone is

54

going to ring – and I can get people to ring me by thinking about them. My mother accuses me of being fey."

The woman nodded, as though satisfied with the answer, "Listen, I'm just trying to perfect my Tarot reading. Will you let me do your cards for you?"

The last thing Fliss wanted was a reading of her future by a woman who admitted to being a novice, but how to say no without being rude?

"Okay," she agreed weakly, knowing she was being pathetic.

She looked around, hoping that Megan would be doing something unspeakably naughty so that she could plead her as an excuse and leave, but she was sat on the floor with a basket of soft, bean-filled creatures, happily playing.

No escape. She reluctantly took the cards and shuffled. As she handed them back the woman grinned teasingly, "No need to look so terrified. There's rarely bad news in the cards and if there is, I promise not to tell you."

"Oh no," Fliss said hastily, "Don't hold back, I'd rather know! Forewarned is forearmed."

"Suit yourself – but you'll have to remember I'm still an amateur, so don't go crazy, will you?"

"I'll take it all with a pinch of salt," Fliss assured her.

"Fine. I'm Jacasta, by the way."

Fliss suspected that even a non-psychic could have made a guess at that name.

"Fliss," she said in return.

"What?" As if she was the one with the funny name.

"Fliss," she repeated, "Short for Felicity."

"Oh, I see."

She said nothing more but began to turn over the cards and peruse the spread with an intensity that made her breath come in snorty gasps.

"The first card is The Tower," she said, after several long minutes, "It's surrounded by a tempest, wind, lightning, waves and it is crumbling."

"Sounds cheerful," Fliss said.

"It's not the disaster it sounds. It's merely warning you of the need for strong foundations in your life. I'd say you are not feeling particularly secure at the moment."

"Correct – but to be fair that could apply to more than half the married women in the world – especially if they have children!"

"Okay," she said calmly, "On to the next card, The Devil reversed."

"Oh, you've found the husband," Fliss quipped.

"Maybe. When reversed it means blocked sexual energy and a lack of vision." That sounded familiar.

"Go on."

"Three of Swords, heartbreak unless you learn to communicate."

"Good advice."

"King of Cups – an emotionally mature man, capable of giving and receiving love."

"Definitely not my husband."

"No, I think you are going to meet a new man. That's the vibe I get. But it's not going to be an easy path to happiness."

"No, I should think that the fact I'm already married might complicate things." Even as she spoke, Fliss found part of her hoping the woman was right. Once she had dreamt of meeting the right man and staying married and in love forever, but four short years with Bryn had killed every last vestige of the old romantic Fliss stone dead.

"Well, thanks, that was very interesting, but I'd better get back."

"Are you staying in the district?"

"Yes, just up the road."

"Merrington Hall?" she guessed.

"Nothing so grand. I'm visiting my husband up at the dig."

"Oh, that's going ahead is it? I thought all the protests might have had an effect."

"Were there protests? I didn't know."

"Heavens yes! Not many of us wanted an ancient monument disturbed. There are some things that should be left well alone."

"Sadly for me, I can see both sides of the argument. Being

nosey I love to hear of all the discoveries these digs make, but like you, part of me says 'what's wrong with a mystery anyway?' But let's face it, nothing you say or do can stop progress. I've tried to block enough new housing on green fields to know that!"

"I suppose so. But Ted Armitage might find he's bitten off more than he can chew. What he forgets is that he has to go on living here, when the diggers have gone, and people have long memories."

Fliss felt there was nothing she could add to that, so she called Megan over to her and said goodbye to Jacasta.

"Bye – and feel free to come in again while you are here. I'd love to help you to explore your psychic abilities."

"I don't think my husband wants to me to stick around for all that long." Fliss didn't add that he would also be horrified if she suggested exploring any of her abilities, psychic or otherwise. He preferred her dumb – in both senses of the word.

She was ready to leave after that little adventure, but just as she was heading for the car she spotted a book shop, almost hidden around the corner of the main street. Now that really was something she was short of – reading material. She had been in such a hurry to pack up and leave home, she'd forgotten to bring her latest paperback. Sleep would be impossible without a chapter or two.

Fliss put her tissue-wrapped crystal in her handbag and led Megan into the shop.

Her first reaction was to stop in the doorway and inhale that lovely, musty smell that only old books and dust exudes and then she looked around. It was a mixture of new books and second hand, most of which, astoundingly, were about the occult and related subjects. Somehow she doubted she was going to pick up some light bedtime reading and rather regretted the impulse to come in. Too late to retreat, though. The bookseller had already spotted her and was smiling in a way which was meant to be friendly, but which was rather negated by the fact that he had a greyish set of extremely large and uneven teeth. They reminded her, irresistibly, of the stone circle up on the moors. What was worse, he had rather obviously had salad for lunch and there were shreds of lettuce adhering to the base of one or two of them. She longed to tell him, but lacked the courage, so every time he spoke, she couldn't help but stare in horrified fascination and had to keep telling herself not to use the words "teeth" or "greens" or any other related comment.

"Can I help at all?"

"Well, I was sort of hoping for a novel of some description, but I see you don't really sell anything like that so I'll leave it…"

"On the contrary, madam, we have a whole section in the back devoted to fiction. Let me show you."

Fliss followed him through a low doorway into another room, also book lined, but this time without scary titles like "Ghost-hunting for Beginners" and "Have You Had A Past Life?"

She was soon browsing happily, and though a good number of the titles were of an esoteric bent, there were enough ordinary books to satisfy her. It didn't take her long to find something that appealed and she went back through to the main shop to pay.

She found Megan sitting happily on a tiny chair, drawn up to a little table, a picture book open in front of her. Apparently the bookseller had been taking care of her while her mother looked at his stock. She looked up at Fliss as she approached, "Look mummy," she said, pointing to the photo in the book, "the pig in the woods."

Fliss glanced down and was surprised to see her daughter was pointing to a picture of a wild boar, recently reintroduced to certain areas in the South of England, according to the text. She turned the book back and read the title, "Wildlife of Britain and Europe." Not the book she would have given a bored three-year-old, but perhaps he hadn't any Beatrix Potter or Noddy.

"You can't have seen that piggy, love," Fliss assured her little girl, "They are no boars in the Peak District – at least not as far as I'm aware," she looked to the bookseller for agreement. He was back behind his counter, perched on a high stool, half-moon glasses balanced on the end of his long nose, reading a paper.

"What was that?" he asked.

"It says in this book that wild boars have been reintroduced in certain parts of Britain – that doesn't include anywhere around here, does it?"

"I wouldn't have thought so. Why do you ask?"

"It's silly really, but my little girl is insisting that she saw one this morning."

"Whereabouts?"

"In Mr Armitage's woods. He's not likely to have wild boars roaming around, is he? I understand they are rather dangerous."

"I think I would have heard about it if he had. You say your little girl thinks she's seen one?" He seemed rather too eager for my liking. There was something rather disconcerting about the way he looked at Megan, as though she was an interesting specimen under a microscope.

"I'm sure she's mistaken. Children have great imaginations. Can I pay you for this. We should be getting back."

"Certainly, madam. Are you staying in the district?"

Fliss felt curiously reluctant to tell him, but gave herself a mental shake to stop being so paranoid, "My husband is one of the team digging at the stone circle."

"Ah, I see. I might perhaps have something that would interest you, then."

"Really?" she answered, in her most bored tone, hoping to discourage him, without being too rude.

"Yes. It's an old map of the district. The circle, barrow and manor house are all clearly marked on it. No one seems to want it, when they can have the more up-to-date and accurate Ordinance Survey maps."

Now he had her attention. She loved old maps. They always have things on them that are far more interesting than endless motorways.

"May I look at it?"

"Certainly." He ducked beneath the counter and she could hear him shuffling papers, moving unknown objects and muttering to himself, "I know it's under here somewhere."

After a few minutes of this he emerged triumphant, "I knew I had it."

Even as he handed it to her, she knew she wanted it. It really was very old and had faded to that glorious yellow colour that nothing but age could bestow.

"How much is it?" she asked, without even attempting to unfold it.

"Nothing. If you want it, you may have it with my blessing. I just wanted it to go to a good home."

"Oh no, you must let me pay for it."

"I wouldn't hear of it. Just let me know if your little girl sees any more boars." He grinned and she tried not to be repulsed by another glimpse of the slimy sliver of lettuce. She hastily paid for the book, picked up her purchases and left.

CHAPTER SEVEN

*"Taranis 'the thunderer' a Celtic sky god whom the Romans
equated with their supreme deity Jupiter"*

Fliss drove back to the farm, her emotions hovering somewhere
between excitement and trepidation. It seemed like years since she
had been out of the house and involved in something truly adult
and important – but she really didn't want to sleep in a barn on a
camp bed. It would have appealed enormously to her teenaged self,
but that was some time ago and now she knew the value of a
comfortable bed and warm duvet.

Within minutes she was pulling up in the yard, which was no
longer deserted, but contained a surly looking man who glanced at
her then went back to his task of hosing the filth off his boots.

He didn't say anything until she had helped Megan out of the
back seat, then he grunted, "This is no place for a little one."

The criticism stung, but Fliss forced a smile, "Maybe – but
where I go, she goes."

To her surprise he seemed to approve, "You're one of a dying
breed," he said, with a grim smile.

"I am?"

"Aye, a woman who wants to look after her own, instead of
palming them off on someone else."

"That's a bit unfair. Most women don't have a choice."

"Yes they do – it's called doing without."

"That rather depends on what you're expecting them to do without," Fliss said, but with what she hoped was a note of finality. She
wasn't prepared to go on with this argument. It was bad enough
having it with her husband.

"Aye, I'll grant you that," he said, "Armitage is the name." He held out his hand and she shook it, even though she could see it was wet from the hose pipe.

"I'm Fliss Elmsworth and this is Megan."

"You'll be the geophys's wife then." She was surprised that Bryn seemed to have made enough of an impression for his name to be remembered – but perhaps the male chauvinism in one called out to the same in the other.

"I am, but I didn't realise you knew everyone that well. They've only been here a short while, haven't they?"

He shrugged, "I have a talent for recalling names and faces – not that it usually does me much good, with only cows and sheep for company. There's not much gets past me."

Looking into his heavy-lidded hazel eyes, she could well believe it. They seemed to look right through her and she found herself wondering what he really thought of her, of Bryn and most of all, the whole enterprise of the dig. It was on the tip of her tongue to ask him, but she managed to restrain herself. She scrabbled around her brain for something farming related to discuss with him, but found herself sadly lacking in country lore. The only thing she could recall at that moment was the Foot and Mouth horror of recent painful memory.

"You must have had a tough couple of years. I suppose Foot and Mouth reached you up here?" she asked.

"Oh, aye. I had three times as many cattle and twice the sheep I have now. Why do you think I'm allowing the circle to be dug up after all these years?"

"I thought farmers had been compensated," she said in surprise.

"Of a sort, but not enough – never enough. I was struggling before it happened. And there's no amount of money can compensate a man for having to hold the head of each of his cows while a bolt is put through its brain."

"Oh my God!" she exclaimed with real feeling, "It must have been horrific."

"It was. Still it's over now – and you don't last long in farming if you can't take death as part of life."

"I suppose not." A sudden loud squeal from the pig-pen reminded her of Megan's "hairy pig" and she added, "Tell me something, will you?"

"What?"

"You don't by any chance have wild pigs living in the woods do you?"

He looked at her for a second before saying warily, "No, why do you ask?"

Fliss forced a laugh, "It's so silly really, but my little girl keeps on insisting she saw a hairy pig in the woods. In the bookshop down in the village, she found a picture of a wild boar and said that it was the same as the one she had seen. I know some people have reintroduced them in various parts of the country, so I wondered if perhaps you had done the same."

"No I haven't – but it's a bloody good idea! I wonder I never thought of it myself. They help with the maintenance of the wood. Thanks for the tip."

She had a sudden moment of panic, "Hey wait a minute, don't take it seriously. Boars are dangerous, aren't they? You can't have visitors to the circle tramping through woods filled with deadly animals!"

"There's no need for anyone to go through the woods. Most of 'em use the road across the moors anyway. I may let people visit the circle, but I don't encourage them to tramp across my land and disturb my livestock."

"Oh." There didn't seem to be much more she could add, though she did have a sneaking suspicion that she had opened a can of worms by telling him about Megan's imaginary piggy.

"Well, I'd better let you get on." she added, weakly, by now desperate to get away from him and his crazy ideas.

He made to turn away, and then looked back over his shoulder, "You sleeping in the barn with the others?"

"I'm afraid so."

"There's a small wood burning stove in there. I'll make sure there's plenty of wood in the barn for you. We can't have the little one getting cold in the night."

"That's very kind, but I'm sure she'll be fine in a sleeping bag with me."

"Maybe, but you'll have the stove anyway."

"Thank you." He walked off and she couldn't help noticing how tall and muscular he was. If his face hadn't been so closed and unfriendly, he might have been quite handsome. She wondered how he had managed to evade wedlock – but then perhaps he hadn't. She didn't know for sure that there had never been a Mrs Armitage; she just knew there wasn't one now. Well, whoever she might have been or might be in the future, Fliss didn't envy her. He was an odd man and more than a little scary.

She took her little bundle of purchases to the barn and tucked the cardboard box under the only bunk that didn't appear to be already taken, hoping that there were no rats around to nibble through the packets.

After that there seemed to be nothing else to do but retrace her steps up the hill, through the wood and back to join the others at the stone circle. There was nothing to occupy her in a deserted barn and she might as well have human company as be alone.

Megan skipped happily by her side as they wended their way, her little cheeks pink with the exertion. Fliss reflected that one of them at least would sleep well that night. The little girl would be out like a light the minute her head hit the pillow.

Now that she knew the way, it seemed to take only half the time to reach the stone circle, which she found to be in a state of organised chaos. As had been announced over lunch, the portaloos had arrived and were being manhandled into position, a few metres from the stones. She could see Bryn several metres away, his head down, walking the site with his various instruments, and a couple of companions. She knew vaguely what he would be doing, sending sound waves or some such through the ground to see if there was evidence of buildings beneath the turf. He had tried to explain the principle to her once, but declared she was too stupid to understand. Her own opinion was that he was too impatient to explain clearly – but whichever it was, she never arrived at a conclusion.

She looked around for the three girls she had eaten lunch with, but couldn't see them, so she asked the nearest man to her where they were. He had a pleasant face, looking far younger than she suspected he was, his soft brown eyes smiling before his lips did, "Fergus and the girls are over by the bog – the digger got stuck in the mud on the way past and they are trying to work out how to move it."

She walked in the direction he had indicated and soon saw the folded arm of the digger sticking up above the peaty undulations ahead of her. She and the little girl scrambled over the last rise and she found herself looking down on an expanse of reddish brown water, still, silent and somehow threatening. Not a ripple broke the surface and the reeds and coarse grasses stood ramrod straight, their reflections making them look twice their length. As she drew nearer and looked down into the water, the racing clouds above were mirrored back and gave the curious illusion of looking down from a great height into a strange land below her feet. No wonder the Celts had believed that such waters were the doorways to their Otherworld.

So deeply engrossed was she in these fanciful thoughts that Fliss almost jumped out of her skin and nearly fell forward into the "other world" when Fergus hailed her, "Hi, Fliss!"

"Hello there," she said, recovering herself hastily, "You seem to be well and truly stuck. Got any good ideas on how to get that thing moving?" she added, nodding towards the digger.

"We were just discussing gathering loads of bracken and stuffing it under the wheels, we should be able to get enough purchase to move it."

"Good idea. I was thinking you would have to drag loads of planks and sacks up here but bracken is right on hand. What made you think of it?"

"Not an original idea – it's an age-old method of crossing bogs. The Celts, Romans and even the Victorian railway men used it."

"Really? Clever old them. Mind you, if I were you and I had a digger right there by the water, I'd be inclined to dredge up a few scoops before I moved it – you never know what you might find."

Fergus looked suitably shocked by her irreverent attitude, "We can't do that," he exclaimed, obviously horrified.

"Why not?"

Angela, Anne-Marie and Helen had joined them by this time and were listening with similarly shocked expressions, "Because," Helen explained patiently, "The site hasn't been surveyed, measured, marked out, photographed or anything else."

"I don't see how you could possibly mark out a bog anyway. What harm would a couple of experimental scoops really do?"

Fergus suddenly grinned, "You're a temptress, Fliss Elmsworth." Before the girls could protest, he had swung himself into the cab and was starting up the engine. A puff of foul-smelling smoke heralded the coming to life of the mechanical monster. The arm straightened, stretched and reached like a dinosaur doing yoga. The bucket plunged into the water as far out as Fergus could make it go, dragged itself along the bottom then lifted with a triumphant slurp, water and mud pouring from it in a black cascade. Fergus dumped the bucketful on his far left and then swung the arm back to plunge again. The girls and Fliss exchanged glances, before, of one accord, they all ran towards the rapidly sinking pile of mud and began searching through it for anything of interest.

The third scoop contained the head.

✳

Back in the barn everyone gathered around the newly cleaned object, a respectful silence prevailed. Fergus was the first person to break it, "Well, I never thought I'd ever dig one of these things up. The last one I saw was in a museum in Ireland."

"Why has it got three faces?" Fliss asked, reluctant to show her ignorance, but compelled to find out all she could about the odd stone head that stood before them on the trestle table.

"To be honest, we don't really know. The nearest we can guess is that the number three was sacred to the Celts, for some reason. Bog bodies have quite often been subjected to the so called "triple" death – a blow to the head, followed by strangulation and the final throat cutting."

"Nice," Fliss commented wryly.

"We do know that they saw the head as the seat of knowledge and power – and to make sure enemies were utterly vanquished, their heads were struck off and cast into pools and lakes."

"So we're lucky it wasn't a real head, then?"

"Depends how you view "lucky" Fliss! Personally I'd give my eye teeth for a bog body or any part thereof."

"Charming."

The young man with the brown eyes, who Fliss now knew was called Conrad, Con for short, said bracingly, "Well, we've all seen it now – and I'm ready for a pint to celebrate – who's with me?"

The invitation was universally accepted. Fliss would have preferred not to take Megan into a pub in the evening, but since that was where their meal was to be had, she didn't have much choice but to agree with all the rest.

As the group broke up and began to make their various arrangements for getting to the village, Fliss turned to get Megan's coat and found herself face to face with her husband. He waited until everyone had trailed out of the barn, heading for the several motor vehicles parked in the farmyard, then spoke roughly to her, "What the bloody hell do you think you're playing at? I suppose you think you're some sort of hero now?"

Actually she was quite pleased with herself. Fergus had been beside himself with excitement when he heard the satisfyingly heavy thump with which the stone had hit the ground when it had rolled out of the digger bucket. Even covered in foul-smelling sludge it had been obvious that the stone was carved and not just a solitary boulder – and it was thanks to her that they had found it.

"Now you come to mention it, yes. Fergus is delighted that my suggestion bore fruit. In case you are not aware, this is the first "find" of the dig," she answered defiantly, furious with his attitude.

"But it wasn't part of the "dig" was it? It was some bloody meddling amateur throwing her ha'porth in where it wasn't wanted or needed."

"What's the matter, Bryn? Jealous that good old-fashioned women's intuition works where all your expensive instruments fail? Too bad."

He looked as though he would like to hit her. He clenched his fist and turned away, stomping through the doorway as though he knew it was too dangerous to stay. Fliss was stunned. In the past couple of years they'd had some real good arguments; vicious, cutting, cruel – but she had never felt threatened physically by him. Mind games were more Bryn's thing. He must be really furious with her – but she didn't really understand why. Had she really undermined his manhood just because she had been the first person to find anything?

Even more surprisingly, Megan followed him out. She usually avoided him like the plague when he shouted at her mother, but now it seemed she would even rather be with her father than stay in the same room as the head. She had been acting oddly ever since they had brought the thing inside, refusing to look at it, hiding her face in her mother's shoulder. Fliss had to agree it was rather ugly – perhaps even frightening to a child.

Alone in the barn she looked, for the first time, really closely at the stone head – and shivered violently. It was as though coldness had descended like a pebble dropping into a pool. Ripples of icy air seem to radiate towards her.

When the girls had first rinsed the mud off the thing Fliss had thought the faces looked serene. The eyes were closed as though in sleep, the features smooth and peaceful, yet now when she looked in more detail, the serenity was gone. The eyes where shut in agony, unable to bear what they might be forced to witness. The few lines etched on cheeks and brow screamed of unbearable pain.

One of the three faces seemed to speak of a stunning blow to the head, vicious pain pulsating from the point of contact; the second struggled in vain to voice the agony, but breath was suspended by the biting knots of the leather garrotte; the third heard the gurgle and spatter of hot blood as it spurted from the slashed throat.

Fliss stared in terror, all too aware that she was allowing her imagination to overtake her common sense. She only felt these things because Fergus had described them to her – and yet... And yet, it all seemed dreadfully real.

Above her head the rumble of distant thunder seemed to shake the building and the head vibrated on the flimsy trestle table.

Suddenly being in the pub with everyone else didn't seem such a bad idea.

CHAPTER EIGHT

"Arawn, king of Annwn, strides through the enchanted forest, accompanied by his flying hounds, the Celtic Hounds of Hell"

When Fliss reached the car, she found Bryn and Megan waiting for her; the rest had already gone. She wondered why her husband had elected to travel with her then realised that he hadn't had much choice. He had found himself in charge of Megan – and she could only travel in her child-seat – also everyone would automatically assume that he would want to enjoy the company of his family. Even though it wasn't true, Bryn was hardly likely to show his true colours and admit that to his colleagues.

Fliss took the keys from her coat pocket and opened the car and whilst she fastened Megan in, Bryn slumped sulkily into the passenger seat. Of course he hated not to be in the driving seat, but her mother's car was not insured for him. Fliss's parents had seen no necessity to include him on the list of named drivers, since he had his own vehicle.

As she took her place and started the engine, Fliss debated making some innocuous remark, in an attempt to get them back onto a half-civilised footing, but one glance at his locked jaw told her that nothing she could say would ever be viewed by him as innocuous. He was spoiling for a fight.

Well, he could sink a few pints in the pub and pick one with someone else. It wasn't going to be her.

Things didn't improve much at the pub. The moment they walked through the door Fliss found herself being hailed by Polly and by the three girls from the dig. She glanced back at Bryn and found his expression thunderous. Of course he would be furious

70

that she had made herself so popular with his colleagues. The three large tables the team had taken over had been thrust together and she was immediately invited to join the throng. Bryn threw them all a venomous glance and retreated to the bar where he sat hunched over a triple vodka.

Fliss sat with the gang and ignored her husband for the rest of the evening.

Fergus rose to his feet when he saw her, "Hi, Fliss, come and join us. Do you know everyone?"

"I've met Angela, Anne-Marie and Helen," she said, forcing a smile. Bryn's behaviour stung even if she didn't want to be in his company.

"Then let me introduce Con, Trev and Shep."

She shook hands, "Don't tell me, your surname is Shepherd," she said to the young man who half stood to greet her, shaking shaggy curls out of his eyes and stroking his beard self-consciously with his free hand.

"No, he looks like a sheep dog," supplied Con with a grin and pulled a chair across from another table for her.

"And the three at the bar are Don, Christian and Will."

"Con and Don?" questioned Fliss with especial emphasis on the 'Don'; she raised an eyebrow and grinned.

"I know, it can't be helped – his mum was a Donny Osmond fan in the seventies."

"Who?" she asked and Fergus groaned, "Don't you just hate the younger generation?"

"Only kidding," said Fliss.

The mood was one of unrestrained joviality and Fliss soon found herself joining in the jokes and good-natured teasing, her troubles, for the moment, quite forgotten.

Polly was an exceptional hostess. She had no trouble recalling who was vegetarian and who was not, and had tasty meals for both. She kept Fliss supplied with hot tea, and the rest with the tipple of their choice. Megan was presented with a pizza-face made with carefully fashioned strips of pepper, carrot and ham. Fliss was tempted by the steak and ale pie, but a sudden memory of Ted

71

Armitage and what he had told her about holding cows heads as they were shot put her off. The cheese and broccoli bake was delicious.

By the end of the evening she was finding her mood had lifted to such an extent that even the thought of an early return, alone, to the barn, couldn't bring her down.

They all begged her to stay longer, but poor little Megan's head was dropping and she reluctantly picked up her daughter and headed for the door. Fergus followed her, on the pretext of going to the toilets.

"Fliss, are you sure you don't want me to come back with you?"

She smiled up at him, "Do you really think that would be a good idea, Fergus? You and I both know you are just being a gentleman, but how do you think my glowering husband and your gossiping friends will view our leaving together?"

"Good point." She knew she hadn't offended him by her straight talking, for his smile was genial, if a little hazy. He had obviously drunk quite a bit himself. He wandered off towards the loos – unimaginatively labelled "witches" and "warlocks" – and she smiled to herself, flattered that he had thought about her welfare. She'd almost forgotten how if felt to have someone express concern for her.

She had quite a shock when she stepped outside for the heavens had opened and it was literally teeming down. She hadn't noticed the rain from inside the pub, since the level of conversation had drowned out the sound of the foul weather. She pulled Megan's hood up and made a run for the car.

It was astounding how heavy the rain was. By the time she had traversed the few yards of road to the waiting vehicle and unlocked it, she was wet through and dripping. When they set off, nothing but double-speed on the wipers would keep the windscreen clear enough to see the road ahead. She erred on the side of caution and took a slow pace, preferring a tardy arrival to an accident.

It was tough struggling across the farmyard, now running almost ankle-deep in muddy rainwater; then, Megan on her hip, floundering across the field to the barn. She had rarely been more relieved to reach a haven.

She flung herself through the doors, slammed them shut against the wind and rain, then leant breathlessly against them, allowing Megan to slide to the floor from her aching arms. It took her a moment to pull herself together sufficiently to notice that the hurricane lamps hung on hooks on several of the beams were shining with a friendly light and the red glow in the corner came from the little pot-bellied stove Ted Armitage had mentioned. Scary he might be, but he had kept his promise and piled loads of wood beside it, as well as, presumably, lighting it in time for her return.

Wet, cold and miserable as she was, this made a tear well in her eye. First there was Fergus with his offer to see her safely back; now the grumpy farmer spending his time hauling wood across a dark field for her. How differently these strangers were treating her from the man who had promised to love and cherish her on their wedding day.

She hastily put such thoughts from her mind. Getting herself and her daughter dry and settled into bed had to be her first priority. Time enough to contemplate her crumbling marriage when Megan was warm and asleep.

She went over to her bed to drag her bag from under it when she noticed a note pinned to her pillow. She unfolded it and found it was from Ted Armitage. If she wanted to use the bathroom for herself and the child, he was going out for the evening and the back door would be open. She knew that the rest of the team had been accorded no such privileges. They were currently using the old outside loo attached to the stables and bathing was an unheard of luxury.

Now she was in a real quandary. The thought of a hot bath was tempting, but then she'd have to struggle back across the wet field in the dark after it. There was also the possibility that if she didn't accept Armitage's hospitality on this occasion, he might be offended and never offer again. And if she was to be here for any length of time, that was not to be risked.

The lure of a long soak could not be ignored. She called Megan back from the far end of the barn, where she had evidently found something interesting to watch – Fliss hoped fervently it wasn't a large spider and decided not to bother finding out – and they slipped back out through the doors and into the storm.

As he had promised, Armitage had indeed left his back door open. Fliss went nervously in, calling "hello" a couple of times, just to make sure he really was gone. The house was deserted, but Fliss did not feel alone. There was an oddly brooding atmosphere about the place, as though there was something hiding in the shadows that did not welcome her presence. It was strange how the light shining through the kitchen window had seemed warm and pleasant when she had staggered across the yard towards it, but now she was under its glare, it merely seemed to light her sufficiently so that unfriendly eyes could examine her more minutely.

She allowed herself one small shudder – a goose walking over her grave – then she sternly told herself that it was all her stupid imagination. There was no one in the house and anyway, far from being unwelcome, she was one of the few people the owner had willingly invited in.

She took Megan's hand and they walked out of the kitchen and into the dimly lit hall. The stairs ascended into the darkness and she was most unwilling to climb them, but Megan skipped happily ahead, "Bath, mummy," she said happily, and began to haul herself upstairs, one hand on the banister. Fliss didn't recall having told her daughter they were to have a bath, but she followed anyway, hoping there would be a light switch at the top.

She found the light, but it didn't help much. Farmer Armitage apparently didn't believe in having a wattage which exceeded 40. She wandered along the passageway, opening likely looking doors and finding nothing but empty bedrooms, or sheeted and shrouded furniture. She opened one door and almost had a heart-attack when a pale frightened face peered back out at her. She drew in her breath in preparation for a scream of terror when she realised that she had seen nothing but her own reflection in a vast, spotted mirror on a remarkably large and ugly Victorian wardrobe. Her

74

heart was still pounding painfully against her ribs five minutes later.

The bathroom, when Fliss found it, was old-fashioned but thankfully clean. It made her smile when she turned on the huge, cumbersome taps and the water sputtered, reluctantly at first, then in a powerful gush. London shops would charge a fortune for modern copies of this bathroom suite, with its cast iron roll-top bath and thick basin and toilet, and here it was, having waited patiently for nearly a century to come back into fashion.

Megan giggled happily at the thought of a splash and Fliss had to keep a strict eye on her to make sure she didn't put her hands under the hot tap, which, she was grateful to notice, was steaming nicely, though that might have had quite a lot to do with the chill in the room itself. Apparently hardy hill farmers didn't feel the need for such blatant luxuries as central heating and radiators.

This being the case, she wasted no time in divesting herself and Megan of their clothes and climbing into the carefully monitored bath water.

They had a happy half hour splashing and playing until the cold began to raise goose pimples on their exposed flesh and Fliss considered it was time to head back to the warmth of the Aga in the kitchen and that promised cup of tea. She wrapped a towel around herself as she dried her daughter and quickly dressed her in her fleecy pyjamas. As she began to dry herself, her teeth chattering, she thought she heard footsteps coming down the passageway and, realising there was no lock on the door, she called hastily, "Don't come in Mr. Armitage, it's me, Fliss. You said Megan and I could have a bath."

The footsteps stopped abruptly and Fliss, rather surprised, opened the door and peered out onto the landing. No one was to be seen in either direction. The house was silent and empty. She must have been mistaken about the sound. Behind her the bath tap gave a gurgle and a large drip fell into the now empty tub. That must have been it. She had mistaken the drip, drip, drip of the ancient plumbing for the sound of footfalls on bare floorboards.

Back in the kitchen everything was just as Fliss had left it.

Megan's damp teddy was still on the rocking chair, steaming gently in the heat, as were their two anoraks which she had draped over the back of two kitchen chairs. Evidently Armitage had not returned from wherever he had spent his evening.

Fliss hadn't noticed him amongst the throng in "The Weary Sportsman" but that didn't mean he hadn't been there. From what she had seen of the village, it wasn't over-burdened with nocturnal hotspots – but what did she know? He could have been at choir practice or the vicar's whist party. As she settled into the rocker with her mug of tea and Megan happily sipping warm milk on her knee, she amused herself by thinking of all the other places Armitage could have found himself that evening. The warmer and cosier she became, the more silly became her ideas, until she realised that Megan had fallen asleep on her lap and she knew she was going to have to face that trudge across the wet, dark field to her bunk in the barn.

Leaving the warmth of the kitchen and heading out into the night was one of the hardest things she had done in a long time. Megan was a dead weight in her arms and she could barely see the ground ahead of her with the hood of her coat falling over her eyes with the weight of the rain battering it onto her head.

Once back inside the barn, she sat Megan on the bed whilst she divested her of her coat and shoes. The child lolled in her arms, still asleep despite the rough handling, and Fliss quickly tucked her into their shared sleeping bag, aware that the air was chilly despite the stove.

As she turned away from the bed in order to hang Megan's coat somewhere to dry she glanced towards the far end of the barn and noticed the stone head, one of its three faces staring directly at her. She couldn't repress a shudder of distaste and hastily went to find a cloth to throw over the horrid thing. She'd never be able to sleep knowing those blank, blind eyes were trained on her.

She found a dusty piece of sacking and wrapped it around the head, standing back to judge the effect. Sadly it merely made it look like a ragged mummified head, or a funeral shroud, but it was better than the head itself – and oddly she couldn't bring herself to pick it up and bodily move it to another location.

She blew out all but one of the lamps, pulled the canvas curtain across and climbed into bed beside her slumbering daughter. It was something of a squash sharing a sleeping bag, but pleasantly warm and cosy. She didn't imagine she was going to find it easy to sleep, but she'd barely had a full night's repose since Megan was born anyway, so what was new?

It was with some surprise therefore, that she found herself waking up some time later. At first she couldn't understand what had woken her. She was still alone in the barn, the rain was still falling outside, nothing, it seemed, had changed.

Gradually she realised that in one major respect there had been an alteration. She was suffering from agonising cramp in her right arm. Megan must be lying on it. Sleepily she tried to shift her weight and it was then that she realised that Megan was on her left. Her right hand was drooping towards the floor, having somehow escaped the confines of the sleeping bag. She tried to lift it and was horrified to hear the squelching, sucking sound of wet mud and to see in the dim light that it was covered in thick, black peat from finger-tip to elbow. She sat up with a cry of alarm. The floor was covered with a surging mass of wet soil. The rain must have caused a landslide and now half the hillside was slithering slowly past her bed.

It was then that she became aware of the smell of rotting vegetation, stagnant water and some other indefinable stench which her mind refused to consider naming.

Panic set in. She had to get Megan out of there. The entire building had probably become unsafe, the pressure of the moving earth must be intolerable against the ancient stonework. It could only be a matter of time before the walls collapsed and the roof caved in.

She struggled to grip the zipper of the sleeping bag, but her stiff, mud-slimed fingers refused to work and she began to sob with frustration and sheer terror. The old timbers above her head creaked and groaned with the weight they were being forced to prevail against and she glanced fearfully upwards, watching huge splits open up in the tortured, twisted wood.

An ear-shattering bang forced a terrified scream from her and she woke and sat up, her heart thumping in her throat.

The barn door was bouncing back from against the wall, a man, shaking the water from his hair, was standing in the doorway.

"I'm so sorry. Did I startle you? The wind whipped the door out of my hand before I could stop it."

Totally disorientated, Fliss looked around her. The roof was sound, there was no mud on the floor. True the rain still fell and the wind still blew, but the mayhem was firmly outside. Her haven was still around her. The landslide was nothing but a bad dream.

She watched as the stranger shut the door against the storm, then turn back to her.

"I've just been told you are here, so I came straight over to tell you that I can't possibly allow you and the child to sleep out here."

She dragged her attention back to him, still painfully confused by the seeming reality of the nightmare.

"Really? And where do you suggest we go at this time of night and in this weather?" she asked coldly.

"That's easily settled. Armitage rented a room in his house to me. I suggest you take that and I shall rough it with the troops."

"Who are you?" she asked, wondering what he was talking about.

"I'm sorry. I didn't introduce myself Mrs Elmsworth. My name is John Norton."

Professor John Norton thought Fliss in a panic. Now Bryn really was going to kill her!

CHAPTER NINE

"Aonghus – an engaging god of courtesy and love, a Celtic equivalent of Eros"

Fliss felt her heart still thundering in her chest and took a deep breath, trying to bring herself under control, "It's very good of you ..." she began, as soon as she felt enough mastery over her voice to trust it not to tremble, "but I couldn't possibly ..."

"Nonsense. I really must insist. Slip your coats on and I'll escort you over to the house."

"But Megan is already asleep ..." she protested weakly.

"Not I'm not, mummy," came the muffled tones of her daughter from under the covers, "bad man woke me up."

John Norton grinned amiably, "There you are then," he said equably, "as your daughter so succinctly puts it, the bad man woke her, therefore the least he can do is give her a proper bed for the night."

Fliss knew when she was beaten, "All right, all right. You win. Who am I to turn my nose up at a warm bed?"

"From what I've seen of Mr Armitage's household arrangements, I wouldn't hold my breath for warm, Mrs Elmsworth."

"Please, call me Fliss."

"Fliss?" he raised one eyebrow in a faintly quizzical way which made Fliss want to giggle.

"Short for Felicity," she explained.

"Now, why would anyone shorten a pretty name like Felicity?"

She shrugged, faintly embarrassed, "I've no idea. It started at school I think. Children always shorten names, don't they? My mother had a friend who was so determined not to have her son nick-named that she gave him the shortest name she could think of – Gary."

"And?" he asked.

"His pals call him Gaz. It infuriates her!"

He smiled, "I imagine it does. Well, I'll go outside whilst you sort yourself out." He headed towards the door, but she called him hastily back, "Please Professor, don't go back out into the rain on my account. I'm quite decent I promise. It's not as though this is a negligee sort of a place, is it?"

She could have sworn she heard him mutter, "Mores the pity," but the sound of the rain on the roof was so loud she could not be sure. She threw him a quizzing glance, but he had turned his attention to the trestle table and its stone occupant.

"Is this our treasure?" he asked over his shoulder.

"It is," she answered, unzipping her sleeping bag and hopping swiftly out.

"I understand we have you to thank for its discovery?"

"Sort of, I suppose," she answered absent-mindedly. She was busily searching for Megan's welly-boot, which had mysteriously disappeared from its place next to its mate, as children's belongings are wont to do at every opportunity.

"I should, of course, admonish you severely for encouraging my staff to ignore every rule of purist archaeology and plunge straight into digging at an historical site without thought, preparation or survey."

"Are you going to?" she asked, slightly perturbed by his suddenly severe tone, her attention drawn away from the search for the boot.

He grinned, looking younger and, she thought, rather attractive, "Are you kidding? When you have unearthed something as magnificent as this?" He had removed the sacking and now drew his glasses from his breast pocket so that he could examine the find more minutely. Fliss watched him, amused at how swift was the transformation from joker back to professor. With spectacles perched on the end of his nose he looked very serious once more.

"You are quite pleased with it, then?" she inquired.

"Pleased is hardly the word. I am stunned."

"Personally I think it's spooky," she admitted, drawing nearer in spite of her revulsion for the object.

"Spooky?" his voice rose slightly in amusement, "Not a word one finds often in academic tomes."

"I don't care. It's still spooky. I don't like the vibes it gives off and I've been having nasty nightmares ever since the thing saw the light of day."

"Have you really? That's very interesting." He turned to face her, removing his glasses and subjecting her to a penetrating look. She felt she was being as carefully scanned as the head had been, and blushed as a result.

"Why is that interesting?" she asked.

"Because the Celts believed that dreams were a way for living human beings to visit the 'otherworld' where dwelt their gods."

She could not restrain a shudder, "Thanks a lot! Now I'm really uncomfortable with that thing!" she nodded her head towards the carving.

He laughed, "Come now, enough of this speculation. Let us get this little lady into her bed. Her eyes are barely staying open."

"I'll have to carry her. I can't find her other boot."

"It's here, on the table behind the head," he said, surprised that she didn't remember where she had put it. Fliss could barely restrain another shudder. She knew that neither she nor Megan had been within several feet of the table since returning to the barn.

"Has anyone else been back here beside you, Professor?" she asked quietly.

"No. They are all still in the pub – and seemingly intending to stay there until the rain stops. I came here as soon as Fergus remembered to tell me that you and the child were intending to camp out." He slipped the boot onto Megan's socked foot, "There you go, little lady. Now shall we brave this horrid weather just once more?"

Megan smiled sleepily at him, "You carry me," she said, stretching her arms out to him. Fliss was astounded. Her daughter did not usually take to men quite so readily, but twice today she had gone quite happily with a stranger. Suddenly Fliss realised that it was not men that Megan didn't like – it was just one man – her father. She made no protest as the professor took the child from her.

"I'm afraid that leaves you carrying the spooky head," he said, his face perfectly grave.

Fliss was startled, "What?"

"We'll have to take the artefact indoors. I can't possibly leave something so valuable in a barn. Fergus was given quite a dressing down for doing so earlier."

It took Fliss a moment to digest this information, "I see," she said, with deceptive calm, "So you really came back for the head, and not out of concern for Megan and me?" It had seemed such a kind, caring thing to do, braving the storm to move a child into a warmer, safer place, but she should have known he would have an ulterior motive – which man wouldn't have? She was disappointed in him and tried not to show it, but he could see the expression on her face and was left in no doubt of her opinion of his actions. Fliss had nothing if not the most startlingly expressive eyes.

He caught her glance and held it, "Most certainly not. The head would have been perfectly safe with you in the barn. My concern, then as now, is that it is not left entirely unattended. If, as I had originally planned, our presence here had been unknown except to a select few, then there would be no need to worry about theft or sabotage, but as it is the entire County – and beyond – knows exactly where we are and what we are doing, I have to prepare for the worst."

"Oh," having thrown herself headfirst towards the wrong conclusion, she was now at a loss, "I'm sorry," she muttered inadequately, after a long pause. He appeared to notice neither her discomfiture nor hear her apology, since he was fully occupied with talking to Megan about her stuffed rabbit, which she had insisted he admire, though it barely resembled the creature it was supposed to represent, so well-loved and cuddled it had been over the years.

As they moved towards the door he said, "Bryn was in the other bar with the locals when I left, but I'll tell him where you are to be found when they all stagger back later. He'll be delighted to have bagged my double bed so unexpectedly."

"Don't do that, for heaven's sake!" she expostulated, then, realising how vehement she had sounded, she added, "There'll be no room for him with Megan next to me – and he'll only wake her if he's had a lot to drink." She could hardly tell Bryn's boss that she would rather sleep with the detested stone head than her own husband. Bryn may have humiliated her in front of his colleagues, but for her to return the compliment would be unforgivable. With Bryn the words, "sauce", "goose" and "gander" had no meaning.

Professor Norton glanced curiously at her, but made no comment.

She wrapped the head back into its sacking cover and hoisted it into her arms, carrying it as she might a bucketful of toads.

"Lead on, Mac Duff," she said, wondering grimly why she was using one of Bryn's stupid quotes. She hoped he hadn't noticed as she followed him out into the wet and windy darkness.

The rain was falling steadily now, but at least the wind had dropped and the noise of the lashing trees had ceased. The smell of wet earth was almost overpowering and she was reminded very vividly of her dream, especially as the cold, dead weight of the carved stone in her arms seemed intent on dragging itself from her grasp to return to the depths of the earth from whence it had come. It grew increasingly heavy and slippery with every dogged footstep. She tried to stop herself from indulging in such fanciful thoughts, knowing it was ridiculous to endow an inanimate object with the capability of rational thought and action. It was a lump of stone. She had to try and remember that and be sensible.

It was with immense relief that she followed the professor into the kitchen and took the thing across to the table where she dumped it with small ceremony. Despite the fact that she felt she had wound the sacking very firmly around it, the moment it stood on the table the cloth dropped away and she found herself staring into one of the three faces – a face which seemed to stare malevolently back at her so that she could barely tear her eyes away.

So intense was her preoccupation with it that she didn't realise that the kitchen was no longer deserted. She started when Armitage spoke gruffly from his seat beside the fire, "'evening Professor. It's not taken you long to pull," he grinned with faint malice as Fliss went three different shades of pink in the space of as many seconds. Professor Norton kindly didn't look in her direction, "Very amusing, Ted. Now, if you've no objections, I've offered the young lady my bed. I can't have a child sleeping in a barn, even if you can!"

"The lady will tell you that I lit a fire for her and the child," muttered the farmer. Norton had evidently hit a raw nerve, though Fliss couldn't imagine why. It was really no one else's responsibility but hers and Bryn's where their daughter slept. She placed the blame squarely on her husband's shoulders – though she could not, of course, explain that to either of the two men, now glaring at each other across the expanse of the stone-floored kitchen.

"Please gentlemen, there really is no need for these recriminations. Megan and I were quite cosy in the barn. It is April after all and not exactly freezing.

Armitage shrugged and rose to his feet, evidently feeling Fliss had justified his actions, "I've another room with a single bed. Do you want it?" he asked the professor, who nodded, "I'd be grateful – unless Mrs Elmsworth would like her husband to have it?"

"No thank you," she left it at that, too weary to think of more excuses.

"Thank you, Ted. I'm getting too old for the delights of roughing it."

This remark made Fliss look curiously at him. She had scarcely been able to see him in the barn, with only the light of the hurricane lamps for illumination, but now she took the opportunity to observe him properly. If she had thought about it, she would have assumed that he was perhaps Bryn's age, early to mid-thirties, but by the harsh lights of the un-shaded electric bulbs

84

she saw that he was probably ten years older than that. He had an interesting face, not handsome exactly, but arresting. The nose was perhaps a little large, but it suited him. His hair was greying at the temples, but was otherwise dark brown and a little too long, but that suited him too. His eyes were the exact shade of melting chocolate that she found the most attractive. Bryn's were muddy hazel.

He seemed to sense her eyes upon him and transferred his gaze from Armitage to her, "You have no objections to sharing the house with two unattached males, Mrs Elmsworth? I think we can both promise you will remain unmolested for the duration of your stay."

"Bummer!" she said flippantly and both men laughed.

"I can see you are going to be quite a handful, Miss. First you lead my staff astray and now you are attempting to do the same with poor Mr Armitage."

"Poor Mr Armitage can take care of himself, thanks!" said Armitage with a roguish grin in Fliss direction – one which, oddly enough, she found amusing rather than intimidating. How peculiar, she thought, everyone warned me against the ill-tempered farmer and I find I like him.

"Do you want a cup of tea? I'm about to brew up."

"I'd love one, thanks, but I'll take Megan up to bed first, if you don't mind."

"I'll show you the way," said the professor, and promptly suited words for action. She followed him through the dim hallway.

"You've made quite a hit with Armitage," he said conversationally as she fell into step beside him, "I've never seen him make such a fuss of a woman."

"You call that a fuss?"

"Believe me, for him, it is."

"You've known him a long while then?" she asked.

"Ages – ever since I found out about the stone circle. I've spent fifteen long years periodically coming up here, trying to persuade the old rogue into letting us mount an investigation. In the end, I suspect I have the Foot and Mouth crisis for his eventual capitulation. It hit most farmers pretty hard and though there was compensation, it didn't cover the trauma they went through."

"It must have been horrific."

"It was – and vastly inconvenient, too, if I may admit to being selfish for a moment. Most digs were affected. There have never been so many trips abroad and so much Industrial Archaeology!"

"Of course, there wouldn't have been much freedom to wander about the fields and hills."

"Not much – but I brushed up on our Industrial Heritage, so it wasn't a complete loss."

They reached the top of the stairs and the professor opened a door at the far end of the landing and held it for her, "Your bed-chamber, madam."

"Thank you."

He flicked on the light and she found herself in a large room, containing a variety of ill-matched heavy Victorian furniture, dominated by a huge double bed, with immense mahogany head and foot boards.

"I hope the sheets are clean. Mr Armitage doesn't strike me as the most domesticated of men."

"Check 'em if you like."

"That seems a little ungracious."

"Perhaps – but eminently sensible."

She pulled back the old fashioned, and rather worn, feather-stuffed, silken eiderdown and was relieved to see pristine white sheets and pillowcases.

"Clean and not damp at all – I'll bet you are regretting your gentlemanly impulses now, aren't you?" she smiled teasingly at him.

"Oh, I often regret them," he said with emphasis.

"I'll bet you do. Well, I shall give you a full report of my comfortable sleep in the morning."

"I shall look forward to it – and I just hope the mattress feels as though it is stuffed with rocks."

"Thanks."

Professor Norton laid his now sleeping burden in the bed and covered her up, "Shall we have tea?" he asked quietly.

"Yes, please," said Fliss fervently, "it's been quite a day."

Not only had Armitage made tea, he had also buttered a pile of hot crumpets. Fliss wanted to refuse, but the aroma was so tempting that she found herself biting into the steamy warmth and feeling the hot butter trickle greasily down her chin. Bliss.

Silence reigned for a good few minutes then Fliss remembered she had a question to put to the farmer, "Oh, Mr Armitage, you might be able to help me with something."

"I'll do my best," he replied, rubbing the back of his work-roughened hand across his mouth.

"I was wondering if you knew of anywhere I could take Megan in the village – perhaps a mother and toddler group or a play school. I don't want her to miss too much normal life whilst we're here."

"Couldn't tell you about that, I don't take part in much village life – but the vicar should be able to help you. Just knock on the door and if she's not there, her housekeeper will direct you."

"Okay, thanks."

Professor Norton was being rather more delicate with his food and was wiping his fingers on his handkerchief, "Do I take that to mean you don't intend to visit the dig again, Mrs Elmsworth?"

"Oh, I don't think so. Bryn has made it pretty clear that I'm only in the way up there."

"You'll forgive my bluntness, but it is I and not Bryn who will tell you should that be the case. I welcome your presence at the dig – in fact, I insist upon it! I have a suspicion you are going to be our good luck charm."

Her cheeks were already pink from the heat of the fire, so she could only hope that he couldn't see her embarrassed blush. She tried to laugh carelessly, but merely sounded stiff, "I'll probably join you later in the day then, but I have to see to Megan's welfare first."

"Naturally." Thankfully he said nothing more and she was able to swiftly finish her tea.

"Well, goodnight gentlemen, and thank you for your kindness –

both of you."

    She fled before either of them could say another word.

CHAPTER TEN

"Mac Da Tho was King of Leinster, who owned a fine hound and a huge boar."

Fliss opened her eyes to complete darkness – not the sort of half-hearted dark of a town night, but real, no street-lights, no moon, can't-see-your-own-hand pitch black. She blinked sleepily, staring around, hoping that when her eyes adjusted she might be able to discern the faint outlines of the windows and door. Nothing. She might still have her eyes shut for all she could see. She lay still for a few minutes, listening to Megan's steady breathing and the erratic thump of her own heart, wondering vaguely what it was that had startled her awake. The rain had stopped and only the occasional drip from the eaves broke the silence though not loudly enough to have woken her.

Suddenly the noise came again and though it was quite soft, still it made her body go rigid with fear. Someone – or something – was outside the bedroom door. She could hear the floor boards creaking under its shifting weight as it moved from side to side. Then she heard an odd snuffling noise that took her a few seconds to place. It was the snorting, sniffing sound an animal makes when it senses something interesting.

Stupid, she told herself, flooded with relief, you are on a farm. It must be one of Armitage's dogs, wondering who the strangers were in his master's house. It was odd though, because she didn't recall seeing any dogs in the house earlier, and judging from the noise it was making it must be bloody huge.

Having convinced herself the noise was of canine origin, she drifted back off to sleep, telling herself that she must ask Armitage not to let his dogs into the house at night. She didn't want to have to wake to irritating noises every night for the rest of her stay.

The next time she woke it was to full sunlight pouring into the room and to sharp pain as Megan used her thumbs to lift her eyelids. The storm of last night was gone and very nearly forgotten.

"Awake mummy?" asked her darling daughter, putting her face up close and giving her the most peculiar view straight up her nostrils.

Much as she longed to roll over and go back to sleep, she knew she had no choice but to get up. She laughed and pushed the little girl off her chest, tickling her and saying, "Yes, mummy's awake, you little nuisance."

Her watch, placed on the bedside cabinet the night before, at first eluded her grasping fingers, but when she finally took hold of it and blearily read its face, she was astounded to realise that it was after nine o'clock. The fresh air and disturbed night had certainly made sure Megan slept beyond her usual ungodly hours.

Imagining the kitchen would be long-deserted by the early-rising farmer and archaeologist, Fliss decided to risk going downstairs in her night-attire. She needed a cup of tea – and she needed it now.

As Megan burst into the kitchen ahead of her, she found she was wrong about the latter. Professor Norton was still sitting at the table in the kitchen, eating toast and reading a bundle of dog-eared notes, looking, this morning, very business-like and severe.

"Good morning," she ventured shyly, suddenly wondering how she could have flirted so outrageously with him the night before. Then it had seemed like harmless fun, born of a relaxed evening in the pub and the excitement of being in a new place with new people – it was so very long since she had been with new people – with any people at all! Her life, these days, consisted of house-work and child-care and nothing else. Even to Bryn she seemed to have become invisible – just there, but of no particular interest. Now, faced with the professor in broad daylight, she felt she had committed some terrible solecism.

She opened her mouth, intending to try to apologise, but he

looked up and grinned so mischievously at her that all her worries faded away. It was obvious no offence had been caused or taken. Her ever-present fear of upsetting the critical Bryn was beginning to colour everything she said and did, but she had to admit he would have been justified in being angry if he had thought that she had been toying with his career.

"Let me get you some coffee," offered the professor, rising to his feet and laying aside his work.

"Please don't get up," she said hastily, "I shouldn't disturb you – anyway I prefer tea."

"Okay, there's plenty of bread if you want toast, but I don't think you'll find any cereal for the little one. Armitage isn't exactly a healthy eater. His idea of a good breakfast is a full English with all the trimmings."

"Fair enough for a man who spends his life outdoors. And I've bought my own stuff for Megan."

"Armitage did bid me to tell you to make yourself completely at home and use whatever you want."

"That's very nice of him, but I'll do my best not to take advantage. He's been very good to Megan and me."

"It'll do the old rogue good to think of someone other than himself for a change." It occurred to Fliss that though the professor kept referring to Armitage as "old" they were actually of a similar age group, but she decided not to remark upon it. She crossed the room and picked up the kettle taking it to the sink to fill it.

"Well," he continued, gathering his papers together, "I must be off to see what is happening up at the dig. The equipment arriving ahead of time has nicely upset my schedule. I'd love to know who was responsible for the co… I mean mistake." He had been about to use a rather stronger expression, Fliss knew, but had hastily moderated his language because of Megan's presence. She smiled to herself, "Was it a mistake by your staff? I rather presumed it had been an error by the hire company," she said, carrying the kettle across to the stove.

"Apparently not. A phone call changed all the arrangements. If I get my hands on the idiot who made it…"

"Look on the bright side – it would have been a great deal more inconvenient if they had cancelled altogether."

This possibility evidently hadn't occurred to him because when she glanced at him, he was frowning, "Very true," he said thoughtfully, "Not exactly sabotage then."

"If it was done deliberately, it looks as though it might have been someone who was rather more interested in annoying you than stopping you."

"How very odd. You have now presented me with an enigma. I can think of any number of people who don't want me to proceed with the dig – but none at all who just want to bug me!"

"Maybe you weren't the target."

"This gets worse!"

She laughed, "I'm sorry. I'll keep my theories to myself in the future."

"Please don't – it's most intriguing."

"Nice of you to say so. Bryn just finds me annoying." She spoke absent-mindedly, her concentration fully upon working out how to get the kettle to boil – she had never touched an Aga in her life before.

"Bryn doesn't have the sense he was born with," he said decidedly, "See you later."

He was gone before she could turn and frame an answer – much to her relief.

After she and Megan had breakfasted on fresh-laid eggs and crusty bread, they bathed, dressed and drove down to the village, or, more specifically, the vicarage.

Fliss parked in what had now become their usual spot by the village green, then crossed to the church, assuming, correctly, that the large Victorian Gothic monstrosity next door would be the abode of the parson.

She was halfway up the lavender-lined pathway when she saw a youngish woman coming out of the front door and slamming it shut behind her.

"Good morning, can I help?" she said, spotting Fliss and Megan as she turned to walk down the path. The smile was automatic, the sort of smile professionals reserved for strangers who might just turn out to be a nuisance.

"Hi, I'm looking for the vicar."

"You've found her."

"Oh good. I was wondering if you could tell me if there is anywhere I could take my little girl to meet other children. Not the nursery school – we won't be here long enough for anything formal, but perhaps something fun?"

The smile became warmer and more genuine as the vicar realised she wasn't going to be dealing with a nutter or a complainer, "Oh, I think we can help with that request."

"Brilliant, thanks."

"I presume you are helping out up at the dig? You don't look like a New Age traveller ... oops; I shouldn't have said that, should I? Not up to me to make judgements like that – not that it would have made any difference if you were New Age – still very welcome and all that ..." she trailed off awkwardly, aware that she had made several glaring errors. Fliss swiftly put her out of her misery,

"Yes, I'm at the dig – or at least my husband is – I'm just visiting."

"Oh, I see. Well, I'm Emma Goodrich – call me Emma, but whatever you do, don't call me after midnight!"

Obviously a well-worn joke, but Fliss couldn't see it going down too well with some of the more straight-laced parishioners. She smiled politely, "I'm Fliss Elmsworth and this is my daughter Megan."

The vicar immediately sank to her knees so that her face was level with Megan's, "Hello young lady, pleased to meet you."

"Likewise," replied Megan confidently. Fliss was astounded. Where on earth had she picked that expression up? The vicar, of course, was enchanted.

"She's a little star, isn't she? Well, let's go and consult the 'mums and toddlers' rota. I know its Wednesdays and Thursdays but I don't want to send you around there if it's half-term or something."

Fliss followed her back into the house, slightly bemused by the speed with which she changed subjects and directions. Once inside her feeling of bemusement was replaced by astonishment. Outside the house bore an uncanny resemblance to a small Borley Rectory, but the interior had been modernised – not just sympathetically redecorated, but seriously up-dated. A white, minimalist hall with beech floors gave onto a large stainless steel kitchen, with black granite worktops. To her left Fliss's glance showed her a purple haze of a lounge, containing the biggest, squarest sofa she had ever seen. It was covered in the purest white leather. Fliss shuddered when she thought of Megan with blackcurrant juice and chocolate buttons.

"Wow!" she exclaimed, not entirely sure if it was a compliment or not. It didn't matter because Emma assumed it was one, "Amazing what you can do with these old places, isn't it? Daddy paid for most of it for me, but the Bishop hasn't seen it yet. I'm not entirely sure he would approve, but one has to feel comfortable in one's home after all."

"One certainly does," murmured Fliss, not at all sure that the argument would convince the Bishop.

"Come into the study, that's where my diary is."

Suddenly Fliss didn't want to see the sacrilege Emma had inflicted on what would once have been a book-lined, mahogany-dominated Victorian Vicar's lair, but she didn't have much choice but to follow, feeling like keeping her eyes shut until the ordeal was over.

She was pleasantly surprised to find that it wasn't so bad after all. Clean and bright, with south-facing French windows, it was virtually untouched by the modern world. Admittedly there were panels of cerise chiffon at the windows instead of the traditional velvet curtains, and the walls were painted apple green instead of something more sombre, but it was a nice room.

"I wanted to paint the bookshelves white, but daddy wouldn't hear of it – he said that was one sin too far! Apparently they are real, solid mahogany! You couldn't do it today – not PC at all to chop down trees in the rainforest."

Thank goodness daddy draws the line somewhere, thought Fliss looking around. Most of the shelves, she noticed, bore odd-looking sculptures and garish pots rather than leather-bound tomes, but at least they were still there – and not obscured by white, non-drip gloss.

"He was right," she said diplomatically, "Don't you think they show off your art beautifully? Those white figurines wouldn't stand out half so well if they weren't contrasted against the dark wood."

Emma apparently hadn't viewed the situation in this light and an expression of grudging approval came over her face, "I do believe you are right. Who would have thought daddy had an iota of good taste?"

"Everyone has a surprise in them," answered Fliss kindly.

"Very true, now where is my book?"

She crossed the room to the only jarring note in the place – a brushed steel and beech-wood computer desk, containing a flat screen monitor and keyboard in transparent blue plastic. The diary was soon unearthed and consulted, "No, you're okay. The next holidays are weeks away – silly me, I should have remembered, we've only just had Easter, haven't we?"

It crossed Fliss's mind that perhaps a vicar might have been more likely to recall this fact than a lay person, but once again she bit her tongue.

"Great, whereabouts is it?"

"In the church hall – which you'll find, amazingly enough, just behind the church. You can't miss it."

"Thanks."

She turned to go, but Emma stopped her, "I say, are you busy right now?"

"Not in the least."

"Then do you fancy a guided tour of the church? I've been reading up about it and I'm dying to try out my style on someone. I need to get the practice in before the summer brings all the usual tourists."

"I'd love it," said Fliss warmly, "I love old churches. And you can tell me about yourself. I'm intrigued to know how lady vicars cope."

"Oh most people are okay – but you still get the occasional old fuddy-duddy who doesn't approve. Mind you the gay vicar issue has taken the heat off a bit! And of course I'm a godsend for a place like this."

She seemed to find nothing even faintly ironic in this turn of phrase so Fliss didn't laugh and simply asked, "Why here particularly?"

"You must be kidding! You need kid-gloves to handle all the undercurrents."

From what she had heard so far, Fliss had found no evidence that Emma even knew what kid-gloves were, let alone how to don them, but this too she let pass, "Go on," she urged.

As they chatted, Emma had led the way out of the house and down another path, which led past the house and towards the churchyard, without the need to go back out onto the road.

"You must have noticed we have rather a large population of – well, I suppose the old-fashioned word for them would be Pagans."

"I suppose it would," agreed Fliss, casting her mind back to the day before, when she had visited shops and businesses founded on anything other than Christianity. Paganism, Wicca, possibly even Devil worship – though to be fair, she had seen no evidence of that. She imagined even belief in fairies might possibly be frowned upon by the church.

"So how does having a lady vicar help?"

"Well, women are so much more tactful, don't you think?"

"Some are," said Fliss warily.

"And I suppose if the church appears to be moving with the times, it makes all this other stuff much less threatening. I must say I really do think people should be allowed to believe what they choose and worship their gods in their own way."

Fliss felt that she more or less agreed with her, but couldn't resist teasing a little.

"Does that include human sacrifice?" she asked seriously.

Emma looked suitably appalled, "God, that isn't going on here, is it? I had no idea!"

It was brought home to Fliss rather forcefully that there was definite danger in being facetious with someone who had no sense of humour and she hastily backed off, "I was joking, Emma! For goodness sake, don't start delivering sermons warning about slashed virgins and Black Masses – you'll cause a panic!"

Fortunately they had reached the porch door and in searching her bag for the huge black key, Emma was distracted, much to Fliss's relief. Literal people, she reflected, are such hard work. Every word has to be weighed and guarded.

As the old oak door creaked open, Fliss was hit by a wave of musty air which she always associated with ancient country churches. A mixture of dust, damp and old books, it was a smell she always thought of when anyone used the expression "the odour of sanctity". She knew that wasn't what it meant, but to her that was exactly what it was. The scent of a building rarely used more than once a week and mouldering slowly away because of it, but to her it smelled holy.

The church held no real surprises. It was a lovely old place, with a special charm of its own, but no different really than hundreds of others all over England.

She was interested to see a large collection of memorial plaques bearing the names of Merrington and Armitage. Apparently the families really had lived in the area for generations. She wondered which were the two who had gambled and respectively lost and won the Manor where she was presently laying her head.

Megan happily skipped at her side and Emma was evidently impressed by her good behaviour. Fliss was astounded by it.

At the end of the tour Emma asked what she thought, obviously as proud as a doting parent.

"It's a fine old church," said Fliss enthusiastically, "I can't fault it – and the smell is just right!"

"Smell? Oh you mean the damp and old hymn books! All old churches smell like that don't they? Of course I've just discovered there's a reason for that."

"Really?" asked Fliss, genuinely interested, "Do tell."

"Lots of old churches – and I mean really old – were built on the sites of pagan worship, druids and all that. It was a deliberate ploy by the early church leaders to make the locals forget the old religions, by supplanting them with the new. It was a case of if you can't beat 'em, join 'em. If people were used to going to a certain spot to worship, then don't stop them going, that just makes it forbidden and therefore irresistible, instead, put your own church in the same place."

"Makes perfect sense," said Fliss.

"It does, except one of the Celts major icons was running water, so nearly all their sacred spots had either streams, springs or wells as the main element. Apparently the early builders didn't let a little thing like that deter them, they simply built over the water. It seems that a lot of old churches have water under them, in one form or another, usually right in front of the altar – and early Christian saints were credited with their origin. Loads of the early Celtic saints had stories about miraculous wells and springs being associated with their demise. Suddenly the damp doesn't seem quite so surprising, does it?"

"Fascinating," agreed Fliss, "And is this church really that old? Surely we must be talking of more than fifteen hundred years."

"It's not quite that old," said Emma, "but it would have been built on the site of an earlier, possibly wooden, church."

"So I suppose there must be some connection between this church and the stone circle?"

"I think so. If you look on a map you'll see the church, circle and barrow all line up to create a triangle."

"Wait a minute, Fergus told me the triangle was formed by the circle, barrow and the peat bog."

"Oh? That's interesting too – but I do feel the church is more likely. After all the bog is a natural phenomenon, but the other three are man-made. I'll have to have another look at my map and see if I can work it out properly."

Fliss recalled her own map, given by the tomb-stone-toothed bookseller. She would do her own little bit of research later, when Megan was in bed.

Thinking of Megan reminded her that her daughter had been astoundingly patient whilst this exploration of the church had been in progress, but now it really was time the poor little mite had some fun.

She explained this to Emma, who was at once contrite, "Of course, the poor kid must be bored to death. You must get off at once and find her something good to do – ooh, I know a place she would absolutely love. It's an Elf Farm."

"Health Farm?" queried Fliss, thinking the woman had finally lost whatever marbles she might once have possessed, "Much as I'd enjoy it, I don't think she's quite old enough to appreciate a massage and a wheatgrass smoothie!"

"Not 'health', I said 'elf' as in Lord of the Rings Elves, Dwarves, Fairies, the lot! It's really just a collection of garden gnomes and other statuary in various poses set in a charming little woodland walk, but the kids love it – running through the trees trying to find the next tableau. It's run by two elderly ladies and you can tell they really believe in it all, which adds a certain something to the experience."

"Sounds perfect," said Fliss with a grin, "Do you have directions?"

"Yep, I'm sure I've got a leaflet – we took the playschool kids at Easter – I'll dig it out and give it to you tomorrow at the baby club."

"Great, thanks. I'll see you tomorrow – and thanks for the tour, it was really interesting."

The sun had come out from behind grey clouds and when Fliss walked down the aisle, she saw the dancing colours cast by the stain-glass windows on the stone floors. Perfect, she thought, just perfect.

CHAPTER ELEVEN

"Geraint, suspecting his wife of infidelity, forced her to accompany him on a gruelling journey."

Megan skipped happily in front of her mother down the path leading from the church to the road. She was glad to be out in the sunshine again, for though she had liked the church, she hadn't much cared for all those strangely dressed people she had seen watching her and her mum as the vicar showed them around. She hadn't been afraid exactly, but it had made her unwilling to run and jump and shout as she usually did. It was much better out here in the fresh air.

As they reached the gate Fliss noticed a BMW parked behind her car on the edge of the green. There was a man leaning on the bonnet but she couldn't recognise him at this distance, yet there was something familiar about the car. She had seen it before – and not so very long ago.

A few steps nearer and with a sinking heart she realised she knew both the car and the man – one rather better than the other.

"Daniel!" she called, as she approached, "What on earth are you doing here?"

Even as she spoke he rose from his slouch on the bonnet and the doors opened to let two men out. All three stood waiting for her and she felt her heart hammering as she recognised them.

"What the hell are you doing with them?" she asked her brother, keeping her eyes fixed firmly on his face. If she allowed her gaze to waver in their direction, she knew she would simply fall to pieces and start screaming.

Daniel grinned, pleased to have shocked her, "These two?" he jerked his head backwards to indicate his companions, "These gentlemen came to mum's looking for Bryn, so I thought I might as well bum a lift off them and collect the car – you did tell me to come and get it, after all."

"But I didn't tell you to bring two thugs with you!" she hissed.

Daniel looked surprised, "Thugs? What are you talking about? They said they were friends of Bryn."

"Oh really? And when did you last meet them at a party at my house?"

"When did you last have a party?" he countered swiftly, knowing as well as she did that he probably wouldn't be invited anyway.

"That's beside the point. You should have asked me before you brought strangers here."

"I didn't know they were strangers – and you told me not to contact you again, remember?"

The taller man stepped forward, "Much as I hate to interrupt this touching family reunion, do you think we could get down to business, Danny?"

Fliss pounced on this as evidence of Daniel's double dealing. She knew her brother too well, "Danny? No one except your cronies call you Danny. These two didn't happen to turn up at mother's, and Bryn didn't find their number in the telephone directory, did he?"

Daniel shrugged and Long-shanks lit a cigarette, "Not quite as stupid as you make out, are you love? Now tell us where we can find Bryn and no one will get hurt."

"I'll tell you with pleasure, but you might as well know he doesn't have your money."

"That's not very good news for you, is it?"

Fliss felt the blood drain from her face, but she tried to be brave for Megan's sake. She lifted her chin defiantly, "Once, out of loyalty to my husband, I might have avoided calling the police, but you've just made one threat too far."

He took a step towards her and though her knees threatened to give way, she managed to hold firm. Just at that moment, out of the corner of her eye, Fliss spotted Ted Armitage walking towards the Weary Sportsman. In a panic, and not knowing what else to do, she shouted across the road to him and gesticulated wildly. On hearing his name and realising who it was calling, he swiftly changed direction and was beside her in seconds.

"Something I can do for you, Mrs Elmsworth?"

"She just wanted to say hi," said Daniel, looking daggers at his sister. She ignored him and began to speak, her words falling over themselves in her hurry to explain.

"These men have been threatening me and Megan," she gasped, "Bryn owes them money and they keep following me."

Armitage was a big man, taller even than Long-shanks. He turned his gaze towards the three men, seemingly not in the least intimidated by the fact that he was outnumbered, "Is that a fact?" he asked, his voice flatly calm and somehow more frightening than if he had roared at the top of his voice.

"Don't be ridiculous, sis!" said Daniel, at his most innocuous and friendly, "You can leave it there, mate. My sister's got the wrong end of the stick, as usual."

"The lady doesn't seem to be the gullible sort to me, sonny – and if there's one thing I can't stand, it's a man who doesn't take care of his own kith and kin."

The other man stepped forward and Fliss tried to scream a warning as she saw the flash of his knife. The sound died on her lips as Armitage sidestepped with the speed of a leaping tiger, smacked the man in the face with the full force of his huge fist and as he lay spread out on the ground, wrested the knife from his hand before he knew what had hit him.

Daniel retreated hastily behind the car and Long-shanks also backed off, though not as far as Daniel had fled.

As the third man lay on the floor, Armitage bent down and for one horrified moment, Fliss thought he was about to plunge the knife into his victim. To her relief he merely thrust the blade between the cracks in the pavement then very slowly and deliberately he trod on the hilt until it began to buckle beneath his weight. When he had achieved a right angle he picked it back up and approached Long-shanks. The knife was placed in his breast pocket, so that the muddied and twisted blade stuck out.

"If you want some good advice, chum, get back in your pretty little motor while it still has some wheels and drive away. Whatever business you have with Elmsworth, leave his wife and child out of it, okay?"

Long-shanks nodded, and gesturing to his bloodied companion they both climbed back into the car and drove off at speed, showering Daniel with dust as the wheels spun and shrieked.

"What the hell are you waiting for?" Armitage asked him, no longer hiding his aggression. Daniel tried to look casual, but failed miserably. He wasn't quite as cocky without his bodyguards.

"I came to collect the car," he muttered. Armitage looked down at Fliss, "Do you want me to see him off for you?"

Fliss was still shaking. She had picked up the bewildered Megan and was hugging her, trying to keep the tears at bay.

"No, let him have the stupid car." She dug deep into her jeans pocket, found the keys and flung them in her brother's direction.

"I'll never forgive you for this, Daniel," she said hoarsely.

"'Course you will – I'm your bro!" He caught the keys with ease and walked towards the car door.

"Not anymore you're not." She walked away with a backward glance. Armitage caught her by the elbow and guided her across the road to the pub.

"I think you need a drink," he said quietly.

"I think you're right."

He found her a quiet seat, almost hidden from view behind a wooden partition, and went to the bar, where Polly glanced curiously at her before going to the optics for the brandy Armitage ordered for her. When he returned she was using a shaking hand to wipe away her tears and trying to smile reassuringly at Megan. Silently he handed her his handkerchief and sat down opposite.

"Drink up, you'll feel better."

"I shouldn't, I'm driving – oh, no I'm not!" The reality of what had just happened suddenly kicked in and she looked at him in anguish, "I've sent Daniel away with the child-seat still in the car."

"Don't worry about that. One of the young mums from around and about is bound to have a spare. The vicar will know who to ask."

She shook her head and managed a small laugh, "That should be the least of my worries."

"I think it should. Do you want to tell me what the hell your husband was thinking, getting involved with ruffians like them?"

"Don't ask me. The first I knew of it was the day before yesterday when they forced their way into my house and threatened to rearrange Megan's face with a flick-knife." He looked positively dangerous and asked grimly, "Is that why you followed Bryn up here?"

She nodded, "Yes, thanks to my lovely husband I've been made to beg for a roof over my child's head. Everyone, including you, must have thought I was a complete idiot, dragging a little girl into the wilds of Derbyshire for no apparent reason – but I could hardly explain the circumstances, could I?"

"Your loyalty does you credit, but I'm not sure Bryn deserves it."

"I know he doesn't – but as my mother would say, I've made my bed and now I'll have to lie on it."

He managed to smile without a trace of humour, "Drink your brandy."

She took a sip and made a wry face. She wasn't usually a spirit drinker.

"What are you going to do now?" he asked, watching her face as she drank.

"I don't know. I'm certainly not going home until Bryn has sorted those two out – and that won't be until he gets paid."

"And Bryn? What are you going to do about him?"

She looked up and met his gaze squarely, "If you are asking me if I'm going to leave him, I'd have to say I really don't know. Just at this moment I don't think I could even bear to be in the same room with him, but I have Megan to consider."

"Fond of her daddy, is she?" he asked ironically, one eyebrow lifted, his head to one side, looking for all the world like one of his own sheepdogs in inquisitive mode.

Fliss began to giggle, which then turned into a full-blown belly laugh, "You are such a rat Mr Armitage! You know she isn't."

His grin made him look irrepressibly boyish, "Well, there you have it, in a nutshell. I'll say one thing then I'll not mention it again. If you want a roof 'til you're back on your feet, there's a housekeeper job begging to be done at my house – no strings attached."

She looked at him, but his face gave nothing away. She couldn't see if he was just being kind to a woman in need or if he had an agenda of his own.

"Thank you. It will ease a lot of concerns knowing that – and in the meantime, I'll do a bit of cleaning for you to say thank you for the bed and breakfast."

"No need. Professor Norton is paying for that."

She groaned and covered her face with her hands, "Oh God, that means I owe him too! Is there no end to this mess?"

"Don't beat yourself up – he can afford it."

"That's hardly the point though, is it?"

Polly popped her head around the edge of the partition, "Excuse the interruption, but a guy who said he's your brother just dropped a child seat in the tap room and said you'd probably be needing it."

Fliss summoned a smile, "Thanks Polly – that's one less problem, anyway."

"You sound down in the dumps. Anything I can do to help?"

"No, really, I'm okay. It's just been a tough couple of days, but I'm getting through it."

"Well, just sing out if you change your mind. If there's one thing villages do well, it is rally around to help out."

"I'm finding that out. And I'm really grateful. Everyone has been very kind."

To her utter humiliation she burst into tears. Polly signalled to Armitage with a jerk of her head that he should make himself scarce, which he reluctantly obeyed, and she plonked herself down beside Fliss and put a comforting arm around her shoulder, "Hey, come on. Nothing is worth all this."

"Oh, Polly, I'm at my wit's end."

"If it's bothering you that much staying at the farm, you can always de-camp to here, you know."

"Can't afford it," sniffed Fliss, "Anyway it's not that. Mr Armitage has been very kind, letting us stay in his house."

Now Polly was shocked, "In the house? I thought you were camping out in the barn with the others."

"I was, but Professor Norton insisted I bring Megan indoors and Mr Armitage has given us free run of the place."

"Bloody hell!" exclaimed Polly, "I've never known him do that before."

"I think it was more for Megan's sake than mine. He seems very taken with her."

"I wouldn't be too sure of that – as far as I'm aware he's never shown the slightest interest in kids before – on the contrary, he usually chases them off his land."

"Correct me if I'm wrong, but isn't that sort of a good thing? Better than the opposite, anyway! And whatever his reasons I'm very grateful."

Polly laughed at her candour, "Good point. Drink up and I'll get you a refill – on the house."

"I'd rather have a cup of tea if that is all right – and thanks Polly, I feel much better now, really I do."

"Okay, but you know where I am if you want to talk."

Polly went off to the kitchen and Armitage, seeing her walk past him in the bar, returned to Fliss and said quietly, "Let me know when you are ready and I'll drive you back to the farm."

"I don't want to be a nuisance. You do your errands first. I'll wait here until you are ready to go back. I'm sure Polly won't mind."

"Never mind that. Just say the word – the child seat is already in the land-rover."

She smiled, truly thankful to have his support, even in so small a matter, "Polly is just making me a cup of tea – as soon as I've drunk that, I'm ready to go."

"Fine. I'll be in the bar."

Polly came back with a small tray, containing tea and a drink of juice for Megan, who was sat on the pew-like seat, her eyes wide, wondering what on earth was going on. She rarely saw her mother cry and she didn't like the experience. Polly had seen the bewildered little face and produced a chocolate bar from her pocket, "There you go sweetheart. I'm not even going to ask mummy's permission, you are having that treat no matter what!"

The tea was almost gone and Megan was happily smeared in melting chocolate when the pub door swung open once more to admit Fliss's husband, who, despite her semi-hidden position, spotted her immediately and swaggered aggressively over to her with the loving greeting, "What the hell are you doing in here?"

Fliss was in no mood to be conciliatory, "Having a cup of tea – and I could ask you the same question. Sneaking off for a pint instead of getting on with your job?"

"Actually, I was asked to collect the lunches today. It seems Polly has somewhere to go later and didn't have time for her usual delivery."

"Asked, or volunteered in the hope of necking a swift one?" said Fliss sarcastically. His deepening colour told her that she had guessed correctly. She decided that now was her best moment to attack. Her natural reluctance to cause a scene in public meant that normally she would have waited until they were alone, but the very fact that she had spent the morning being frightened out of her wits, whilst the worst thing he had to worry about was a warm beer, just made her see the proverbial red.

"Sit down," she hissed, "I have something to say to you."

"It can wait," he growled and started to walk away.

"Bryn, I'm warning you now, if you don't sit down and discuss this, it'll be the last time you see me outside a courtroom." Her voice was quiet, but he evidently heard her clearly enough, because he turned back and looked at her. Something in her face told him that for once she was in deadly earnest for he walked back and sat opposite her, "Make it fast," he said, "I've better things to do with my time than listen to your whining."

She stared at him for so long without speaking that he grew

unnerved and shifted uncomfortably in his seat, "What?" he snapped eventually.

"Did you ever love me, Bryn?"

"Oh for God's sake, do you really think this is the time and place to start all that rubbish?"

"No, you're right. That wasn't what I wanted to talk to you about, I don't know why I said it. I just thought I ought to warn you that Daniel brought those two characters here. They threatened Megan again, but Mr Armitage smacked one of them in the nose and they left – but they are not happy."

Fliss watched in fascination as her husband's previous high colour faded swiftly to a sickly whitish green, "He did what?"

"Who, Daniel or Armitage?"

"Don't bother to repeat it, I heard you. Now it'll really hit the fan."

"Good, it's just what you deserve, you rat!" Fliss's tone belied her words, for she tried to keep her voice even so that she would not frighten her little girl again. The child had witnessed enough adult violence, verbal and physical, for one day.

"Don't be so eager to see me go down, Fliss. This involves you too."

"Not as long as I stay here it doesn't – and if you think I'm leaving the safety of the farm until you've sorted this mess out, you are very sadly mistaken."

He gave a mirthless laugh, "That's what you think. Exactly how long do you think that miserable old straw-sucker is going to tolerate a kid running around his precious house?"

"According to him – as long as I want."

She stood up, "Come on Meggie, Mr Armitage is taking us back to the farm now."

A backward glance would have shown her an expression of disbelief on Bryn's face, but she never bothered to look at him again.

CHAPTER TWELVE

"Morrigan, an Irish Goddess of death on the battlefield – her favourite form was the crow"

Armitage said nothing until they were in his vehicle and on the bumpy road back to the farm, then he glanced sideways at his passenger, noting her grim expression.

"I gather you had a word with your husband about what just happened back there?"

"I did."

He waited for her to volunteer further information and when she did not, he asked, "You'll forgive my interest, but am I likely to have unwelcome visitors at the farm?"

This was not something she had considered and was at once contrite, "I'm so sorry Mr Armitage, it never occurred to me that you might have reason to worry."

"Call me Ted, everyone else does."

"Do you mind if I make that Edward? Ted makes you sound about a hundred years old."

He laughed, "Actually it's Theodore – but I try to keep that quiet."

"Why? Theo is a nice name."

"Use that if you like, then – and don't get the wrong idea about your two thugs. I'm not worried – I'd just like to be prepared in case I need to protect my livestock and property. I know how that sort work. If they can't get you, they take it out on whatever they can."

"Oh God, this is just awful!" she exclaimed tearfully, "Now I've put you and yours in danger."

"No you haven't. I'm just erring on the side of caution. Chances are they'll realise that though you would be reluctant to go to the police, I certainly wouldn't hesitate. I'm sorry I mentioned it; now forget it, for God's sake."

She subsided into silence, staring out of the window, so she didn't have to catch his eye should he chance another glance at her. She need not have been concerned. He kept his attention firmly on the road.

As they approached the lop-sided gateposts that marked the start of his land, she shivered as she realised that two huge crows were perched atop of each, their seemingly malevolent yellow eyes watching as they passed. He noticed her revulsion and grinned, "Not enough for a 'murder'," he remarked.

"What?" asked Fliss, startled.

"A gathering of crows is called a 'murder', but I don't think two counts."

"Nasty looking creatures, aren't they?" she ventured.

"Nasty habits, too. If they hang around, I might have to go out with my shotgun. They take the eyes out of young lambs if they get the chance."

Fliss shuddered, "Did you have to tell me that?"

"Not really, but a townie should know the facts about these things. If I just told you I was going to shoot crows, you'd think I was unspeakably cruel, wouldn't you?"

She had to admit that she probably would, but the memory of the evil looking birds made her shiver. She turned to check on Megan and saw that she too seemed repulsed by the creatures, her hands were covering her face, but she was peeping between spread fingers back over her shoulder, as though she couldn't bear to take her eyes off the birds, but was also too terrified to look directly at them.

"It's all right, baby, the nasty birds have gone now," she said soothingly, pulling the little girl's hands down.

"Nasty birds," said Megan decidedly.

They drew into the farmyard and something made Fliss look up. The crows were now circling over the house, looking like a pair of wheeling vultures. She shuddered and hurriedly released her daughter from her straps and took her into the house.

Armitage followed looking amused, "Seems to me you've been watching too many movies. Hitchcock has been dead for years you know."

"I know I'm being irrational, but they really looked as though they'd like to dive bomb us."

"I can assure you they won't – they are more afraid of you that you are of them."

"I'd feel happier if they looked it."

"Well, there's nothing I can do about that. What are your plans for the rest of the day? I've got to get on with things now, but I won't be far away if you're worried your friends might resurface."

"Actually I thought I might do a little housework for you, if you wouldn't be offended. It would make me feel better about taking your hospitality."

"Feel free. Do whatever you like – but don't work too hard, it's really not worth shattering yourself."

"If I do go out later, do you want me to lock up?"

"I don't usually bother – but given the present climate, I think that might not be a bad idea. I've got a spare set of keys somewhere. I'll dig 'em out for you."

When the keys were found and Armitage gone outside, Fliss looked around and began to regret the impulsive offer of domestic drudgery. The place really hadn't been touched with a duster or a vacuum cleaner for years. With a sigh, she headed for the pantry and the cupboard under the sink, where she assumed she might find cloths and cleaning fluids. She did, but the minute sums of money indicated on the price tags told her just how long ago they had been purchased. The rusty tin of "Ajax" was even marked in pre-decimal figures. She could only hope they didn't lose their power with the passage of time. She made them a sandwich and a drink then set to work.

✳

It was late afternoon by the time she decided she had done enough for one day. Megan had been a treasure, dusting with her mother and standing on a stool to reach the sink and wash unbreakables, but the last thing Fliss wanted her to learn was that housework was a woman's lot in life. Time to show her little daughter that housework had its place, but that place wasn't the centre of a woman's universe.

She put a cautious head outside and was relieved to see that the crow couple had apparently grown weary of waiting and had taken themselves off elsewhere. She put on their coats and taking Megan by the hand, she led the way across the garden to the path leading through the woods and up onto the moors.

Low cloud had brought an early dusk-like light, making the woods even darker and more menacing than usual. They hurried on, Fliss ignoring the rustle of undergrowth and the whisper of the breeze amongst the leaves. She just wanted to escape the trees and get to the dig. Once there the light wasn't much better and Fliss could barely discern the figures of the diggers amongst the standing stones – so much so that she had no idea which were human and which were rock. She felt very alone and vulnerable under the foliage and hurried across the uneven ground towards them, telling herself that it was more than imbecilic to allow herself to be spooked by a couple of birds and inclement weather conditions, but she still couldn't shake off the feeling that she needed to be near other human beings.

Though the site was now littered with the paraphernalia needed on the dig, nothing had managed to disturb the tranquillity of the place. The portaloos had been shrouded by the mist and could almost have been standing stones themselves, draped as they were by a veil of Mother Nature's making. From this distance she could almost imagine there were no people around even though common sense told her they were there. She tried to listen for their voices, to reassure herself that she wasn't going to be alone when she finally reached the stones, but the wet peat seemed to absorb sound as surely as it absorbed water.

She found it wasn't much better when she reached her

objective. The atmosphere around the biggest carved stone was heavy and unpleasant, almost as though some invisible force was dragging her towards the ground. She felt she could barely put one foot in front of the other and when she looked around she found that Megan had released her hand and was stood just outside the entrance to the circle, a stubborn expression on her little face.

"Come here sweetheart, to mummy," she said coaxingly, but Megan shook her head and folded her arms in a caricature of adult refusal, "Nasty in there," she said firmly.

Fliss looked around for Fergus or John Norton and seeing neither she gladly removed herself, joining Megan at the two gate stones. Helen and Anne-Marie, at the far side of the circle and previously hidden from her view, looked up briefly from their sketching and measuring and greeted her warmly, "Looking for your husband?" asked Helen.

"Not really, but is he around?"

"Over at the bog with the Prof," she answered, "They've been there all afternoon, scraping the bottom and sieving the mud. I think they've had quite a few interesting finds. It seems it was a place of worship and ritual offerings."

"Yeah, and we're stuck here with the bloody boring measuring stick," muttered Anne-Marie mutinously, "Trust the men to get in on the interesting stuff and leave us to do all the donkey work."

"Typical," agreed Fliss absent-mindedly.

"Hey, what's it like in the house with the scary farmer?" asked Angela, sliding between two half-fallen stones and walking across to join them. Fliss noticed that she seemed entirely unaffected by the stone circle, strolling easily and smiling as though she had not a care in the world.

Just me then, she thought, perhaps my mother is right and I am 'fey'.

"He's been very nice actually," she answered, returning the smile, "A real gentleman. He's given me the run of the place."

"Charming! He wouldn't even let us use the loo. We've been having to go in the old servant's outside lav, behind the stables."

"Oh he thinks I'm a damsel in distress – I have Megan to thank for my different treatment, I can assure you."

"Yeah right," said Anne-Marie, with an edge to her voice, "Have a kid and you rule the world. It gets you everything from a seat on the bus to a council house."

"Huh, I wish that were true," she snorted contemptuously before she could stop herself, then realised she had been a little too emphatic, so added a little more mildly, "I haven't been given a seat on a bus for years – not since I was young and single!"

"Yeah, yeah, what you mean is young with big boobs!"

Fliss decided not to rise to this bait, merely saying that she would see them later and headed off in the direction of the bog.

The low cloud had settled over the surface of the water in a dense fog and Fliss watched in fascination as it curled and spread, billowed and retreated with the disturbance caused by the dip and scoop of the huge excavator.

Fergus saw her first and hailed her enthusiastically, "Hi, Fliss come and look at our finds."

Professor Norton and Bryn both looked up when they heard him shout her name. The professor smiled and waved, but Bryn hunched his shoulders and turned his attention back to the black, muddy water.

Two of the men Fliss had been introduced to in the pub were busy shovelling the pile of excavated mud into a large box-like contraption which Fliss realised was actually a sieve, held at waist level on a rough wooden stand. It looked like back-breaking work, but would have been more so had the sieve been simply laid on the ground. Shep was wielding the spade and Trev sifting the debris.

"What have you found then?" she asked and Fergus was immediately by her side, ready to show off the fruits of their labours, which were lying just at the far side of the sieve, neat rows of plastic trays and boxes, and one or two tarpaulin sheets for the larger items. Con and Don were there busily sorting the wet offerings placed in a pile by Trev.

Con seemed glad enough to stand up, arch his obviously aching back, and tell Fliss what was going on.

"A first basic glance sorts the rubbish from genuine artefacts –

one man's bit of old wood might be another's Celtic carving. Then there's a further sub-division depending on age. So far we've found stuff from Celtic, Roman, Iron Age and Bronze Age. This has evidently been a place of worship for thousands of years. We've even found Victorian coins and a couple of fifty pence pieces."

"So people are still throwing in offerings today?"

"Looks like it – but most people can't resist throwing a coin into water – the Trevi Fountain must earn bucket-loads for the Italian Government!"

"I think it goes to Charity. Do you mind if I take a closer look?"

"Not at all, but if you pick anything up, make sure you put it back in the same tray – or I might have to kill you." He added with mock severity.

She laughed, "I'll be careful, I promise."

Most of the objects were unrecognisable to an amateur like Fliss, muddy bits of wood, green-stained lumps which apparently were metal and stuff that just looked like stones to her until it was pointed out that they had holes bored through them and had once been strung together to form a necklace. Most of it still had a layer of sludge adhering to it, which didn't help with identification and Fliss wondered how Con could see the good stuff amongst the bad. One or two things, however, were quite obviously special and even Fliss could see it. There were several wooden carvings, mostly representing vaguely human forms, but roughly carved, and one or two were just heads, reminding Fliss too closely of the stone triple head for her to want to touch them. The one thing her hand did stretch out for, before she could stop herself, was a little metal pig. She picked it up and examined it closely. Pig was too modern a term to describe it. It was a boar, with a stiff little ridge along its back, meant to look like bristles, and two long, tusk-like teeth. It was so like the picture that Megan had insisted was the same as the pig in the wood that Fliss felt a little shiver of deja-vu. She put it hastily back where she had found it.

Two stone carvings also caught her eye. These were flat stones with picture cut in relief and she marvelled at the artistry of the unknown maker. With only rudimentary tools, he had cut pictures showing a central figure of a horned man, seated, cross-legged on what seemed to be almost a throne. There was a stag and a boar at his cloven feet and acolytes behind him. In his hand he held a horn of plenty. The second was a 'close-up' showing just the face of the same figure. This showed more clearly that his horns were like antlers and around his neck he wore a torc.

Fergus had wandered off and he now returned to see her looking at the carving, "Handsome fellow, isn't he?"

Fliss shuddered, "Not really, he looks like the Devil."

"Ah," said Fergus meaningfully, "That's what you are supposed to think."

"Meaning?" she asked, slightly impatiently. She was getting a little tired of her ignorance being continually paraded for everyone else's amusement.

"It's Cernunnos, Celtic god of prosperity, amongst other things. But the early Christian Church wanted to discredit the old gods – so what better way to do that than attribute his most prominent features to Satan. Horns and cloven hooves were suddenly the epitome of evil."

"So that's why Paganism became almost synonymous with Devil Worship?"

"And witchcraft – anything that harked back to the old religion."

"PR in the early church was pretty damned effective, wasn't it?"

"Certainly was – and male chauvinism won the day too. Suddenly Eve became responsible for the whole sorry mess."

She reached for something else; a large oval-ish pebble – or so it seemed to her, "Why this thing? It's just a big stone."

"Not quite," replied Fergus, "Look closer and you'll see that it has been fashioned into that shape. It's not natural at all." Fliss did as he suggested and could see that the stone had indeed been chamfered all around to give it a distinctive shape, pointed at one end and flattened at the other.

"I see – but what was it for? It must have had a use, since they went to so much trouble to shape it."

"It was a ceremonial axe – very probably used in the sacrifice of humans. You know that the Celts performed the triple death? Well this was probably the axe that delivered the stunning blow, just before the garrotte and the throat cutting."

She dropped it hastily back into its box, "Thanks for filling me in one that one," she said with distaste. She looked across to check on Megan and noticed the little girl had wandered away from her side and was now pulling at Professor Norton's coat, demanding to be picked up. Fliss hastily replaced the other items and headed over to stop her daughter from making a nuisance of herself. She needn't have worried, Norton looked down, smiled and lifted the little girl into his arms, pointing at the digger and obviously telling her all about it. By the time Fliss arrived at his side, he was talking quite happily to his young companion.

"I'm so sorry, Professor, you must be busy. I'll take Megan away now."

"Don't worry, Mrs Elmsworth, she's fine. She likes the digger."

"Are you looking for the man?" Megan suddenly asked the Professor.

"What man, sweetheart?" he asked.

"The man over there, the Robin man." She pointed out across the water. Fliss wondered what on earth she was talking about. She looked out across the misty water.

"What does she mean?" asked Norton, genuinely puzzled by the reference.

"I don't know," answered Fliss, adding, "What do you mean, Megan? Who's the Robin man? Do you mean Robin Hood, like in your cartoon?"

"No," she answered scornfully, "Not that Robin. Robin like the birdie on Christmas Card, he's got a red chest."

"A red chest? Where is this man?"

Megan pointed unwavering in the same direction as she had before, straight out across the water, "Over there, in the water."

As Fliss squinted, trying to see in the gathering darkness and through the mist, she could almost swear that the fog had swirled into the vague silhouette of a man for the briefest second before dispersing again.

Professor Norton was suddenly serious. He thrust Megan into Fliss's arms and approached the digger, "Trevor, take the arm out over there, as far as you can," he shouted above the sound the motor.

He returned to Megan, "Is that the place, Megan?" he asked.

"Bit more that way," said Megan with a wave of her hand.

"You are not planning on listening to a kid, are you?" said Bryn, coming nearer as he realised what was happening.

"We've nothing to lose," answered Norton shortly.

He gave Trev the instructions and the scoop plunged into the muddy water.

The second time it rose out of the water, it was obvious to all that there was something solid in the bucket. It looked like a piece of wood until a segment fell away and hung in mid air, still attached to the main trunk. A dangling arm, muddy water dripping from the fingers.

"Jesus Christ Almighty," whispered Con, "That's a body."

CHAPTER THIRTEEN

"Nemain, one of the dreadful goddesses of war, sometimes seen as the washer at the ford, rinsing the bloodied raiment of those destined to die in battle."

A stark silence greeted this pronouncement then suddenly everything became business-like.

"Mrs Elmsworth, I don't think this is the place for Megan just now."

"No, I'll take her back to the farm, but before I go, could I offer a little piece of advice?"

He was obviously distracted, but even so maintained his courtesy, "Of course, what is it?"

"The three girls back at the circle are already feeling a little left out of things, with all you men here doing the interesting jobs. Don't you think it would be a nice gesture to call them over. This is a really exciting find, after all."

He smiled briefly, "Invaluable advice. Never alienate your staff if you can help it." He turned to Don and asked, "Could you run and fetch the girls?"

"No need," said Fliss, "I'll tell them on my way back down."

"You could do me another service, if you would."

"Certainly. What is it?"

"Any find of human remains has to be reported to the local coroner, by law. Could you use the telephone in the farm to ring the police and find out what the number is? Under normal circumstances I would have the number ready but I must admit I didn't think this site would yield bones let alone anything more."

"Of course. Do you want me to speak to the coroner's office, or just get the number?"

He glanced down at his watch, "Umm, it's getting late. By the time I've finished here and walked back to the farm, office hours will be over, though in theory, the coroner should be available whatever the hour. Do you think you could handle the phone call yourself?"

"I don't see why not. I only need to tell them who you are and what the find is, don't I?"

"And the location. Very well, I'll leave that in your very capable hands. Thank you Mrs Elmsworth."

As this conversation progressed, the arm of the excavator had been swinging gently towards them, extra care being taken to ensure that the precious cargo didn't dislodge and sink back into the waiting waters.

Just as it reached the edge of the pool, Fliss took Megan's hand and began to lead her away, with many a longing backward glance. She was as intrigued as anyone else to view the find, though slightly repulsed too, but she agreed with Professor Norton. A dead body, no matter how old, was not a fit sight for a three year old girl.

As she passed the stone ring, she called out to the three young women, who had evidently decided to give themselves a break and were sitting on the fallen stone she had utilised the day before.

"The professor wants you over by the bog. They've found something."

"Anything interesting?" called Angela back.

"Oh yes!"

They needed no second bidding, notebooks, clipboards, pencils and measuring tapes and sticks were abandoned and they ran as fast as their legs could carry them. Fliss watched them enviously for a moment until they were lost to her sight, then with a sigh led her daughter back towards the wood.

✳

DI Matt Piper was sitting at his desk, looking at a pile of paper-work in his "in-tray" and debating whether to make a start or just go home and come in early tomorrow. TWOCs, shop-lifting and drunk and disorderly weren't exactly riveting stuff and there was a cold lager in his fridge with his name on it. Briefly he tried to remember what exactly had attracted him to a life in the police force, but he couldn't recall a single defining moment.

The phone rang and made him jump, so much so that he laughed at himself. Big, strong copper who is scared by the ringing of a telephone.

There was still a laugh in his voice as he answered, "DI Piper."

"Hiya, Matt, it's Lucy out at the front desk. I've got some woman on the phone, reckons she's found a body. Shall I put her through?"

The slump left his body and he shot bolt upright, "What?"

"A body," she repeated succinctly.

"Oh God, yes, put her through!"

There was the usual short delay whilst the switchboard did its stuff, then Piper found himself speaking to a young woman, who, he thought, sounded remarkably calm considering she had a dead body on her hands, "This is DI Piper speaking. Can I help you, madam?"

"DI? Oh, I'm sure I didn't need to disturb you. The young lady could have given me the Coroner's number."

"We'll arrange for the Coroner if necessary, madam. Now, would you like to tell me exactly what happened."

"Professor Norton asked me to ring. He has uncovered a bog-body at Broadbarrow Loe Farm and I understand from him that it is necessary to inform the Coroner."

Piper felt his excitement plummet, "A bog body? You're from the archaeological dig?"

"Yes. I did try to explain to the young lady, but the moment she heard the word 'body' she transferred me to you."

"She would. Just hold on a second and I'll find the number for you, Mrs …"

Fliss gave her name, then waited as he put down the receiver and began shuffling the papers on his desk. A few seconds went by then she heard his voice again, "Here it is. Do you have a pen?"

Fliss took the number and thanked him, but just before she could hang up she heard him say, "Excuse me, but do you think Professor Norton would object if I popped over to have a look? I'd be really interested."

She didn't quite know what to say. It was probably best not to upset the local constabulary, but on the other hand, the professor wouldn't want all and sundry invading his site. She made a quick decision, "Well, I'm sure he wouldn't object to you coming, but I must ask that you don't bring a crowd of sightseers with you."

"No, just me, I promise."

"Okay. Perhaps I'll meet you later then."

"I'm looking forward to it."

Piper grinned to himself as he hung up. A look at a bog-body and a meeting with a young-sounding woman. What more could a lonely, divorced policeman ask for?

✳

As the afternoon wore on, Fliss began to feel more and more dejected. Everyone, it seemed, had some important task to accomplish, whilst she sat at the farmhouse window and watched the world go by. She briefly met the DI, whose name she had forgotten, when he pulled into the farmyard and she went out to direct him to the dig. She thought that somehow he matched his voice. Dark brown. His voice, on the telephone had been deep, resonant, reassuring. Now that she looked at him, he was just the same. His hair was the darkest brown, without being black, his eyes the sort of hazel that had more brown flecks than green. His face was ordinary, but pleasant. A man you could feel safe with. She would like to bet that he had become a policeman for all the right reasons. He would not be a little tin god who did a 'stop and search' just because he didn't like the look of you.

Cutting across her thoughts, a man from the Coroner's office arrived literally seconds after him, so he took over and led them away across the field. Fliss was left feeling frustrated and useless. She was dying to know what was going on, but with Megan in tow, she had no choice but to sit tight and pretend she wanted to read to her little girl.

She must have read at least eight stories, but she didn't recall the content of any of them. Megan seemed quite contented, but was evidently fully aware of her mother's feelings for she suddenly said, "Mummy, why don't you make a cup of tea? You'll feel better."

Fliss couldn't help laughing. The tone, the sentiment, were her own mother to a tee.

"Thanks honey, I'll do just that. Do you want to watch television?"

There was an ancient set in the corner of the parlour, which still worked, but was so basic that it could barely receive Channel Four, let alone Five. Fliss wouldn't have been surprised to have switched it on and found the old test-card picture of the girl and the clown.

Leaving her daughter happily settled in front of the box, she went to the kitchen to make the tea. A knock at the door startled her, but she quickly recovered herself and flew to answer it, pathetically grateful for the chance to speak to an adult.

It was the DI and she stared at him in surprise for a few seconds before remembering her manners and trying to explain why she couldn't invite him inside.

"I'm so sorry. This isn't my house. I'm only staying whilst my husband is on the dig. Mr Armitage is ..."

"Don't worry, madam, I know Ted Armitage. There's no need to explain. I just wanted to call and see if you were all right. It must have been a nasty shock, digging up the body."

She didn't like to explain that her over-riding emotion had been excitement, not shock. It was slightly embarrassing to be credited with finer feelings that one obviously didn't possess. She couldn't even understand herself why the passing of time should make a difference, but the fact was that a thousand year-old body was much less horrifying than a new one.

"I'm fine," she said eventually, "Once I realised it was a bog-body I was more interested than anything else."

"I can understand that – but why aren't you still up there now?"

"I have a three-year old daughter, so I thought it best to get her out of the vicinity."

"Oh, I see," he looked thoughtful, "well, I'd better be on my way."

She found her hand fluttering out towards him in a vague effort to stop his departure, "Oh, just a minute, don't go. Tell me what is going on up there? I'm dying of curiosity."

"Okay. The Coroner's officer has spoken to Professor Norton and they've agreed that for the moment the body should remain up on the moor, so they are erecting a tent over it. They'll have to keep it submerged in bog water or decomposition will set in fairly rapidly. I'm afraid a couple of your lads are going to have to spend the night up there with it."

Fliss was surprised and showed it, "Why has it to stay up there?"

"It's too dark to manhandle it back through the woods and to get a vehicle up on the moor at night is nearly as difficult. It just seems easier to leave it where it is for the present. It will help to preserve it until they can get it under lab conditions."

"Do they know anything about it?"

"Only that it is male – and in a remarkable state of preservation. There's lots of excitement, but we've all been sworn to secrecy. The professor doesn't want a crowd of journalists bothering him until he has had chance to examine it more closely."

"Megan was right," she murmured without thinking.

"What?" His sharp tone made her realise that she had spoken out loud and she hastily tried to explain the comment away, "My little girl said she could see a man in the water. It was nothing, just a vivid imagination."

The policeman in him was intrigued, but he tried not to show it, "You said she was only three. That's a very vivid imagination for one so young?"

Her grin wasn't very convincing, "She takes after her mother," she said lightly, then added,

"Do they think it was a sacrificial killing? It's not just some poor soul who fell in the water?"

"No chance! Not unless he smacked his head, strangled himself and cut his own throat on the way down."

Fliss pulled a face which showed her distaste, "They didn't leave things to chance, did they?"

"Nope. He was well dead by the time they put him in the bog."

"Thank heavens for small mercies."

"Very small mercies. He would have been stunned, but still alive when they forced his head back with the garrotte and cut his throat."

Shuddering, Fliss reflected that she had been wrong. Time didn't make death any less horrific.

✳

Theo's Land Rover pulled into the yard just as the policeman and the man from the Coroner's office left. He joined Fliss on the doorstep from where she had been waving farewell.

"Something going on?" he asked tersely, nodding towards the retreating cars.

She gave him a shortened version of events, watching carefully for his reaction. How would he feel to know his land contained a place of sacrifice? She wasn't sure how happy she would be to know there were bodies in her back garden.

"It's a man?" was all he asked and she nodded, "Why?"

"It's funny. I always had the sort of feeling that it might be a female." He walked past her into the house and put the kettle on. She followed him, dumbfounded, "What?"

"What do you mean, what?" he responded, infuriatingly calm.

"You sound as though you knew there was a body."

"I suppose I did, in a way."

She drew in a deep breath and tried to marshal her thoughts, "Would you like to explain exactly what you mean, Theo?"

He turned around and looked at her in surprise, "I'd have thought that you of all people would have felt it."

"Felt what?" she asked – she wanted to scream at him, but managed to restrain herself.

"There has always been a tradition of a ghost up on the moors. Vague and misty, enticing people off the path and into the bog. Mostly it's assumed it's a man, but personally I always felt it was a woman."

She laughed nervously, "You are pulling my leg, aren't you?"

"Never been more serious, love."

He meant it. Fliss was stunned. This whole situation was becoming more and more bizarre with every passing second.

A knock at the door precluded further conversation. It was Angela, who had been sent by the professor to ask Fliss if she needed a lift down to the pub for supper. Bryn, apparently, had offered to stay with the body on first watch. Con and Don would eat and come straight back up to relieve him and Trev. Norton and Fergus would do the over-night guard duty from midnight to dawn.

Fliss was about to accept the offer when Theo intercepted, "The child seat is already in my Rover," he said, "I'll take Mrs Elmsworth down for her meal. That way she can leave when Megan gets tired."

Angela shrugged, "Okay. See you later, Fliss." With that she was gone. Fliss's first reaction was to assure Theo that he didn't have to keep running around after her, but she bit her tongue and left well alone. Let the man do whatever he wanted to. She was tired of being grateful and under obligation.

She went to fetch Megan from in front of the telly and found her curled up on the settee with the two black and white collies. That reminded her of the night before and she went briefly back to the kitchen to speak to the farmer, "Theo, could you do me a small favour?"

"Certainly, what is it?"

"The dogs disturbed me last night, snuffling at my bedroom door. Can you make sure they don't do the same again tonight?"

He was sat at the kitchen table, drinking tea and reading the paper. When she said this, he looked up at her, a slight frown between his brows, "The dogs never go upstairs, Fliss. They have the run of the place downstairs to deter burglars, but they never go near the bedrooms."

126

"Well, they did last night."

He looked unconvinced, but was apparently not prepared to argue about it, "I'll shut 'em in the kitchen."

"Thanks, I'd really appreciate it. I was frightened to death until I realised what it was."

He grinned, "We can't have that, now can we?" She was glad he hadn't taken offence, but she felt so strongly about the matter that she had no choice but to mention it. He said nothing else but put down his cup and paper and shrugged himself into his jacket.

She went back to the parlour and taking her daughter by the hand, led her through the house and into the yard where Theo was already waiting for them and within a few minutes she was in the Land Rover next to him heading back down to the Weary Sportsman.

CHAPTER FOURTEEN

*"One of Arthur's warriors, Peredur, grew up strong and agile,
but devoid of courtly manners."*

When she entered the pub Fliss was immediately summoned to a table at the far side of the room by an excited Helen, "Come and join us, Fliss," she called. Fliss glanced at Armitage in case he was expecting her to keep him company, but he had already spied a couple of his own cronies and was heading for the tap room, "Call me when you are ready to go back," he said as he walked away.

"Okay," she answered diffidently and went towards the waiting girls. The situation was beginning to feel distinctly odd. Her husband and her own car were back at the farm, but she was here at the beck and call of a man she had known for only two days – and was happier with that than she would be in the company of the man with whom she had exchanged vows. It felt like Bryn was the stranger.

Helen had shifted along the pew-like bench so that she and Megan could sit and barely waited for them to do just that before she began a breathless regaling of their exciting afternoon. Fliss was torn by the story. She was delighted that the professor had told the girls that it was she who had told him to call them over to the bog, but hearing all the news second-hand was rather painful.

"Where are the men?" she asked, noticing for the first time that apart from Con, the others were nowhere to be seen.

"Oh, they all wanted to stay a bit longer. We were starving, so we made Con drive us down," said Angela.

"I'm taking my driving test as soon as we get back," muttered a glowering Anne-Marie, "I'm sick of having to wait around and beg for lifts." It was obvious she was still annoyed that they had been left out of the excitement of the discovery until the last minute – and even then only had Fliss to thank for their inclusion.

"What happens next?" Fliss asked, valiantly trying not to let her disappointment show.

"As soon as we can move the body, it'll be taken to the lab so that proper tests can be carried out. Then we should know exactly how old he was when he was killed, how long ago that was, everything he ate and drank – the same as a modern autopsy really, but it will give us invaluable information. In the meantime, we keep digging! As soon as the measurements and diagrams are finished, the professor wants to excavate one of the standing stones so that we can find out exactly how long they have been there. If we can match the ring with the body, it will tell us an awful lot. We may know, once and for all, if henges were built to perform ritualistic killings." Helen scarcely drew breath as she quietly explained all this and Fliss had to hide a smile. It was the most she had heard the young woman say since her arrival.

Polly came over and they ordered their meals, "You all look flushed. Has something exciting happened?" Since they were all under strict instructions not to mention their find, this was vehemently denied, but Polly didn't appear to be fooled for a second. She raised one quizzical brow, smiled knowingly and went off to fetch their meals.

They were half way though their respective dinners when the men arrived. They went straight to the bar, but Professor Norton headed towards the girls. He couldn't keep the smile off his face and Fliss thought what a difference it made to his demeanour. He looked young and full of vitality. It made her want to smile too, though she was still gutted that all the good stuff was happening without her around.

"Here's my little psychic," he said to Megan as he sat down. For some reason this description of her daughter unnerved Fliss to such an extent that she felt obliged to deny the suggestion.

"I'm sure it was merely a coincidence," she said, her tone sounding stiff even to her own ears. The subtlety was not lost on the professor and he immediately backed off, smiling disarmingly.

"Of course it was – but a lucky coincidence for us."

She was grateful he didn't pursue the matter and her manner towards him softened considerably, "This must be a very satisfactory event for you, professor. Have you ever found anything like this before?"

"Never. I've had my moments – who hasn't? But this is something special." He glanced around the table and made sure that everyone else was, for the moment, preoccupied, then he said quietly, "And whether you like it or not, Mrs Elmsworth, I have you to thank for that."

There was a note in his voice that made the blood rush into her face. His eyes held hers for a moment then confused, she looked away. He swiftly patted her hand then said jovially, "Can I get you ladies a drink? No champagne today, I'm afraid, but as soon as the news is out, I shall make it my business to buy a few bottles."

Fliss felt that she could quite happily throw back a large glass of wine, and then another, but she shook her head, smiling slightly, "Not for me. A mother is never off duty."

"An orange juice then? What about you Angela? Your usual? Anne-Marie, I can't afford your usual! You can have half a lager and like it." Amid the laughter and banter, Fliss managed to hide her emotions and forced herself to calm down. He had meant nothing by his comment, so why was she colouring up like a silly schoolgirl? She couldn't have been more relieved when the advent of a newcomer took attention away from her crimson face.

She had no idea who he was, but every head in the pub turned when he walked in and she realised he must be someone fairly important.

"Good evening, good evening one and all!" he said heartily, pausing to shake the occasional hand, slap a back or give a friendly punch on the arm. Fliss knew his sort, 'hail-fellow-well-met' to one's face, but ready to stab the back of a rival should the opportunity arise. She could see it in his smug expression, the wide smile never quite reaching the eyes. He didn't miss a trick. He noticed the people who were friendly back, but those who were luke-warm towards him received a second, more incisive glance.

He had the sort of unruly, reddish, curly hair with which it was hard to look good, and he had managed to grow it to just the wrong length. An inch or two longer and it would have hung in bouncy tendrils giving him a sexy, slightly Charles II élan; a bit shorter and it could have been crisply tamed with gel. As it was he merely looked like an aging, debauched cherub, his face too chubby and red for the style. He obviously spent a great deal of time outdoors, but sadly didn't have the olive-toned skin which would have benefited from constant weathering.

She watched his progress across the room, hoping he would confine himself to greeting the locals and ignore herself and the other 'incomers', but in that she was to be disappointed. His trek ended right beside their table. The slap he bestowed upon Professor Norton was none too gentle and Fliss almost winced on his behalf.

"Well, Jack, it seems that congratulations are in order!" His booming voice could easily be heard in both halves of the pub and a silence descended on the drinkers as they waited avidly to hear the rest of the conversation.

"I don't think we need discuss that here," said Norton quietly, "Can I get you a drink Douglas?"

"Aye, why not? I'll have my usual, Polly, love," he said, turning his head. Fliss observed him with renewed interest. She had heard the name Douglas before. This must be the Douglas Merrington whose family had once owned Theo's farm. She hoped Professor Norton wouldn't feel the need to introduce her. She didn't particularly want to be seen consorting with the enemy.

He turned back to the table, his grin encompassing them all, "I know your boss is being coy. I've heard the news, so as a special treat I want you all to be my guests at the Hall tomorrow, for a day of pampering. What's the point of owning a Spa if you can't give out freebies to your loyal staff."

Norton looked pained, "Douglas, please, keep your voice down. I thought we agreed that there was no need to make an issue of this."

Fliss's mouth dropped open slightly. So Douglas Merrington was the big money behind the dig. No wonder Professor Norton hadn't wanted Armitage to know that little gem of information. He would be utterly furious.

"Oh, what can Armitage do about it? The thing is entirely out of his hands now you've discovered the body."

"Douglas, who told you about that? I had intended to come over to the Hall this evening and speak to you personally."

For the first time Merrington looked slightly shifty, "Does it matter? I've been told now – and I might say that I would have preferred to be informed immediately. I've put a lot of money into this little venture."

"I realise that, but I prefer not to use the telephone to convey news of this sort."

"That's a little paranoid isn't it? Who do you think might have bugged old Armitage's phone line?"

"I wasn't thinking of bugging, more of eavesdropping – and stranger things have been known. It's no secret that the dig is going on, Douglas, and there are people who are very interested. I don't think you realise just how big a scoop this would be for some journalists. Public interest in archaeology has never been greater."

The mention of publicity made the businessman in Merrington pull up short,

"Good point, old man. We really do need to keep a lid on this for a while, don't we?"

"I really think we do, yes."

Fliss had been assuming that Merrington had arrived alone, but just then he was joined by a tall blonde, who had evidently been visiting the ladies. She took his arm and pouted playfully, "I thought you'd have my usual waiting for me darling," she said, in the huskiest voice Fliss had ever heard.

"How the hell should I know what your usual is?" said Merrington dismissively. Fliss wondered how the woman would react to this deliberate rudeness, but she merely laughed,

"You are such a pig, Douglas, I don't know why I stick around,"

"Because you look ten years younger after all the free

treatments I allow you at the spa," he said with a grin, "Bring us a gin and tonic as well, will you Poll?" he called and Polly acknowledged the request with a nod of her head.

"I'm Tanya, by the way," the blonde added, as she pulled up a chair from the next table and sat with them, "I'll wait forever if I wait for Douglas to deal with the social niceties."

Somehow Fliss had just known she would be called something like Tanya. She noticed how the other women around the table were rather intimidated by this newest arrival – and with every good reason. Not one of them could quite believe their eyes. This was a stunningly attractive example of the human form. Even the hard-to-please Anne-Marie could find nothing to criticize. Her figure was a perfect size ten, possibly even an eight, her face gorgeous, with a straight little nose and violet blue eyes, her hair was long and silky, and if it was bleached it was done with such mastery that not the vaguest hint of a dark root spoiled the effect. Her clothes were elegantly understated, black trousers that fitted every curve, and a cream cashmere jumper adorned with a small gold brooch. She wore impossibly high heels to her black boots, but her gait was a smooth and unhurried stroll. She could have just descended from a catwalk, yet nothing about her spoke of pretension or snobbery. Her enthusiasm towards them was genuine and warm.

"Douglas has told me he intends to invite you all for a day at the spa. Do tell me you've all accepted. The place is an absolute drag during the week and I'm desperate for some decent company." Her glance encompassed the whole table and they all found themselves nodding their assent, except Fliss, who opened her mouth to speak, then closed it again.

"Fliss – you did say your name was Fliss, didn't you?" The reply was a swift nod, "Now, why," continued Tanya, barely taking a breath, "aren't you agreeing to come too? Don't tell me you're a spoilsport."

Fliss finally found her tongue, "I'm sorry, I don't mean to be, but I have Megan to consider."

Tanya smiled and her hand came across the table to touch

133

Megan's cheek. Fliss winced as the beautifully manicured nails picked up a smear of ketchup from the chubby faced youngster, "Oh, we can sort little Megan out. There's a crèche at the Hall."

Fliss handed Tanya a paper serviette to wipe her fingers. She wondered how she was going to wriggle out of this one. Going for a day of pampering sounded like bliss to the young mum, who had barely had time for a bath which stretched to ten minutes since motherhood had dawned, but she felt a certain loyalty towards Armitage – and this seemed like marching into the enemy camp.

"It's really very nice of you, but I've arranged to take her to the village play group tomorrow and the vicar will be expecting me."

"Actually," intercepted Professor Norton, "I could do with you making it the day after tomorrow if that's not inconvenient, Douglas. There's still a lot to do at the site and I can't have you poaching half my diggers."

"Yeah, yeah, whatever," said Merrington, evidently bored with a conversation that didn't have him as the main topic, "Make it whenever you like. We're not exactly swamped with paying guests at the moment anyway – though I'm expecting that to change when we have exclusive viewing rights to the latest bog body to be found in England."

Fliss thought that Professor Norton looked entirely taken-aback by this comment, but he managed to restrain himself from shooting a sharp denial towards his sponsor. She caught his eye and he raised an eyebrow at her. The message was clear enough. Why on earth did I ever let this man become involved? She sent a small sympathetic smile back across the table.

"Megan and I have finished eating, so if everyone will excuse us …"

"Oh, must you go?" said Tanya, "I was hoping to hear all about the dig."

Fliss smiled at the woman, realising, with a slight shock, that viewed close to, Tanya was actually quite considerably older than she first appeared. A web of tiny lines around her eyes and lips were skilfully hidden by make-up, but they very definitely existed. Tanya was forty if she was day, but she looked about twenty-eight.

Gathering her thoughts, Fliss replied,

"Oh, the others can tell you everything. I'm just a bystander. Good night all. Nice to meet you, Tanya. Perhaps we'll run into each other again before I leave."

"I hope so. And I must say, your little girl is simply gorgeous. Have you ever thought of putting her in for child modelling?"

"I can't say I have," said Fliss, trying not to sound stiff and unfriendly. She realised child models were necessary, but not for her daughter.

"I'll get you some addresses. My agent will know the best places for you to go."

"Oh please don't go to any trouble," she protested, wondering what on earth she could say without being rude.

"No trouble at all."

She left it at that, after all, she didn't have to follow up any leads the agent might give her. Professor Norton rose to his feet as she did, but she noticed Douglas Merrington stayed firmly in his chair and barely acknowledged her departure. But then if he could treat a stunning blonde like dirt, what chance did a small, brunette, mum-of-one have in gaining his attention?

"You have a lift arranged, Mrs Elmsworth?" asked the professor quietly as she slipped past him.

"Yes, thank you. Mr Armitage has kindly offered to take me back to the farm."

"Very well, but you need only ask, you know that, don't you?"

She smiled up at him and for a moment their eyes met and held, leaving her confused and blushing.

"Everyone is very kind," she murmured.

"You don't make it a chore," he said softly.

The words were still ringing in her ears when she went to find Armitage.

He came across from the far end of the bar as soon as she appeared in the doorway, "Ready for home?" he asked.

"Not quite. Would you be putting Megan in the car whilst I pay a quick visit?" she asked, suddenly realising that she was never going to make it along the bumpy track. Megan, by now

135

thoroughly at home in the pub, had been by herself twice since they had arrived. Fliss however, had been ignoring all the signals whilst in the professor's company, ready to die before admitting she needed the loo. Theo was different. He knew all about nature's calls and she felt no embarrassment admitting her need to him.

"Sure, no problem. I'll draw up to the door so you can hop straight in."

"Thanks Theo, I won't be long."

As she came out of the toilets and into the long dark passage that led to them and thence on to the kitchen at the back of the pub, she found Fergus leaning against the wall, his hands in his pockets.

"Hello," she said in surprise, "What are you doing here?"

"Waiting to have a word with you."

"Really? What about?"

He stood up straight and reached out to take her hand, "I want you to tell me if it's all over between you and Bryn."

She slid her fingers dextrously out of his grasp, "How many have you had, Fergus?" she asked lightly.

"A lot, but that's only given me the courage to speak to you. Look, you only need to tell me that you and Bryn are making a go of it, and I'll not say another word."

She wanted to say the words, even if they weren't true, just to get herself out of this awkward situation, but the lie stuck in her throat. At her obvious hesitation he stepped forward and pressed himself against her so that she was trapped between him and the wall, "Tell me I'm in with a chance, Fliss," he whispered hoarsely, his lips brushing her neck and cheek. She could feel the heat of his body even through her thick fleece, and his breath upon her face, though beery, was not unpleasant. She found that even though she didn't fancy Fergus much, it was still nice to have a man pay her some attention. It took all her strength to push him away, because she found that suddenly, though there was no chemistry at all for her, she would have quite liked him to have kissed her. She couldn't remember the last time Bryn had kissed her – properly, with feeling.

"Hey, back off, pal. I'm not the sort of girl who takes advantage of a drunken man," she said, placing her hands squarely on his chest and thrusting him back. He grinned, "I am drunk," he admitted.

"You'd have to be to go after me, love. There are at least three unattached girls on the dig, not to mention all the talent in the village. Take my advice and find yourself someone who's unencumbered. It'll be much more fun for you."

"I can't imagine any more fun than you, Fliss."

"That's because you've not yet experienced a ruined evening out because the babysitter lets you down. Or the sleepless nights when a tummy-bug strikes and you spend three hours cleaning up sick."

"I'd do it for you."

"You think so now, while you've got your beer goggles on. Now come on, let me by. Mr Armitage is waiting outside and you don't want him to come looking for me, now do you?"

He looked suddenly aggressive, "What's with you and him? You seem mighty close very quickly."

"Until I agree to date you, pal, you don't have the right to ask me any questions at all. Now move, or I'll lose my temper."

Sheepishly he stood aside and watched her as she walked away.

CHAPTER FIFTEEN

"Nodens was a British god of healing, whose magic hounds were also believed to cure the sick."

In the Land Rover beside Theo, Fliss was torn between two vastly differing loyalties. She liked Armitage a great deal, and had known nothing but kindness from him. He had even offered her a home should she need it. But Professor Norton did possess deep brown eyes and a charmingly boyish grin.

That thought pulled her up short and sharp. What the hell was she thinking? She was a married woman with a young child – and just now she owed her loyalty to Theo and no-one else.

"Theo," she ventured diffidently, still not fully sure she ought to get involved in any of this.

"Yes," he replied, copying her slightly shy tone teasingly.

"I found something out this evening that I think you ought to know."

He glanced briefly at her, then his eyes were back on the road, "And are you going to impart this nugget?" he asked. She could hear the amusement in his voice. Ha, she thought, he imagines there can't be anything going on in this village that he doesn't know about. Well, I'll show him.

"Yes. I know who has been financing the dig at the stone circle."

"So do I. It's Douglas Merrington."

Her mouth dropped open, "You knew and still you let them dig?"

"Of course. John Norton is an old friend. He wouldn't have taken Merrington's money without telling me."

"But I thought you despised Mr Merrington."

"Doesn't stop me taking his money – in fact it makes me a little more inclined to."

She suddenly laughed, "You crafty devil! I'll bet Douglas doesn't know you know."

"He hasn't a clue."

"And I suppose you have negotiated a huge fee?"

"Of course – and I've made him wait! It must be fifteen years since John first asked me if he could dig on my land. Naturally he knew nothing of the feud and told me quite innocently who was behind the scheme. I refused, but told him why and assured him that the day would come when he would either find another backer, or I would force the price high enough to make Merrington's eyes water. It's taken a long time, but we finally reached an agreement. It wouldn't have happened even yet, but for the down-turn in my fortunes." He grinned suddenly, "By God, it must stick in Merrington's throat to think that he'll be financing my continuing to live in his ancestral home."

"I must admit, that does puzzle me. Why should he want to give you money? I thought the whole idea was to try and starve you into submission. He seems desperate to have the farm back in Merrington ownership again."

"He thinks it will drive me crazy having people trampling all over my plot. He hopes it will send me hot-foot to the estate agents to sell up. He knows as well as I do that there's always been a tradition of a burial up on the moor – we just all thought it would come from the tumulus. He hoped if he could prove the rumours true, I'd be swamped with nutters wanting to get in touch with their mystical pasts."

"You may very well be! Won't it drive you crazy? The bog body is going to be huge news when it gets out. There'll be media swarming everywhere."

"It'll die away eventually," he said confidently, "And I'll be all the richer for it. That makes the inconvenience worth while."

Fliss stared at his profile in the gathering gloom of the spring dusk, wondering if he really knew what he was in for. Media frenzy was nothing to treat lightly.

After another short silence she said, "Didn't you feel a little bit mean towards the professor – if he's your friend, you must know that he's been aching to do this dig for years."

His grin remained firmly in place, "You don't really think he's spent at least two weeks up here every year of the past fifteen just wandering aimlessly about the place and playing whist with me in the evenings do you? I can assure you he's done plenty of poking around. I should think John knows as much about Broadbarrow Loe as I do by now."

"But don't you both feel that's a little dishonest towards Mr Merrington?"

"No more dishonest than him trying to ruin my peace using John as a front. Douglas Merrington deserves everything he gets for assuming that he can buy a man's loyalty with a few lousy quid."

Fliss sank into a thoughtful silence. She was beginning to wonder if anyone ever told the truth about their intentions, or whether every action always had to have an ulterior motive. It made her life seem naively open and simple. Even Bryn had his own secrets from her – and what secrets did she have? Five hundred pounds in a savings account for Megan's future – and that was all. Hardly on a par with all this subterfuge she was suddenly encountering.

"Well," she said decidedly, after a moment, "I'm not going to consort with the enemy. Mr Merrington can keep his invitation to spend the day at his spa. I wouldn't dream of going there now."

"I wouldn't have thought it was your cup of tea anyway, is it?" he asked, genuinely surprised that she should have even considered the prospect.

She gave a snort of incredulous laughter, "You have to be joking, right? A whole day of luxurious pampering, with nothing to do but lie back and relax whilst every bit of my poor, old, knackered body is pumiced, pummelled, massaged and soothed! I'd kill for it! Do you have any idea when I last had the time to even sit in a bubble bath for more than ten minutes? I only wear jeans all the time because my legs were last shaved before Christmas."

"Well, you daft beggar! If it means that much to you, go and do it! It won't bother me." He sounded amused, but she still wasn't sure he meant it.

"No, I'm not going to let Douglas Merrington think he's bought me too. I stand by my friends through thick and thin."

He took his eyes off the road to look at her for so long that she panicked slightly and said, "Watch out, I don't want to end up dead before I've had my pampering," and giggled nervously. He withdrew his gaze saying, "Don't worry; I know this road like the back of my hand."

"Yeah, and I know the next line to that one, 'ooh, where did that freckle come from?' Just drive Mr Armitage!" She kept her tone light because she had been slightly perturbed by the intensity of his glance. He had looked genuinely moved by her comment and she began to worry that he might have been given the wrong impression. Bryn was always telling her that she spoke too impulsively and that she grew too fond of people too quickly. One day, he had warned, she would be too openly friendly with the wrong sort of person and she would end up dead in a gutter after being stalked or similarly plagued by some nutcase who wouldn't take no for an answer.

Not that she placed Theo in either of these categories. She liked him a lot and felt that she had known him for much longer than two days – but she didn't really need any added complications just now. And his thinking she might be angling for a romance would definitely be a complication too far! It was bad enough that she had just had to fight off the drunken advances of Fergus. She was still deciding whether to end her marriage – to begin an affair would be madness.

As they pulled into the farmyard she already had her hand on the door catch ready to leap out as the rover drew to a halt. She wanted to be away before she could embarrass herself any further. To her surprise he laid a light, restraining hand on her arm, "Don't be daft, Fliss. Have a day out at Merrington's expense. You deserve a bit of fun and I don't want you to miss out on that because of me."

She felt compelled to meet his eyes, but found nothing to frighten or dismay her in them. He just looked as he always did. Slightly amused, but calm.

"Okay," she said, relieved, "I'll think about it."

"Good, now I'm off to check on the livestock. I'll see you later." With that he opened his door and strode off across the twilit yard.

She helped her sleepy little daughter out of the back of the vehicle and carried her indoors.

Within an hour Megan was bathed and put down to sleep in the big old bed. A quick story, a hug and a kiss then the light was switched off and Fliss went downstairs, leaving the door a little ajar so that the landing light could illuminate the room and so that she would be able to hear should her daughter wake and call for her.

Once back on the ground floor, Fliss found herself wandering aimlessly about wondering how on earth to fill her time until she too could retire. She didn't particularly want to be hanging around in the kitchen when Theo came in. He might want to revisit their conversation without the saving presence of the little girl.

She remembered from her cleaning that there was a television set in the parlour – and that she had had the foresight to clean the grate and reset the fire. It would only need a match to encourage a cheerful blaze. She made herself a cup of tea and took it with her to the room, shutting the door carefully behind her. She didn't want a muddy dog jumping all over her when Theo came back in.

A convenient lamp on a table next to the sofa invited her to plump up some cushions and kick off her shoes so that she could put her feet up. A glance at the bookshelves in the alcove beside the fireplace changed her mind from television to reading. The only thing she could find that appealed was a Sherlock Holmes that she had read before, but it was preferable to some of the other tomes on offer, "The Pig Breeders Annual 1948" and "Dairy Farming for the Hill Farmer".

It was incredibly peaceful in the quiet house. There was not a sound but the crackling and spitting of the dampish logs on the fire. Megan had obviously drifted straight off and the team had not yet returned from the pub. The warmth of the fire began to have a soporific effect and Fliss found the words she was trying to read were running into one another and making no sense at all. It was a struggle to keep her eyes open and she wondered why she was bothering to do so. There was no one to see her take forty winks – and who cared anyway? Much as she was enjoying her trip to the foggy streets of Victorian London, she laid the book aside and allowed her head to fall back on the cushions. They were rough and cold under her cheek, but still she sank deeper into them, aware of a musty odour as her nose brushed the material.

It was some minutes later that she became vaguely aware that the musty odour was growing stronger. She sighed and shifted in her sleep, a frown furrowing her brow as the smell changed gradually from musty to earthy and finally to the stench of decay. She had smelt that before, she knew. This afternoon on the moor when the excavator had stirred up the bog with its intruding claw.

She was startled awake by the sudden feeling that she was no longer alone in the room. Even with her eyes still closed she could sense a presence, could feel the sudden chill as a body came between her and the heat of the fire.

She opened her eyes with difficulty, feeling that she had been in a deep sleep for hours and had not merely drowsed. It was hard to make her eyes focus and she blinked and frowned as she tried to adjust to the swift alteration from slumber to wakefulness. She could see someone beside the sofa, but it took a moment before her vision cleared enough to see the details. When it did, a scream of pure terror was wrenched from her and she thought she might pass out.

The man who stood beside her was no one she knew. He was naked, his flesh white and bloodless, his hands were raised to his slashed throat as though to stem the gushing flow of blood that streamed down his chest. Gobbets of blood oozed between the clutching fingers and the blood tricked slowly down his arms to the bent elbows, where it dripped with a steady noise like her own heartbeat onto the wooden floor.

Even as she screamed and screamed again she looked into his eyes and read a message there of hopelessness, of agony. He silently beseeched her help, but she had no help to give. She could not, in that moment, have moved to save her own life, let alone his. She could not bear his pain and closed her own eyes again to blot out the vision of horror.

She heard the door burst open and forced herself to look and see who had entered. She hoped to God it was someone who could help the injured man for she knew she could never bring herself to touch him.

Professor Norton was beside her in two strides, kneeling beside her and taking her hands between his own, "Felicity, my dear, what is it? Has something happened?"

Has something happened? Was the man blind or mad? She couldn't believe he was asking so obvious a question when there was a blood soaked man in the room with them.

"God, yes! You've got to help him!" She turned her gaze to the spot where the man had been standing, but to her astonishment and consternation the room was empty but for the two of them.

Norton followed her gaze over his shoulder, "Help who?" he asked, concerned, but puzzled.

She sat up, trying to see beyond him. The floor was entirely bare of bloodstains, but the tap, tap, tap of the drops hitting the floor was still echoing in her horrified mind. The fire flickered brightly, no longer shielded from her sight by the mysterious stranger. The fact that it was still in full flame and had not sunk into embers told her that she couldn't have been asleep for more than a few minutes.

The professor was still speaking and she had to summon every vestige of concentration she possessed to understand what he was saying to her, "Felicity, what is it? What on earth made you scream like that? I thought you were being murdered!"

She shuddered at the word, "Not me," she whispered tearfully.

"What?"

She shook her head. How could she explain to him when she

144

couldn't even explain the incident to herself? As she looked over the room once more, desperate to make sure the man had not merely collapsed and fallen out of view, she caught sight of the open desk. Standing upon it, an ugly leer upon its one exposed face, was the carved stone head. Fliss gave another small cry of alarm just as Theo burst in through the door, "I thought I heard someone scream. Is everything alright?"

Professor Norton hastily released Fliss's hands and rose to his feet, "Mrs Elmsworth seems to have dropped off to sleep and had a bad dream, Ted. She's fine now."

"Mummy!" called a small voice from up the stairs. Fliss tried to get to her feet, "Megan ..." she said brokenly.

"You stay there," said Theo briskly, taking one look at her shocked expression, "I'll see to her."

The fact that Fliss sank back, ashen-faced, onto the sofa, and let him go to her daughter, showed the professor how profoundly she had been affected.

"I'll get you a brandy," he said, suiting action to words and going over to a corner cabinet and opening the door to get a glass and a decanter.

He placed a half-full glass in her shaking hand and said briskly, "Drink that." She took a sip and shuddered gratefully as the heat hit her cold innards.

"Care to tell me what happened now?" he asked softly, sitting on the sofa beside her.

"I don't know how to. I've just seen the most appalling thing ..."

He obviously didn't know what she meant. He glanced across to the television, "But the TV isn't switched on."

"It wasn't on the TV; it was here in this room."

"But there was nothing here when I came in ..."

She looked at him, swallowed deeply then tried to explain, "Professor Norton, I can tell you why Megan said the bog body was a 'robin-man'. It's because he had a red chest – red with blood. The blood from his cut throat flowed down his chest."

He looked back into her eyes, a slight frown between his brows.

He searched her face, as though to convince himself of her sanity.

"Are you trying to tell me that you think you saw the bog body here in this room?"

She nodded, "Except that I saw him as he was before the peat claimed him."

His look of disbelief cut her to the quick – but what else could she expect? She didn't believe it herself.

"You know I haven't seen the body, nor heard it discussed?" she asked, determined to convince him. She couldn't bear the expression of pitying scepticism on his face.

"As far as I'm aware, that is true," he replied evenly.

"Then if I tell you that he had a ginger beard, short curly auburn hair and a large mole on his left shoulder?"

His demeanour scarcely altered, but she knew he was shocked.

"The hair would have a reddish tinge anyway, due to the action of the acids in the peat, but the mole – you could not have known that detail."

"But I do know it."

He said nothing more, but absent-mindedly lifted her hand towards her mouth with his forefinger, "Drink your brandy," he said.

CHAPTER SIXTEEN

"Rhiannon's singing birds were the heralds of the otherworld.
Their beautiful and enchanting song was said to be
able to wake the dead."

Fliss felt the brandy glass clatter against her front teeth as she tried to take another sip and it made her realise just how badly her hands were still shaking. She tried to pull herself together. She could already see by the worried expression in the professor's eyes that he thought she had completely lost the plot. She had to show him that she was sane, lucid and most of all sober. She couldn't bear him to think that she might be a secret drinker when she had a child in her care.

She took a deep reviving breath and spoke again, willing her voice to be steady and calm, "I'm perfectly alright now, thank you professor, and I'm very sorry for startling you. It must have been the strain of an exciting day, coupled with my over-active imagination."

He smiled at her, looking relieved, "Please don't apologise. Dreams can be extremely realistic – and anyone would be horrified by something as graphic as you've described."

So, it was to be written off as a dream. Very well, she could accept that; in fact she wanted to believe it was true. Anything else was unthinkable, incredible ... and totally horrific.

Theo came back into the room at that moment and she didn't think she had ever been more pleased to be interrupted. Being alone with the professor, watching him eye her warily, as though he was wondering what further madness she was going to subject him to, was rather more than she could bear.

"That's a bloody curious thing," he said musingly as he walked through the door. Fliss almost started up off the settee, but the professor stopped her, noting that her white face betokened a faint if she stood up too quickly, "Stay where you are," he ordered quietly.

"What is it?" she asked Theo breathlessly, sinking back obediently into her seat, "What has happened?"

"Nothing very important, just odd, that's all. The old Grandfather clock in the hall has suddenly started working again. To my certain knowledge it hasn't moved a hand in fifty years. I've always intended to have it looked at, but never got around to it."

"And it's working now?" asked the professor curiously.

"Yep. I couldn't help but notice the tick as I came down the stairs – and what's more, it's telling the right time."

Professor Norton hadn't believed that Fliss could go any paler, but she blanched and looked ready to pass out. He felt it was imperative that he change the subject and steer both she and Theo away from the odd events to the severely practical.

"Is Megan okay?" he asked, knowing this was the one thing guaranteed to take Fliss's attention away from the odd events of the evening.

"She's fine. Jemima Puddleduck sent her back off to sleep – especially with the promise that I would take her to the river to feed real ducks tomorrow."

"Thank you, Theo," Fliss said warmly, thankfully distracted as the professor had planned, "I'm really very grateful."

He dismissed her thanks with a wave of his hand, almost embarrassed, "Think nothing of it. Are you alright now?"

"I'm fine," she assured him, "it was just a particularly horrible dream and I feel such a fool for screaming the place down like I did."

"Then let's go into the kitchen and have a cup of tea. That will put everyone back on a firm footing – we are British, after all!"

Fliss and the professor both smiled at this sally and followed him into the kitchen, Fliss having to concentrate fully so that her still wobbly knees didn't collapse beneath her and give her the further humiliation of falling, splayed, at the feet of her two companions.

Theo opened the door of the Aga and did some vigorous rattling with the poker, which apparently helped to boil the kettle in some way which Fliss couldn't fathom. She sat on a decrepit old armchair in front of it, tucking her now cold feet up under her. Professor Norton and Armitage took wooden chairs at the big old oak table and when the boiled water had been transferred to the big, brown earthenware pot, the farmer poured tea for them all.

They sat in silence and Fliss felt that they were all studiously avoiding the subject of her odd behaviour. She searched her mind for a safe topic of conversation.

"Oh, professor, I felt I should ask you first, since I am here under false pretences. Would you object if I joined the others at the hall? Mr Armitage thinks I ought to go, but I'm really not a member of the team."

The professor appeared to rouse himself from a reverie, and Fliss couldn't help wondering what had so preoccupied him. She hated the idea, but suspected he was still harking back to the incident and felt that the more he dwelt on it, the more peculiar he was going to think her.

"What? Oh, the spa, you mean? Certainly, you must go, by all means. You were invited after all – and I can't imagine Bryn wanting to spend a day smothered in mud and wrapped in hot towels. Merrington may have his faults, but his establishment is flawless. You'll have a wonderful time."

"Thank you."

She could think of nothing else to say and so sank into the comfort of the chair, cradling her mug in her hands to warm them, watching the two men as they began to talk to each other, the awkward silence finally broken.

She was still feeling shivery and unsettled, but gradually the utter terror of the past half hour was fading away. When she closed her eyes, she could see again the blood-spattered victim, but the vision was beginning to take on the misty unreality of a rapidly fading dream. Perhaps the professor was right. The strain of the day had made her imagination run away with itself. She tried to forget her experience and concentrate on what the professor and the farmer were saying to each other.

"Say what you like, but Merrington is the worst kind of idiot," Armitage was saying gruffly, "a bloody malicious one! Don't try and convince me that he pulled that little stunt tonight by accident. Nothing he does is ever unplanned."

The professor was altogether milder in his assessment of the situation, "He's just thoughtless," he countered calmly, "what would be the point of telling the whole pub of our discovery? The excavations would simply be over-run with sightseers and ghouls."

Armitage reached for the teapot and topped up his mug, "You still don't get it, do you John? Merrington isn't interested in archaeology. He doesn't give a tinker's cuss about your investigations or the bog body. He just wants to hack me off! He wants to make my life impossible so that I'll sell him this place for a song."

"Don't you think you are carrying paranoia to extremes, Ted? The Merringtons haven't owned this property for three generations – and Merrington Hall is a magnificent building, far larger and grander than this. I rather think he's over the loss by now."

Armitage gave a 'huh' of cynical laughter, "Believe what you want, my friend, but I know the Merrington clan. This isn't just about property, it's about pride. Old Merrington lost this house because he thought he could fleece a mere peasant. It stuck in his craw that his luck ran out – and to an inferior! And it chokes his great-grandson that he's still being laughed at nearly a hundred years later."

The professor evidently didn't have a response – or one that he was prepared to voice, anyway, so he poured himself more tea then carried the pot across to Fliss, who shook her head when he offered it. The tea had been far too strong for her when it first came out of the pot – now it was going to be undrinkable as far as she was concerned.

Having, he felt, won the argument, Armitage rose to his feet and gave a full stretch, groaning with pleasure as he did so, "Well, some of us have to be up early in the morning, so if you don't mind, I'll wish you both goodnight."

"Goodnight, Theo," said Fliss.

The professor turned around, "Goodnight – and don't concern yourself with Douglas. I'm keeping my eye on him."

"Be sure you do – you'll find yourself with a knife in the back if you're not careful."

With that he was gone.

Norton put the teapot down and said, "I'd better be on my way too. It's a long walk up to the moor in the dark."

Fliss looked aghast. She had been convincing herself all evening that she had suffered nothing more than a particularly nasty nightmare, but the reality of being left downstairs alone – or on her bedroom for that matter! – in the house hit her like a blast from a water cannon.

She said nothing – in truth she was speechless anyway, but the terrified expression on her face made Norton stop dead. He had known she had been badly affected by her experience and he had been fully aware of how bravely she had tried to hide her continuing fear, but he had been hoping that a period of calm, coupled with his own studiously pragmatic explanation of the affair would have restored her serenity.

It was now obvious that no such transformation had taken place – and Norton had absolutely no idea how to deal with the situation. He was overwhelmed with sympathy, but had no solution.

"My dear," he began softly, then realised what he was saying and hastily added, "Mrs Elmsworth. Please don't look so tragic." He suddenly decided that ignorance was his best defence. It was perhaps wisest to change the direction of the conversation, "I can assure you there is no need to worry. I've found my way a dozen times before in the dark."

She was inexpressibly relieved that he thought her fears were for him and not herself. She forced a smile, "It's silly, I know, but those woods must be treacherous in the dark. Do you really have to go?"

"I'm afraid I do. Now that Mr Merrington has let out our little secret, it's even more imperative that the body isn't left alone. Who knows who heard him mention our find?"

"I suppose so," she whispered.

It was with the greatest difficulty that he turned away from her and headed for the door. Her anguished cry stopped him as he reached for his coat hanging by the door.

"Please don't leave me. I can't bear it!"

His jaw clenched as he contemplated merely walking through the door and leaving her, but he found he could not do it. When he came back across the room he found her flying towards him and before he knew it she was in his arms, sobbing hysterically against his chest. Reluctantly he put his arms around her and patted her ineffectually, "Felicity, I really do have to go," he pointed out gently.

"Please, please don't leave me here alone. He'll come back, I know he will. The moment I close my eyes he will be there."

He didn't even bother to pretend that he didn't know what she was talking about,

"He was never really here, my dear. You must know that," he said softly.

"It doesn't matter whether he was real or not – don't you understand? I can still see it all, the blood, and the look in his eyes. Even if it was all in my head, I'm still haunted." He could barely hear her, muffled as she was against his chest, but he discerned enough to know that he was lost. He rested his chin lightly on the top of her head and gazed out of the window, contemplating his next move.

A flickering shadow flitting across the yard outside alerted him to the danger he was inviting. The uncurtained window, in a room starkly lit by a bare bulb turned their every movement into a tableau for anyone outside to see. This most innocent embrace could look anything but to a biased observer. Gently, so that she would never know his thoughts, he pushed her away from his body and held her at arms length.

"I'll ring Fergus on his mobile and tell him that my old war wound is playing up. He'll be furious at my desertion, but I'll weather the storm."

He offered her a tissue from his pocket and she took it and scrubbed her face, "Do you have an old war wound?" she asked with a small laugh.

"No, but I'll invent one."

She looked into his eyes, "You think I'm completely mad, don't you?"

"I think you are a very sensitive girl who has had a very vivid and unpleasant experience."

She nodded slowly then said, "Shall I make some more tea?"

"I think so. It's going to be a very long night."

"I'm so sorry, but I really couldn't bear to go to bed just yet – the very thought …" she shuddered and he said hastily, "Then don't think. You make the tea and I'll go into the parlour and build the fire up. If we are going to be up all night, we might as well be warm and comfortable."

She didn't really want to go back into the room, but she knew he was right. She could hardly expect the poor man to sit up all night on a wooden kitchen chair. She gave her nose one last blow then went to the sink to wash her hands and refill the kettle. He locked the back door then searched his coat pocket for his phone.

Fergus seemed curiously calm and unsurprised to be left holding the fort. He accepted Norton's excuse of a back spasm without comment. It was a call that left the professor with a distinctly uneasy feeling. Fergus was not usually so accommodating. He had resented being second fiddle to Norton from the very first, knowing that his CV was more than equal to the job, and feeling very strongly that Norton was pulling strings to which he had no access. Norton had become friends with Armitage over the course of the years, and Douglas Merrington trusted him implicitly. For the sake of peace, Norton had tried to pull rank as infrequently as possible, but on the odd occasion he had been forced to make decisions, Fergus had made it obvious he would have done the complete opposite. This capitulation was uncharacteristic and Norton briefly wondered what game was behind it.

He was still cogitating when he realised that Fliss was looking at him, two mugs of tea in her hands and an air of expectation surrounding her. He waved her ahead of him, "After you, Mrs Elmsworth."

"You are joking, aren't you? I'm not setting foot in that room until you have made sure the coast is clear." She sounded almost back to normal and though she spoke in a jocular manner, he knew she was speaking nothing but the truth. He would have to go ahead of her into the parlour.

"Come on then, let's scare away the bogey-man."

"You mean the 'boggy-man' don't you?" It was a valiant attempt at a joke and he smiled amiably, "We shall have to think of a name for him. 'Pete Marsh' is taken."

He made sure she was settled on the sofa, with an old rug over her legs, before he sank gratefully into the arm chair by the fire.

"I can't say I'm entirely sorry not to be tramping across a dark moor tonight. I'm whacked."

She bit her lip, looking suitably guilt-stricken, "I'm so sorry. If it wasn't for me you would be asleep by now. I really shouldn't have ..."

"Please forget it. I'd have to be a half-wit to prefer the moor to a warm fire. I'll wait here with you until you feel you can face going to bed."

"I don't think I can," she whispered.

"Then I'll sit down here with you."

They were both silent for a few moments, then he spoke again, "You'll forgive the presumption, but am I to assume that you will be leaving tomorrow and going home?"

"If only I could. Talk about a rock and a hard place," she said dejectedly.

He looked across at her, one eyebrow raised slightly, "Would you care to elaborate? I hate to pry, but you make it terribly difficult not to."

"I'm sorry. I know I haven't explained anything, but I really felt I ought not to discuss mine and Bryn's personal difficulties with his boss – but frankly, I'm beginning to see that I owe him no loyalty whatsoever." She avoided his glance, playing with the

154

fringe of the blanket with nervously plucking fingers.

"As I say, I really don't want to pry, but you must understand that I really need to know that you have a genuine reason for not leaving a house that has obviously frightened you nearly witless."

She felt she had no choice but tell him everything. He listened in silence as she described her terror when the two thugs had forced their way into her house and threatened her child. At first his face was expressionless, but as the story developed he looked increasingly grim. When she reached the part that Armitage had played in the saga, he swore gently under his breath and she looked up at him in surprise.

"I do beg your pardon," he apologised, "but I had no idea Ted had allowed himself to become involved."

She was stung by the implied criticism, "I didn't expect him to start hitting people," she said, "I just thought they would back off if I had someone with me."

"They probably would have done so. Ted always was too handy with his fists. The inclination has had him in trouble before."

"Are you telling me he has a record?" she asked incredulously.

"I'm afraid he has a name that is not unknown to the boys in blue."

"Oh dear me," said Fliss inadequately, "But surely those men won't dare to complain to the police – they must both be known criminals."

"Not necessarily."

Fliss felt rather sick. This was more trouble than she had anticipated.

"This is all my fault," she said miserably.

"If we were to do anything so futile as lay blame, I think it lands squarely on your husband's shoulders, Felicity."

"Yes, but I'm the idiot who married him."

He laughed, "And I'm the idiot who employed him, thus encouraging him to purchase the over-priced technology in the first place! Let's settle the argument by splitting the blame equally between us."

"Why are you so nice to me?" she asked, before she had time to think.

"I may be an idiot, my dear, but I'm not stupid enough to attempt to answer that question. Now drink your tea."

CHAPTER SEVENTEEN

*"Sadb, a gentle goddess, the mistress of Finn MacCool,
compelled by an evil druid to spend much of her life as a deer"*

She sipped her tea and looked at him, "Keep talking," she said, "I don't like the silence."

"What would you like to talk about?" he asked, willing but momentarily without ammunition.

"You know all about me, now. So tell me about yourself."

He shrugged, "I'm an ordinary sort of a man," he said deprecatingly. She thought he was anything but and smiled slightly, "What about where you were born, and your family? Your wife must hate you staying away from home for so long."

"I don't have a wife," he said shortly.

"Never married?" she asked in surprise.

"I'm a widower. My wife died ten years ago. I have a daughter of seventeen."

Somehow it wasn't what she had been expecting to hear. She thought he might be divorced – or horrifically happily married to a gorgeous blonde. A dead wife and a teenaged daughter were a shock.

"I'm so sorry. I had no idea. You must think me incredibly insensitive."

"Not at all – how could you know? And plenty of men have a teenaged daughter, I'm not alone."

Of course he had known full well that her apology had referred to his wife, but his comment lightened the situation and made Fliss giggle, "Oh, you!" she chastised him, "I'm beginning to think you might be a dreadful man."

"I sincerely hope so," he smiled cheerfully.

"Where is your daughter?"

"Staying with friends – and due to join me here in the next few days."

"That will be nice for you."

"I'm not so sure about that. She thinks the diggers are around for her entertainment. I spend most of my time breaking up fights over her – knowing full well that she has absolutely no intention of dating any one of them."

"She's a bit of a handful, then?"

"That might be a fair way to describe her."

"I don't suppose I shall meet her. I expect I will have to leave fairly soon."

She sounded so wistful that he found it difficult to make any other comment and they fell into a friendly silence.

They had both chosen a book from Armitage's meagre stock and for half an hour or so they sat saying nothing, with the occasional crackle from the fire the only sound. Fliss could hear the sonorous, ponderous tock, tock of the big old clock in the hall, but she tried not to think about why it had suddenly and mysteriously begun to keep time. The echo of its tick pounded into her brain like an annoying finger-beat on a table or the drip of a tap. It began to mesmerise her so that she couldn't read or concentrate on anything but the noise it made. That ticking hadn't been heard in this house for years – and now she couldn't hear anything else. She almost jumped off the sofa when it struck the hour and the whole house seemed to reverberate. She felt sure that it must wake Megan, but though she strained her ears to listen beyond its clamour, not a sound issued from the bedroom upstairs. She might find the clock loud and invasive, but apparently her daughter did not.

Had she been a little less preoccupied with the elderly timepiece, she might have noticed that though Norton held a book, he rarely turned the page. It seemed that he too had more on his mind than an antiquated novel.

"Felicity." She started violently when he spoke, so deeply

engrossed had she been in trying to turn her thoughts from the darkness that threatened to engulf her. She steadied herself and looked up at him, "Yes?"

"There must be a way out of this dilemma of yours."

"I suppose there must be, but for the moment it eludes me," she tried to sound light-hearted and very nearly succeeded.

"What if I were to offer Bryn a loan to pay off the debt?"

"Dear God, no!" she exclaimed, before she realised quite how rude and ungrateful she must seem, "Please don't even think of suggesting it. Bryn is a proud man and if he knew I had even discussed this with you, my life would be utter misery."

His expression – or rather the stony-faced lack of expression – told her exactly what he thought of Bryn and his pride. To save her own face she tried to back-track a little, "I'm so sorry. That must have sounded terribly ungrateful – and I really didn't mean it to. You and Theo have both been so good to me. But Bryn wouldn't want pity. He would rather we found our own way out of this mess."

"Alright, I understand that it was a bad idea," he said in a care-fully neutral tone, "But we have to do something. It's obvious you don't want to stay here, and equally apparent that you have no wish to go home in the present circumstances, so do you have some-where else to go? Your parents perhaps or a friend?"

"It was my brother Daniel who introduced Bryn to those thugs, so I would scarcely be any safer at my mother's. As for friends – I lost contact with them when I married Bryn. He doesn't really encourage me to foster relationships with anyone other than him. He made things so unpleasant that slowly but surely they all faded away."

It felt to Fliss as though she were listening to someone else saying these things. She hadn't even admitted any of this to herself, let alone a third party. Perhaps it was the lateness of the hour and the residual trauma of the day, but it all came pouring from her like a stream of bile. For years she had accepted it as normal that her old friends should cease to visit now that she had a husband and a child and they were still free and single, but suddenly she knew that there was nothing normal or natural about it. She recalled how friends had tried to contact her and Bryn had failed to pass on messages, lost phone numbers, and frankly been downright rude to callers. Slowly but surely he had brainwashed her, alienating her friends, weaning her away from her family. Little bits of poison had been poured – and she, poor fool, had drunk in the toxins believing it was nectar.

"Oh my God!" she looked at him despairingly, "I've been such an idiot. I've laid myself out on the floor and let him wipe his feet on me! He's controlling every aspect of my life and I didn't even realise it."

He tried to sooth her, but even she could see that though he spoke the words, he didn't believe a single syllable, "You're tired and frightened, that's why things look so bleak. I'm sure that Bryn has been caring for you in his own way."

"No he hasn't. Bryn has never cared for anyone but himself. What sort of a man puts his wife and child in danger? Things look bleak because they are bleak. I've been a bloody fool – and because of it I now have no one to turn to except the husband who dropped me in the mire in the first place!"

He obviously had nothing to say and tears of utter humiliation welled in her eyes. Hadn't things been bad enough without this emotional outburst? What the hell would this man think of her now?

"If you really feel that way then I don't think you have any alternative but to go to the police and make a complaint against the two men. It has only been loyalty to Bryn that stopped you before, hasn't it?"

She nodded slowly, "Bryn will be furious, but I can't let that stop me. I have to think of Megan. I'll go to the police tomorrow after the toddler group."

"I think that is very wise."

"It doesn't really solve my problem though."

"Why not? You'll be able to go home."

"That's the problem – I don't want to. It isn't my home any longer. I've been miserable there – and happy here, in spite of

160

everything. You see, you couldn't be more wrong. I don't want to leave here. I just want the odd things to stop."

She had never been more grateful when he maintained his serious expression. If he had laughed at her, or even tried to jolly her along by denying anything peculiar had happened, she would surely have burst into angry tears.

"Perhaps the vicar could help you with that?"

It was as though he had lifted a huge weight from her breast. A tremulous smile hovered around her lips, "Why didn't I think of that?"

He grinned amiably, "You don't get to be a professor for no reason, you know. I am actually quite brilliant."

She laughed, and as she did so her eye lighted upon the stone head on the bureau. It seemed to be grinning maliciously at her.

"That's it!" she exclaimed incredulously, "It's that horrid thing!" He turned to look where she pointed, asking in surprise, "What? The stone head?"

"Yes! I was fine in this house until you brought that evil thing in here! It's that bloody head! I should have known. I felt it was emanating malevolence. Even Megan didn't like the thing."

He turned back towards her, "That's easily remedied. It will be removed in the morning."

She looked at him for a long time and he returned her gaze steadily.

"It would be easier for you if I just packed my bags and went home, wouldn't it?" she said softly.

"I've never been a man who took the easy way, my dear,"

"If you told me to do it, I would have to go," she admitted.

"I suspect you've had quite enough of men telling you what to do."

"I have – but I would respect your wishes, Professor Norton."

"My wishes are that you do precisely what you want to – and I think you have earned the right to call me John – after all, we have spent the night together."

"Have we?"

"We have. It's almost five in the morning – Ted will be up very shortly."

161

"Good God! Doesn't time fly when you are having fun?"

He laughed, "I think you are probably the strangest woman I have ever met. Now, why don't you try and get some sleep? I shall take the stone head out to the car and you should go up and tuck yourself into bed."

She stood up and crossed the room, holding her hand out to him, intending to formally shake his hand in farewell, "I don't think I'll ever be able to express how grateful I am to you for this night."

He took the outstretched hand and lightly kissed her fingers, "I wouldn't have missed it for the world – now go to bed."

She floated up the stairs as though on a cloud, a silly smile adorning her features. It was still there when Megan woke her up several hours later.

*

Fliss had waved Megan off to feed the animals with Theo and was in the midst of a huge, eye-watering yawn when Bryn walked, uninvited, into the kitchen, his face more than usually grim and bad-tempered. The absurd expression on his wife's face did nothing to lighten his mood.

"Tired Fliss? Still, that's hardly surprising, is it?"

Fliss hastily shut her mouth and blinked away the sleep. His sudden appearance threw her into turmoil but she did her best to disguise the fact. She gave silent thanks that Theo had taken one look at her exhausted face and had taken Megan off her hands for an hour so that she could 'come round' in a civilised manner. Her husband was spoiling for a fight and it was obvious that he wouldn't have cared if their little girl was there to witness it.

Seeing him now, suddenly there before her in the flesh, made her realize that all the happy plans she had made a few hours before as she listened to the five bongs from the clock in the hall had just one major obstacle. She would actually have to face her husband and tell him that she was leaving him.

Cuddled into the warm sheets, her pink-cheeked cherub asleep beside her, it had seemed a simple matter to get Bryn out of her life. She would simply tell him that their marriage was over, they had grown apart and it was no-one's fault.

But here was Bryn, large, strong and in a very unpleasant frame of mind. The words stuck in her throat until she realized he had said something very odd – and in an extremely arrogant way – which she had utterly failed to understand. She looked at him stupidly, a slight frown creasing her brow, "What?"

"Don't play stupid with me, Fliss. I know you. And you ought to know me well enough by now. Do you really think I'm going to take this lying down?"

The frown deepened as she took offence at both his tone and demeanour, which was both sarcastic and aggressive.

"What are you talking about?"

"Your little tête-à-tête last night. Don't bother to deny it. I saw you through the kitchen window."

"Saw what? There was nothing to see. I haven't done any-thing!" Half of her was wondering why she was bothering to argue with him, but her innocence demanded that she deny his accusations. She was genuinely surprised, but he was too angry to be convinced.

"You call falling into some man's arms nothing, do you? I don't know which of the bastards it was, but when I find out, I'm going to kill him. No one makes a fool of me and gets away with it. To think I believed you when you claimed you came here because you were afraid. You've been carrying on with someone and you followed him here. Who is it, Fliss?"

With startling clarity she recalled the feeling of John Norton's arms around her – and how swiftly he had removed them and guided her away from the window. Perhaps the embrace would have been longer had he not realized the danger of the lighted room in contrast to the darkness outside. She shook her head slowly, trying to make sense of everything. Would something more have happened? She realized now that she had desperately wanted it to.

"I notice you are not denying it," he took another step closer to her, his voice low and gruff, his face thrust in front of her, so that she could feel his breath on her skin and smell his body odour. To think she had once rather liked his smell. Feeling slightly sick she recoiled from him, "I don't have to confirm or deny anything to you, Bryn. I have only one thing to say. We're finished. I'm staying here with Mr Armitage and you can go where you like and do what you want."

"Jesus Christ – don't tell me it was Old MacDonald! You are having an affair with the farmer?"

"I'm not having an affair with anyone. Amazingly enough I haven't needed another man to show me what a useless lump of filth you are."

He laughed coarsely, "You think I believe that? I know what a stupid bitch you are. You couldn't possibly find the guts to leave me without some encouragement – well, let me tell you, darling, you'll never leave me. I'll see to that."

"I think you'll find I already have." Her knees were trembling but she was proud to hear that her voice was steady.

Armitage walked into the kitchen just at that moment and in a calm voice said, "I don't believe you were invited into my house, son."

"I'm speaking to my wife," said Bryn, spinning around and fronting up to the farmer in a way that could not be interpreted as anything other than a threat.

"I don't give a toss what you are doing – get out before I throw you into the cess pit with all the other crap."

Bryn gave a "huh" of derisive laughter – but he went.

Fliss sank into the easy chair, covering her face with her hands.

"Cup of tea?" asked Armitage serenely.

"Oh, Theo, is tea your answer to everything?"

"Pretty well. Do you want some or not?"

She gave a small laugh, "Yes please."

"Here catch," he said and she lifted her head in surprise, "What?"

Something small and metallic flew through the air towards her and she instinctively did as he said and caught it.

"What's this?"

"Car keys. I get the impression you've just lost your rights to

164

the family vehicle."

"I suspect so."

"I haven't the time to be running you here and there, so use the Land Rover whenever you need it."

She looked down at the keys, "Are you sure, Theo? It's a dreadful inconvenience for you."

"No it's not. I shall expect you to do all my errands for me. You'll be taking a load off my mind. I hate bloody shopping – so now it's your job."

"Thank you," she said, the sentiment was heartfelt and warm.

CHAPTER EIGHTEEN

*"Pwyll, disguised as a beggar, laid in wait with a hundred
horsemen to trick Gwawl, a rival suitor
for the hand of Rhiannon"*

As Fliss drove gingerly into the village (she had never driven a
Land Rover before) she found it a very different place than she had
previously experienced. Gone were the deserted streets and quiet
houses. Chaos confronted her and she almost turned around and
drove back to the farm. She told herself not to be so silly and such
a coward and forced herself on. Megan needed to meet other
children, she had been too long in the company of adults as it was
– and was probably the explanation for her odd behaviour, seeing
men who weren't there and taking instant dislikes to lumps of
stone and birds.

Finding a parking space proved to be something of a challenge,
for her favourite spot opposite the pub was now taken by a
dilapidated ex-post office van, still pillar-box red, but lacking the
lettering, though the ghost of the words "Royal Mail" could be
vaguely discerned beneath a layer of grime. The roads were lined
with other similarly bizarre vehicles and had they not been so rusty
and generally decrepit, Fliss might have assumed the circus had
come to town. They were Travellers alright, but she doubted there
was a single drop of Romany blood flowing through any of their
veins. She could catch the waft of Cannabis and Patchouli oil
before she had even opened the car door – having said that, to be
perfectly fair, she had whiffed a spliff once or twice at the dig too.

A large group were gathered by the picnic benches on the grass
verge outside the pub, though Polly wasn't likely to open the pub

doors for at least another two hours. In a way which mildly irritated Fliss, they were dressed just as one would expect New Age Travellers to dress, in tatty jeans, highly coloured and holey jumpers, voluminous tie-dyed cotton skirts, leather or flowery embroidered waistcoats that had seen better days, and other generally dirty and scruffy Charity-shop rejects. Why couldn't they break the mould for once and wear something neat and clean? Did their hair always have to be in braids and dreadlocks or long and unkempt? Was there some law against looking vaguely nice? It was such a cliché.

Not quite knowing how to handle the situation she put her head down and made straight for the church hall, avoiding eye contact. It was not that she had any particular aversion or animosity towards travellers, New Age or otherwise, but she hated confrontation of any kind, especially when she had Megan with her, and with the distinct smell of drugs in the air, she couldn't be sure of the reaction she might provoke. It hadn't occurred to her that in her present garb of muddy-at-the-knees jeans, manure-caked walking boots and big, sloppy jumper, she didn't look so very different from the objects of her caution. Her appearance caused not a ripple of interest and she walked by unmolested, for which she was silently, but fervently grateful.

It was a different story in the church hall, however, for as she entered it became immediately obvious that Emma the vicar was having her own difficulties with the travellers and was handling it rather differently than Fliss had done. The village mums were at the far end of the room, in a rather defensive circle, their children playing happily and obliviously on a patch of carpet, looking to Fliss like a ring of bison protecting their young. A harassed-looking Emma was just in front of the door where Fliss had entered, facing a group of unkempt individuals, who were all red-faced and obviously angry.

As soon as she saw Fliss, Emma pounced on her with relish, "Here's someone who can help you – her husband is a member of the dig team."

Fliss almost quailed under the assault of several pairs of angry eyes which turned instantly upon her. She threw an accusatory glance at Emma, who was evidently only too happy to throw her to the wolves, if it took the heat off her.

Their spokesman stepped towards Fliss in a way she found very intimidating, but she bravely stood her ground.

"So, you're one of the desecrators, are you?" His chin was thrust aggressively out and Fliss couldn't help but flinch slightly, though she really didn't want to show him that he was frightening her. He wasn't very tall, probably only 5.5, with straggly grey hair pulled into a greasy ponytail. He had at least two days growth of beard, also grey, and the sort of dilated pupils that told Fliss that if he wasn't high, he was certainly under the influence of something illegal. He wore a dirty T-shirt which bore the legend, "Trees are people too", a jacket that had once been a colourful Aztec design, but which was now faded to universal earth-tones, and jeans which were more hole than denim, showing thickly haired though muscular flesh.

Fliss's normal reaction to such a challenge would be to back slowly away apologising for being alive as she did so, but she was still smarting from her run-in with Bryn and the man's unfounded accusations just made her indignant.

"You don't know what you are talking about. No one is desecrating anything."

"Oh really?" The sarcasm was unmistakable, "And what would you call digging up dead bodies that have been lovingly laid to rest? How would the vicar here like it if me and my mates went over to her churchyard right now and started opening up the graves?"

Emma intervened, though hardly in a manner likely to intimidate, "That would be horrible. There are people living here who have loved ones buried in that churchyard."

He turned on her, "So what? We consider ourselves to be the natural descendants of the people buried on the moor. We're offended by that – and what do you do about it? Nothing, that's what."

"There's no comparison," said Fliss firmly, realising that Emma was going to lose any battle of wits with the man, merely because she had allowed herself to be swayed by his arguments, "for a start, no one is even digging on the moor. At the moment all the surveys carried out are electronic ones. And Stone Circles don't contain graves, so even if they do decide to dig, it won't be disturbing anyone's eternal rest."

"Tell that to the bog-man, you jumped-up bitch!"

Fliss's mouth dropped open. How could he know about the bog body? It was supposed to be a closely guarded secret. Fortunately she was saved from further comment by Emma, who finally found something to give her leverage, "There are children here and I won't have swearing – or any more raised voices. Now, you can either settle down with your children and let them play nicely, or you can leave right now. The choice is yours."

One of the women spoke from the back of the hall, "If they stay, I'm leaving. I'm not having my daughter playing with their filthy little nit-carriers."

"Oh nice, very nice!" said the man, "Very Christian. You don't allow a bit of bad language, but bigotry and hatred is quite okay."

Emma managed to be very dignified when she answered him, "I can't be held responsible for the comments of individuals. I have already said you are welcome to stay and I repeat it."

"No thanks, we've places to go."

He turned back to Fliss, "Hey you, tell us how to get up onto the moor."

"I don't know," answered Fliss, "I've only been here a couple of days and when I've been up to the dig it has been through the farm. And I wouldn't advise you to try that way. The farmer doesn't welcome trespassers."

"Forget it," he growled back, "We'll find our own way. Thanks for nothing."

There was a collective sigh of relief when they were gone. Emma headed towards the little kitchenette at the back of the hall, "I think we'll have our tea early today – we need it!"

Slowly normality was resumed. Emma set the urn to boil then introduced Fliss to the other mothers and their children, though she evidently felt the need to remonstrate mildly with her ladies, "You know Pam, You really shouldn't have said that about not wanting Tilly to play with their children – if they are dirty, it's really not their fault, now is it?"

Pam bristled a little, but was conciliatory, "Oh, I know, I know! But it just makes my blood boil when I see the state of some of them. They go on and on about saving the earth from evil exploiters like us, just because we choose to live in a house, but they can't even be bothered to care for their own little ones. How much would it cost to buy a bottle of Tea Tree Oil and treat their head-lice? And what about education? It's all very well for them to decide to drive around the country in a death-trap of an old van, but don't bring your children into it. That's my opinion and I'm sticking to it!"

There were murmurs of assent and Emma was forced to calm things a little, whist still attempting to defend the New Agers. She was nothing, thought Fliss, if not a true fence sitter!

"Well, I can see your point of view, but saying it like you did made you sound awfully bigoted and unfriendly – and that just plays right into their hands. It is a free country after all. You wouldn't like it if someone told you how to raise your youngsters."

"You've got to be joking, Emma, you really have! The Church, Government and social Services do it all the time! The only people they don't inflict their petty rules on are the very ones they should! Scum like that loud mouth!"

This immediately began a debate on Society, Politics, Liberals, Do-gooders and on how they couldn't even smack their own children anymore – not that they would want to, but that's not the point! When they hit upon Christianity and how Christmas was forthwith to be known as the "Winter Festival" and soon the Nativity Play would be banned in schools, Emma obviously thought it was time to draw a halt to the proceedings, "Kettle's boiled, let's have tea," she said brightly, "Danielle, do you want to gather the children in a circle and we'll sing a few nursery rhymes."

"Are you sure they're not too politically incorrect, vicar?" said

Danielle, and was given a very sharp look, however the sally was greeted with laughter from the rest of the group so Emma was forced to let the comment pass.

Tea was made and once the children began to sing the atmosphere lightened and Fliss and Megan spent the rest of the morning playing and singing with the other mums and toddlers, without further conflict to mar the occasion.

At the end of the session, and after locking the door, Emma accompanied Fliss down the path towards the gate, "Do you fancy a spot of lunch at the vicarage, Fliss?" she asked kindly, "I suspect you should avoid the pub for at least another couple of hours. I know that man said they were leaving, but I doubt they will do so before they have sunk a few jars!"

Fliss considered the invitation for a few seconds before replying, "Yes, thanks, I will. I have to go to the Police Station in Feldon later, but another hour or so won't make any difference."

Emma looked surprised, "The Police? Nothing serious I hope?" The classic, "you can tell me if you want to" gambit thought Fliss, amused.

"No, not really, just something minor I have to sort out."

"I had noticed you were driving Ted's Land Rover – has someone pinched your car?"

Since Emma was not going to cease fishing until she had at least a nibble, Fliss thought it easier to go along with that explanation and gave the sort of non-committal grunt that could have been either assent or dissent. She didn't want to actually lie to a vicar – even one who had so callously dropped her in the mire a couple of hours ago.

In the vicarage kitchen Emma became very business-like. She sat Megan on a high stool at the counter and gave her paper and crayons then she took a quiche from the fridge and transferred it to the oven. Whilst she chopped and diced to make a salad, Fliss brewed a pot of fresh coffee.

"So, tell me about the dig," she said, popping a slice of cucumber into her mouth, "Have you really not found anything yet?"

Fliss didn't want to discuss the body as she knew Professor Norton had hoped, in vain as it turned out, to keep the find a secret, but she also wanted to get Emma's advice on the stone head and the nasty experiences it seemed to be engendering.

"Well, they've not started digging at the circle yet, and the surveys my husband has been carrying out haven't revealed any buried structures like house foundations, but they have found one or two things in the bog."

"Really? How interesting. What sort of things."

"Actually, I'd like a bit of advice from you on one of them."

Emma looked stunned, "Me? I don't know a thing about archaeology. I couldn't tell you anything useful."

"It's not archaeological advice I need, Emma, it's spiritual."

Fliss gave her a brief outline of the several eerie incidents that had occurred since the finding of the stone head. Though she mentioned the man she had seen with the slashed throat, she didn't admit a body with similar wounds had been pulled from the bog.

Emma looked thoughtfully at her, "For someone as pragmatic as me, it's very hard to understand the sensitive and imaginative mind. I'm afraid I would see a stone head as just that – a lump of carved stone, interesting, thousands of years old, but inanimate and unthreatening. To you, however, its previous usage has endowed it with supernatural significance – and the power of the mind is very strong."

"That's a polite way of saying that you think its all in my mind," intercepted Fliss, indescribably disappointed that this was the most comfort the vicar could offer. She didn't quite know what she had expected, but it was more than this!

Emma was quick to disabuse her of the notion, "Don't under-estimate what the mind is capable of, Fliss. I've known the very sick become completely cured simply because they believed so strongly in a miracle. I've no doubt that what you saw was very real to you. Your imagination has enabled something primeval to have free reign."

"Okay, I can accept that, but what I really want to know is how do I put the lid back on the box?"

172

The vicar smiled, "The same way you took it off – by the power of your mind. You have to believe that when Professor Norton takes that artefact out of the farmhouse, he'll take the spirit, or force or whatever it is, with him."

"And will he? Take it away with the head, I mean?"

"I think so. The head seems to be the focus of the power. When it goes, so will your ghost."

"I hope you're right," said Fliss doubtfully.

"Don't hope it – know it!"

A tinny bell began to ring, making Fliss jump, until she realised it was the timer on the oven.

"Ah," said Emma, "Lunch is served."

As she cut and served the quiche, she asked brightly, in a very obvious change of subject, "So, tell me about your husband. It must be fascinating being married to an Archaeologist. Who was it said that every woman should marry one, because the older you get the more interested in you he becomes?"

"He's not an archaeologist," said Fliss dully, "And it was Agatha Christie."

Emma stopped mid-salad-tossing, "The crime writer? Are you sure?"

"Positive," said Fliss decidedly, "She was married to one."

"Oh."

They ate the meal and talk turned to other matters – less dangerous ones on both sides.

When she rose at last and made her excuses, Fliss found she had almost forgotten all the negative things about Emma and had grown quite fond of her. She had led an interesting life – much more exciting than Fliss's own - and that always endeared her to people. She liked to hear other women's adventures – to live vicariously so to speak. She wanted to repeat the pun to Emma, but wasn't quite sure she would "get" it. She seemed to be one of those seriously intelligent people who are actually quite dense when it came to everyday life and ordinary things.

For once Emma was on the ball, "I say, why don't you leave Megan with me? I'm not doing anything this afternoon, and a police station is no place for a little one."

"I couldn't possibly put you to the trouble," protested Fliss, fully intending to allow herself to be persuaded. She had been putting off the evil moment for just that reason. Not only did she not want to take Megan anywhere near the police, she also dreaded what the little girl might overhear and understand. She was so quick-witted these days and though in many ways she still seemed to be a baby, in others she showed an awareness that sometimes disconcerted her mother.

"No problem at all," Emma assured her, "I'd love to have her. It will give me an excuse to play silly games and watch children's television."

Fliss conceded with good grace, and within a few minutes was following the careful directions given by Emma and was on the road to the nearby town of Feldon, where she knew she would find the nearest police station.

CHAPTER NINETEEN

*"Merlin was enchanted by the Lady of the Lake and
allowed himself to be bound by his own spells"*

On the way to where she had been told she would find the police
station, Fliss thought about what Emma had said. It seemed far too
glib and convenient – Emma was sitting on the fence yet again.
She hadn't come right out and stated that there was no such thing
as ghosts. To do so would almost be to deny the existence of an
after-life and that of course was the whole basis of her religious
belief. If there was no after-life and therefore no heaven and hell,
then there was really no point in behaving well in this life because
there would be no punishment or reward in the next. No eternal
damnation, no blissful paradise.

On the other hand the vicar could hardly admit that she believed
Fliss was being haunted because then she would have to come to
the farm, bearing bell, book and candle and be ready to cast out the
unquiet spirits.

It really was much easier to blame all the odd events on Fliss's
over-active imagination.

Fliss felt vaguely ripped-off as she searched for a parking spot
then carefully made sure she displayed her ticket in a prominent
place on the dashboard – illegal parking just outside a police
station wouldn't be the brightest move.

The building was the original Victorian edifice, still with a blue
lamp over the front double doors and a stone lintel carved with the
word "POLICE" just below it. Inside, however, technology had
overtaken the old-fashioned charm. The mahogany desk was still
the main feature, but instead of being open as it had been in times

past, it was now faced with plate-glass and the doors which led off in several directions could only be accessed with swipe cards or the keying-in of a PIN.

Fliss went to the receptionist and spoke through the tiny microphone and the holes drilled in the window. She had already decided that she would ask to speak to the pleasant young man who had driven out to the farm to see the bog body. It would be so much easier to explain the details to a friendly and familiar face instead of a complete stranger.

"Hello, I wonder if you can help me."

The young woman on the other side of the glass smiled pleasantly, "I'll do my best, madam."

"I'm Mrs Elmsworth. Is DI Piper available to have a word with me?"

"DI Piper is interviewing at the moment, but if you want to wait I'll see if I can find out if he's going to be long. Just take a seat over there."

Fliss turned and looked to where she was indicating and saw a row of steel-framed chairs, bolted to the floor. What an indictment to modern society, that the chairs have to be secured so they can't be pinched or used as weapons, she thought sadly, doubly glad she hadn't brought Megan with her.

She sat down and the receptionist, true to her promise, went off to find Matt. She bumped into him just as he came out of the interview room.

"Oops! What's your hurry?"

"Sorry Luce. Were you looking for me?"

"Yep. There's a young lady out in reception, asking for you by name."

"How does she look?" Lucy knew this wasn't a question of attractiveness but degrees of danger.

"Not bad. Bit scruffy, but tidy scruffy if you know what I mean. Dirty jeans, but a good make."

"Did she give her name?"

"Elmsworth, I believe."

He searched his memory for a few seconds, and then light

dawned, "Oh, I know. She's one of the archaeology lot. Yeah, I'll see her, no problem. I'll just go and dump this lot on my desk. Tell her I'll be with her in five minutes."

He was with her in considerably less.

"Shall we talk in my office, Mrs Elmsworth?"

She looked up when she heard his voice and smiled at him, rather shyly, and nodded her assent. He tapped in his number and held one of the big, old doors open for her to go through then fell into step beside her as they walked briskly down a series of corridors.

They didn't exchange any conversation until he showed her into a glass-partitioned cubicle off a larger room full of desks and computers with about half of them occupied. Her advent caused not a stir of interest.

Fliss noticed that he didn't have much around to personalise his work-space. No photos of wife or family, no plants, no posters of his favourite football team.

"Now, how can I help you?" he asked and she dragged her attention away from her surroundings and back to her companion.

"Well, it's sort of hard to explain," she began.

"Try," he instructed, not unkindly, but firmly, so that she had no choice but to comply, suddenly realising that he was probably a busy man.

"There was an incident yesterday and I felt I ought to explain what happened in case there were consequences."

"What kind of an incident and what sort of consequences?"

She blushed a little, "It would be easier if I began at the beginning if that's alright with you."

"Fine. Go ahead."

"A few days ago my husband left me alone with my daughter to come up here and work with Professor Norton. After he left, two thugs burst into my house and threatened me and my little girl with a knife. They claimed they had loaned my husband a large sum of money and he had reneged on the repayments."

"He hadn't mentioned this loan to you?"

"Not a word. I was stunned. And of course I had no money to

give them – not nearly enough anyway. I persuaded them that I didn't know the exact location of the dig and promised to contact my husband for the payment if they came back the next day."

"And they accepted that?"

"They didn't have much choice. It must have been obvious to them that I had no money – and I can be very persuasive when I try."

"I'm sure you can. What happened next?"

"As soon as they went I rang my mother and asked to borrow her car so I could drive up here and confront Bryn."

"Bryn is your husband?" She nodded and he continued, "And did he admit he had borrowed the money?"

"Yes," she answered bitterly, "so that he could have a new computer. Can you believe he put our little girl's life in danger for the sake of the latest bloody mega-drive or whatever the stupid things are called?"

When she hesitated, evidently expecting an answer to what he had considered a rhetorical question, he murmured diplomatically, "I don't suppose he thought you'd be in any danger when he agreed the loan. People usually believe they can keep up with the repayments when they sign on the dotted line – it's only later they realise they were kidding themselves."

"Yes, well, he is a husband and father; he should have been more than sure!"

"And then?" he prompted, determined not to be side-tracked again.

"I refused to go home without him or the money – which he doesn't have – so Mr Armitage let me stay in the farmhouse."

"Unusually generous of him, from what I've heard."

"I won't hear a word said against that man," bristled Fliss, "He's shown me and Megan nothing but kindness."

Piper raised an eyebrow but said nothing more on the subject, "So now we come to the incident you mentioned?"

"Yes. I had gone into the village to ask about a playgroup where I could take Megan and then I saw my brother, Daniel. He had come to collect my mother's car – and I couldn't believe my eyes when I saw that he had those same two thugs with him. My own brother had led them straight to me."

"Perhaps he was unaware of their agenda,"

"Oh, he was aware all right. The rat! It turns out he introduced them to Bryn in the first place."

Matt looked grim for a moment, "Charming. Are we likely to know this brother of yours?"

"Is that the royal 'we'?"

"No, we as in the Police Force."

"In that case, very probably. Anyway, the same old threats started to come out. They wanted their money and they were pretty annoyed that I had done a runner and tried to give them the slip."

"I presume there was no help to be had from your brother?"

"You must be kidding. He led them to me – and I'll bet he would have held me down while they slashed me."

"I'd like to hope not," he said seriously, "So who did turn out to be your knight in shining armour?"

"Mr Armitage. I saw him going into the pub so I shouted him across. I was nearly hysterical with fear, not just for myself, but I had my baby with me."

"I understand your dilemma. Did Armitage respond to your plea for help?"

"He certainly did. I told him what was going on – though my brother tried to deny anything was happening to scare me – then the taller of the two thugs pulled a knife on us, so Mr Armitage knocked him down."

"How? Fist or implement?"

"He just punched him." DI Piper looked thoughtful then said slowly, "That's interesting because I have Armitage in my interview room even as we speak and he's denying ever meeting the two men let alone striking one of them. They've lodged a complaint that he swung for them with a baseball bat. A claim your brother – Daniel is it? – is upholding."

Fliss was white with ill-concealed fury, "They are nothing but slimy liars – and you are just as bad! How could you let me go on knowing that you had Mr Armitage in custody? You've arrested the wrong man – but that won't bother you, will it?"

"Watch what you're saying, madam," he warned, his voice deceptively calm.

"Why? What are you going to do? Throw me in jail? You had no right to interview me without reading me my rights and offering me a solicitor."

She looked so furious that Matt couldn't help notice how pretty she was with two spots of red on her cheeks and her eyes glistening furiously. He suddenly grinned, "Come off it love. You've been watching too much telly. You weren't being interviewed – you asked to speak to me, remember? – and Mr Armitage isn't under arrest. He's helping me with my enquiries."

"Well, now that I've told you what really happened, you can let him go home with me," she said decidedly.

"It's not quite that simple. I'm going to be straight with you, Mrs Elmsworth. This isn't the first time Ted Armitage has had complaints laid against him. He's a farmer and he owns a gun – which he's swung in the direction of trespassers once too often. He's potentially dangerous and it's up to me to make sure he knows just exactly how far he can go before we throw the book at him."

"I'm sure he'll behave from now on. He really is a good man – and I'd like to bet any complaints about him have come from a certain Douglas Merrington – or his cohorts."

The blank expression on the policeman's face told Fliss she wasn't far off the mark, but she wisely decided not to pursue the matter, "I've told you what really happened, so why does it have to go any further?"

"Forgive my bluntness, Mrs Elmsworth, but I've been given two conflicting stories – and my only witness for Mr Armitage has a vested interest in keeping him out of jail – do you really think that will stand up in court?"

She looked not only shocked but deeply offended, "Are you saying that you think I'm lying?"

"No, I'm saying that what I think doesn't matter. A good Brief would tear your story to shreds. You've just admitted that Armitage has offered you a home – it's only one step away from there for a lawyer to hint that you are co-habiting with him. Suddenly your testimony holds no water at all."

"But those two ... creatures are nothing but a pair of loan sharks, who threatened my little girl with a knife!"

"That's not the story they tell."

"And have you checked to see if they have 'form' – I believe that's the police parlance."

"I'm doing it even as we speak – or at least a member of my team is – but the sad fact is that if those two have sailed close to the wind, but never actually been caught, then I'll have nothing to prove they are lying and you are not."

"And you wonder why I didn't come to you for help right at the beginning."

"I'm sorry, but I'm powerless to act. They've made a complaint and they have an injury to prove their story. All Armitage has is you and teeth-marks on his knuckles – and it's not a good combination."

"What if I can get my husband to tell the truth about those two?"

"That would be a start."

"And I'll stand guarantor for Mr Armitage, if that's any help."

"It will be eventually – but I still need to hold him for a few more hours. He needs to cool off."

"I understand you think he needs a warning, but what you are forgetting is that he has animals that need feeding and caring for. I don't know where to begin – and the RSPCA won't thank you for ill-treating his stock."

"I think you'll find that word will have travelled fast in the village. The animals won't go without, I assure you."

"I hope you are right."

"I am."

"Well, can I see him for a few minutes?"

"No. Go back to the farm and he'll be brought home later."

"I really need to see him."

"Why?"

"Because I want him to know that I didn't mean to drop him in it."

She gave him her most appealing look.

"Alright, you can have two minutes – but that's it."

"Thank you, Inspector."

He didn't bother to point out that he was a Detective Inspector.

Theo greeted Fliss with a sheepish grin, "Nice of you to visit. Got a cake with a file in it?"

"Don't joke, Theo, I feel awful. This is all my fault."

"Rubbish. It's all my own fault. If I didn't let my fists fly at the first sign of trouble, I wouldn't be here."

"But you only did it to protect me and Megan."

"I wouldn't say 'only' to protect you. I didn't like the man's face and I enjoyed flooring him, so don't feel too guilty."

She managed a small laugh and he chucked her under the chin, "That's better. I like to see you laugh, Fliss. You don't do it often enough."

She looked at him and he met her eyes squarely, "I've not had much to laugh about recently," she faltered, suddenly aware that there was more going on in his mind than she knew how to deal with.

"We'll soon alter that."

"Theo," she began, realising that she was going to have to put a halt to whatever he was thinking.

"Don't worry," he interrupted, "I know we're just good friends, as the saying goes. I may be a country bumpkin, but I'm not blind or stupid."

"What do you mean?" she asked, genuinely puzzled. He gave an enigmatic grin then the policeman came down the passageway and led him back to the cells.

CHAPTER TWENTY

*"Arthur's war-band assisted Culhwch in one of his hardest tasks,
which was to retrieve a comb, razor and scissors from between
the ears of a terrible, enchanted boar"*

It was almost tea-time when Fliss arrived back at the farm, having called at the vicarage to collect Megan. Emma had shown great concern at hearing of Theo's sojourn at the police station but, as Fliss was unsurprised to realize, she had little help to offer. She agreed with DI Piper that the livestock would by now have been taken care of by neighbouring farmers, but apart from that she had nothing. She studiously ignored Fliss's suggestion that she might perhaps ring the police and personally vouch for Theo herself and simply started to tell Fliss what a good girl Megan had been, what a credit she was to her mother and how delighted she would be to offer babysitting services again in the future. Fliss left it at that.

The lights were ablaze in the Weary Sportsman as Fliss left the vicarage and she was sorely tempted to enter and claim her evening meal, but the thought of having to explain, yet again, how she had spent her day was tedious in the extreme. Worse still was the idea that she might have to actually converse with her husband when she knew he was behind Theo's plight. That sent her indignation level soaring to an alarming height. She knew if she found him gloating in the snug, bragging at his cleverness at ridding himself of one whom he thought of as his rival, she might just end up spending the night behind bars herself.

It was a struggle finding a space to park in the yard as there were two new vehicles she hadn't seen before, but the owners appeared from various directions when they heard her motor. One of the young men hailed her, "You must be Fliss."

"Yes."

"Hi, I'm Malcolm and that's Jason and Gavin. We had a call from Ted's solicitor asking us to take care of the animals and make sure you were okay."

"Oh, brilliant. Thank goodness for that. I would never have known what to do. Is everything alright?"

"Yes, fine. It's all done and dusted. We're just off. One of us will come over first thing and then Ted should be back. He seemed confident he'd be home by lunch time at the latest."

"I'm really grateful, thanks so much."

"No problem – he'd do the same for us – in fact, come to think about it, he has! Remember the cider drinking competition, boys?" The two other men had joined them by this time, and Fliss was amused to see that they were so alike that they even blushed at the same rate when Malcolm mentioned cider.

"Anyway, I've left a bit of paper with all our numbers on if you have any problems."

"Thanks again. Can I offer you all a drink or something before you go?"

"No, thanks. There was a chap in the kitchen who made us all a cuppa about half an hour ago. See you around."

"Bye." Even as she was waving them off the premises Fliss felt her heart lighten. The "chap" in the kitchen must be John Norton. He would know what to do about Theo. She didn't wait to see their tail-lights disappearing down the rapidly-darkening lane but flew indoors with a happy smile and Megan in her arms.

She plumped the little girl down by the door and told her to take off her Wellingtons, then she went inside, fending off the two sheepdogs who immediately ran at her, tails wagging, obviously wondering where on earth their master might be.

The feeling of apprehension that had persisted all the way home and had only ceased when she thought she was going to see the professor came flooding back when she saw that the "chap" was none other than Bryn. The archaeologist was nowhere to be seen and she suddenly realised that of course he would be at the Weary

Sportsman with the others, eating a hearty meal and thinking of anything in the world but her.

As soon as he saw Fliss, Bryn grinned maliciously, "Been to visit 'Lover Boy' in the clink?" he asked, with an air of innocent enquiry that didn't fool Fliss for a moment.

"You unspeakable bas..." she trailed off, suddenly remembering the presence of her daughter. She turned to the little girl, who was still just outside the door, struggling to remove her boots, "Do you want to go into the other room and watch TV while mummy makes tea, honey?"

Megan looked up, her intense concentration on the job in hand broken, and nodded happily.

"No, she doesn't," Bryn intercepted gruffly, "she wants to come and sit with her daddy."

Fliss wondered what was behind his sudden fraternal interest, but before she could say anything Megan piped up, "No I don't, I want to watch telly."

"You'll come here and do as you're told," he snapped back, rising to his feet. Megan strolled across to him and Fliss could see that she was determined to get the unwanted cuddle over and done with quickly so that she could make her escape.

"Leave her alone, Bryn," she said quietly. He ignored her and lifted the reluctant child into his arms where she reposed, as stiff as a plastic doll with her body arched slightly away from her father so there was as little physical contact as she could possibly manage. She dutifully kissed his cheek when he asked, with false heartiness, "Don't you have a big kiss for your daddy?" then wriggled to be let down to the floor, "Telly now," she said firmly. Bryn set her on her feet with very bad grace.

"Been pouring your poison, Fliss?" he asked harshly. At the sound of his voice the two dogs, who had settled by the Aga, rose of one accord and growls rumbled in their throats. Bryn threw them an evil look, "Lie down and shut up!" They did so, but all pretence at sleep was gone and they both watched him warily.

"Megan doesn't need me to tell her what sort of a man you are," replied Fliss with dignity and took Megan into the parlour, switching on the television for her and instructing her to be good, "I'll just be in the kitchen if you want me," she added, but Megan was already fascinated by the flickering images on the box in the corner.

In the hall on the way back to the kitchen, Fliss took a moment to take a deep breath and think about what she intended to do next. Bryn was obviously spoiling for a fight and much as she would have liked to give into her feelings of anger and frustration, she knew she had to protect Megan from as much of their mutual bitterness as she could. Bryn must not be allowed to provoke her. She silently promised herself that she would be civil to him no matter what he said or did.

She walked back through the kitchen door and straight over to the sink where she began to peel potatoes. She could feel his gaze on her back and it seemed with every passing second that it burned deeper until she could stand the silence no longer.

"How come you are not at the pub with the others?" she asked conversationally. She didn't care where he was or what he did, but it was the only thing she could think of to say.

"Where should I be but where my little wifey is?" he said, his voice slick with false charm.

"How sweet. That's the first time I've ever been put ahead of a pint in terms of desirability. Tell me more nice things, Bryn; I've had a long day." She felt quite proud of herself. She had managed to speak without a pinprick of sarcasm. He seemed to think so too, because he rose to his feet and walked over to her, putting his arms around her waist and nuzzling her neck, "Oh, come on, Fliss. We've had our ups and downs, but you know you're the girl for me, really."

"Have you ever asked yourself if you are the man for me?"

"Don't need to, love."

She decided a different topic of conversation was called for, "What's going on at the dig? Have they moved the bog man yet? I feel as though I'm missing everything, stuck down here with Megan."

"You were the one who wanted a kid," he said gruffly, "And no, they haven't moved him yet. Shouldn't think they will be for a while."

"Oh? Why not? I would have imagined they'd want him in a lab pronto."

"Under normal circumstances they would – but thanks to you there's a complication."

She pulled herself out of his embrace and turned to face him, "Thanks to me? What do you mean?"

"Well, you're the idiot who told those New Age scumbags where the dig is, aren't you?"

"No, I most certainly did not!"

"Don't be naïve, Fliss. You went into the village and the next thing you know they are up on the moor, dancing around the stone circle with protest banners and accusing us of all sorts."

"I told them to stay away," she protested, "I warned them that Armitage doesn't welcome trespassers – and I told them the only way I knew up there was through the farmyard."

"Well, you didn't make much of a case. They are up there now and Fergus and Professor Norton are ruing the day they met you. Neither of 'em dares to leave the finds unattended. They are going to be up there for days because all the nutters' old vans are blocking the only road across the moor."

Fliss was horrified – not just because of the situation that Norton found himself in, but also that he might think for a single moment that she was responsible.

She moved swiftly away from him and went to the fridge to fetch the sausages. She moved now on autopilot, cooking the food, but neither seeing nor hearing anything. She couldn't get the thought of the professor stuck up on the moors out of her mind. What on earth must he be thinking of her? A flappy-trap who couldn't wait to get into the village and gossip – and it was so unfair because the New Agers had obviously known all about the dig before she even walked into the village hall.

Bryn was sitting back at the table, watching her. After a moment he said something, but she didn't hear so he repeated it, loudly. She stared at him blankly, "What?"

"I said, is Armitage happy in his new digs?"

"You just can't resist it, can you?" she asked wearily, "You couldn't leave the subject alone and let us have a relatively peaceful evening. I was prepared to be reasonable, but you always have to win, don't you?"

"I wondered what you were thinking about just then – and now I know, don't I?"

"Give it a rest, Bryn."

"No, I bloody well won't. Who the hell do you think you are fooling?"

"I'm not trying to fool anyone. I don't know how many times I have to tell you that I'm not having an affair with Armitage or anyone else."

"I know what I saw," he said grimly, "and now the man is paying the price."

"I don't know why you think you've done something clever." She strove to keep her voice level and calm, "The police aren't going to hold him forever – and when he does come home, he's going to know exactly who was responsible."

"Ooh, I'm shaking in my boots," he responded sarcastically.

"It's easy to say that now, but your friend with the knife wasn't exactly laughing when Theo confronted him."

Bryn had obviously heard the story in full, because he declined to pursue the subject, merely adding, "Well, he won't be back before tomorrow, so I'll take advantage of his absence and have a decent bed for the night."

"And which bed precisely are you planning on occupying?" she asked coldly.

"Why, yours of course, my dear. You are my wife, after all – and you don't seem to be fussy who you take to bed these days."

She stared at him for a long time, taking in every feature, every line of his face, as though examining a stranger – for, in truth, that was what he had suddenly become. She could hardly believe that she had lived with this man, slept with him, had a child with him. Their life together had become as hazy and ill-remembered as a dream. This was not the Bryn she had fallen in love with.

Somewhere along the way they had both turned into different people and each had been too busy with their own development to notice and adapt to the changes in the other.

She had become a mother, had grown responsible, always aware that now another life depended on her. He had drifted on in his own sweet way, refusing to grow up and admit that things had to change. Her new persona simply made him feel guilty – and with that guilt came an anger that could only be directed at her. She could see the hate in his eyes as he looked back at her and she went cold with fear. In his head all the changes were bad – and it was her fault.

"Take my word for it, Bryn," she said with icy clarity, "I am fussy who I sleep with."

She went to fetch Megan for her tea.

He waited until she sat down with her plate in front of her before he said, "I'd like some of that."

She knew that he was fully aware that she had only made enough for herself and Megan, but still she rose and passed her own food to him. He began to eat with gusto, a triumphant smirk on his face.

Fliss said nothing. She actually felt now that she couldn't have eaten a bite and he was welcome to her sausage and mash, but it made her silently fume that he had callously let her cook and serve the food before asking for some. It was just another of his petty mind-games, a method of control. She wondered why she had been submitting to it.

She knew now that she had to leave the house without him knowing it. She would pluck her own eyes out before she would sleep with this man again – but she wasn't prepared to face the scene that would ensue if she refused him.

When she had finished eating Megan showed a flash of insight that would have scared Fliss to death had she not been so relieved, "Mummy, you said I could say night-night to the pigs."

Fliss opened her lips to deny she had made any such promise, then realised that her little girl had just offered her an escape route.

"So I did sweetheart, but I have to wash up first, feed the dogs and make your daddy a cup of tea." She knew it was imperative that she did not show too much eagerness. If Bryn suspected for a moment that she intended to run, he would never allow her out of the door.

He evidently thought he had won because he rose and said, "I'll make the tea while you wash up." She knew she was supposed to grovel with gratitude at this generous gesture so she forced a "thanks" as she picked up the dishes and carried them to the sink. She made herself take her time over the task, but if her hands were slow, her brain was scurrying from plan to plan like a mouse looking for cheese. It was too risky to try and drive into the village, though she knew that both the Weary Sportsman and the vicarage would offer safe havens. Bryn would hear the engine starting and be out of the door before she had thrown the car into reverse gear. Her only hope was to sneak around the side of the house and make her way up onto the moor. She knew Fergus or John Norton would help her. All she needed was their company as far as the car. Bryn wouldn't dare to try and stop her from driving away if his employers were on hand.

The only problem was that it was now getting dark and she would have to find her way through an even darker wood and across open moor land with a small child.

She fed the dogs with a sack of dried stuff she had seen Theo use then put it back in the pantry, where she knew there was also a torch – in case of power failure. Cleaning the house for Theo was now paying dividends because she knew where everything that might be of use to her was kept. She slipped it in the waistband of her jeans, almost gasping as the cold metal slid against her stomach, and pulled her jumper over it to hide it. It was now or never.

"Come on, Meggie. Put your coat on. The pigs want to say night-night so they can go to sleep too."

Bryn looked at her, "Don't you think it's a bit cold for tramping around a farmyard?"

"No we'll be well wrapped up and it'll only take a few minutes – why don't you come with us?" She knew him well enough to

190

realise that if he was invited he would say no – but if she gave him the slightest indication she didn't want him along, he would insist on accompanying them.

"No thanks," he responded, "Pigs smell bad enough from in here – I'm certainly not going to hang over the side of their pen and get a noseful!"

"Please yourself. We won't be long. Why don't you go and watch the TV? And put a match to the fire while you're in there. I'll be perished when I come back in."

He shrugged non-commitally, but she noticed he glanced longingly towards the hall. He had taken the bait and it wouldn't be long before he had his feet toasting in front of the fire, a glass of Theo's whisky in his hand and the television churning out some mindless, violent rubbish of the sort he seemed to enjoy.

She took Megan's hand and led her out of the back door and into the enclosing darkness.

CHAPTER TWENTY-ONE

"Calatin was a misshapen Druid who was said to have studied sorcery for seventeen years"

As she skirted around the side of the house, Fliss could have sworn she heard Bryn's voice calling her name, but she prayed that it was only her imagination and ploughed on. He couldn't possibly know what she intended to do.

She walked faster, stumbling on the uneven garden path, Megan dragging on her hand. The little girl was struggling to keep up and loath as she was to admit it, Fliss realised she would have to slow down a little or risk a twisted ankle or worse. Nothing could be more fatal to her plans.

Megan, in spite of her laboured breathing, seemed unfazed by this nocturnal adventure, plodding stoically on, neither questioning her mother nor attempting to make conversation as she usually did when they walked together. Perhaps she sensed her mother's panic.

Soon the garden gave way to the field and presently they plunged into the gloom of the woods. Was it her imagination or was there a curious mistiness spreading before her, dark and foreboding? Fliss pulled out the torch and clicked the switch, hoping against hope that the batteries wouldn't be flat. The beam illuminated the way ahead and solved the mystery. The bluebells had flowered and their nodding heads covered the floor of the woods in a blanket of darkness. She could hardly believe they had blossomed so completely and in perfect unison in so short a time. Surely it had only been yesterday when she last walked through the woods, and there had only been the faintest hint of the blue to come then? The soughing of the trees was eerily secretive and shivers ran up and down her spine. Anything could be hiding in that encroaching blackness and neither of them would see or hear it until it was too late.

Fliss mentally shook herself. "Stop it," she whispered under her breath, "Just stop it. There's nothing here but trees." But somehow she knew that wasn't quite true. That same brooding stillness, which had unnerved her the first time she entered the wood, now extended about her, despite the breeze that rustled the leaves above her head. It was as though the wind had tried and failed to penetrate the tree trunks and could only dance high up amongst the leaves, desperate to find a way in.

Suddenly something disturbed the undergrowth and though common sense told Fliss that it was merely some large animal like a badger or a fox, she still let out a tiny bleat of fear.

"It's alright, mummy, it's only the hairy pig." Somehow this didn't console Fliss at all.

"It's going to show us the way," Megan added confidently.

Fliss knew that the last thing she intended to do was to follow a wild boar, which, if the pictures she had seen were correct, had huge, sharp, yellowing tusks, around a dark wood at night – especially one that only her four year old daughter could see.

"We don't need to, sweetheart. We can follow the path."

That was true to a certain extent, but she realised now that it was remarkably difficult to follow a mud track in the dark, with only the beam of an old torch lighting the way. She gritted her teeth and continued, hoping and praying that her sense of direction wouldn't lead them astray.

What the hell had she been thinking? She must have completely lost the plot to have brought her child into a wood, in pitch darkness. Would it really have been so bad to stay in the house with her husband for just one more night? As soon as the question formed itself in her mind, the answer came swiftly back – yes it would! She didn't know what the future held. She had no idea how she would manage for money or how she would convince Bryn that he had to leave her alone – but she knew she was never going back to him – not for a night, not for a second.

Soon she was stumbling along, the meagre light only making the surrounding wood darker and more menacing by contrast. She kept glancing up just in case she might walk slap bang into a tree branch, but mainly she looked at the ground. She could only see her feet and Megan's by the torchlight, but felt they were the more important just at that moment – a black eye would be easier to cope with than a twisted ankle. Brambles tore at her jeans, and she almost fell on her face a couple of times when fronds of fern or tree roots tripped her, but somehow, miraculously, she found herself being led along by her little girl, who seemed to know, unerringly, which was the right way. Fliss was too afraid to ask if she was still following the "hairy pig". She didn't want to know. A snap of broken twig behind her set her heart pounding in her throat, but she pressed on, determined not to look behind. All that mattered was that Megan was keeping to the path and slowly the trees were thinning out and vague glimpses of light told her that she was at least nearing her destination. She still had to find her way across a few hundred metres of moor but at least there were no trees, nowhere for mysterious things to hide and watch her with silent malice.

There seemed to be a bonfire lit in the centre of the stone circle, and she could see figures moving around, black against the dancing flames. She knew that could only be the travellers, for Fergus and John would never dream of lighting a fire just there. She skirted carefully around, making sure she was well out of range of the flickering light. The last thing she needed just now was an angry confrontation with the New Agers.

She became aware that she actually had no idea where John Norton had pitched his tent, but a process of elimination told her that he was more than likely by the bog. The original tent had been pitched to protect the bog man from the elements and prying eyes until he could be moved, and Bryn had mentioned him being steeped in bog water to keep him stable until he reached a laboratory. Common sense told her that where the bog man was, she would find the professor.

A tiny light led her to the place, but it flickered and died as she came upon the tents and she wondered what it had been. They were lit from within by the vague, steady glow of battery-powered lanterns – what she had seen had looked more like a tiny flickering flame, like a candle or a match.

She called cautiously, trying not to startle the two men too much by her unexpected approach. The only visitors they would be expecting up here would be travellers and she didn't want them to smack her first and ask questions afterwards.

Fergus came out of the nearest tent asking, "Who is it?" in a more aggressive tone than Fliss had previously heard him use.

"It's me, Fliss Elmsworth."

He seemed stunned, lifting aloft his hurricane lamp, as though to prove the truth of her statement, "What the hell are you doing up here in the dark? How did you get here? Have the buggers moved their vans?" She didn't bother to answer the succession of questions, merely responding to the last one, "No, we walked up."

He stared at her, then glanced down towards Megan, "You did what?"

"We walked. I need to see the professor. Is he here?"

She heard the ripping sound of a tent being unzipped and the shushing of the material as Norton swept the flap aside and emerged, demanding, "What's going on, Fergus?"

"You've got a visitor, John," said Fergus wryly.

"What the devil…?"

John stopped short as he recognised Fliss. She strained her eyes to see his reaction to her presence, but the lamp shining into her face sent him into stark relief against the blackness and she could only see his outline. He was silent for a long time – or so it seemed to Fliss, then he said coolly, "What can I do for you, Mrs Elmsworth?"

"I'm so sorry, I know this is a dreadful imposition, but I had to get out of the farmhouse."

"There's really no need for you to be afraid. I did as you requested and moved the stone head." Was it her imagination or did he sound cold? She suddenly recalled what Bryn had said about him believing she had directed the travellers onto the moor. She opened her lips to explain to him that she wasn't responsible, but Fergus's presence stopped her. She couldn't pour forth the passionate denial, the heartfelt assurance that she would never betray him, when Fergus was listening so avidly to her every utterance. She drew in a deep breath and tried to speak calmly, "You don't understand. I'm not afraid of the house. It's Bryn."

"Bryn?" Fergus spoke sharply, "What has he done to you?"

"Nothing, really, but he won't leave the house. He says he's staying the night and I ..." she trailed off, the blood rushing to her face. How to explain to two relative strangers that she didn't want to sleep with her own husband?

"So what?" asked Fergus, almost rudely, "He's your husband, so why shouldn't he sleep with you while Armitage is out of the way? I certainly would."

He didn't seem to think he had said anything amiss, though Fliss's cheeks burned at the implication.

"I've left him," she said blandly. She couldn't think of anything else to say.

"Then tell him to sod off," advised Fergus.

"That's easier said than done," said Fliss coldly. She wished Fergus would do as he had just suggested Bryn do, so that she could speak to John Norton alone. This was excruciating.

"I don't see why," said Fergus matter-of-factly, "Bryn has always seemed a perfectly reasonable fellow to me."

"Then you don't know him as well as you think you do," snapped Fliss, "It's his fault Mr Armitage is in jail. He and his thuggish friends have cooked up this whole scheme between them."

"And why should he do that? You told me in the pub the other night that your marriage was solid. Why are you suddenly splitting up?"

Fliss glanced at the silently listening Norton, feeling that his unspeaking condemnation was cutting into her like a razor sharp blade then she turned back to Fergus, "I think you'll find that I avoided telling you anything about my marriage at all, except that it exists! And Bryn is mad as hell because he saw me being hugged

196

through the kitchen window and has convinced himself that I'm having an affair with Mr Armitage."

Fergus laughed mirthlessly, obviously annoyed with her frankness. He had asked the questions, but now it seemed he didn't particularly like the answers, "Dear God, how desperate would you have to be?"

"Shut up, Fergus," said Norton harshly, "That is one step too far. This is neither the time nor the place."

Fergus turned to look at his colleague, "Bloody hell, it's not true is it?"

"No it is not," said Fliss savagely, "Not that it would be any of your business if it was. At least Armitage has treated me with respect. He didn't expect a quickie up against the wall of a pub toilet!"

Finally Fergus realised that perhaps he ought to keep quiet.

John Norton approached Fliss and indicated that she walk in front of him, "I'll accompany you down to the farm, Mrs Elmsworth, and see you safely off the premises. I'll have a word with Bryn in the morning."

"There's really no need for you to do that, professor. It isn't your responsibility to sort out my difficulties, but I really cannot risk having a screaming match with Megan looking on. I only ask that you help me to leave the farm without a scene."

"Very well," he answered quietly then addressed Fergus with icy disdain, "I trust you have no objection to my leaving you here for an hour or so, Fergus?"

"No," said Fergus, sarcasm dripping from every word, "Go right ahead and help our damsel in distress. God forbid that she might have to take care of her own affairs for once in her life."

Fliss thought she sensed a slight movement in the professor towards Fergus, but if he had felt prompted to respond to the baiting, he managed to restrain himself.

"If I don't make it back, I'll make sure a couple of the other lads come up here to keep you company."

"In other words, a couple of the other lads will be keeping me company," said Fergus furiously, "Seems to me that it isn't

Armitage that Bryn has to worry about."

Norton lifted Megan into his arms and took Fliss's elbow with his free hand, apparently not having heard Fergus's parting shot. Fliss could gladly have died of embarrassment there on the spot.

They said nothing as they walked across the moor back towards the woods. Norton carried Megan, who rested her now weary little head on his shoulder. He had released Fliss's arm, but she felt as though the skin still burned where his fingers had gripped her. She didn't trust herself to speak, though she longed to explain everything to him. Fergus was right. She was a completely useless wimp who didn't even dare to confront her own husband and tell him to get the hell out of her life. How did she think she was going to manage as a single mother in the big, bad world without a man to rescue her every five minutes?

As they approached the stone circle, Norton finally spoke to her, "We'll take a slight detour, if you don't mind. I'd rather not be spotted. It wouldn't help for them to know that Fergus is now alone."

"No, quite. I understand."

They skirted the stones by a rather wide margin, both their torches temporarily doused.

She stumbled a couple of times and his hand shot out to steady her, but she gently withdrew from his grasp as soon as she regained her footing.

Once they reached the trees they put their torches back on and in the few seconds they stopped to do so, Fliss found the courage to speak to him, "Professor, I very much need to tell you that it was not me who told the New Agers about the dig. They were already in the church hall arguing with Emma when I arrived."

He glanced at her in surprise, "I never supposed otherwise. What made you think I blamed you?"

"Bryn told me."

"I'm surprised you are still listening to anything Bryn tells you."

She laughed quietly, "So am I. But it hit a raw nerve when he said it."

"I see."

They walked on, but in single file now, with the professor leading the way. He seemed very sure-footed and Fliss could only suppose that he not only strolled around at night quite a lot, but also he knew the way through the woods rather better than the back of his own hand.

Suddenly her feet slipped from under her just like a cartoon character on a banana skin and she found herself slamming into his broad back, completely unable to control either her feet or her body. Her arms went out in a desperate attempt to keep herself upright, and in a movement so dextrous she wondered how he managed it without dropping Megan, he turned and caught her about the waist.

"Are you okay?" he laughed softly, his breath warm on her cheek. She nodded, too breathless to speak. Seconds passed and still he retained his hold, "Felicity ..." he whispered.

"Yes?" Her voice too was scarcely discernible above the rustling leaves. His lips were close to her face and she wondered how it would feel to be kissed by him. The flutter of excitement in her stomach made her feel light headed and almost a little sick. She wished she could see his eyes more clearly. They were dark shadows in the poor light.

"Want to go home," murmured the sleepy Megan, breaking the spell. Norton released Fliss,

"Watch your step," he said in his normal voice and Fliss thought that she had been mistaken and he had never breathed her name.

"I will. I'm sorry. I almost had us both flat on our backs."

"Life is full of regrettable things," he said enigmatically.

They walked on and presently the path widened a little and they were able to walk abreast again.

"I owe you an apology, Felicity."

"No need. I've had men grab me around the waist before," she joked, seeking to lighten the atmosphere and distract herself from the sudden alteration of her feelings towards him.

"Not for that – I refuse to apologise for saving you from a most undignified tumble," he said with a smile, "I meant about this latest trouble with Bryn. He has entirely the wrong idea about you and Armitage – and that is my fault."

"It has nothing to do with you," she said firmly, "Bryn saw something which was totally innocent and immediately jumped to the wrong conclusion. It is his own stupidity that split us up – long before he saw me hug you. If anyone deserves an apology, it is poor Theo – and even he wouldn't be in his present predicament if he hadn't punched someone," she added severely. Nothing could make her approve of physical violence – now that she had forgotten how satisfied she had been to see the arrogant bully floored with a single blow.

John's lips twitched as he hid an unkind grin. Ted Armitage was famed for talking with his fists and not his mouth.

"Very true," he admitted with mock seriousness, "But I have to say in Bryn's defence that if I had a lovely young wife, I would do my utmost to keep her too."

She glanced sideways at him, "Am I lovely?" she asked.

"Never more so than at this moment," he assured her light-heartedly. Fliss grinned, knowing that her hair looked like a bird's nest of dead leaves and broken twigs, her face was grubby and scratched and her clothes wouldn't look out of place in the travellers' camp on the moor.

"Thanks."

By this time they had reached the garden gate and the realisation that Bryn was probably looking for her and would find her in the company of John Norton made Fliss quail, all her courage fizzled away like a spent match.

The yard was deserted and Norton directed her to his car and unlocked the doors for her, "Get Megan's child seat and strap her in. I'll be back presently."

"What are you going to do?" she asked, her voice low and trembling.

"I'm going to tell Bryn where you are spending the night."

"Be careful, I don't want ..."

"Don't worry, I will assure him that a scene enacted in front of Megan will be unacceptable."

That wasn't what she had been about to say, but she didn't bother to correct him.

Her fingers wouldn't work because her hands were so unsteady and it took every grain of concentration she could muster to work out how to transfer the child seat from one car to another. She had only just accomplished the task when she heard footsteps approaching and whirled around, ready to confront Bryn, should it be him.

She need not have worried. Professor Norton joined her, a strange smile on his face,

"I found Bryn in the parlour, as white as a sheet. He tells me that the house gives him the creeps and he has no intention of staying another minute. He was only waiting for your return to tell you that he intends to spend the night on the moor with the artefacts."

Her mouth fell slightly agape with genuine surprise, "What?"

"It's true. I have no idea what has changed his mind, but it was a chastened Bryn I left in the kitchen just now, clutching a cup of tea as though his life depended on it."

"Then I don't need to trouble you any further," she said, still stunned by this unexpected turn of events.

"On the contrary, you are still sleeping elsewhere tonight. You deserve a night in a comfortable bed."

"No, honestly …" she began to protest, but he raised a hand to cut her short.

"I insist. You've had a hell of a day."

That she had to agree with. She climbed into the vehicle and waited for him to start the engine.

"Are you going to take me to the pub? I hope Polly will have a room made up, I'm exhausted."

"We will be calling at the pub whilst I tell Con he needs to join Fergus up on the moor for the night, but you are not sleeping there."

"At the vicarage then?" she inquired tentatively.

"No. I have a room at my disposal at Merrington Hall. You will be using that."

She looked down at herself, "Oh, no John, I couldn't. Look at the state of me! Douglas Merrington wouldn't allow me over the doorstep."

"Most people walk around in towelling dressing gowns, my dear. It's a health farm. You won't be out of place at all, once you've had a shower."

With that assurance she had to be content.

CHAPTER TWENTY-TWO

*"Owain set off in search of the Castle of the Fountain,
which was guarded by the Black Knight"*

Megan was asleep almost before they had pulled out of the farmyard. Fliss looked around to check on her and smiled softly when
she saw the tousled head nodding. Poor little lamb must be
exhausted after trekking through the woods and stumbling over the
grassy tussocks and crumbling peat.

She returned her gaze to the front and repressed a shudder as
she looked out into the darkness. They were amongst the trees now
and she could barely discern the lane. With the headlights
sweeping across the tree trunks they looked almost as though they
were blocking the road, only to shift reluctantly, silently out of
their way, seemingly unwilling to give them passage, but forced
out of necessity to do so. Like a voiceless, condemning crowd
gathered in front of a police van containing a particularly hated
criminal, they parted with malice.

Yet she felt safe in the car. There was an odd intimacy in the
warmth and dark.

"You are very quiet," said John in a low voice, wary of rousing
the sleeping child.

"I was just thinking," she answered, equally quietly.

"About what?"

She could hardly admit that she was now afraid of trees too! She
searched for something less incriminating to tell him.

"I was wondering what Bryn meant about the house being
creepy," she said at last.

"I've no idea. He didn't elaborate. I suppose any old building seems a little daunting when one suddenly finds oneself alone."

"Huh! I suppose so, but he's never been much over-burdened with imagination before. I'm surprised to hear him say something like that."

"Forgive me if I sound rude, but to be honest, I can't say I care a great deal what Bryn is feeling just at this moment."

She gave a small laugh, "That makes two of us. It just seemed odd – especially after what happened to me last night."

"I'd forget about that if I were you."

"I'm trying."

They fell silent, but there was no awkwardness in the atmosphere. Fliss wasn't left feeling that she had said something she ought not. He had not made her feel stupid or weird. He had not denied that something had happened to her, though he evidently didn't want to discuss it, either.

It was some moments later when he spoke again, "What did you mean back there, Felicity?"

"When?" she asked sleepily.

"When you mentioned Fergus expecting a quickie against the pub wall. Has he been bothering you?"

That made her sit up. She had forgotten she had lost her temper and what she had retorted to the annoying Fergus and now she would have to explain it.

"He was drunk and tried it on," she said calmly, as though it had been unimportant – which, in truth, to her it had been, "It was something and nothing, but it made me mad when he started on Theo. The man has done nothing to deserve all this abuse."

"I see."

She thought that perhaps he didn't see at all, but there wasn't much she could do about it. Why did everything always have to be so complicated? All she had wanted at the beginning of this eternal week had been a break from her husband and some time alone in her little house with her small daughter. Now she felt as though she was constantly fending off amorous drunkards, an abusive husband, a bolshie policeman, aggressive New Age Travellers … the list seemed endless.

When he said nothing more, she settled herself more comfortably in her seat, glad to see that they had now left the trees behind and in the open again. The headlights, with nothing to bounce off, faded away into gloom ahead of them.

Though Fliss knew it was quite a way to the village, still it seemed to be taking an uncommonly long time to cross the empty fields. Her eyes began to shut from sheer weariness and boredom. It was hardly surprising she was tired. How many hours actual sleep had she had last night? Not many, and all she longed for now was a bath and a bed. Would this journey never end?

Strangely it was the cessation of movement that woke her with a start. She opened her eyes and found the car in utter darkness. She could barely see John next to her and Megan was completely lost in the dimness of the seat behind, "What's happening?"

"The car just stalled. Heaven's knows why. There's plenty of petrol. It just slowed down and came to a complete halt."

"Can you fix it?"

"Well, I'm going to be incredibly macho and open the bonnet – but what happens after that is anyone's guess."

"I don't think it can be petrol," she observed, "the headlights are out too." John glanced out of the windscreen, "So they are. Perhaps the battery is flat."

He tried to restart the engine but was rewarded with not so much as a cough or a splutter. There was an unpleasant clunk from under the bonnet, then nothing more.

"Bloody hell," he muttered, "This is all we need."

"What now?"

"A phone call, I think. Bryn is the nearest, I'll call him. It will only take him ten minutes to get here."

"But you said he was leaving the house."

"I'll try his mobile."

He could not have stunned her more if he had suddenly struck her. She asked in a tight little voice, "What did you say?"

"Look," he said, imagining she hated the idea of seeing her husband again so soon and trying to placate her, "I know you and Bryn aren't the best of friends but ..."

205

"It has nothing to do with that," she interrupted hastily, horrified that he should think her so petty, "I don't care who rescues us – but I've just caught Bryn out in yet another lie."

"I don't quite know …"

"Did you not think it was odd that I drove all the way here to speak to Bryn the other day?"

He smiled. She could just see the glint of his teeth in the dimness that surrounded them, "Well, as I've grown to know you better, nothing you do surprises me."

"That's beside the point," she dismissed his flirting. She was too furious to be bothered just at that moment, "Don't you think that if I'd known he had a mobile phone, I would simply have rung him and not dragged my little girl half way across the country?"

The smile faded, "He didn't tell you he has a mobile?"

"No. I must be the only idiot who doesn't know her own husband's phone number! That bastard has made sure that whenever he leaves home is he free to do whatever the hell he likes, hasn't he? What I want to know is why? God, I'm such a stupid …"

"Hey, hey, that's enough. This isn't down to you, Felicity. All you have done is placed your trust in a man who didn't deserve it."

She sank into a brooding silence and much as he didn't want to remind her of her grudges, he took out his own phone and tried to get a signal.

"Damn!"

"What now?"

"The battery is flat on this too. It looks like it's down to me to get us moving again."

Fliss wasn't unhappy that Bryn would not be joining them. She couldn't be sure she would be able to keep her hands off him. What a fool she had been all these years. Why on earth had she put up with it?

John moved to release his seatbelt and let himself out of the car when there was an almighty bang which reverberated through the interior of the vehicle making them both jump. Fliss gave a tiny startled scream and Megan whimpered slightly, moving grumpily but thankfully not waking up.

"What the hell was that?" breathed Fliss, her heart still pounding with shock.

"God knows," John responded, looking over his shoulder to see if something had run into the back of them, though he couldn't understand how he would have missed oncoming headlights in the mirrors. There was nothing outside in any direction. His hand went to the handle again but before he could pull it the car began to rock gently from side to side, as though someone was rhythmically pushing it, waiting for it to rock back then pushing again.

Fliss gasped and John sat aghast looking all around and trying to work out exactly what was happening.

The rocking suddenly became much more violent and Fliss found herself having to grip tightly to the edges of the seat to stop herself from sliding first into the door then onto the handbrake and gear-stick.

"What's going on?" she asked tearfully, "How can this be happening?"

"It must be the wind," he said firmly, "It can blast across these hills at a terrific rate sometimes. There's no other explanation."

There was another bang then another and another. A volley of sharp blows seemed to hit the bonnet, the windows and the roof above their heads. Fliss covered her ears in horror and cowered in her seat, trying desperately to get as far away form the noises as the confined space would allow. She was almost out of her mind with fear, tears dripped down her cheeks and though she whimpered, she managed not to give voice to the shrieks that echoed around her own skull. Inside she was screaming and petrified, but as always Megan was at the forefront of her mind. Miraculously the child still slumbered, as though she were immune to the evil thing that pounded the vehicle – and even in her own terror, Fliss was determined that she stay that way.

After an eternity of about three minutes the noises ceased as suddenly as they had begun. The headlights flickered into life and the car engine hummed cheerfully as though it had never died. John's white-knuckled hands both gripped the steering wheel, nowhere near the ignition.

He glanced at the ashen Fliss and without a word he slammed the car into first gear and roared off down the lane, spurting gravel and mud from under his wheels, as though the hounds of hell were literally on his tail.

Within seconds they saw the welcoming lights of Broadbarrow Loe ahead of them.

Fliss sat up, bemused at the sudden alteration from terror to normality. She brushed away her tears with shaking fingers, "Thank God," she whispered.

"Are you alright?" he asked, his own voice far from steady.

"Just about. That was probably the worst five minutes of my life. What about you?"

"I've been better," he admitted ruefully, "And I rather think I've changed my mind about stopping at the pub. I'll ring Con when we get to the Hall."

"What about Fergus?"

"Be blowed to Fergus," he said succinctly.

✳

For all she had sworn not to consort with Theo's enemy, Fliss could not have been happier to see the welcoming lights of Merrington Hall.

When she climbed out of John's car, she found her legs were trembling so violently that she could barely stand. She had to close her eyes and force herself to focus before she could reach into the back seat and release her daughter. Then she allowed herself to look at the building. It was stunning – an immense Victorian monstrosity of stone and glass, with towers, crenellations, battlements. Fliss couldn't decide if it was incredibly ugly or fantastically beautiful, but it was certainly a masterpiece of showmanship. Merrington's grandfather had certainly made up for losing Theo's farm. Nothing could more clearly have said, "Keep the grotty old farmhouse, I can afford this!"

John's mobile had worked well enough to allow him to ring ahead and tell Douglas to expect them, so as soon as the wheels swept up the gravelled drive, people were out on the flight of stone steps to greet them.

Fliss found herself relieved of the burden of Megan by a middle-aged lady, plump and friendly, who introduced herself as Mrs Burton the housekeeper, "I'll put the little one to bed, for you Mrs Elmsworth. We have a full babysitting service, so you don't have to worry about her."

"Thank you," responded the bemused Fliss.

Now that her child was no longer her responsibility, Fliss found herself almost collapsing. John was by her side, taking her arm and bearing her up, "Are you alright?" he asked softly. She looked up at him, "I will be." He smiled bracingly, "You'll feel better when you've had something to eat."

Something suddenly occurred to her. She had no idea why the thought popped into her head, but nevertheless it did and she found herself asking, "John, when you said the stone head was gone from the house, what did you do with it?"

He seemed surprised at the suddenness of the question, but answered her frankly,

"I put it into the boot of one of the cars."

"And after that?" she persisted. He looked uncomfortable and shrugged, "Nothing. It's still in the boot."

"Which car?" she asked, her voice tense and wary.

"That one," he admitted ruefully, with a gesture towards the vehicle they had just travelled in.

It was her turn to simply say, "I see."

Then she found herself being linked on her other side by the beautifully-scented Tanya, "Fliss, I'm so delighted you are here! I was almost out of my mind with boredom. There's hardly anyone here at the moment. You've positively saved my life."

She let Tanya lead her up the steps. As she did so, Tanya spoke over her shoulder to John, "Douglas is waiting for you in the library, Jack. Tell him to put some champagne on ice and we'll join you in about an hour."

John grinned ruefully at Fliss and did as he was bid, murmuring, "I'll look forward to it," and went up the stone steps two at a time. Fliss watched him go with mixed feelings.

"I'll bet you are ready for something to eat," said her hostess, "I know I am." Since Tanya looked as though she lived on coffee and cigarettes, Fliss took this comment as a polite nothing. She was about to deny the suggestion when she remembered that Bryn had eaten her supper – and now, despite the shock of the journey, she was ravenous.

"Yes, I am, but I can't eat in a posh dining room dressed like this," she gestured towards her grubby jeans and floppy jumper. Even in her bemused state she hadn't failed to notice that Tanya looked as stunning as always – so much for John saying everyone would be wandering around in dressing-gowns!

"Oh, no problem," exclaimed Tanya with her tinkling laugh, "I'll have something to fit you, don't worry."

"Something stretchy?" asked Fliss wryly, glancing down at her own ample figure then at Tanya's size eight.

"Listen honey, I've been every size in the book. I have a wardrobe full of 'thin clothes', 'fat clothes' and 'who ate all the pies tents'."

"That sounds about right," Fliss managed a giggle.

"Nonsense, you are a size twelve."

"Actually I am. How did you know?"

"I don't know much, honey, but I do know clothes," answered Tanya.

"Have you really had all that trouble with your weight?" asked Fliss diffidently. It seemed a rude question, but Tanya looked so elegant, it was hard to imagine her carrying an extra ounce, let alone a few stones.

"God, yes," said the older woman frankly.

"This must be a really good health farm, then," mused Fliss, wondering exactly how much a night in such a place would have cost her, should she not be a guest of the management.

"Health Farm?" Tanya's laugh rang out loud and clear this time. No polite tinkle of girlish laughter, but a huge guffaw, "Sweetie, you are so naïve I just want to hug you!"

"Why, what do you mean? Isn't it a health farm?"

"Only in the sense that food is an addiction like any other."

"I still don't know what you mean," said Fliss. They were inside by this time and she was gazing around in awe, too stunned by the baronial grandeur to be offended by Tanya's tone.

"If you come to Merrington Hall, Fliss, you're in rehab. We're just a little more discreet about it, that's all. You come here to kick cocaine, not chocolate cake."

Fliss's mouth dropped open slightly, "Oh, I didn't realise that."

"Well, don't let it worry you too much. We don't have any real ravers here at the moment. In fact, as I was complaining the other day, it's stone dead – as opposed to dead stoned! The trouble is we are just that little bit too far from London for the real stars to come – you know the sort who want the public to know they're in rehab! We tend to get people who want to get clean quietly – or whose families want them to."

"Oh," said Fliss again. There didn't seem to be any other response she could give just at that moment.

Tanya led her to her own suite of rooms and immediately turned into the perfect hostess. She ran Fliss a bath, and poured in copious quantities of oils and bubbles. She produced a disposable razor, shampoo, scented soap and huge white, fluffy towels, which were draped over a towel warmer until Fliss should need them.

With Megan safely tucked up in bed and a child alarm in her possession, Fliss at last felt relaxed enough to strip off her thoroughly unpleasant garments and slide into the hot, aromatic water.

Tanya left the connecting door open and chatted aimlessly whilst she pulled clothes from the fitted wardrobes in the dressing room and decided what would suit her new playmate.

When her guest was scrubbed and exfoliated, her legs and armpits shaved, and her hair washed, Tanya insisted on blow-drying her hair whilst Fliss was let loose with her make-up bag.

It was a little more than an hour later when Fliss, feeling self-conscious and thoroughly out of place, walked into the bar and approached the waiting John and Douglas Merrington. As Tanya had said, this room had obviously once been the library – in fact it was still lined with bookshelves and filled with books, but one wall had been converted into a bar. The bookshelves remained, but now held ranks of bottles. The bar had been created out of the same wood panelling that adorned other parts of the room. Beautifully and cleverly done, but Fliss still thought it was a shame. This should be a room dedicated to peaceful and erudite pursuits, not somewhere for oiks to get steaming drunk.

The two men were sat in two plushly-upholstered chairs, their drinks on a table in front of them, and were obviously deep in conversation.

"Here we are," said Tanya loudly from across the room. She fully intended that her creation would make an entrance and cause the stir she richly deserved.

John looked into Fliss's eyes and smiled, "Wow," he mouthed.

Douglas was less impressed, "Thank God, she scrubbed up so well. I thought we were going to have to feed her in the kitchen." His grin was supposed to take the sting out of his words, but Fliss just thought what an utter pratt and a bore he was.

They walked across the room to join the men and Tanya immediately made Douglas join her at the bar whilst she decided which of the three choices of champagne they ought to drink. Fliss felt as though she was tottering clumsily on the high-heeled sandals Tanya had insisted she borrow. She thought that perhaps her simple black dress was a little too low-cut and short, but the look in John's eyes reassured her as she sat opposite him.

"I was wrong earlier – now you really have never looked lovelier."

"Thank you."

"Are you fully recovered?"

"I think so – what about you?"

"A double whisky was surprisingly comforting, but of course it means that I can't drive back to join Fergus on the moor."

"Oh, but I've taken your bed – again," she exclaimed then went faintly pink when she realised the implication of her words, "I seem to make a habit of that," she added as she tried and failed to reclaim her dignity.

"It is one of your more charming failings," he assured her, grinning at her discomfiture, "and I live in hope."

"In hope of what?"

"That I won't always be required to give up my bed to you."

She was silent while she thought about that, not quite sure what he meant by it. He could see she was confused and leant forward to pat her hand, "Don't worry, Douglas has endless rooms that he can place at my disposal. You are not causing the least inconvenience. Now, shall we eat?"

"Yes please," she breathed, "I'm absolutely starving!"

CHAPTER TWENTY-THREE

"From Camelot, the questing knights set forth on journeys of adventure and discovery"

The first glass of champagne went straight to Fliss's head. With no food in her stomach the alcohol hit her like a physical blow. Suddenly she understood the meaning of the phrase "punch-drunk". She really did feel that she had been smacked on the head. Her surroundings took on a curious unreality and it seemed the world had suddenly slowed down. She felt an urgent and curious desire to sing, but the only tune she could recall was "The Dingle Dangle Scarecrow" and even in her present state that seemed hardly appropriate. Megan would like it though – should she go and find Megan and sing to her?

When Douglas suggested they adjourn to the dining room, she wanted to giggle. Silly man, they weren't in court. All rise. She found herself walking very carefully. The shoes might give her killer legs, but they were very difficult to control.

She felt John Norton take her elbow and she wondered vaguely if he had noticed she was slightly unsteady on her feet – or if he simply wanted to escort her to their table. When she stumbled a little and almost went over on her ankle she felt his grip tighten and she suspected that it was the former.

She felt a little less light-headed when she had eaten her starter, and was mortified to notice that she had cleaned her plate well ahead of everyone else. No one seemed to notice and she helped herself to a bread roll and wolfed that too.

"Fliss, a little bird tells me that you are going to need a good divorce lawyer," said Douglas, as the waitress gathered up the dishes.

For a moment she thought she was still drunk. Had she imagined he had said that?

"I'll give you the number of my man. Barry Morgan of Morgan and Fentiman. He'll make Bryn's eyes water, take my word for it."

Apparently she hadn't imagined it. She glanced towards John, a question in her eyes and he shook his head almost imperceptibly. The tale-telling hadn't come from him then. She tried to recall if she had mentioned her split to Tanya, but they had discussed so much whilst dressing that she really couldn't be sure.

"Thank you, Mr Merrington," she heard herself saying, with the slightest hint of a slur, "But I really hadn't thought that far ahead."

"Well, may I suggest you do? If your man gets his story in first, you might find yourself being divorced for adultery and desertion – and believe me, that won't do you any favours if he decides to sue for custody."

The very thought made cold chills spread over her entire body, "But I haven't ..." she spluttered, almost incoherent with rage.

"It won't make any difference, sweetheart. To all intents and purposes you are living with another man – and one who is not exactly squeaky clean where police records are concerned. Wait until you have to try convincing a judge you're not sleeping with him!"

Fliss went quite white and John hastily intercepted, "Alright Douglas, I know you mean well, but all this is Mrs Elmsworth's own business."

Douglas held up his hands as if in surrender, "Okay, okay, I'm only trying to help."

It suddenly occurred to Fliss that the man was right. If there was one thing she had learned over the past few days it was that she needed to protect Megan and herself. Bryn had proved himself to be pretty well capable of anything.

"I'll take that number, Mr. Merrington, thank you."

He at once became expansive in response to her polite acceptance of his advice, "No problem – and call me Dougie, my friends do." He smiled warmly and patted her hand. He loved nothing more that being the magnanimous Lord of the Manor, dispensing wisdom and justice to his adoring and obedient peasants.

Having, he felt, successfully solved Fliss's problems, he turned his attention to John Norton's little dilemma, "That reminds me Jack, I've sorted the scum on the moor out for you."

For some reason John looked far from reassured by this pronouncement. He eyed his host warily, "What exactly have you done, Douglas?"

"I've hired you a couple of heavies, my friend. Believe me, when you and the boys show up tomorrow with these two bruisers behind you, the lentil-chompers will be packing up their vans and moving on to bother someone else."

Even though Fliss was halfway through her third glass of champagne, the fuzziness in her head cleared faster than the bubbles in the wine were popping.

"Did you say two heavies?" she asked incredulously.

"God above, Douglas! What were you thinking?" John cut across her question, but she persisted. She had to know if the awful notion that had just occurred to her was true.

"Please don't tell me you've hired the two men who put Mr Armitage behind bars."

Douglas grinned unkindly, "As a matter of fact, I do believe they did have a run in with Farmer Ted. It just so happened that Barry Morgan was the on-call solicitor when they made their complaint. Of course Ted refused to have him and called in his own man, but not before Barry met up with the two fellows and had a pleasant little chat with them. He knew I was being troubled by the New Agers, so he gave them my number."

"I'm sorry, Douglas, but that is not the way I conduct my affairs. You'll have to un-hire them. I refuse to threaten and coerce anyone – even if their presence is a vast inconvenience."

"It's more than an inconvenience, my friend! How the hell are you going to get your precious bog body to the safety of the lab with that rabble standing watch?"

"I've arranged for the body to be looked at on site. Professor Houghton and Dr Cottrell are coming up tomorrow."

"That's all very well, but what if your New Age pals won't let them past either?"

This was a distinct possibility and for the first time John looked a little uncertain. Douglas saw the hesitation and dived in for the kill, "At least let the fellows escort your two boffins onto the moor and off again."

John looked apologetically at Fliss, "We'll discuss it later."

Wisely Douglas accepted that this meant he had won. He said nothing more on the subject. He poured more wine into Fliss's glass and began to tell her all sorts of amusing tales. It took a while, but eventually she began to thaw towards him – after all, she wouldn't have to see the two men. She was unlikely to be going back up onto the moor anyway. Theo would be home in the morning and if Bryn was stationed on the moor for the foreseeable future, then she intended to stay well away. Let Douglas have his hired 'heavies', she didn't care. If they were gainfully employed for a few weeks, it might take the heat off her – and it would certainly be uncomfortable for her husband. In fact, the more she thought about it, the more amused she became. Bryn was going to love working right alongside the two thuggish debt-collectors.

When John saw that she had relented, he too relaxed. Soon the laughter and the wine were flowing.

✳

Fliss woke with the slightest hint of a headache. When she lifted her head from the deep, soft comfort of the Egyptian cotton pillow, the headache hit with its full force. Blinking in the sunlight pouring through the window and groaning with pain, she dropped her face into the pillow once again. Why, oh why had she let Tanya keep filling her champagne glass last night? The answer came back swiftly. Because she had been having fun! For the first time in years she had felt beautiful, desirable, funny, clever. After four glasses of bubbly, even Douglas Merrington had seemed charming and amusing. The evening had been hugely enjoyable. The food had been superb, the drink had flowed and once the one little hiccup had been overcome, she had been made to feel welcome – not only welcome, but a part of the group. When she spoke people had listened. When she had joked they had laughed – not at her, but with her. She had had an identity of her own. She was Fliss – not Bryn's wife, Megan's mother, Daniel's sister. Just for a few short hours she hadn't belonged to someone else. And she had loved it.

There was a knock at the door. With a groan she rolled over and called, "Come in."

"Good morning," said a male voice, and with a wince of very real pain, she realised that it was John Norton who spoke. She sat up hastily and pushed her unruly hair off her face.

"Hello," she said shyly.

"How are you feeling?"

"Just off dead. Why didn't you stop me from drinking so much? You should have known I wouldn't be used to it."

"I was hoping you would throw yourself at me," he said matter-of-factly and crossed the room. She saw, through half-opened eyes, that he was bearing a tray, "I thought you might need coffee," he added.

"I do," she agreed and reached eagerly for the cup and saucer, "What? No breakfast in bed?" she was disappointed.

"I'm afraid not. We have to be on our way in the next hour or so – and Megan is asking for you."

Back to reality so soon? She sipped the coffee and watched him as he walked to the window and looked out.

"Do you usually help out with the room service?" she asked.

"No, not usually – but I don't usually bring girls here with me, either."

She smiled into the coffee cup, "Don't you?" He turned and looked at her, "No, I don't. Can you be ready to eat breakfast in about ten minutes?"

"I think so – if you have painkillers."

"They are on the tray. I'll see you downstairs presently."

When he was gone, she looked for the aspirin and found a packet, as promised, on they tray beside a small vase containing a single red rose. Either very corny – or a house speciality, but she

still smiled and picked it up to sniff it.
She found a note from Tanya too.

> *"Dear Fliss,*
> *Keep the dress – you looked fabulous in it! I've*
> *also found you a pair of jeans and a couple of*
> *nice tops! I'll never wear them again – not*
> *really in keeping with my image!*
> *Thanks for last night, it was fun!*
> *Yours, Tanya.*

The jeans were designer as were the shirts and they had obviously never been worn. Tanya might not feel at home in them, but Fliss felt undeniably glamorous. It was amazing how quickly a bit of happiness made a headache wither away. She wondered if she ought to feel insulted that Tanya saw her as a charity case – then dismissed the thought. Who cared? The jeans had probably cost more than her whole year's clothing allowance – and even she wasn't too proud to accept charity once in a while. In fact, she might as well get used to it, because once she and Bryn made their split official, he was extremely unlikely to dish up any maintenance. Living on charity was probably going to be her life – at least for the next year or two until she could go back to work full time.

She was dressed in her new gear and downstairs well within the ten minutes John had requested.

Breakfast was served in the conservatory at the back of the house. Fliss could not have chosen a more idyllic spot to eat a meal. The sun was hot on the glass roof, but one of the waiters came and pulled across a shade. Outside perfect lawns sloped down towards landscaped grounds and a lake.

She thought she would not be able to face a full English, but once she had thirstily downed two glasses of orange juice, she suddenly found her appetite. John watched with some amusement as she tucked in heartily.

"I presume you want to come back with me?" he asked.

"Is that stone head still in your boot?"

"I'm afraid it is."

"Then no, I don't! Would you ask Mr Merrington to order me a taxi?"

He smiled, "Don't you think you are being a bit melodramatic?"

"After what happened to us last night?"

"It was the wind," he protested, "I told you it was."

"The wind my eye!" she hissed back, warily observing the milky-chinned Megan in case she understood the conversation and was scared by it, "The wind might have rocked the car, but it certainly wasn't responsible for the banging."

He was about to protest further, but Douglas joined them, "Is there a problem?" he asked, in his usual jolly manner, "Trouble in paradise, eh Jack?"

"Not at all," said John with dignity.

"Do you think one of your staff could arrange a cab for me, Douglas?" asked Fliss sweetly, glancing at John with a determined look on her face, "It seems Professor Norton can't give me a lift back to the farm."

"No need, sweetheart. I'm going that way myself. I'll take you in my motor."

"Thank you, Douglas, I'm most grateful – if you are sure it is no trouble."

"None at all. Have you been happy with your stay?"

"It's been fantastic," enthused Fliss, "I haven't been this spoilt for years. I really do want to thank you very much."

Douglas grinned, "Any time, sweetie. It's always a pleasure to have appreciative guests."

He pinched a slice of her toast and wandered off, saying over his shoulder, "The car will be outside at ten."

Fliss looked at her watch. That gave her twenty minutes to finish her breakfast and clean Megan up.

"I'll go and put the child seat in Douglas's car," said John, wiping his mouth on his napkin and rising to his feet.

Fliss looked up at him, "Now you are making me feel awful," she said.

"Why? I'm not offended."

"No, you just think I'm crazy."

"I assure you, I don't. Last night was a nasty experience and I can understand why you were frightened. I just don't believe an inanimate object can cause such events."

"I'll bet you wouldn't sleep with that thing under your pillow just the same," she countered.

"You're right – I wouldn't. It's far too bulky."

"Okay, have it your own way. But I'm not changing my mind about it. No doubt I'll see you back at the farm sometime later."

"No doubt." With that he was gone.

Douglas was in a 4x4 when she joined him and it took quite an effort to lift Megan up into it and hoist herself after. The thing was huge.

"Hope you don't mind, but I thought I would take the road across the moor and have a look what's going on."

She could hardly protest when she was accepting favours from him, so she smiled weakly, "Of course. Whatever you say."

It was even more of a circus in broad daylight. The road was blocked by the old vans and trucks belonging to the New Agers, but Douglas simply drove off the road and went around them. Fliss clung to her seat as she was thrown hither and thither by the ruts and dips, thanking God silently that Megan was well secured in her child seat. If she had known this was going to happen she might well have risked John's car and the stone head.

There was another surprise waiting for them. Once they managed to get past the last van they found a circus of another sort had descended. The media was out in force. Apparently the New Agers had been willing to let someone pass. Row upon row of Outside Broadcast vans, cars and more 4x4's were parked alongside the stone circle. The waiting journalists saw Douglas's approach and flocked towards him, cameras clicking, microphones and booms thrust in his direction before he had even climbed out of his vehicle. Fliss wound down her window so she could hear what was being said, but it was almost impossible to make out a single word in the shouting for attention.

Douglas was obviously loving every second. He grinned all over his face and held up his hands for quiet, "One at a time ladies and gentlemen, I can't answer all your questions."

One, obviously the loudest, boomed from the back of the crowd, "Is it true, Mr Merrington, that you've found a bog body – another 'Pete Marsh'?"

"Indeed it is true – but this one is complete. It is probably the most important discovery of the past ten years."

"Any chance of a peep, sir?" asked a gorgeous blonde in a dark grey suit.

Douglas pretended to think about it then smiled broadly, "Why not? Follow me." He began to walk towards the marsh and the tent. Fliss panicked and called after him, "Douglas, I really don't think the professor ..."

"The professor isn't here, now is he? And what harm can it do?"

Fliss watched helplessly as the journalists and camera-men struggled valiantly after the swiftly disappearing Douglas.

"Oy, you!" She turned and found the New Ager from the Toddler Group standing at the far side of the vehicle. His face was contorted with fury, "What the bloody hell is going on?"

"I ... I don't know..." she faltered.

"That bloody maniac is taking the press into see the bog man, isn't he?"

"I've told you I don't know!" she returned.

"Liar!"

He turned back to address his fellow travellers, who were gathered in a silent, but threatening group just behind him, "Come on lads, it's just as we thought. Merrington is letting the press see our bog man. It's time we put him back in the bog where he belongs!"

They set off at a run after Merrington and the press.

Fliss bit her lip. What the hell was she going to do now? John would be furious – and devastated.

She clambered out of the car and unfastened Megan, "Come on sweetheart. It's time for us to leave, I think."

She was some metres from the edge of the wood when she saw

a couple of figures just emerging from the gloom. Gladness gave her feet wings and she hauled Megan up into her arms and ran towards them, "John, thank God."

He looked astounded to see her there, "Felicity, what the devil..?"

"You need to get to the bog man, John. Douglas has taken the press into the tent and the New Age Travellers are hot on his trail. They were talking about throwing the body back into the water."

"What!"

He ran past her, not waiting to hear more. Behind him Bryn came out of the woods.

"Well, Fliss, you can always be relied upon to be slap bang in the middle of any trouble, can't you?"

"Shut up!" she retorted, "Go and help the professor – or you won't have a job to do – and believe me, you're going to need one when the CSA comes after you!"

He looked as though he wanted to say more, but she barged past him and headed for the path through the woods.

CHAPTER TWENTY-FOUR

"Lugh, the Celtic sun god, who slew Balor
with his magic sling shot"

Bursting into the kitchen, Fliss nearly knocked Theo off his feet. He had obviously only just walked in and hadn't even taken off his coat. The two dogs were fawning over him, both giving voice to rapturous whines and barks. Before he knew what was happening, Fliss had cast the dogs aside and thrown herself into his embrace. There was a look of wonder on his face to find a beautiful young woman in his arms.

"Oh, Theo, thank God you are back."

"If that's the welcome I can expect, I'll go away more often."

She laughed self-consciously, "I'm sorry," she said, letting him go and turning back to make sure Megan had removed her boots, "It's just that it's all kicking off at the stone circle and I had to bring Megan away."

"Poor you, missing all the fun," he teased.

"Oh, no, you don't understand. I think it's really serious. Douglas Merrington has really done it this time."

"What the hell is he doing up there?" asked Theo, suddenly aggressive.

"Causing trouble as usual."

"Then I'd better get up there," he said decisively, but she thrust out an arm to stop him going out of the door, "Oh no, you don't. You are in enough trouble with the police as it is. We'll ring them and let them go and break up the fight – if there's going to be one! It's nothing to do with you."

He seemed easily persuaded out of it, for he shrugged and

started to unzip his anorak,

"Suits me. Put the kettle on, will you? I'm gagging for a decent cuppa. But you'd better ring the police first, I suppose."

"Okay."

She went into the hall to use the telephone and as she picked the handset up she heard the back door closing softly. She dropped it onto the hall table with a clatter and ran after him, shouting out of the door to his retreating back, "I can't believe I fell for that!"

He turned and gave her a friendly grin, "Neither can I!" he said and headed for the woods.

Fliss went back indoors, rang the police and asked to speak to DI Piper, who luckily was available. He listened to her story with increasing irritation, "What possessed Mr Merrington to inflame the situation like that? We were working on having the Travellers moved on in a legal manner. A couple of days and they would be gone."

"Mr Merrington marches to the beat of his own drum from what I can gather," said Fliss wearily.

"I'll get some men there as soon as I can."

"Thanks, I appreciate it. Of course nothing might happen but ..."

"Better safe than sorry. Are you okay?"

"Yes, but I wish I'd managed to stop Mr Armitage from going up there and joining in."

"So do I. He's a pain in the neck when he's in the cells."

"I'll bet he is. Well, I'll let you go and do whatever it is you have to do."

"No doubt I'll see you later."

"Yes, bye."

Fliss spent the next hour pacing the floor. Megan drew in her colouring book, and watched her mother, a slightly puzzled frown between her brows. Grown-ups were funny. Why didn't mummy sit and watch TV or something. Why did she keep going to the window when there was nothing out there to see?

Fliss had finally given up her pointless (and rather tiring) pacing and was nursing a mug of tea at the kitchen table when the back door opened and admitted a grinning Theo. His cheeks were ruddy with health and fresh air, and he was stamping the mud off his boots and rubbing his hands together when John came in behind him. He was rather pale and sombre and was sporting a nasty graze on his jaw line.

"What happened?" demanded Fliss, jumping up and crossing the floor towards them. She was breathless with tension and could barely get the words out.

"Nothing much," answered Theo with a rumbling laugh. He was evidently enjoying himself immensely, "Your man here took a punch from Zak Oldthorpe, but the Rozzers arrived just in time to save him from an assault charge."

"I should have floored the little twerp," muttered John, obviously furious, but still in control of himself enough to remember to remove his boots at the door.

Fliss led him to the chair she had just vacated and examined the wound, "Who is Zak Oldthorpe?" she asked absently, more interested in the injury than the cause of it.

"He likes to think of himself as the leader of the New Agers, but I know him as a thieving little scumbag who couldn't resist helping himself to anything that wasn't nailed down."

She looked at Theo, a baffled expression on her face, "Is he the mouthy one with the ripped jeans and stringy ponytail?" she asked.

"That could actually describe most of the buggers," said Theo ironically, "but yes, that's him. Why? Do you know him?"

"I've met him. But if you know him of old, why did he act dumb and ask me how to get up onto the moors?"

"He'll have had his reasons. He's as slippery as a bucketful of fish entrails. It was probably all for show in front of the others. They'll know he has a record, but they'll think it was for action aboard the "Rainbow Warrior" and not for stealing and killing sheep and selling joints in the pub on a Saturday night."

As she listened to Theo's diatribe, Fliss bustled around finding cotton wool and filling a bowl with water from the kettle. John submitted to her ministrations without protest. She could see that he was still seething that Zak Oldthorpe had managed to get in a blow without him being able to reciprocate. She guessed his male

226

ego was more bruised than his face. She lifted his chin towards the light so that she could see exactly what she was dealing with and found herself looking into his eyes. When he caught her glance the frown slowly faded and was replaced with a rueful smile, "Ignore me. It'll take me a while to get over it."

"Being on the receiving end – or not getting the chance to swing back?" she asked softly.

"A bit of both," he admitted.

"Tell me exactly what happened," she said, as she dipped the cotton wool in the salty water and began to bathe the wound. There was a bruise forming under the skin, but Zak had evidently been wearing a ring or something, because the skin was broken.

"I was too late to stop Douglas, who, in his usual brash way, had swept Fergus's protests aside and he didn't feel he could argue with the man who was paying his wages. The press were swarming all over the site when I arrived. They were trailing through both tents, taking photos, filming, handling artefacts. It was chaos and I don't mind admitting I was furious. The New Agers were everywhere, mingling with the journalists – God knows what damage they have all done. They were giving interviews, claiming that we were defiling the dead, desecrating a religious site and said they were going to put the bog man back where he belonged before our sacrilegious actions released Armageddon."

"What did they mean by that?"

"They have some madcap idea that the Druids put male sacrificial victims into bogs because they knew the body would be preserved forever. Only very special rites were used to protect the surrounding area from the deepest evil. They say that because these men were so young and fit – and a very real loss to the community – that they were only ever killed in times of greatest need or fear."

"They really think that something evil was loose in the area and only the bog body can contain it?" she asked, a tremor of fear in her voice. She had seen for herself how powerful these forces could be and it frightened her to think that there might be more to come. The terrifying assault on the car was too fresh in her mind for her to take the matter as lightly as he evidently did.

"Come now, Felicity, be sensible." He said gently, trying to reassure her with his own prosaic view of the incident, "These are people who also think that it hurts vegetables to be pulled out of the ground."

"Maybe it does," she said bleakly, "what happened next?"

"Oldthorpe, if that is his name, saw me and steamed towards me, screaming abuse. I was trying to calm him when the little rat took his chance and clobbered me."

"It wasn't much of a punch," intercepted Theo, with great amusement, carrying two mugs of tea to the table.

"Yes, well thank you, Ted, but I didn't notice you coming to the rescue," sniffed John, accepting the tea and wincing when he opened his mouth to sip it.

"Me? Oh no, I've learned my lesson. Who was it told me not to think with my fists?" he grinned happily as John cast him a look of loathing.

"You did the right thing, John, not striking back."

"I know – but sometimes civilisation proves to have a remarkably thin veneer. I'm not a violent man, but my first reaction was to fight back, especially when I saw that idiot man handling the bog man. I've waited all my life for a find like that and he can't see how important it is. He'll tell us so much about how our ancestors lived – but that fool prefers to remain in ever-lasting ignorance."

Fliss thought it wiser to steer him away from the subject of Zak Oldthorpe, "What time are your two experts due to arrive?"

"Two o'clock, so I would be grateful if you could make me look a little less like a prize fighter."

"Believe me, that's the last thing you look like," said Theo dryly. Fliss threw him a reproving glance, "It's not that bad, John."

"I won't be permanently scarred then?"

"Hardly. There. You'll do." Without thinking she laid her hand against his cheek, just as she would if it had been Megan she had been tending. It was only when his hand came up and covered hers that she realised what she had done. She blushed and pulled gently away.

A knock at the back door distracted everyone's attention and the moment was gone. Theo opened it and DI Piper stood on the step. "Do you think I could have a word with the professor, Ted?"

Theo held the door open and swept his arm in a gesture of old-fashioned courtesy,

"Be my guest, Inspector Morse," he said.

Piper ignored the sarcasm and walked past him into the kitchen. John pulled a chair from under the table with his foot, "Take a seat, Matt. Do you want some tea?"

"I'd love some," said the policeman taking the chance to sit, "but I'll have to get back, thanks all the same. I just thought I'd let you know the situation is under control. I've left a couple of uniformed officers to guard the bog man. Oldthorpe and three of his cohorts are in the cells, cooling their heels, but I'm afraid the ladies of the camp have decided to register their protest at police brutality by dancing around the stone circle."

"They can dance to their heart's content," said John forcefully, "as long as they stay away from the bog man."

"Normally I would agree with you sir, but to use their own parlance, they're 'sky-clad', so I thought I'd better warn you."

"Sky-clad?" repeated Fliss, puzzled.

"Stark, staring naked!" explained Theo with a grin, "I'll bet your boys are enjoying that, Piper."

DI Piper glanced towards him and a wry smile drifted across his face and was gone in an instant, "I wouldn't be too sure about that. In my experience it's usually those with the least to be proud of that are the most eager to let it all hang out."

John looked pained, "And I have to march two senior members of the University hierarchy right past them. Marvellous! Still, it's not exactly warm up there," he added hopefully, "Perhaps the ladies might have to cover up?"

"I wouldn't rely on it, sir. The ones I saw had a goodly layer of fat to keep 'em warm."

John closed his eyes in the deepest pain and gave a shudder of abhorrence, "Oh, dear God."

"Sorry, professor, but there's really not much I can do about it.

They are on private land and they're not offending public decency – well, not in the eyes of the law anyway. And frankly, if I arrest them, then the kids will have to be taken into care. It's a logistical nightmare."

"Correction, Inspector, it's a nightmare, full stop. Have the press gone?"

"Most of them have what they wanted – a picture of the bog man. One or two are sticking around to interview you."

"They can forget that."

"They also want to interview Mrs Elmsworth."

Fliss was astounded, "Me? Why should they want to speak to me?"

"Someone told them that it was the little girl that found the body. You can imagine how that little nugget had the newshounds baying for blood."

She felt the blood draining from her face and had to sit hastily, "Who the hell told them that?"

"Couldn't tell you, madam, but I would expect phone calls and knocks at the door."

Theo stood up aggressively, "They'd better not try it," he growled.

"You just remember you're still in my black books, Ted Armitage," warned Piper, "Well, I'm sorry to be the bearer of bad tidings, but I've done my best in the circumstances. It's not against the law to be hacked off about something."

"No shit, Sherlock," grunted Theo. Piper ignored him, but Fliss felt a slightly hysterical giggle coming on.

"I'll bid you all good day. Hopefully I won't be required any time soon." He saw himself out, never imagining that his hopes were to be dashed within three hours.

*

Fliss was bored. She had prepared the vegetables for tea, cleaned the kitchen, played with Megan, made a snack for Theo when he came in mid-afternoon for a brew before going off again. She was

230

now cuddled up with her little girl on the big old sofa in the parlour, reading a book of nursery rhymes and wondering what on earth was happening up on the moor with John and his experts. She had been tense all afternoon, not only worrying about John and the bog man, but terrified in case the phone rang and the media frenzy became directed at her. She could cheerfully have strangled who-ever it was who had mentioned Megan's name in connection with the discovery of the body. It had been nothing but a fluke, but she knew the press would turn her daughter into some kind of psychic freak show.

It was nearly five when John walked in and flopped onto the sofa beside her. He rubbed his hand wearily over his face, "Oh, Felicity," he muttered, "How could I have been so utterly wrong?"

She pushed the book into Megan's grasp and took hold of his hand, "What is it, John?" He gripped her fingers as though they were a life line, "It looks as though Piper will be back sooner than he thought."

"Why? What is it? I wish you would tell me, you're frightening me."

"I'm sorry. I didn't mean to." He kissed her hand and released it, "It's the bog man. I have it on the authority of one of the country's greatest experts that far from being an ancient body, our man has lain in the bog for less than ten years. Probably nearer to seven."

Fliss was appalled, "What! But he has the injuries of the triple death. How can he be a modern victim?"

"I dread to think. But I can assure you that he was killed very recently using ancient methods."

"Dear God," she breathed as the implications of what he was saying slowly sank in, then she took heart and tried to cheer him, "But how can they be so sure? They can only have had the time to do a very cursory examination."

"Well, the fact that the ligature was nylon baling twine was a bit of a give-away," he answered grimly.

"Oh dear," she said, biting her lip. That must have been painful for him to discover.

"To be fair to me, the cord was buried deeply in the skin of the neck and was covered in a thick layer of mud. I had only glanced over the body before we had to submerge it in bog water to preserve it – but it was a vastly unpleasant moment."

"It must have been," she sympathised.

"That's not all," he continued, "Several artefacts have also 'walked' from the cache of finds. I was hoping that at least the stone ceremonial axe-head and your dreaded carved head would be the genuine article. Both are gone. One taken from my car and the other from the tent."

She looked at him, her sympathy shining in her eyes. She knew how much all this had meant to him, "I'm so sorry, John."

"Don't be. I'm an idiot. I so wanted it to be true that I let my enthusiasm blind me. I should have seen that the state of preservation was far too good for a three thousand year old body."

"You can't blame yourself for that. You haven't really had a good look at it and I understand that the preservation process begins to tan the skin the moment the body is in the water."

He smiled slightly at her, "It does, but how do you know that?"

"I've been doing a bit of reading," she admitted, slightly shame-faced, "They have quite a good library in Feldon and I wanted you to be able to discuss things with me."

"My darling girl, I don't think I have ever been more touched."

Her heart began to pound, "John," she whispered.

"Is it tea-time, mummy?" asked Megan loudly, "I'm hungry."

She gave a small breathless laugh, "I'll always be mummy first," she said apologetically.

"That's as it should be. We'll talk later. In the meantime, I have to ring Matt Piper and explain why he has had to wait two days to begin investigating a crime scene."

CHAPTER TWENTY-FIVE

*"Laeg, charioteer of Cuchulainn, cast himself
in front of a spear meant for his master"*

DI Piper was surprisingly understanding, "Don't be so hard on yourself, professor. That body had me fooled too. Who could imagine there would still be a lunatic around who was bumping people off by knocking them on the head, half strangling them then cutting their throat? It's a bit of a bizarre MO by any standard."

Norton had to agree with that assessment.

"And it's not as though you've disturbed a crime scene, since the body was found in the middle of a marsh."

"True. And the body has been preserved in the bog water and not touched by human hands until today."

"I trust your two experts were suitably gloved and robed?"

"Of course. We have no more desire to contaminate a body with modern life than you have when at a crime scene. I suspect we're similarly suited and booted in both cases."

"Then everything that could be done has been done. It's a pity the press were allowed to swarm all over the site, but it can't be helped now – and none of them actually touched the body, did they?"

"Zak Oldthorpe may have had his hands on it, he was certainly threatening to, but I think Fergus managed to hold everyone else off."

"Okay, we'll cross that bridge when we come to it. In the meantime, I'll be there as soon as I can with the Scene of Crime Officers. I'd be grateful if you could make sure nothing else is disturbed before we get there."

"I'll do my best. It would have been better if I had been able to ring on my mobile from the moor instead of having to tramp down to the farm, but as ever, I couldn't get a signal."

"Miles away from the nearest mast, that's the trouble."

"I suppose so. Is there anything else you need me to do?"

"We'll have to question everyone who has been involved in the dig. Is you entire staff still on the moor?"

"No. The women have been staying at the 'Weary Sportsman' in the village. As soon as I knew the travellers were at the site and liable to cause trouble, I arranged for them to stay at the pub."

"Good. I'll send someone to interview them and then I'm afraid you might as well send them home for the duration. I'm going to have to close down the dig until further notice."

"I suppose there is no other choice?"

"I'm sorry, but no. Until we know who our victim is, where and when he was killed and of course who did it, the area around the marsh is a crime scene."

"Alright, I'll clear my people out as soon as I can."

"And I will take great pleasure in telling the New Agers that they will have to pack up their vans and park them elsewhere."

After he had hung up, Piper leaned back in his chair, a satisfied smile on his face – from a policing point of view; a ten-year-old corpse was far more challenging than one that had clocked up three thousand – more chance of catching the perpetrator for a start, he thought with a small laugh. He picked up the telephone again and began to make his calls.

✳

Fliss decided that perhaps it would be better if Megan was off the farm when the police arrived. She suspected they would remove the body via the road on the moor, but they were still bound to swarm all over the farm.

What she did not admit, even to herself, was that she wanted to be absent herself when they brought the corpse down. She couldn't bear the idea that she might catch even the slightest glimpse of the face of the dead man. She knew that if she recognised him from the apparition she had seen in the parlour, then she would never be able to sleep in the house again.

She was in the kitchen when John came back from nearly half an hour on the hall telephone. He heaved a huge sigh, "That wasn't the easiest task I've ever had to perform."

"What were you doing?"

"Breaking it to the girls that once they have been interviewed by the police, they are on indefinite leave."

"Who protested the loudest? Let me guess, Anne-Marie," she said with a smile.

"She was vociferous," he admitted, finally seeing the humour of the situation. Anne-Marie had given him hell on the phone. She blamed him for just about everything that had gone wrong with the dig, from Fliss's arrival to the advent of the New Age travellers. She also told him frankly that if he had done things by the book, the bog body wouldn't have been found until the site had been well and truly logged and examined.

"Poor you," she said sympathetically.

He noticed that both she and Megan were donning their coats, "Going out?" he asked in surprise.

"I thought I might remove Megan from the vicinity while the police were here. We're going to the Elf Farm for the afternoon."

"The what?" She briefly explained about the two elderly ladies who had turned their large house and vast garden into a tiny theme park for little children.

"Emma told me about it," she said, "they have statuettes of elves and faeries hidden all over the garden, gnomes too, I think. Little ones adore running all over the place trying to find the secret spots."

"Sounds charming," he commented, "But if you were hoping to use Ted's car, I'm afraid he had the same idea as you and decided to disappear until the police have done their job."

"Oh, but I've promised her now," she said, disappointed. She hated to break a promise, especially to Megan.

"No problem. I'll take you."

"I couldn't ask you to do that," she protested, "It will be unbearably tedious for you – and the police may want to speak to you."

"I doubt that. They will want to perform a post-mortem before they begin asking questions. Anyway, if they do, it's just tough. They'll have to wait until we get back."

"Okay, if you are sure."

"I can't think of a nicer way to spend the afternoon."

"I can," she said frankly, "But it's the sort of thing a mum has to do."

As it happened, she enjoyed her afternoon very much. The Elf Farm was probably one of the oddest places she had even been. Because it was so early in the season, there were very few other visitors, which meant that they were the focus of most of the attention from the two eccentrics who ran the place.

Far from being merely a money-making, touristy exercise, the two women obviously believed wholeheartedly in the 'little people'. They were convinced that real faeries lived at the bottom of their garden, in the woods and by the stream and that their little statues were mere representations of the real thing.

Megan, Fliss and John were required to don pointed, pixie hats for their trek around the garden, so as 'not to frighten the elves and pixies'. Megan chose a green one, Fliss red and John chose the most ridiculous he could find in the hamper, pink with yellow and green spots. Megan and Fliss giggled every time they looked at him. He seemed determined to join in the fun and Fliss found it hard to believe that he was a serious-minded professor of archaeology, with umpteen letters after his name.

They were given a long, involved lecture on faeries, elves and all the other 'elementals'. They learned of their likes and dislikes, their habits, some nice and others not so pleasant. Megan was fascinated, and Fliss wanted to laugh out loud when she saw John paying close attention and nodding sagely at some of the comments.

"Now," said Miss Sylvia, "One has to be on one's guard the whole time, because faeries can appear and disappear in the twinkling of an eye. You'll see my faeries and elves in the glades and amongst the tree roots, but real faeries are much harder to see."

Megan was looking up at her in solemn silence. Fliss threw a conspiratorial smile at John, but he was listening intently, "So who do you think the faeries really are?" he asked.

"It's very hard to know everything about faeries – they like to keep their secrets, but perhaps the nature faeries are what the Celts saw as the gods of the trees, lakes and streams. They were reputed to be the ones who magically produced the stone circles," explained Miss Sylvia seriously.

"Yes," intercepted Miss Evelyn, "And perhaps Professor Tolkien wasn't far wrong when he wrote about the Ents. Our ancestors believed that it was terribly bad luck to cut down an oak tree, because the dwarf-like oak-men would haunt the axe-man forever after. They would never venture into a place where oaks had been felled after dark. One only has to think," she shook her head sadly, "what happened to poor Lord Nelson."

Even John looked mystified by this, "I don't quite see..." he murmured.

"Well, he was killed so tragically on board his ship."

"Yes?" prompted the professor, trying not to sound impatient.

"And what were his ships made of? Why, English oak, of course. Perhaps the oak-men felt he was responsible for the felling of so many great oaks for his ships."

"One can't argue with that logic," agreed John, kindly hiding his smile.

"Sometimes the little people felt the need to strengthen their stock, with marriage to a human being, but of course a faerie wife must never be touched with iron, or ever struck, or she would take all her riches and disappear back to faerie land," it was Miss Sylvia's turn to speak. The two ladies uncannily followed each other in conversation, even when they were distracted from their tourist script. There was barely a breath between one falling silent and the other speaking.

"This has led to the belief that faerie folk are really the spirits of the Stone Age people who lived in these islands before the Celts invaded. Gradually their simple stone and bronze weapons would have been overcome by the iron weapons carried by the invaders. Slowly, quietly they slipped away to live in the deepest forests, the caves on high hillsides, until they became merely a memory. They must have dwindled in size from lack of decent food until they faded away altogether."

"So sad," mourned Miss Evelyn, "And it may perhaps be true, because ancient burial mounds are often taken for gateways to faerie land."

"When they were first found and we knew no better, Stone Age flint arrowheads were called 'fairy darts' or 'elf arrows'," said Miss Sylvia, briskly, as though to pull her sister out of her self-imposed depression, "witches used them as powerful talismans."

"Fascinating," said John and Fliss could almost believe he meant it.

"We have chattered on for far too long – if you don't begin now, it will be too dark to look around the grounds," said Miss Evelyn, suddenly businesslike, "Off you go."

Fliss and John considered themselves dismissed – and did as they were told.

Megan ran ahead, eagerly searching every bush and shrub and squealing with delight when she found yet another tableau of petrified faerie folk frozen forever in various pursuits. There were faeries dancing around rings of garishly painted toadstools, elves at their cobbler's last, dwarves tending a sleeping Snow White.

Fliss and John strolled behind her, enjoying the beautiful spring weather and the gleeful laughter of the little girl.

"It was very nice of you to bring us here," said Fliss, "You must have far better things to do."

"Not at all. I wouldn't have missed it for the world."

"You're just saying that," she insisted, feeling sure he must be bored to tears and astounded at the naivety of the two ladies.

"I promise you, I'm loving every moment. How often do you think I get a chance to come to places like this?"

"Why would you want to?" she asked cynically. She had liked the two ladies, but their credulity was a little embarrassing. And one couldn't laugh because it would be a case of most definitely laughing at and not with, and that would be rather cruel.

"You don't realise how lucky you are, Felicity, you have a ready made excuse to go back to the innocence of childhood whenever you want to. You have a child. Don't you ever want to remember how it felt not to have a care in the world?"

"Is that how your childhood seems now?" she asked wonderingly, "I don't think mine was. I only ever recall being rather a worried little thing. I did believe in faeries, but I was rather afraid of them I think. All the stories I heard seemed to paint faeries in rather a poor light. They stole babies and left changelings, they played mean pranks and when people went to faerie land they came back years and years later, having only been gone, they thought, for a few hours, to find all their friends and relations were dead and buried."

He looked appalled, "Dear God, you did have a dreadful time of it, didn't you?"

She laughed, but real mirth was absent, "I'm rather afraid I did."

He put his arm around her shoulder and gave her a comforting hug, "You make me want to put things right for you."

"I wish you could," she hadn't meant to sound so sad, or so sorry for herself.

He raised her chin with a gentle index finger and kissed her softly on the lips, just once and very briefly, then released her.

"It's time we were getting back," he said, as though nothing had happened. Fliss found herself feeling as though she had been dragged apart and trampled on. He was walking away down the path, calling to Megan to say goodbye to the faeries and elves, and she had no idea what to think or how to feel, she only knew that her mind was spinning and her heart pounding. There was a sick feeling in the pit of her stomach and she didn't know if it was fear, or excitement, or perhaps a mixture of the two. All this was moving too fast – or maybe not fast enough? She didn't know.

✳

Piper decided to be present at the autopsy. He could have waited for the results in the warmth and comfort of his office, but he had been fascinated by the body since he had first heard of its existence – and the fact that it was now a murder had not altered his feelings.

It was odd seeing it now, laid out on the stainless steel dissecting table. Everything about it suggested age and it seemed unkind to tear it from the past and lay it in the clinical sterility of the modern world.

The resemblance to the ancient bog body he had once travelled to Manchester University Museum to see was remarkable. Not that 'Pete Marsh' was still in Manchester. The British Museum had claimed him, as they did with anything worth having, and very generously allowed him to go 'home' once in a while.

The skin was the deep, dark brown of old leather. Tannic Acid in the peat acted on human skin just as it did in the leather making process. The hair had a faintly reddish tinge – both caused, he was assured, by the acidity of the wet peat in which it had been buried. And buried it had been. The fact that it had been found in a couple of feet of water was distracting. It seemed that the summer when the murder was committed had been a particularly dry one and the edge of the marsh had receded far enough for the victim to be buried in a shallow pit. Perhaps it was merely good luck – or perhaps the culprit had known the moor well enough to realise that before long the water would be back to cover the grave – probably forever, if fate had not taken a hand.

Piper listened and watched as the post-mortem proceeded. The body was first measured and weighed, but Piper could see that despite the ravages of time, it was a well-nourished male and about five feet ten or eleven, aged around twenty seven. One of the hands had become detached – but that was often the case with decay. The wrist is the narrowest major joint on the body and therefore the most likely to fall apart first. The thicker skin on the palms of the hands and soles of the feet tended to hold the bones in place a little longer. The plastic sheet in which the body had been wrapped was bagged for later, minute examination. After such a passage of time, and immersion in water, it was unlikely that the area around the body would hold any clues, but it had to be examined anyway. Then began the painstaking task of removing the clumps of peat and cleaning the body. Norton had left the body as untouched as possible, for almost the same reason as the police had. He had been in search of clues too – but he merely wanted clues to tell him about the past.

When the worst of the mud had been rinsed away, the pathologist began the painstaking task of trying to comb through the tangled hair and beard. Norton would have been looking for ancient pollen, lice, anything that told him about how the man had lived. The police were looking for how he had died. Samples of hair were taken for DNA and drug analysis. The nails were checked and the underside scraped. Bog man might just have fought with his attacker and some skin might have been retained.

Normally the clothing would be removed, but here it was unnecessary. Bog man was naked. No clue to his identity would be found in pockets in this case. The body was minutely examined then swabs taken from all the orifices. Piper turned away for that one. There is no dignity in suspicious death – but that didn't mean he had to witness it.

When the pathologist began his examination of the hands, Piper was prompted to ask hopefully, "Any chance of a finger-print, doc?"

"Possibly," was the reply, "The preservation is good. We'll have to see."

If the man had a record that might make identification a piece of cake – if he hadn't, however, it took them no further forward.

Once this thorough examination had been completed, x-rays were taken then out came the knives. This was one route Professor Norton would never have followed. An ancient body would have been carefully handled, leaving little trace of man's interference, so that the body could be displayed in a glass case for all the world to see, his eternal peace ever-lastingly broken. This man was a murder victim and his appearance was of little consequence. The Y shaped incision opened up the body for all to see. The heart and lungs removed, the stomach so that the contents could be analysed, along with the rest of the organs.

When it was done the pathologist, Dr Mills, joined Piper, peeling off his gloves with a snap and casting them into the nearest bin.

"What's the cause of death, Alan?"

"Just as Norton and his team thought, blow to the head, cracking the skull, but not causing instantaneous death, merely stunning the victim. I suspect he would have dropped to his knees if he wasn't already kneeling. The ligature was pulled back and up forcing the head back. Then the throat was slit from behind, using a cut so deep it actually nicks the anterior surface of the cervical spine."

"Not an accident, then?" asked Piper cynically.

"Nor suicide," agreed Dr Mills.

"How long ago?"

"Tests will tell us more precisely, but at least seven years."

"Better start looking at the Missing Persons Files."

CHAPTER TWENTY SIX

*"Lancelot and Guinevere's love for each other
wounded the jealous Arthur"*

They pulled into the farmyard to find the policeman's car already there.

"So it begins," said John with a sigh, "Back to earth with a bump."

"Suits me better than fairy-land," said Fliss rather grumpily. She was confused by what had happened and rather inclined to take that out on him – after all, it was he who had caused all the upheaval in her life.

"We are a little ray of sunshine, aren't we?" he teased.

"Well," she excused herself, "I don't know why you are so bothered. It must be obvious this has nothing to do with you."

"You think so? Perhaps you are right, but frankly I was rather more concerned about Ted. The body was found on his property, after all. Shall we go in and face the music?"

Fliss's mouth dropped open as the full import of his words hit her, "Oh dear God. Theo – of course they'll want to pin this on him! It never occurred to me."

"Why would it? One doesn't usually suspect that there might be a murderer in one's immediate circle."

She couldn't argue with that.

They went indoors. DI Piper was sitting at the kitchen table, opposite Theo. They were both drinking tea and they both looked equally grim. Fliss felt that perhaps she ought to take Megan through to the parlour and sit her in front of the TV again. It was something she tried not to do on a regular basis at home, but this situation was far from regular.

John greeted them both then addressed himself directly to the policeman, "Is there any news, Matt?"

Piper glanced up at him, then returned his gaze to his mug, "Not really, professor. It will be a while before forensics give us any definite information. I just came to ask Mr Armitage a few questions." The formality of his reply was not lost on anyone in the room.

"Anything I can help with?" asked John. He glanced towards the door as Fliss quietly re-entered, and smiled briefly at her as she went to the Aga and poured them both a cup of rather stewed tea.

"Not unless you can remember any time in the past few years when the summer was hot enough to dry out the marsh where you found the body." said the policeman, without much hope in his voice.

"As a matter of fact, I do recall that. Let me see. It must have been '96 or '97, I believe."

"'96," growled Ted, "I remember we had to bring the sheep down so we could water them. The marsh must have shrunk by about half, I would think."

"I do believe you're right."

Piper looked slightly taken aback, "You were here then, professor? I thought this was your first visit to the district."

"No, I've been coming here almost every summer for the past fifteen years."

"Sixteen," countered Ted.

"Oh. That puts rather a different complexion on things," the policeman said slowly, and, in Fliss's opinion, rather ominously.

"Why did you want to know about the marsh drying out?" inquired John.

"I'm afraid I can't tell you that at the moment, sir, but I must now ask you to avoid leaving the area when you have dismissed the rest of your staff – unless any of them have visited with you in the past, that is."

Fliss looked horrified. Such a request could only mean one thing. John was now a suspect too. His face had stiffened into a

244

mask of disbelief, "Are you trying to tell me that you think I might have committed this murder?"

"I'm sure you know that I'm not saying anything at all, sir, merely asking you to remain in the area for further questioning should the need arise. The rest of your group have now been interviewed, their names and addresses taken and they are now free to leave."

"Very well," the professor had quickly regained his equilibrium, but Fliss had seen how shocked he had been by the sudden shift in the policeman's attitude. It had, in an instant, gone from deference to defence. Strangely she felt very little shock. It was as though she had been expecting this development. Part of her had sensed something bad was going to happen – and now it had. Ever since that damned stone head had been brought to the surface of the bog, she had known it was going to spell trouble. Now two men she had grown immensely fond of were both under suspicion of murder – and she and her daughter were living under the same roof. Yet she felt perfectly calm. Some instinct told her that neither John nor Theo had blood on their hands, that they were not capable of such brutality. It had been a very different character that had been able to perform the 'triple death' on a healthy young man.

However, this sureness did nothing to comfort her. Errors had been made before, and no doubt they would be made again. Theo and John were in a very dangerous situation and it was that thought that made her blood run cold, not the idea that she would be sleeping in the same house with them.

Piper asked Theo a few more questions, most of them relating to his use of bailing twine. It must have been perfectly obvious to the policeman that he found this line of questioning baffling, thought Fliss. He knew nothing about the ligature around the neck of the victim. He responded with perfect honesty, if a little impatiently, and then Piper took his leave.

There was an awkward silence in the kitchen, which Theo tried to break by making one of his usual, insensitive remarks, "Well, John, looks like we're both in the same boat for once. Hope you know a good lawyer."

"As it happens, I do, but I'm rather hoping I won't need her."

"Well, no, why should you? You are an educated man – it's only brawny countrymen like me who smash people's skulls in, isn't it?" Fliss knew that Theo didn't mean to attack his old friend, it was only the strain of his situation that made him talk so stupidly. John looked grim, and his fists clenched under the table, "Don't be so bloody ridiculous, Ted. Jordan knows we, neither of us did it – he just has to be thorough."

"Some maniac did it, John," said Theo tensely, "And if the police don't find out who, they might just go for the easy option. They've already got me down as a loose cannon. It's alright for you. You can drum up any number of big-wigs to vouch for you – including Lord of the bloody Manor Merrington. Who can I turn to for a reference?"

"Me," said John staunchly.

"And me," said Fliss, "I'm moving in with you. Would I do that if I thought you were capable of murder?"

Oddly enough it was that comment which calmed him, and he turned to smile warmly at her, "Bless your heart, Fliss. Do I take that to mean you've made up your mind to take up my offer of a home and a job as my housekeeper?"

"I have. In fact, I'm going to leave early in the morning, go home and pack up as much of mine and Megan's stuff as I can fit in your Land Rover – if that's okay with you."

"Fine. I just wish I could come with you and help, but unfortunately it would be viewed with rather a lot of suspicion if I suddenly headed for the motorway."

"It's okay, I'll manage. I'll just bring clothes and a few toys for now. The rest will do later."

"It looks as though I'm unable to help either," said John wryly, "And much as I hate to be the bearer of bad tidings, it doesn't seem to have occurred to you that Bryn will probably be heading home in the morning too. The police have suggested I dismiss all my staff, remember?"

Fliss looked abashed for a moment then cheered up, "Can't you think of an excuse to keep him here for a day or two more? He certainly won't be happy about losing his wages if you sack him."

"Not really, he's a geophysicist, not an archaeologist. I intend to ask Fergus to stay and help clean and catalogue the finds, but Bryn can't do that."

"Has he analysed all the data he's collected yet?"

"No, but he needs the computer to do that."

"Can't you set him up in the pub for a few days with a plug socket for his machine?" suggested Ted, being as technical as he was ever likely to be.

John smiled, "I think that might be arranged."

✳

It felt incredibly odd to Fliss driving down her own street in a battered old Land Rover that, now she thought about it, smelled rather strongly of dogs and sheep.

It felt even more odd when she pulled onto her drive and realised that the "For Sale" sign she had noticed from the top of the street was actually placed in her own front garden and not next door as she had supposed.

"The absolute bastard," she murmured under her breath.

"What?" demanded Megan, "What did you say, mummy?"

"Mummy was just saying that daddy has been busy on the telephone whilst we have been away."

Her first task when she unlocked the door was to ring the Estate Agent whose number was so prominently displayed.

"Oh, hello, Mrs Elmsworth, I'm delighted to tell you that we have had one or two enquiries already. I was hoping to speak to Mr Elmsworth soon and make arrangements for viewings."

Fliss had to wait for the manager to draw breath before she managed to intervene, "Well, since my husband has put our house on the market without my knowledge or consent, I rather think any viewings will have to wait."

There was a blank silence at the other end of the phone, then a world weary sigh, "I see. That does rather complicate things, doesn't it?"

"Just a little. I'm sorry he has inconvenienced you like this, but I can assure you that I will be moving out and the house will be going on the market – but not until I have spoken to my solicitor."

"Of course, very wise – but did you say you were moving out?"

"I am."

"Forgive me for saying so, but that might not be your best course of action. Of course, it has nothing to do with me, but possession is nine points of the law."

"I know that, but nothing would make me stay in this house for another night. I will take your advice and ring a solicitor this very moment though and we will be in touch presently about the sale, but if you could take your sign down in the meantime, I would be grateful."

"Of course. Goodbye Mrs Elmsworth – and good luck."

Fliss felt horribly deflated when she hung up the phone. She thought she would feel triumphant to have so neatly turned Bryn's nasty little trick upon him, but all she felt was terribly, terribly sad that he had felt compelled to do something so underhand and plain nasty to her. What on earth had happened to the attraction that had created Megan?

She searched her handbag then made the call to the solicitor on the business card that Douglas Merrington had given her. Mr Morgan seemed to take an unsavoury delight in her story and assured her that Bryn would be getting away with nothing. A letter would be on the way to him in the last post, care of the Weary Sportsman, telling him exactly what happened to men who tried to sell joint property without the other party's permission, and exactly how much maintenance she would be requiring for the upkeep of herself and her daughter. It was a phone call that depressed her even more than the first.

Having made two thoroughly unpleasant calls, she thought she might as well go for the hat-trick and dialled her mother's number. She knew she should really break her news personally, but it was really more than she could bear just at that moment – and if she said nothing, Daniel was bound to let the cat out of the bag – and then she would be in ever more trouble.

To say Mrs Cottrell was displeased with the information her daughter imparted was a vast understatement. She was scathing in her condemnation, "Don't be ridiculous, Felicity, you can't just announce you are leaving your husband and are going to take my granddaughter to live in the God-forsaken back of beyond in the house of a complete stranger. What do you know about this man? He could be a child-molester – or a murderer!" Fliss had a sudden vision of her mother picking up a newspaper in a couple of days time with Theo's face splashed over the front. The "I told you so" rang in her ears. She winced slightly, but was determined to stand her ground, "I think I'm a fairly good judge of character," she said quietly.

"Oh really? Why is your precious marriage failing then? You always were headstrong and melodramatic! I don't know how poor Bryn has coped with your vagaries for this long. The man is a saint."

She could not have said anything more calculated to send Fliss's temper over the edge.

"A saint? You really do have to be joking! But then of course you only have Daniel to compare him to and in those circumstances I suppose Bryn is a saint!"

"Oh, here we go again. When will you ever get over this silly idea that I favour Daniel?"

"When you start showing it," was the bitter rejoinder. There was an impatient sigh on the other end of the line, "I really don't know what you want from me," she said in a martyred tone as though Fliss had asked for the impossible. Fliss supposed that for a confirmed fence-sitter, who treasured her own peace above everything else, this was one task too many, however she could not have said anything worse. Fliss suddenly felt as if the ring-pull had been removed from a shaken can of pop. Words poured out so fast that they tumbled over each other, but her meaning was quite clear. She wanted to be heard. A procession of minor injustices had grown into a festering, boiling rage that she could no longer suppress. She had been ignored, passed over, put aside in favour of her siblings and she was sick of it. Because she had been loving and compliant she had been taken utterly for granted. Those in the family who had yelled the loudest had been given all the attention, while she sat quietly waiting for the storms to pass until her turn would come – but it never did. She was always left with the dregs. She had been told – more times than she cared to recall – "I know you won't mind, Felicity." Well, she did mind – she minded very much, but she had been too afraid of losing what little affection she was ever shown to protest at the unfairness of it all.

She didn't know where it all came from, but it flowed, as hot as molten lava, ripped from the depths of her soul. All the heartbreak poured out and tears began to trickle down her cheeks. She paused for a moment to try and compose herself aware that perhaps she might be saying too much and with too much bitterness and it was then that she realised there was an unnatural silence at the other end of the telephone. Her mother hadn't hung up on her. There was no dialling tone.

"Mother?" she said tentatively, unable to quite believe the truth – that her mother had carefully, quietly laid the receiver down on the table and walked away, leaving her talking to no-one. With an almost unbearable physical pain in her chest she suddenly understood that her passionate outburst had been in vain. Right at the beginning of her diatribe her mother had rejected her claim for attention. She had not wanted to listen, but more than that, she had made a complete fool of her. She had let Fliss unburden herself to the ether.

Fliss knew now, without any shadow of doubt, that she was not considered important enough to warrant a hearing. She could have regretfully accepted it if her mother had just had the guts to admit she didn't want to hear the list of complaints, that she didn't want to acknowledge her failings as a mother – but to simply walk away was cruel beyond the point of forgiveness.

"Oh, mother," she whispered despairingly, "you wouldn't even attempt to care on the one day I needed you most."

Sadly she replaced the receiver, knowing that she was never going to contact her mother again. Any approach now would have to come from the other side – but she wouldn't be holding her breath.

She had just walked away when the phone rang and she raced back to it, part of her hoping it was her mother. Inside she was still that quiet little girl patiently waiting a turn that never came. Her hands shook as she gripped the handset, her breathlessness making it almost impossible to speak. She heard John's voice saying, "Felicity? Is that you?"

"John? Yes, it's me," Anguish, then relief flooded over her.

"Are you alright? You sound odd."

"I've had a couple of shocks, John, but I'm alright now."

His voice was sharp, "What is going on? Do you need me to come?"

Her reeling world righted itself. She knew he couldn't come – but if she said the word he would move heaven and earth to get to her. Just in that moment, that knowledge meant everything to her.

"No, no, I promise, I'm alright now."

"Do you want to tell me what happened?" Her first reaction was to hide all the shameful events of the past few hours, but suddenly she realised that yes, she did want to tell him everything. He wouldn't think badly of her because her husband despised her and her mother detested her.

She tried to be objective, to tell the story without any self-pity and to keep a reign on her emotions. Her voice was quiet but steady and she was proud she managed not to cry. She wanted to weep until she had no tears left. The pain was so great she almost wanted to die, but the sound of Megan playing upstairs pushed that thought away.

He was silent when she finished telling her tale. For a dreadful moment she thought he had gone too, had walked away and left her talking into a dead telephone and she felt sick to her stomach but then he said softly, "My poor darling. I wish I was there."

"I wish it too," she said fervently, wondering even as she spoke how she could be saying something like that to a man she scarcely knew.

"Felicity, come back soon."

"As soon as I can."

"I'm sorry, but there's something else I needed to tell you.

251

That's why I rang – apart from wanting to hear your voice."

She smiled, "What?"

"I think Douglas has finally lost it. He's hired those two thugs as his personal bodyguards and he's strolling around the place with them in tow, looking like a second rate actor in a bad gangster film."

She felt a strange desire to laugh, "They deserve each other."

"It won't bother you to know they are still in the district?"

"I can't say I'm deliriously happy about it – but now I have left Bryn, they can't use me to threaten him, can they?"

"It would seem a little pointless," he conceded.

"Then let the Lord of the Manor enjoy the weather on Planet Douglas!"

John laughed, "I miss having you around, Felicity."

"I've only been gone a few hours."

"All the same. Drive carefully."

"I will. Goodbye."

When she put the phone down this time, she immediately took it back off the hook. There was no one she wished to speak to now. She went upstairs to do the packing.

CHAPTER TWENTY SEVEN

*"Sualtam Mac Roth's severed head rallied the Ulstermen into
battle even after his death"*

Driving into Broadbarrow Loe felt like coming home. Fliss found
her tight grip on the steering wheel lessening as the stress of the
journey faded away. There was probably half an hour of daylight
left, so when she began to see notices plastered onto every
available tree trunk, telegraph pole and wall, the light was so poor
that she had to stop the car and jump out to read one.

She was grim-faced when she returned to the car and drew away
from the verge. An emergency meeting of the Residents'
Association had been called, to be held that night in the church
hall. It was co-signed by Daphne Cook (owner of 'Wicca Works')
and Everett Thomas (Druid). The topic under discussion was the
disruption caused by the Archaeological Dig on the moor. The
point was to ask the said Dig to pack up and leave the area forthwith. Since it said "all welcome" Fliss reckoned that might have to
include herself and John Norton.

When she had calmed down a little it mildly amused her to
think that witches felt the need to be members of a 'Residents'
Association' – she couldn't help feeling that it was something of a
contradiction in terms. Surely for centuries witches and their ilk
had delighted in being 'outsiders' and defying convention – now
they were calling meetings for the purpose of driving out and
persecuting others. Ironic, to say the least.

The house was deserted when she arrived back, so after having
a quick cup of tea, she went in search of John and Theo. Both men
were in the barn. Theo was folding the now deserted camp beds and

John was sat at the long trestle table helping Fergus clean and catalogue the numerous finds. They all looked up as she and Megan walked in. John smiled warmly at her, but with Fergus beside him, he seemed curiously reluctant to approach her. Fliss was inclined to be disappointed by this reaction, but on reflection she decided it was probably wise. She had enough trouble to face without her husband beginning to suspect that she might be heading for an affair with his boss – and Fergus, in his present mood, would be sure to mention it.

"What time are we going into the village to attend this meeting?" she asked.

John raised an eyebrow, "We? You are intending to come too?"

"Wouldn't miss it for the world," was the determined reply. Fergus grunted and began to scrub a bit of stone with unwonted vigour.

"Do you have a problem with that, Fergus?" asked Fliss politely.

He put down his nailbrush and faced her, "As a matter of fact I do. What the hell has any of this to do with you? You're not an archaeologist – you are no longer even co-habiting with a member of the team. Why don't you just stop interfering in things that don't concern you?"

Fliss saw Theo open his mouth to come to her defence, but she quelled him with a sharp look, "I wonder at your arrogance, Fergus! What makes you think I'm attending on your side? I happen to be a resident of Broadbarrow Loe as of today – and as such I'm perfectly entitled to my say."

Fergus looked stunned, "What?"

"I've just been home to fetch mine and Megan's clothes. We are now officially residing here. So I'll see you at the meeting tonight."

With that she turned on her heel and walked off.

＊

All circumstances considered Fliss felt it was better for her to travel into the village with Theo rather than John – not that she had been invited to accompany the professor. She was disappointed because she had not had a moment alone with him since she arrived back at the farm, but the sensible part of her brain knew that they now had to tread extremely carefully. One of the warnings she had been given by the smarmy solicitor on the telephone that morning was that she now had to be squeaky clean until the divorce came through. He conceded regretfully that she could just about get away with living at the farm so long as it was clear to all parties that she and Megan had their own rooms and that she was paying rent, but any other misdemeanours would be viewed very poorly in the eyes of the divorce courts.

She had explained all this to Theo when he came into the house for his tea and he was enthusiastic about making everything homely for her. They went upstairs and chose a small bedroom for Megan (there were six bedrooms in all) which he promised to decorate for her the following weekend. They then spent a happy hour or so emptying all his late mother's clothes and knick-knacks from the room presently occupied by Fliss and Megan and replacing the contents of the drawers with Fliss's stuff. Soon there were several black bin bags lined up in the hall ready to be taken to the Charity Shop in Feldon. Another three were filled with rubbish.

He also rang Malcolm and arranged for his younger sister to come and baby-sit Megan whilst they were out that evening.

Fliss had a quick bath, kissed her little girl goodbye and told her to be good for Kelly and when she had satisfied herself that the youngster knew how to get hold of her on John's mobile phone, they set off. John and Fergus had already gone into the village some hours before, to have their evening meal at the Weary Sportsman. Fliss wondered vaguely if Bryn would accompany them to the village hall, but somehow she doubted it. He had very little interest in anything that didn't directly affect him, and since he knew his employment with the professor was short-lived now, he would hardly be interested in the outcome of a local debate. It could be weeks before the police allowed the work on the site to begin again, depending on the outcome of their investigations, so there was very little point in planning ahead.

The meeting was just about to begin when they arrived. Emma was stood at the front of the hall, her cassock looking pristine as though it was newly washed and pressed. Fliss suspected that she rarely wore it. She had certainly never seen the vicar thus arrayed. She called for silence and bade everyone take their seats.

"I would just like to say a few words of welcome to you all. I realise that some of you feel no affinity to the church at all, and that is perfectly fine. Please don't feel that even though this is called the church hall that you are not welcome in it. I myself would prefer to think of it as a community hall."

"Why don't you call it that then," came a voice from the back. A few sniggers were heard, but Emma successfully ignored the interruption and continued, "I would like to thank professors Norton and Ripley for agreeing to hear our comments and answer our questions. I'm sure by the end of the evening we will all understand each other and be able to continue with our various pursuits in perfect amity."

"I wouldn't count on it love," said another voice. This time Emma took the hint and sat down, handing the reins to her colleagues on the dais.

Fliss could see Polly and her husband sitting near the front, next to the man from the bookshop – she hoped he finally managed to dislodge that dreadful wisp of lettuce from his front teeth. She also saw the very fat lady who had read her Tarot cards and she recognised a few other people whose shops she had visited at various times, but she didn't know the Chair – a very tall, slender woman who had passed the first flush of youth and was frankly ill-advised to carry on sporting such very long hair. Streaked with grey and falling straight from a centre parting it did nothing to soften her face and made her look rather like a witch. It was some minutes before Fliss realised that was exactly what she was. She was seated behind a long table on the raised dais which served as a stage for the occasions when there was a play or concert. With her was an equally thin man with long white hair and very bony features who could only be the Druid. Emma was also sat with them, but she looked decidedly uncomfortable and Fliss noticed that for the rest of the evening she said nothing beyond her initial introduction of the committee members. John and Fergus were also on the top table and Fliss was quite surprised that they had agreed to be there, but then she supposed it was only fair that they should have equal rights to answer the criticisms directed at the dig. It would hardly be a debate without an opposing team.

As she and Theo sneaked quietly in and took two of the last three seats in the room, the talking began – and it went on for some considerable time with various people making known their objections to the dig and the inconvenience of the media invasion. Others jumped to the professor's defence, Polly amongst them, citing the jump in tourists and thereby profits for their various enterprises. Fliss felt that she could quite happily fall asleep as the conversation bounced to and fro, with balance sheets seeming to be the major issue at the forefront of most of their minds. She found herself waking up and taking notice however, when a plump woman rose to her feet and addressed the panel, "I don't think you people have any idea what you are doing," she said briskly. Fergus was quick to intercept, "Madam, we are all fully qualified to carry out…"

"Qualified!" she snorted, "this has nothing to do with what you have learned from a University, my boy. You are playing with forces you neither understand nor respect."

Fergus sank into silence, his face a dull red at the indignity of being called a 'boy'.

"I think you will have to be a little more explicit, madam," said John gently, "I don't think you can accuse any of my team of having a lack of respect for the past. On the contrary, we do what we do so that we can all learn from our ancestors."

"I have no problem with archaeology, per se," she said graciously, satisfied that she had put Fergus in his place, "But there are certain places in this country that have a greater significance than finding out how we used to live."

There was a murmur of assent through the room. People turned to one another to whisper their support, so Fliss took the chance to look around and see if she knew anyone else. She was horrified to realise that most of the New Age travellers were also present. This boded ill for John. Their leader was bound to want his revenge for his arrest and of course he would blame the professor, even though he had brought it entirely upon himself. She could see his profile when she craned forward and he did not look conciliatory.

"You all seem to be under a misapprehension," said John calmly, "I understand that you are trying to tell me that you feel the circle and the marsh had a religious significance – but I am fully aware of that fact. But surely the religion of our ancestors should be as fully explored as every aspect of their lives. It was as much a part of them as what they ate, and where they slept."

"Yes, but you wouldn't go smashing your way into the Vatican or the Blue Mosque to find out about religion, would you? You wouldn't dig up a graveyard to find out how a coffin was made. Because you have the excuse of research, you think you have the right to do anything at all – and if we poor plebs object, we are accused of refusing to move with the times. We are ignorant and you have the weapon of education to wave over our heads like a sword. It doesn't enter your heads that there might be some things we won't ever know – and that perhaps we shouldn't know. Religion may be the opium of the masses, professor, but we are as entitled to our drug as you are to be hooked on knowledge."

"You make knowledge sound like an evil thing, madam. You surely can't want your children and grandchildren to be raised in ignorance?"

"If the goddess had wanted us to know, she'd have told us," another disembodied voice from the rear of the room. John squinted against the light shining directly into his face to try and see the speaker, "Perhaps that's true – but perhaps it is also true that we were given the intelligence and the tools to discover things for ourselves by God, or the goddess, or Mother Earth or the spirits of the trees and streams."

Zak could keep silent no longer, "You just don't get it do you, Norton? Bog bodies weren't sacrificed just for a religious rite. It wasn't an every day occurrence that was performed with no thought or emotion. It wasn't like you going to church on Christmas Day and not bothering again until Easter. These men went willingly to their deaths to protect their communities from very real dangers. For a young man to give up his life, to pass up the chance to bring his children into the world – that's powerful magic, man!"

"I'm aware of it, Mr Oldthorpe, but it was made magic by the power of belief. I'm not destroying anything tangible by delving into the past. It's over and done with, the page is turned. You can't possibly imagine that there is still any residue of either the old evils or the old cures for that evil."

"That's where you are wrong mate. I believe it completely. That sort of power doesn't just fade away. Only a bloody idiot couldn't feel it every time he walks amongst those stones."

Fergus had evidently recovered himself sufficiently to make a valid point, "What you all seem to be overlooking is that the bog body we dug up wasn't put in the marsh by our ancestors three thousand years ago. Do you people really think the police would be bothering to investigate otherwise?"

One of Zak's female companions rose to her feet, "You think you know it all, don't you, pal? Has it occurred to you that the body you disturbed is the latest in a long line of sacrifices? Someone realised that the magic was dwindling away and they made damn sure we'd be protected for another thousand years – until you desecrators interfered."

This pronouncement was greeted with a stark silence then pandemonium broke out. Most of the room were utterly appalled that the woman seemed to be suggesting that any member of their community might be responsible for the terrible crime. One or two looked uncomfortably aware that such a thing might not be entirely impossible.

Zak took advantage of the chaos to leap to his feet and head for the table, but this time John was ready for him. He leaned forward and gripped him by the lapels, "Don't even think about it. I spend half my life wielding a pick axe. You won't be picking a fight with a bookworm."

Zak wrenched himself from John's grasp and walked away, spitting on the floor to show his contempt. When he whistled his group ceased fighting and followed him out of the hall, "You've not heard the last of this, Norton," he called from the door, "we're not going to stand for you desecrating our sacred sites any longer."

There was an embarrassed silence when they had gone. The Chair turned to John, her face grave and forbidding, "I must apologise for that outburst, professor. No matter how strongly we feel, we should not have made physical contact."

"Madam, I understand. But you must know that this is so much nonsense. There is nothing malevolent lurking on the moors – and killing a human being wouldn't tame it even if there was."

"I hope you are right, professor, because if there is such an entity – and I'm afraid I believe there is – you have released it amongst us."

Even as Fliss was shivering at the sombre tone and sepulchral warning, she was trying to tell herself that it was scare-mongering of the worst sort. The only danger on the moor was a very human one – a nut-case who wanted to copy the old ways of death for his or her own bizarre and perverse pleasure. But part of her remembered the apparition of the bog man standing by her in the farm parlour, the blood from his slashed throat rolling down his arms and dripping from his elbows onto the floor. She could not forget the terror she felt even though she had tried to convince herself that it had merely been a particularly nasty and graphic dream. She couldn't forget the violent rocking of the car and the hammering blows that had faded away as though they had never happened. She shivered when she thought of the stone head and how each of its faces seemed to speak of the three agonies that the triple death inflicted. She looked up at John, hoping that an exchange of glances would comfort her, as his voice had comforted her that morning, but he was talking quietly to Emma. Suddenly she was aware that Theo was speaking to her and she roused herself from her very unpleasant reverie, "I'm sorry, Theo, what did you say?"

"I said, it's time we were getting back. I promised I'd have Malcolm's sister home by eleven at the latest."

"Okay," she said absently.

"Are you alright? You've gone white as a sheet."

"Yes, I'm fine. I was just afraid it was all going to get out of hand and people would be hurt. I hate violence." She shuddered and he grinned, "I'd forgotten how sensitive you ladies can be," he said teasingly, "You wouldn't dream of hitting a man over the head with a frying pan when he comes home late smelling of another woman's perfume."

"Well, I certainly wouldn't do any such thing," she said, "Unless it was Bryn, then I think I would be able to suppress my finer feelings."

"Come on, let's go home."

It was a subdued gathering that filed out of the hall and away to their various dwellings.

CHAPTER TWENTY EIGHT

"Morholt, the Irish champion, fought Tristan, who dealt him a mortal blow, lodging a piece of sword in his brain"

John arrived back at the farm about an hour behind them by which time Theo had gone to take Kelly home. Fliss was lounging in front of the television, pretending to herself that she wasn't scared to be in the house alone, but jumping out of her skin at every sound the old house made. The clunking radiator had been bad enough, but when one of the logs on the fire gave a loud crack and spat out an ember like a miniature firework, she almost had kittens.

She was so relieved to hear John call her name that she almost ran and pawed him as the two dogs were doing, but just managed to restrain herself.

"You were a long time. I hope there wasn't any more trouble."

"No, I had to go to the pub. Bryn had sent a message saying he had some results for me."

"Anything interesting?"

He flopped down on the sofa beside her, "Unfortunately, like everything else on this bloody jinxed dig, it appears to be bad news."

"Why," she asked, concerned at his demeanour. For the first time since she had known him, he really did seem utterly tired and defeated.

"From his soundings, I really don't think the base of the stones go deeply enough into the ground to have allowed them to stand for three thousand years. If I didn't know better I'd say they had been erected as recently as a hundred years ago."

She was as baffled as he was, "How can that be possible? Surely people would know about it if the circle wasn't ancient."

"I agree with you. I admit I'm mystified. I've searched ancient documents and there has always been a tradition of the stone circle being here."

The word 'documents' brought something to her mind, "Actually, I have something that might help. When Megan and I first arrived, the man in the book shop gave me an old map of the district."

"How old?" he asked tensely, "Please don't say 1934 or something!"

"No, older than that. I'll fetch it."

She was back within minutes and they spread the map on the dining table which was the only space big enough to accommodate it.

John pored over it for quite a while before he blew out a long, low whistle, "Ted, you old rogue," he said quietly, with an almost awed admiration, "You've been holding out on me."

"What is it?" asked Fliss impatiently, "What do you see? It all looks okay to me. The stone circle is there – they've even drawn it on – well, a representation of it, anyway." She pointed to the mark on the chart that seemed to be the disputed feature. John shook his head, "Just one minute. Let me check this out." He went upstairs and returned presently with a ruler and a pocket geometry set including compasses, which he proceeded to utilise in a manner which completely mystified Fliss.

"Just as I thought," he said at last, "The stone circle may be marked, but it's not in its present location."

Fliss was even more baffled, "What on earth do you mean? Are you trying to say a huge stone circle has been moved? That's impossible."

"You would think so, wouldn't you?" he mused cynically, "But it looks as though that's exactly what someone has done – though I would say 'faked' rather than moved."

"But how? And why?"

John cocked his head and listened, "That sounds like Mr Armitage coming in right now. Let's ask him."

Theo had evidently heard their voices because he came to join them. As soon as he walked into the dining room and saw the map coupled with John's expression, he knew the game was up – and he at least had the grace to look sheepish.

"I see you've unravelled the family secret," he said wryly.

"We've certainly half unravelled it," conceded John, holding his temper in check with admirable restraint, "We know someone faked the stone circle I've spent the past fifteen years trying to interpret. What we don't know is who, how or why."

Theo pulled out a chair and sat down, gesturing to the other two to do the same, "This could take a while," he said by way of explanation.

"I'll bet," muttered John. Fliss glanced at him, trying to read his expression, but his face was deliberately blank. She imagined he was feeling pretty irate, but he gave nothing away.

"The 'who' was my great grandfather – pretty well as soon as he took ownership of the property. In fact the stone circle was one of the reasons he had always wanted to own the place. He followed the 'old religion' you see."

Fliss wanted to ask what he meant, but this did not seem the moment to disrupt the flow of information. John had waited fifteen years for this and she didn't feel she could make him wait any longer.

"How he did it was fairly simple, believe it or not," continued Theo, "He used a clan of gipsies who used to pass through the district every year. They were itinerants who helped mainly at lambing time and with the shearing. The stones didn't have to be moved far – they were lying about up on the moor. And the gipsies had horses that were used to dragging loaded caravans."

"That's the labour explained – but how the hell did he maintain secrecy?"

"The gipsies weren't exactly welcomed by the community – nothing changes much, does it? A bribe of a few guineas and an offer to let them camp on the moor whenever they wanted to was enough to secure their silence. Actually they thought it was a hoot to get one over on the villagers."

"But how could he build a stone circle and have no one know about it?" asked Fliss, "It must have been a hive of activity up there for a couple of weeks at least."

"Longer than that," corrected Theo, "They did it very subtly over a period of about two months. And don't forget, it was now his land. He simply continued with Old Merrington's edict that no one could trespass on his land. It didn't go down too well, let me tell you. They thought that now one of their own had the moor, they would be freer to roam, but granddad had his own agenda. It's one of the reasons why we Armitages have never been particularly popular. The locals thought we'd risen above our station, so they shunned us. Years went by before any but a select few went up on the moor. By the time they did, no one recalled exactly where they had last seen the circle – would you be able to tell one bit of moor from another?"

Fliss shrugged, "I suppose not."

"Don't forget, people then didn't have much time for wandering aimlessly about anyway. We're talking about the late nineteenth century here and most agricultural work was still being done without the aid of machines. Leisure time is a modern concept. When a man had been slaving his guts out all week in the fields, the last thing he wanted was to drag himself up a bloody steep hill and ramble over a moor. City dwellers wanted to, but not country folk."

"True enough," murmured John, "And I suppose to hide the real circle he just let the perimeter of the wood spread out a little?"

"That's right. No one noticed that the wood was a bit wider at that point, and the circle a bit further away from the trees than it used to be. To be honest, nobody was really that interested back then. There was none of this obsession for getting 'back to nature' and 'finding our roots'. It was just a few old stones that had always been there."

"But the triangle Fergus talked about," said Fliss, still trying to work all this out, "He said the barrow, the bog and the stones form a triangle on the map."

"They still do," said John, "Look I'll show you. The present circle and the other two form a right angle triangle, but move this line," he pointed it out on the map, "to here, and you get an equilateral one."

"So the whole thing is a fake?" asked Fliss disgustedly – and with more than a little embarrassment. Thank heavens John didn't know about her feeling all wobbly and faint when she went into the circle. It was obvious now that it was caused by nothing more than her over-active imagination. She was a weak-minded idiot.

"It's not all fake," said Theo, rather hurt by her reaction, "One stone had been there since the original circle was created, but it was a monolith. It gave my great grandfather the idea of where to build his decoy circle."

"The carved stone opposite the entrance?" guessed Fliss, realising that it was not the whole circle that had made her feel odd, but just the one stone, when she approached it.

"Yes."

"But why, Ted? Why the hell did he generate this elaborate hoax? And why did you let me make a fool of myself?"

"I told you," said Theo grumpily, knowing that he was in the wrong and hating it, "He followed the old religion. He wanted the circle kept sacred for him and the few others who felt the same way. They had been sneaking up on the moor for years behind old Merrington's back, risking man-traps and being prosecuted for trespass. Can you blame them for wanting to keep the circle just for themselves?"

John raised a cynical eyebrow, "Are you trying to tell me that your great grandfather was a pagan?"

"We all are," said Theo defensively, "What of it?"

"Not a thing," said John, "It just wasn't what I was expecting to hear."

There was a short silence then Theo said quietly, "You know that I regret all this, John, for only one reason. I would never have kept this from you if you hadn't had Merrington as your backer."

"Ted, you've made a prime idiot out of me."

"I know – and if I could change it, I would, but I made a vow to my father that Merrington would never be allowed to set foot inside the real circle."

John looked into the face of the man he had considered his friend for so many years now and didn't quite know how he felt about the betrayal. It was painful to him to know that he had trusted the man and had allowed himself to be hoaxed along with everyone else – but in honesty he had to admit that Ted had never made a secret of the fact that Douglas Merrington was an insurmountable barrier to their full co-operation. He could have chosen at any time to tell Merrington to keep his money and tried to find finance elsewhere, but it had been easier to stick with a man who seemingly had bottomless pockets as far as the Armitage farm was concerned.

At last he said, "For two weeks every summer for the past sixteen years I have wandered over this place – how the hell have you managed to keep me away from the real circle?"

Theo grinned for the first time, "By God, you made it hard on occasion! I've had to be very inventive to keep you out of that section of the wood. Luckily for me you were never very interested in exploring the woodland, only the moor and the barrow."

"You're not going to tell me your grandfather transported all his barnyard muck up there and built that too, are you?"

Theo laughed, "No, the barrow is real enough. And tradition has it that it is a woman who is buried there – a female warrior, not a man."

"She must have been quite a woman to warrant such a burial," said John musingly, "How do you feel about us digging into the side and trying to find the tomb?"

"After what I've done to you, feel free," said Theo, "But for God's sake, dump Merrington!"

John smiled back, "I'll see what can be done," he said, "But in the meantime, I think the least I deserve is a glimpse at the real circle."

"Alright," said Theo reluctantly, "But I'm serious about this, John. Merrington must never know."

"Agreed," said John and offered his hand. Theo shook it.

"Be up at first light and I'll take you up there,"

"Can I come?" said Fliss breathlessly.

John looked dubious, but Theo trusted her implicitly and said immediately, "Of course, but will the little one object to being woken so early?"

"You know Megan by now. She never objects to anything, bless her."

Fliss thought she would never fall asleep that night. The entire bizarre story spun in her brain and she found it hard to believe that Ted and his forebears could have planned and executed so complex a lie. She could only imagine how strongly they must have felt about their beliefs. She also wondered who else in the village were part of the 'select few'. She thought about those she knew and tried to picture them dressed in druidic robes enacting strange rituals under the light of a full moon. Polly at the pub she could see, with her long red hair hanging free and glinting in the moonlight – on the other hand, would pragmatic Polly not think it would be too cold for prancing about in the dark? The jury remained out as far as Fliss was concerned – and she doubted Theo would ever tell her. If he had managed to keep his family's secret all his life, and in spite of John's investigations, he was hardly likely to open his heart now.

✳

It was still dark when a light tapping on her bedroom door woke Fliss, but she was immediately alert. This was something she wouldn't miss for the world.

Within half an hour they met in the kitchen and drank a swift mug of tea before setting off. Fliss and Megan had only stumbled a few steps when John lifted the little girl into his arms, "Are you sure you want to do this, Felicity? You could be snuggled beneath the covers."

"I could – but I'd rather be here," she assured him with a smile.

There were moments when she changed her mind. Staggering through the still dark wood was not easy, especially when they left the path and had to force their way through closely packed under-growth. Theo really had made sure that his secret was well hidden. Fliss was disorientated within minutes. If the men left her, she knew without doubt that she could never find her way back.

The bluebells smelt earthy and sharp as they were trodden underfoot and Fliss wondered how much damage they were inflicting on the ecology of the place. She was probably crushing all manner of little creatures and the first tender buds of rare plants.

Then suddenly they were in a clearing and the stones stood, silent, beautiful, brooding. The rising sun hit the tallest and it looked as though it was stained with running blood. Fliss stood transfixed. She heard Megan asking to be put down and she heard John setting her on her feet, but he said nothing.

The child walked slowly into the centre of the circle then turned and lifted her face to the rosy glow. Fliss was scared. She didn't know why, she only knew that she didn't like her little girl looking so old and serious. There seemed to be a knowledge in her eyes that frightened Fliss out of her wits. It occurred to her that Megan had been here before.

"I want to go," she whispered.

John glanced at her, "Just give me at least a few minutes," he pleaded, surprising her with the passion in his voice.

"Then bring Megan to me," she replied, swallowing to moisten her dry throat, "I can't go into the centre of the stones."

He didn't argue, merely fetched the child and placed her into her mother's arms.

Fliss retreated a few metres and found a convenient tree stump where she sat and watched the two men as they examined the stones. It seemed to take an eternity before they came and joined her.

"It's incredible," said John quietly, "And I have to say, Ted's grandpa made a remarkable job of copying it. He obviously felt that the facsimile ought to do the original justice."

"I still think it was an utterly loopy thing to do," said Fliss under her breath, she didn't want Theo to hear her, but she wasn't going to lie to John.

"Oh, I don't know. It sort of makes sense, when you think about it. Even places that are open to the public have certain spots that are roped off, where they don't want the masses to intrude. Some things are sacred after all. And you have to feel that about this place."

Fliss felt it all too deeply, "Can we go now?" she asked, restraining a shudder.

"Certainly – but since we have come this far, do you mind if I make a short detour to the standing stone on the moor? I need to view it in its new context."

"I suppose not," she said reluctantly.

There were still remnants of mist on the moor, wisps of low cloud that moved in swirling drifts before them, dispersing rapidly in the wind and sun. Fliss could almost see them forming into ghostly figures which hovered for a few seconds then disappeared. She told herself that she was, yet again, being an over-imaginative idiot. She held Megan's little hand tightly, as though their roles were reversed and she was the child and Megan the old and wise one. It was odd how much comfort could be gained from a tiny hand.

When they were within sight of the stones John strode on ahead and she let him go, making no attempt to keep up. She was over-come with tiredness now and longed for her warm bed. She must have been mad to agree to this trek, when she could have stayed warm and cosy indoors.

She stopped in her tracks when two crows suddenly flew up out of the middle of the stones, cawing bad-temperedly. She hated those evil-looking birds. What on earth were they doing landing there, she wondered? It wasn't a usual spot for them to haunt. They normally stayed down nearer the farm, where there was always a chance of a free meal in the shape of discarded food or even road-kill on the lane.

"Jesus Christ almighty!"

It was not only the words of blasphemy but the tone of panic in which they were spoken that halted Fliss in her tracks. She saw John run out from between the stones, white-faced and staggering he made his way towards her.

"Don't come any further," he shouted.

"What is it?" called Theo, who had been walking beside her.

John had reached them and sank to his knees, retching and coughing. Theo made to walk past him on to the circle, but John gripped his wrist, "Don't Ted. We need to go back, now!"

"What the bloody hell are you talking about?"

"There's a body."

"What?" Theo was genuinely stunned by this pronouncement. It was obvious he had heard the words but couldn't quite bring himself to believe them.

John looked up at his friend, "Send Felicity away. She mustn't see it."

In that moment Fliss knew, as clearly as if she had walked between the stones herself and seen with her own eyes. It wasn't just a body that lay in the centre of the stone circle. It was a body that had been ritually sacrificed with a blow to the head, a ligature around the neck and a slashed throat. That was why the crows had been there – taking advantage of a free meal. They would only be attracted by the smell and sight of blood. She felt sickened and faint. Her legs buckled under her and she joined John on the spongy peat, the wetness seeping into her jeans and sending the chill through skin, muscle and tendon and so deep into her bones so that she thought she would never be warm again.

"Tell me it's no one I know," she whispered.

"You know him," said John shortly, looking into her eyes and suddenly recovering himself. He knew it was up to him to get her away from this place, that he had a duty to care for her. He rose to his feet, deathly pale, but determined, and gripped her under her arm, "Now get up. We have to get Megan away from here."

"Who is it?" she breathed, looking pleadingly up at him and resisting his attempts to get her to her feet, "I have to know."

"Later. We'll discuss it later. This is no place for a child."

Subdued and silent they returned to the farm house and John, grim-faced, lifted the telephone and dialled DI Piper's number.

CHAPTER TWENTY NINE

"Morgan Le Fay, Queen of Avalon, and other dark sorceresses such as Nimue or the Calatins, used their supernatural gifts to bewitch and manipulate mortals for their own ends"

They sat Megan in front of something mindless on the television and retired to the kitchen to discuss what would happen next.

Theo made tea – as Fliss had known he would – and she accepted a mug, but her eyes were on John. He was still pale, but seemed curiously detached. She could not know that he was haunted by what he had seen. It was an entirely different matter to see a human being butchered than to speculate on those same injuries when the only evidence was a skeleton or a preserved corpse. In those circumstances the injuries were interesting and academic. Every time he closed his eyes he saw the truth. The reality was blood, ripped flesh, slashed tendons, exposed bone.

"Now tell me who it is," she demanded.

John rubbed his eyes with slightly shaking fingers and she had a sudden terrifying thought – terrifying because she didn't quite know how she felt about it, "Oh dear God, it's not Bryn?" she cried on the verge of hysteria.

He reached out and took her hand, holding it firm and warm in his own, "No. It's Fergus."

She had no words. She looked into his eyes for a long time, hoping that if she said nothing, if she refused to break the spell, then what he said would not be true. It could not be Fergus lying up there on the moor, cold, dead, and covered with his own blood.

"I'm so sorry, sweetheart. If I could have spared you this, I would have."

"You're sure? You could not have been mistaken? You were only there for a few seconds, perhaps you did not see clearly ..."

"It is Fergus," he said softly.

Fergus, nice, kind, infuriating, sulky Fergus. Fergus who had wanted to kiss her. She wished she had let him, now. Would the pain she felt be less if she had not refused him?

"Who has done this, John?" she asked, tears trickling down her cheeks. She lifted her hand to brush them away. Funny, she didn't even know she had begun to cry.

"God alone knows."

"What's going to happen now? What did the Inspector say?"

"He asked that we all remain indoors. He wants me to ring the pub and tell Bryn to stay there. He'll be going up onto the moor with the SOCO and when they've finished, he'll come and interview us."

"So, we've just to sit here and wait?"

"I'm afraid so."

"What about Fergus's family?" she asked, slightly hysterical, "Someone ought to tell them."

"We have to leave that to the police, Felicity," he told her gently, "It's out of our hands now."

The interminable morning wore on. Theo went out to feed the animals, despite the policeman's request. Fliss, desperate for something to occupy her, brought Megan into the kitchen and they baked bread and cakes. Soon the kitchen was sprinkled with an almost imperceptible layer of white flour and Megan was happily playing with a rapidly greying lump of dough.

John sat and read a book by the Aga, smiling occasionally at Megan's happy squealing when the crusty bread came out of the oven, or when her mother let her lick a bowl clean of cake-mixture.

The door burst open just as they sat for home-made cake and coffee. Fliss looked up and was horrified to see not Theo, whom she had been expecting, but her husband.

"What the bloody hell is going on?" demanded the ever-charming Bryn, "I've been kicking my heels in that pub for hours. Where the hell is Fergus? It's typical of him to do a disappearing act when there's work to be done. He's supposed to be helping me sort out this bloody mess on the computer."

John had rung and told him to stay at the pub, but on the instructions of DI Piper, he had not told of Fergus's murder.

"I thought I told you to wait at the pub until I called you," said John harshly. He was still suffering from the shock of seeing Fergus cold and bloody on the moor and it was all he could do to control his fury when he heard Bryn speak disparagingly of the dead man.

"Who the hell do you think you are ordering about?" growled Bryn. The sight of the cosy scene in the kitchen had begun a suspicion in his mind and suddenly he didn't give much of a damn if John Norton was his boss. A vague memory of Fliss in the arms of an unknown man came to him and it seemed to him now that perhaps the shape and size had not been so very reminiscent of Ted Armitage after all.

Fliss could see the truth dawning in her husband's eyes and she intercepted hastily,

"Be quiet, Bryn, for God's sake. Something serious has happened."

As if only just reminded of her presence, he turned a furious face to her, "I'll say it has. I've had a phone call from the Estate Agent. I believe you've taken it upon yourself to take the house off the market – you interfering bitch!"

"Watch your language in front of my daughter!" she hissed back, "Yes, I did instruct the Agent not to sell OUR house."

"What are you trying to do? Do you realise you could be visiting me next in hospital with two broken legs?"

"Oh believe me, love, I won't be visiting you!" she said sarcastically.

They squared up to each other, the hatred crackling between them in almost visible blue sparks. John took a deep breath and decided the moment had come to intercept, loath as he was to come between a husband and wife.

"Might I say something?" he asked.

"Go ahead," snarled Bryn, never taking his eyes off Fliss for a

274

second, "Though what the hell this has to do with you, I don't know."

"I merely wanted to say that your services will no longer be required. I am suspending this dig for the foreseeable future – but I intend to pay you to the end of the contract. I can write you a cheque here and now, if you wish."

For the first time Bryn looked at him, his face white with fury, "Salving your conscience, Jack? How long have you been sleeping with my wife?"

Fliss gasped, but John didn't even flinch.

"One more word, Bryn and I'll retract the offer."

"Retract it and go to the devil! If you think you can buy my wife with a few lousy quid ..."

Fliss slapped him, hard, "How dare you! What do you take me for? And don't bother to answer that, I know! You are despicable, Bryn, and I couldn't hate you more if you had been the evil scum who killed Fergus ..." she faltered to a stop. Of course she should not have told him that Fergus was dead. The policeman had asked them to keep the fact quiet until he had chance to view the body and begin his interviews.

Bryn looked more stunned at the news than he had at the stinging blow she had dealt him, "What did you say? Are you telling me that Fergus is dead?"

Fliss suddenly became aware of the indrawn breath of the child behind her. Megan knew what dead meant. She had owned a hamster earlier that year – emphasis on the 'had' and her mother had given a careful explanation of death and heaven and being reunited at some dim and distant future date when she was very old and grey.

She glared at her husband, "I'll never forgive you for this, Bryn," she whispered, then went to her daughter and said breezily, "Come on, Meggie, time to get cleaned up. Let's go upstairs and wash your hands."

As she passed John she threw an apologetic glance in his direction, but she could say nothing. It was too fraught a situation to try and explain or excuse anything that her husband said or did.

She heard them continue to talk after she left the room, but their voices were lower now. The anger seemed to have left Bryn's tone and John merely sounded his usual measured self. If nothing else, at least the shocking revelation had knocked the wind out of Bryn's sails. He had lost all his bombast. And if she knew him, it had all been for show. He would take the money that John offered – but probably only on the condition that she was never told how much he had been given.

Let him keep every filthy penny. She would rather beg her bread on the street than accept anything from him now. The heat burned her cheeks as she recalled his accusations about her and John Norton having an affair. How humiliating it was to be defamed by her own husband – and in front of the man she now accepted she had fallen head over heels in love with – and whom, she had to admit, had never made one single wrong step. She still had no idea how he felt about her. He had been kind – exceptionally kind – but had he been lover-like? Not really. No, she thought wistfully, not at all. He had kissed her hand, and given her only one light peck on her lips. He had embraced her, but only when she had thrown herself into his arms. He had sat up all night with her, but only because she had begged him to do so. What was going on? Anything or nothing? Was she really in love – or did John's kindness merely seem wonderful when contrasted with Bryn's brash insensitivity? She had no idea.

She decided that Megan was safer away from the vicinity of the kitchen, so when they came back down, fresh and clean, she sat her at the dining room table with her paints and a plentiful supply of paper. Luckily there were plenty of old newspapers around to line the mahogany table.

When she returned to the kitchen some minutes later, she found both Theo and the Inspector had joined the throng.

"Good morning Mrs Elmsworth. Can I say how sorry I am for the loss of your friend?"

She thought that was rather sweet of him in the circumstances and said so, "Thank you Inspector. It's nice of you to say that."

"I'm afraid I'm going to have to ask rather a lot of questions.

Do you feel up to answering them?"

"I think so. They'll have to be answered, sooner or later, so let's get it out of the way, shall we?"

"That would be best. I know it seems harsh, but while it's all still fresh in your minds is the most helpful time to ask."

"I understand."

He invited them all to sit – including Bryn, who was looking rather less sure of himself now that John had explained exactly what had happened to Fergus. He had become uncomfortably aware that he had probably been the last person to see Fergus the evening before – well, the last person apart from his murderer. And Bryn was bright enough to know that being the last person to see a dead man was never a good position in which to find oneself.

Piper took out his notebook and suddenly began to look very businesslike and serious, which for some odd reason made Fliss want to giggle. She realised it was hysteria and bit the inside of her cheek so that she wouldn't embarrass herself, for in truth she had never felt less like laughing, but still the feeling was there bubbling away in her chest like an odd sort of heartburn.

"I understand it was you, professor, who found the body?"

"It was."

"The time logged at the station was a little after six o'clock. Would you like to tell me why you were up on the moor at that time – considering that the dig is now suspended?"

John looked a little bemused. How could he answer that question without explaining about the false ring of stone that Armitage deceased had created? Fliss came to his rescue,

"I'm afraid that was my doing, Inspector. I wanted to see the sunrise over the stones."

Piper raised an eyebrow and gave her a long, speculative look, "The sunrise?" he asked quizzically. Of course he didn't believe her, but she stood by what she had said, looking straight into his eyes.

"Yes, the sunrise," she repeated firmly, "I hadn't slept well, Theo was already up as he always is, then Megan woke the professor playing on the landing, so we decided to make the best of a bad job and go up on the moors to see the sunrise over the stones. I thought it would be ..." she faltered and made a winding gesture with her finger, as if trying to stir the cogs in her brain to churn out the right word for her, "er..."

"Romantic?" suggested the policeman.

"Yes, romantic," she caught Bryn's furious look and backtracked hastily, "Not romantic, no ... er ..."

"Atmospheric," supplied Theo helpfully, just as John came in with, "Spiritual."

"Okay, I'll buy that – for now. Did you see anyone else up there?"

"Not a soul – just a couple of big crows," said Fliss.

"Well, they didn't do it," said Piper cynically.

"So exactly what time did you wake up this morning?"

"I don't know exactly. About five I suppose."

"And both Armitage and the professor were both in the house then?"

"Of course."

"They were both here all night?"

"Yes," she said, trying not to show her contempt for his line of questioning.

"How the hell would you know," growled Bryn, "Unless you were in bed with the two of them!"

As she went white with suppressed fury, the policeman shot her husband a keen look, "Mr Elmsworth does have a point, madam. Can you be sure that either or both of them were here all night?"

"I told you, I slept badly. I would have heard them go out – or come back in. The house was quiet all night. No one went in or out."

Piper turned his attention to Bryn, "Can you explain why you left the pub and came here when you'd been asked to stay where you were?"

"I didn't know what had happened, did I? I just got an odd call from the professor asking me to stay in the pub – but why should I? He's not my boss anymore – and I wanted to speak to my wife. We had family business to discuss."

"I see. Well, that's fair enough I suppose. Now, let's turn to the events of last night. What time did you last see Professor Ripley?"

"About midnight, I suppose. To be honest, I wasn't that aware of the time. I'd had some bad news and I'd been drowning my sorrows for most of the evening. Fergus had sunk a few himself and was pretty damned offensive, if you must know the truth of it."

"So, you quarrelled?"

"I wouldn't say that exactly, but we didn't part on the best of terms."

"You're being very honest, sir, if I may say so. Most people wouldn't want to admit to falling out with a man who was subsequently found murdered."

Bryn looked shifty, "There's not much point in trying to cover myself," he said almost sulkily, "Half the pub heard us have a go at each other. If I lie now, it will look the worse for me when you ask around later."

"That's true enough," Piper accepted the explanation with a wry smile, "Having gone thus far, would you like to tell me what you argued about?"

"Not really," grunted Bryn.

"Let me hazard a guess – a woman?"

"Full marks, Sherlock," said Bryn, throwing a poisonous glance towards his wife, "He had plenty to say about what an idiot I was for letting my little diamond slip through my fingers."

Fliss had been looking down at her hands, minutely examining the broken nail of her left thumb, but she transferred her gaze to her husband when he said this – he had sounded almost wistful, and she wondered if he meant it, however the expression on his face was anything but benign and she looked away again.

"That seems a little tame to cause such animosity," suggested Piper gently.

"He needed to mind his own business," said Bryn.

Theo spoke up, determined to set the record straight, "If Fergus did as he told me he intended there was a little more to the conversation than that, Bryn."

The inspector turned to Theo, "Do tell, Mr Armitage," he said pleasantly.

"It would be my pleasure," said Theo ignoring the fact that Bryn half-rose out of his chair, his fists clenched, "Fergus had found out that Bryn was behind all the leaks to the press and the New Agers. He was furious and fully intended to tell Bryn exactly what he thought of him."

Fliss let out a gasp of shock and even John looked stunned. Now Bryn did get to his feet and took a step towards Theo, "He was a bloody liar," he spat furiously, "He wanted to slap the blame on me, but I wasn't having any of it. There may have been a mole, but it wasn't me!"

He could see that not one person in the room believed him and with a look of disgust, he turned on his heel and headed for the door.

"I'd advise you not to leave, Mr Elmsworth," said the policeman grimly.

Bryn hesitated then returned to his seat, "Just so long as you take note that I stayed under duress."

"It is duly noted, sir."

"Good. Now can you give me an explanation as to why I'm being asked all these questions when it must be obvious that I have a rock solid alibi? I was in the pub all night – and not in any fit state to leave and commit a murder!"

"I'm just trying to get to the truth, Mr Elmsworth. Someone killed Fergus Ripley – and you had a grudge against him."

"Yes, but I didn't have a grudge against the other fellow, did I? I'd never even heard of this god-forsaken spot seven years ago."

"I only have your word for that."

"Brilliant! You have two men here who admit to being at the scene of both murders, but still you pursue me."

"No one is pursuing you, sir."

"It doesn't feel that way."

"Why don't you shut up, Bryn?" asked Fliss wearily, "Tell me, Inspector, do you know who the other man is yet? If you knew that, it might help find the real murderer."

"The only thing we know about him is that he was pumped full of illegal drugs – so what he was doing here is a mystery. It's not exactly the perfect place to score a hit."

"Oh, I can solve that little mystery for you," said Fliss airily, "I was told the other day that Merrington Hall isn't really a Health Farm, but a rehab clinic. They don't broadcast the fact because it would freak out the locals."

"Are you sure of this?" asked Piper incredulously, "Because it's the first I've heard of it – and the local police should really be informed of something like that."

"Unless Tanya was pulling my leg, yes, I'm sure. And I can't think of any reason why she should. As for keeping the police informed – we are talking about Douglas Merrington! A law unto himself. I don't suppose there is anything official at all about his methods. If your body was a drug addict, then he could have been in rehab."

Piper looked thoughtful, "That's very interesting – and it actually solves two mysteries; why he was here and how he was enticed up onto the moor. You can bet his murderer offered him something he couldn't refuse."

"But as far as I'm aware, Fergus wasn't into drugs. Why did he go up onto the moor in the middle of the night?" asked John suddenly. He had been listening to all this in bemused silence. Was there no end to the surprises Fliss could spring on them all? She had been in the district only a few days and she had discovered more than the police had.

"I'm sure the reason will become clear."

Bryn shifted moodily in his chair, "This is all irrelevant to me. He didn't go on the moor to meet me, so do you think I could go now?

"I suppose so, but stay in the village!" warned the Inspector, "I will be wanting to talk to you again soon."

"Don't worry, I'm not going anywhere without my wife," he replied and slammed the door behind him.

Fliss stared after him for a long time, sickness growing in the pit of her stomach. He meant it. There was never going to be any escape from him.

Then she felt John Norton's hands resting on her shoulders and she felt briefly safe.

CHAPTER THIRTY

"La Belle Dame Sans Merci, described by the poet Keats, was a Banshee who attracted mortal lovers, causing them to become hopelessly infatuated and bereft of will or purpose"

John touched her only for a moment then returned to his seat, "Is there anything else you need to ask us, Inspector?"

"I have a few more questions, professor," said Piper. Fliss thought he sounded tired and rather depressed and she wondered why. Of course investigating a murder couldn't be pleasant, but surely he was used to that?

"Ask away."

"Were relations between you and Ripley amicable?"

John hesitated, "Not always," he admitted guardedly at last, "There was some professional jealousy on his part."

"Anything more personal?"

Though she didn't look up, Fliss felt John's eyes on her.

"Perhaps," he said quietly.

"Would you like to be a little more specific?"

"Not really."

"What about you, Mr Armitage? Did you have any quarrel with the victim?"

"No."

"But you are a member of a cult who see the Stone Circle up on the moor as a sacred place?"

There was yet another blank silence, then Theo blustered, rather unconvincingly Fliss felt, "Who the hell told you that? As if I couldn't guess! It's total and utter rubbish. I don't know what you are talking about."

"Oh, I think you do. I have it on very good authority that there is a long established Druidic cult in this village and that as owner of the land on which the circle stands, you lead it."

"You've been listening to malicious gossip again, Inspector, and you and I both know it," said Theo firmly.

"That really is ridiculous, Matt," protested John, "I can assure you that Ted Armitage does not lead a murderous cult who make human sacrifices in a stone circle."

"How can you be so sure, sir?"

Fliss felt compelled to answer, "Inspector Piper, do you really think I would bring my child into this house if there was the slightest doubt in my mind about either the professor or Mr Armitage?"

"Smarter women than you have been blinded by affection, madam."

"But ..." she began, but he cut brutally across her excuses, "Look, the facts are these: I have two bodies, murdered in exactly the same way, dumped in the same place, at least seven years apart. And here I have two men who were both here at the time of each murder and who each have an obsessive interest in Celtic history and that bloody stone circle. In fact just about the only thing they have in common is the stone circle since one is an academic and one is a farmer. What do you expect me to think?"

"I know neither of them is capable of murder," she insisted, but his words sent ice through her veins. It seemed he had already made up his mind who the culprits were.

"Sadly what you think you know is neither here nor there," he said stiffly, "I'm sorry gentlemen, but I'm going to have to ask you both to accompany me to the station."

Theo laughed out loud, "How very clichéd, my dear Holmes."

"Sherlock Holmes would never have said that, sir. He wasn't a policeman," said Piper tetchily.

"Is this really necessary, Matt?" asked John wearily.

"I think it is."

"Very well," he said resignedly, "Do you think I might have a moment alone with Mrs Elmsworth?"

284

"I'm afraid not."

"Come on, Inspector Morse, have a heart," said Theo with some amusement, changing his detective, since he had been asked to, "If I promise to go quietly, let the man speak to his girl."

Piper glanced down at the still seated Fliss who was blushing to the roots of her hair, but who looked pleadingly back at him.

"Alright, you have five minutes." He laid a stern hand on Theo's shoulder, but Theo hesitated for one last word with Fliss, "Don't worry about the animals, Fliss. I'll use precious police resources and ring Malcolm from the station. Everything else is sorted, I think – oh, and the clock in the hall is fully wound up."

"I know how it feels," responded Fliss with a stern glance at the policeman. Theo laughed and allowed Piper to lead him outside to the waiting police car.

John took her hand and pulled her to her feet and into his arms, "Felicity, I don't have the time to say everything I want to …"

"I know," she whispered.

He stroked her face, her hair, "God, this is a mess. I have no idea what to say to you. This is the last thing I intended to happen. I'm too old for you – and you are still raw from all you've been through. It's all madness, you know that, don't you?"

She nodded, "I wish you would kiss me," she said softly. With a small groan of despair he did as she asked him and she knew then that it was right. Despite all the wrongness that surrounded them, she belonged in his embrace.

It ended too soon and she felt bereft and cold when his lips left hers.

"Don't stay here alone, Felicity. Go to Emma at the vicarage. I don't want you in danger. Inspector Piper thinks he has it all worked out, but the maniac who did this is still out there."

"I'll go right now. I'll get a few clothes together and I'll take Megan there straight away, don't worry."

"I'll be worried about you for the rest of my life," he said simply and she forced a smile,

"Don't say that or I'll think I'm more trouble than I'm worth."

"You could never be that. Goodbye, my love."

He took his mobile out of his pocket intending to make his phone call before he ever arrived at the police station, but, as is always the case when one needs it the most, the battery was dead, "Damn," he muttered, then turned back to her, "Do me a favour, Felicity, will you? Ring Merrington and tell him I need a solicitor."

"I don't know his number," she said. He handed her his phone, "Plug it in and you'll find the number in the address book."

"But won't you need it?"

"It's not much use to me in its present state – and I'd feel happier if I knew you had a phone. Recharge it and then don't let it out of your sight!"

She went to the door and watched him get into the back of the car with Theo then with tears rolling down her face, she waved him off.

As she turned to go back into the house, she noticed there was another policeman standing in the yard and she hastily wiped her face.

"Has the Inspector left you here on guard or something?" she asked.

"No madam, I'm here to wait for the pick-up truck. We are impounding the vehicles of the professor and Armitage. Forensics needs to examine them."

"What? Both of them? But I need a lift into the village."

"I can call a cab for you, if you like – or send for another police car."

She thought for a moment, then dismissed the idea, "No, it doesn't matter. I'll ring for a lift myself, thanks."

She went upstairs to John's bedroom, where she assumed she would find the battery-charging lead. The room smelt ever so slightly of him and it brought tears to her eyes. Beside the lead there was a picture by the side of the bed and she picked them both up, thrusting the lead into her jeans pocket, then examining the portrait. His daughter, she thought, as the pretty teenager smiled up at her. She replaced it and went towards the door, feeling that she was trespassing, but when she saw one of his discarded sweatshirts hung over a chair, she grabbed it and sniffed deeply. Odd how she

286

had only been close enough to him to smell that faint, pleasant odour just once, yet now it brought her incredible comfort.

She went down to the hall, plugged in the mobile and did as he had asked. It took a couple of minutes to get Douglas himself to the telephone. She spoke to at least three PA's before she convinced them that she really did need to speak directly to the 'boss'.

He sounded impatient, "Fliss? What is it? I'm rather busy."

"Yes, I know, I'm sorry. John asked me to ring. He's been taken to the police station and he wants you to send a solicitor."

"John's been arrested?" he asked sharply, "What the devil for?" She didn't know what to say. She didn't know if he knew about Fergus, or if the police wanted her to keep his death to herself. No one had instructed her and she floundered for a moment, "Er, I don't really know. He's helping with their enquiries."

"Dammit all, this has disrupted things nicely I must say. I hope that they have at least arrested bloody Armitage too."

She bit back a tetchy riposte and merely answered, "Yes."

"Well that's something at least. Everyone knows he's behind all these murders."

He had said 'murders' so he must know about Fergus. It didn't take long for bad news to spread. They had only found Fergus at five that morning and now it was a little after twelve. She wondered vaguely who had told him. Bryn in all probability. He seemed to keep the man informed of everything else.

"I must go now, Douglas," she said swiftly, wanting to be off the phone, "Don't forget to send a solicitor for John, will you?"

"I'll do it now. Do I take this to mean you are at the farm alone?"

"Not for long," she reassured him, "I'm about to ring Emma Goodrich and get her to pick me up and take me to the vicarage for the night."

"Don't bother her. Hop in John's car and come over here. I'm sure he won't mind and I think he'd want you to stay here in comfort instead of in a draughty old vicarage."

"I can't. The police have impounded both his and Theo's cars."

"Have they indeed?" he said thoughtfully, "They certainly seem to mean business."

"That's hardly surprising, is it?"

"I suppose not. Stay there. I'll send Tanya to pick you up."

"No, really, I couldn't impose," she protested, but she knew it was in vain. He simply spoke over her, "Nonsense. She'll be there in less than half an hour." He rang off leaving Fliss biting her lip in consternation. Determinedly she placed a finger on the cradle and having gained a dialling tone, she rang Emma and briefly explained the situation, "Can you get to me before Tanya? I don't want to go to the Hall, but I can't be rude enough to refuse outright."

Emma assured her she would do her best.

By the time she had packed a holdall the policeman and the two cars had gone. She felt a little afraid but comforted herself with the thought that it would only be a few more minutes before Emma arrived to pick her and Megan up.

It was over half an hour later when she heard a car pull up in the yard and she took Megan's hand and led her to the back door to go and meet Emma, to save her any unnecessary waiting around. However it wasn't Emma who greeted her, but Tanya.

"Hi, honey," she called cheerfully, extending her long legs out of the 4x4, "Douglas told me your car-less state, so I thought I'd better come and get you."

"That's very nice of you, Tanya," said Fliss, unable to help smiling at the other woman's elegance even when clambering out of a large vehicle, "But I've already rung Emma. She's on her way to collect us."

"No, she's not darling. As I arrived in the village she was just getting into her car, so I waylaid her and told her she needn't bother. Being a nosy sort of soul, I couldn't help stopping and asking where she was going."

Fliss hadn't wanted to go to Merrington Hall, but she knew when she was beaten. She felt uncomfortable in the place, as though she didn't really belong in such august surroundings and she certainly didn't like or trust Douglas Merrington but she found herself at a loss. There was also something disquieting about the fact that Tanya felt she could hijack her plans and instruct Emma that her services were no longer required. Her instincts told her loud and clear that she would be better off at the vicarage, but Tanya was smiling so pleasantly, and had gone to so much trouble to collect her and Megan, that she didn't have the heart to argue.

She fetched the child seat that the policeman had so thoughtfully removed from John's car before they towed it away, and Tanya made a pretence of helping her secure it into the car. She actually didn't have the faintest idea how to fasten it in, or how to buckle Megan safely, but she fluttered around, trying to be helpful, but really just getting in the way.

It seemed to be ages before Fliss's bag was stowed in the back and they were on their way.

"You've been having quite a time of it, haven't you?" she asked sympathetically as they drove away, Fliss gazing wistfully over her shoulder at the house fast receding into the distance.

"You could say that," answered Fliss, "But not as bad a time as Fergus, Professor Norton or Mr Armitage."

"I was sorry to hear about Fergus. He was fun. But don't you worry too much about the prof. Douglas doesn't let his friends down. He is with his lawyers right now, sorting the whole sorry mess out."

"He's going to get them out of Police custody?" asked Fliss eagerly, leaning forward so that she could look into Tanya's face.

The other woman eyed her warily, "Well, he'll certainly do his best for Jack," she said carefully.

Fliss sank dejectedly back into her seat, "Of course. I forgot. He won't lift a finger to help Theo."

"I don't want to be the one to point this out, Fliss," ventured Tanya hesitantly, "but you seem to have a real blind spot where Ted Armitage is concerned. Doesn't common sense tell you that he really is the most likely culprit for these murders?"

Fliss wanted to argue with her, but something stopped her. What was the point? She would be wasting her breath. Tanya was very firmly in Douglas's camp and if she was going to have to spend the next few hours, possibly even days, in her company, there was very little point in rousing her enmity.

"He's always been kind to me," she said quietly.

"I suppose that is important," agreed Tanya then added brightly, "What do you want to do this evening?"

Fliss tried to be enthusiastic, but failed miserably, "I'm really sorry, Tanya, but I've really too much on my mind to even contemplate enjoying myself. I'll probably just have an early night. I was up early this morning."

"I know what you need – a jolly good massage. I'll arrange it when we get back."

"I don't think so. I have Megan to think about."

"Nonsense. I won't take no for an answer. Megan has been safe enough with Mrs Burton in the past. You need to make some time for yourself." She smiled and cast a sideways glance at her companion, "Besides, you don't want to look like something the cat dragged in when Jack comes home, do you?"

As she had known it would be, this was the deciding factor. Fliss shrugged non-commitally but Tanya knew she had won. Fliss would leave Megan to Mrs Burton and would submit to the ministrations of the masseuse.

✳

As they turned into the huge iron gates that wouldn't have looked out of place on a medieval castle, Fliss was amazed to see the New Age vans and caravans parked on the wide expanses of lawn that surrounded Merrington Hall.

"What on earth..?" she gasped. Tanya shrugged eloquently, "Don't ask me. You know Douglas has his own way of doing things and nothing will stop him. For some reason he took pity on them when they were chucked off the moor by the police."

"But aren't they supposed to be sworn enemies?"

"Money talks," answered Tanya succinctly.

"What do you mean?"

"Douglas realised that it wasn't really in his interests to be painted as a villain in all this. He wants Armitage to be the bad guy.

As things stand the farmer's boy is the man who looks after our heritage and he's the wicked lord of the manor who is desecrating it."

"I'm surprised he cares," said Fliss cynically.

"If nothing else, Douglas is a shrewd operator. More and more people are seeing everything New Age as our salvation. It doesn't do his business any good to be lumped with insensitive Toffs who only care about making money."

"But he does only care about making money," protested Fliss.

"Yes, but looking that way is not how to do it."

Fliss fell silent. She was disgusted with the self-serving Merrington and even more reluctant to take his hospitality, but she was committed now and there was no going back. She toyed with the notion of ringing for a cab when they reached the house.

Tanya took over completely, as was her wont. She took Megan's hand and began to lead her up the steps, "I'll find Mrs Burton and get Megan sorted out, you bring your bag in," she instructed Fliss over her shoulder. Fliss did as she was told and went around the back of the car to hoist out her bag. A voice behind her made her start painfully – she hadn't fully realised just how shredded her nerves were.

"Well, if it isn't Mystic Meg." She spun around and found Zak Oldthorpe strolling towards her, a hand-rolled cigarette dangling from his lips and one eye scrunched against the smoke.

"What did you call me?" she asked in astonishment.

"You're not going to deny being the prof's own personal little psychic are you? I've heard all about your magical powers."

She turned away from him, hoping to hide the discomfort she felt. She wasn't quite sure she knew to what he was referring but she certainly wasn't stupid enough to fall into the trap of denying something that he was trying to bluff her into saying.

"I don't know what you are talking about."

"Oh, I think you do. Fergus Ripley had a very big mouth when he had a few bevies inside him. You've seen a man who wasn't there!" He laughed harshly and Fliss felt sick to the pit of her stomach. Was there nothing secret in this place? How could Fergus have been stupid enough to broadcast the tale of Megan's imaginary robin-man to all and sundry in the pub?

"I'm surprised you waste your time listening to the ramblings of a bitter drunk. He was just hacked off that John found the bog body and not him – he had to make the reason airy-fairy instead of just admitting that John was the better archaeologist."

The smile swiftly left Zak's face, "There's nothing clever about disturbing the peace of the ancient dead, love," he said viciously.

"Yeah, well it turned out it wasn't all that ancient, didn't it?" she returned sarcastically, unable to bear this self-righteous bully for a moment longer.

"That doesn't excuse what your smart-arse pal does the rest of the time."

"Look, I'm not discussing this with you, now or ever, so why don't you just go back to your air-polluting old rust-bucket and leave me alone?"

"I'll go, but don't think this is over. Your professor is behind bars, where he belongs, and with any luck, that's exactly where he'll stay."

"I wouldn't count on it. Your new best friend, Mr Merrington, is trying to get him out even as we speak."

Zak's expression clouded and he threw Fliss a look of pure hatred, "No one else is going to dig at that circle – I'll make sure of it."

"Good luck with that then," she answered as airily as she could and went into the hall.

*

As she lay almost naked on the couch, with warm fluffy towels spread over her, Fliss had to admit that Tanya had a point. The subdued lighting, soft music and the aromatic scents of the essential oils in a burner all combined to make her feel relaxed for the first time in days. The masseuse was more than good, her strokes pleasantly firm, her only comments related to the massage and she made no small talk to break the atmosphere. She even

292

warmed her massaging oil so that there was no nasty cold shock when she spread it on the bare flesh. Fliss felt herself drifting into a sort of dreamy half-sleep that was incredibly comfortable.

The back was the last part of the body to be done, and took the longest, so it was the most soporific. When it was over and Fliss felt the towel being pulled up over her shoulders, it was more effort than she could summon to open her eyes and acknowledge the therapist as she said quietly, "All done, madam. You stay there whilst I fetch you a drink of water, then take your time getting up. There's no hurry."

Fliss drifted into a light sleep and was only vaguely aware of the door opening again. She wanted to say something, but the effort was too great and she stayed where she was. She could drink the water in a few moments. The woman had said she didn't need to hurry.

It was only when a different voice spoke softly and menacingly in her ear that she jerked awake, suddenly terrified.

"Don't move, Mrs Elmsworth. I want you to listen very carefully to what I have to say."

She didn't dare to disobey. She opened her eyes and tried to look over her shoulder, but she could make out nothing in the candle-lit gloom, "What do you want?" she whispered. Her first thought was that she was naked except for her panties and that he intended to rape her, and she began to plan wildly what she would do if he tried to uncover her. She recognised the voice and nothing in her past experience told her that she was safe in any way. The more things began to fall into place in her mind, the more terrified she became.

"In a moment, when I tell you, you are going to get up and we are going to walk through the changing rooms and out to the swimming pool."

"I can't. I'm not dressed."

"You don't need your clothes in the pool and you have a towel."

"Why are we going to the pool?" she asked.

"Because you are going to have a nasty accident. Stupefied by your massage, exhausted and half asleep, you are going to stagger

293

into the pool." His voice was icy cold and Fliss began to shiver uncontrollably. She knew what he was telling her. For some reason she was going to die – but why? What had she done to deserve this?

"Please don't do this," she begged, lifting her head, "I have my little girl. Just go away and leave me alone and I promise I'll forget this ever happened – in fact it didn't happen, " she was babbling almost incoherently now, the terror making her words fall over each other in her panic to get them out, "I had a bad dream, that's all."

He gave a low laugh, "You have a lot of dreams, don't you, Mrs Elmsworth? Well, one particular dream has dropped you into a whole heap of trouble."

"What are you talking about?" she asked breathlessly.

"You are the only person in the world who knows what the bog man looked like seven years ago, before the peat tanned his hide for him."

"What?" Now she really was astounded. How the hell could anyone but John know that she thought she had seen the bog man in the farmhouse parlour? Dear God! He had not told everyone, had he? Was there not a single man in that team who could keep their mouth shut?

"Surprised that I know about that, are you? Well, I'll put you out of your misery, since it makes no difference now. Fergus Ripley was snooping around and he overheard you telling John Norton about seeing the apparition. You were a little too accurate for comfort, my dear."

"But the police don't know," she said desperately, "I swear I won't say anything, ever."

"I can't take that risk."

"But if you kill me that's just one more murder – and even then it may not save you. What if someone else comes forward and identifies him? He must have had relatives, friends."

"He had no-one. He was a junkie and junkies don't have families. They drive everyone who loves them away. He did have a sister. That was why I ended up having to bury him. I miscalculated. My original plan was to leave him on the moor to be found, safe in the knowledge that Ted Armitage would go down for his murder. I'd even stolen baling twine from his barn to use to strangle him. Then his bloody sister turned up. He'd told her where he was going. It meant I had to get rid of the body because suddenly it could be identified. I've waited a long time to do the same again, but this time nothing is going to go wrong. Armitage is going to jail and he'll have to sell his farm to pay his legal fees."

She raised herself up on her elbow and twisted her head towards him, "You killed Fergus in that horrible way just to get the farm off Theo?"

He walked across the room to her, "Get up. We're going to the pool."

"No," she whispered, her throat suddenly dry with terror, "No, please don't do this."

"You either walk, or I knock you out and carry you, it's your choice."

"Someone will see us. You can't get away with it." She was trying to buy time, to delay the inevitable, but she knew he had thought of this and that he had planned against their being disturbed, "The girl who massaged me said she was coming back with some water," she added, without much hope.

"She won't be coming back. I met her in the hallway and told her you had gone back to your room."

"She will come back. She has to come back and make sure I'm okay. She won't take your word for it. I know someone will come."

"The pool is closed for cleaning – and everyone is at dinner at the other end of the house. No one will hear you scream, Mrs Elmsworth. No one will save you from drowning."

CHAPTER THIRTY-ONE

"Annwn's magical cauldron, guarded by nine maidens,
healed the sick and restored the dead to life"

Fliss thought quickly. She had no choice but, for the moment, to do as he directed. She was better off conscious as that way there might be some hope of escape – and she had no doubt at all that he was quite capable of knocking her on the head, as he had threatened; after all he had done it twice before, very effectively. She hastily pulled the towel around her body and slid to the floor.

"There's no need for this. I won't say a word. All I want is my little girl and me to be safe. I'll never endanger her, you know that."

He ignored her, merely holding the door for her to go out before him, "This way," he gestured her to turn to the right. As the door of the massage room closed behind them, closing off the pleasant aromas of the oils, she was suddenly aware of his body odour, sharp and unpleasant, with an overlaying hint of cannabis. Was there anyone around here who didn't use and abuse drugs? It occurred to her to wonder if perhaps Bryn did too – was that why he never seemed to have any money, no matter how much he earned. Well, it hardly mattered now except that he would have the raising of her daughter in his hands – still better him than Fliss's mother!

She looked around her as she walked slowly ahead of him. Her teeth were chattering but whether from fear or cold she didn't know – probably both, she thought, suddenly aware that the last time she had been this afraid was a couple of days ago, when she thought she saw a dead man standing by her side. Now she had a man who was very much alive, and it was more terrifying than she could ever have imagined.

Her gaze darted from side to side, trying to see an escape route, but she quickly realised it was no use trying to run in here. Row upon row of changing cubicles, showers and lockers made the place a maze of dead ends and corners with unknown destinations. She had no idea how to get out – and he, of course, would know the place well.

Through two more sets of doors and suddenly they were at the side of the pool. Her bare feet hit the tiles and she shuddered, partly from cold but mostly because she knew that this was where she was going to die. He wouldn't change his mind; he wouldn't take pity on her. His only thoughts were for himself and what he wanted. In his narrow world other people were merely appendages, for his use or disposal, as he thought fit.

It was dim in there, with only the late evening sun casting a slight orange glow through the huge windows at the far end. There was another glow there and it gave Fliss a sudden surge of hope. It was the green exit sign above the fire escape door. If she ran and pushed with all her strength, she should be able to open the fire door. They were never locked, were they? Not in a place like this.

She didn't wait to analyse the situation any further, and just began to sprint towards the far end of the pool, but fate conspired against her again. She had forgotten she was slick with oil from her massage – and the girl had soothed almost every inch of her body. As soon as she tried to gain purchase enough to run, the oil reacted with the smooth tiles and their surface sprinkling of water that had trickled from the bodies of the last swimmers. Her feet slid wildly and she seemed to be moving in painfully slow motion. He had no difficulty at all in catching up with her and throwing her to the ground in an unnecessarily violent rugby tackle.

She lay winded and bruised and he rose to his feet, laughing softly, "You're feisty, I'll say that for you. Goodbye, Mrs Elmsworth." Before she had time to gather her wits enough to understand what was happening, he had simply grabbed the edge of the towel and used it to flip her into the pool.

The water was freezing and hit her with a shock that almost made her gasp, until she realised that to do so would be to suck water and not air into her lungs. She began to kick and struggle her way to the surface, the bubbles rushing past her face, and the water filling her ears, so that all she could hear was the muffled rushing of her beating hands and feet.

She managed to lift her face above the water for a brief moment and drag some air into her lungs before she felt his hand grasp her hair and plunge her back beneath the surface. She reached up and tried desperately to loosen his fingers, scratching and clawing at his flesh, praying that she was hurting him enough to make him let go. She might have been swiping at him with a feather for all the notice he took. Every time she moved her arm, sharp pains shot down her side and her lungs burned as the air in them became spent and useless. She was tiring rapidly and knew she was going to have to give up. She thought of Megan's little face, smiling at her and it gave her the strength for one last effort, but still he would not release her and she felt icy blackness stealing over her. He held her until the struggling stopped then with one final contemptuous shove, he pushed her deep under the water and away from the side.

Miraculously she felt the floor of the pool beneath her feet and the darkness receded. With the slightest movement she could manage, she pressed her toes onto the bottom and lifted her face upwards to the top, stealing a silent gasp of air before letting herself drop once more. Her only chance now was to let him think she was dead. If she could convince him of that, he would go away and she could clamber out of the bone-chilling water. Hopefully the fact that it was rapidly darkening outside would ensure that he couldn't see her clearly enough to suspect she was still alive. The desire to cough and choke was overwhelming, but somehow she controlled it. The delicate lining of her nose burned unbearably with the chlorine in the water, and her hair was draped annoyingly over her face, but still she lay still, barely daring to breathe.

Suddenly there was a commotion outside and it took all her will-power to ignore it and lie perfectly still on her back, letting herself sink and rise with the movement of the water, which was still disturbed from her frantic struggles seconds before. She could feel his eyes on her, hard, unfeeling, searching for any sign of life.

Police sirens screamed outside on the lawn and the blue flashing lights lit the pool then faded in quick succession. Suddenly all the lights came on and she heard a male voice shout, "Christ almighty, she's in the pool!" There was a splash as someone dived in, but she kept her eyes firmly shut. It could be a trick of his to test her. She felt hands grab at her waist, but she slid from their grasp, her oily skin making it impossible for the man to hold her.

"Felicity!" her name was wrenched from his lips in despair and she opened her eyes, "John? Is that you?" With speech came the longed-for cough and soon she could not stop, choking and spluttering and treading water in a desperate attempt not to sink again.

"Thank God!" he said fervently, "I thought he'd killed you."

"He tried," she said.

"Are you alright?"

"No, I'm in agony. I think I've broken a rib."

"Can you get to the side?"

"I think so." They reached the ladder and she managed to hoist herself up and out, using only her left arm. Her right side felt bruised and swollen and she could barely raise her arm at all. She felt him try to help her with his hand in the small of her back, but once again the oily skin defeated him and she had to take the hand of the waiting police woman, who thankfully had had the presence of mind to pick up the towel and wrap her in it the moment she emerged from the pool. It was then that she remembered that she was practically stark naked except for her panties. She clasped the towel around her, still shaking, her knees so wobbly that she would barely stand upright.

As Douglas walked past her, a policeman on either side, he said softly, "Your daughter is upstairs alone with Tanya. I just rang her on my mobile phone."

For a split second she was frozen to the spot, trying to make sense of what he had just said to her then she began to scream hysterically and tried to run for the door, "Megan! She's got Megan!"

The policewoman grabbed her shoulders and pulled her back, "No, she hasn't love. We went and found Tanya first, that's how we knew where you were. Megan's safe."

"What?"

John was climbing out of the pool, his clothes dripping onto the tiled floor, "It's alright, Felicity. Megan is perfectly safe, I promise. There was a policeman standing next to Tanya when she took Douglas's call."

She closed her eyes and sent up a silent prayer of thanks, but the shock coupled with overwhelming relief made her sway unsteadily and she found herself being swept up into John's arms, "We're going to get you to the hospital, Felicity. Don't worry about a thing."

"No," she murmured faintly, "I want Megan. I'm not going without Megan."

"Megan will come with us, don't fret."

＊

Afterwards she could never recall how she arrived at the hospital. She supposed she must have passed out, but she didn't remember that either. She recalled being put into the ambulance, and Megan's frightened little face level with hers as she stood by the side of her mother's stretcher – then nothing, until she was tucked up warm and safe in a private room, with John and Megan both watching her as she opened her eyes.

John smiled at her, "Feeling better?"

"I'm not dead then?" she asked facetiously, wondering why and how she could joke. Perhaps it was the sight of his drawn face, trying to be casual and comforting, when he was so obviously concerned about her.

"Not quite. Though I'm not quite sure how you managed to avoid it."

"Nor am I. He was very determined. Thank God for older

300

brothers always trying to hold you under when you went swimming as kids."

He smiled grimly then commented, "I'm still not quite sure why he felt the need to do away with you. I suppose trying to get Ted jailed was reason enough in his sick mind for his other murders, but why you?"

"He thought I could identify the bog man," she explained quietly. He evidently didn't understand what she was saying, because the frown deepened, "He thought what?"

"Fergus overheard us talking about the apparition in the farmhouse parlour. He told Douglas that I knew what the bog man looked like and he knew if I could tell the police who he was, the trail would lead straight to Douglas and Merrington Hall."

"Oh, my God! A bad dream nearly cost you your life?"

"Douglas seemed pretty confident that it wasn't just a dream."

"Douglas is a homicidal maniac," he replied decidedly, without a trace of humour.

She found herself laughing anyway, then winced as it pulled on her broken rib,

"Don't, it kills!"

"Sorry. Do you want me to call the nurse?"

"Yes, but only if she has my clothes so that I can go home."

"I don't think they're planning on letting you out just yet."

"I think you'll find they can't stop me," she said, determination writ all over her face.

He was spared the need to respond when a light tapping on the door heralded the arrival of Emma, who peeped in and asked brightly, "Do I disturb?"

"Not at all," said Fliss politely if unenthusiastically.

She wondered why Emma looked a little sheepish, but she didn't have long to wait to find out.

"I want to apologise to you, Fliss," said the vicar rather breathlessly, "I really do feel most responsible for this terrible event."

"Why should you?" asked Fliss, genuinely surprised, "It wasn't your doing."

"No, but if I hadn't let Tanya persuade me out of collecting you myself, Douglas would never have been able to do what he did."

"Oh, that," exclaimed Fliss, "Think no more about it. I'm a big girl now, I should have known not to go off with strangers – and let's face it, they don't come much stranger than Douglas Merrington!"

Emma smiled weakly, "Even so ..." she murmured, "Anyway," she added, rallying,

"Is there anything else I can do for you? Do you need anything?"

"No, I'm fine, thanks. In fact as soon as the doctor gives me the okay, I'm going home."

"You're going to have to stay here for the next couple of hours at least," intercepted John,

"The police want to question you as soon as you feel fit enough."

The vicar glanced at Megan, sitting so quietly, her big eyes going from one adult to the other as they spoke, "Well, at least let me take Megan off your hands. This is really no place for her, is it?"

Fliss looked uncomfortable at the very suggestion, "I don't think ..."

"Oh, please, Fliss. Let me do something for you. I really do need to be of use – you have no idea ..."

Fliss began to feel utterly weary and under pressure. She just thought, "whatever" but kindly didn't say it merely substituting the stock answer of any mum with young children,

"It's really nice of you Emma, but she's going to fall asleep, then I'll have to disturb her later when I collect her."

"Nonsense, she can stay the night! I have a lovely spare bedroom. That will give you a whole evening and a good night's sleep to recover from all this."

Fliss had to admit that the prospect sounded tempting, "If you're really sure ..." she said uncertainly.

"Positive. I'd love to have some company and you'd like to come home with Aunt Emma, wouldn't you Megan?" turning the little girl who stared at her wide-eyed for a moment before nodding obediently.

"That's all settled then," said Emma joyfully and within a few minutes she had put the flowers she had brought into a vase, put Megan's coat on, and led the little girl off down the corridor.

John looked at her as she watched them walk through the door together and as soon as it had closed behind them he commented, "If you are really not happy about that arrangement, sweetheart, I'll go after her and bring Megan back. I can watch her while you speak to the Inspector."

She smiled gratefully, but shook her head, "I'll have to learn to let her out of my sight sooner or later."

"You are a remarkable woman, do you know that?"

She gazed at him in surprise, "Me? Why on earth would you think that?"

He shook his head, "You just are. Not two hours ago you were on the point of being drowned and now you can sit calmly here and do what is best for your daughter, even though it's causing you distress."

"That's just being a parent. You would do the same for your daughter, wouldn't you?"

"I'd like to think so."

"Well, there you are then – nothing special, just a mum."

He took her hand, "I really thought we'd lost you back there. It was one of the most horrific moments of my life, seeing you in that pool."

"Was my naked body really that bad?" she joked, suddenly aware that he was getting too serious and she was at a loss how to react. Was he seeing her as a friend – or something more? He had kissed her, but she had asked him to – and how many men would refuse the offer of a kiss?

"What?" He looked confused for a moment, then light dawned and he laughed, "I'd like to be able to assure you that I hadn't noticed you were unclothed, Felicity, but it would be a lie. Actually, that made your loss seem even more of a waste."

It served her right, she thought, as the blush spread over her cheeks. Never make light of something unless you know you can take the ensuing banter without embarrassment!

"Oh dear God, how humiliating this is!" she admitted, covering her face with her hands, "I don't know why I'm trying to make jokes about it, when you and several policemen, including, as I recall, Mr Piper, have seen me in the buff! Why couldn't bloody Douglas Merrington try to kill me when I had my clothes on?"

"I'm so sorry. I would never have mentioned it if you hadn't done so first."

"I wish I hadn't now."

"If it is any consolation at all, I can assure you we were all thinking about how to save you. Your lack of swim suit was the last thing on my mind, at any rate."

She dropped her hands into her lap, "John, I want to ask you something."

"Anything at all, my dear."

"How do you ..."

The door opened and DI Piper walked in, "Feeling fit enough to talk to me now, Mrs Elmsworth?" he said.

CHAPTER THIRTY TWO

"Thomas the Rhymer, slipped in and out of the Otherworld, drawing on divine sources for inspiration. Bards, Like Druids possessed supernatural powers of prophecy"

John rose hastily to his feet, "I'll go and get a coffee or something and leave you to it. I'll come back later." Was it her imagination, or was he glad to be given a chance to escape? He certainly seemed eager to be gone, for he shot through the door the policeman was holding for him before she had chance to protest. There was no way in a million years she was going to continue with the question she had begun, when he came back – if he ever did.

Piper seemed to notice the melancholy expression on her face because he asked sympathetically, "Are you sure you're okay? Because we can delay this a little if you need to."

"No, I'm fine. Ask me anything you like."

He took the chair that John had so recently and abruptly vacated and as he did so, Fliss found questions of her own flooding into her mind, "Actually, Mr Piper, do you think I could ask you something first?"

"Certainly. What is it?"

"How come you suddenly turned up at Merrington Hall, blue lights flashing? You had arrested Theo and John for the murders."

He shifted uncomfortably in his seat, "They were never arrested," he protested mildly.

"Alright, if you are going to be pedantic, they were assisting you with your enquiries," she countered, "But why the dash to the Hall. You couldn't have known I was in any danger."

"If you must know, it was Professor Norton. He was pacing the station like a caged lion, fretting about what had happened to you. In the end, just to shut him up, I rang the vicar to check you were there and safe."

"And she told you I was with Tanya?"

"Yes,"

"But so what? You had no reason to suspect Douglas and Tanya at that point, had you?"

"Not really. But there were several things that didn't quite add up. For a start Merrington hadn't sent a solicitor even though Emma said you had asked him to. Then she told us that you said that Merrington knew about Fergus's murder – but we hadn't released any information."

"That didn't worry me overly because unfortunately I had told Bryn and I know how Bryn loves to gossip."

"I thought of that, but when I confronted Bryn he swore he had not been in touch with Merrington – or anyone else for that matter – since hearing of the murder."

Fliss looked contemptuous, "I've learned to my cost that you can't believe a thing Bryn says."

Piper smiled grimly, "Maybe not, but he sounded sincere enough to worry me. Then I remembered you had told me that the Hall was a covert rehab clinic. Everything fell into place. A murdered drug addict will never be very far from a source of help or drugs. I decided to check and found that both Tanya and Zak Oldthorpe have past records for drug dealing. Tanya also has one for drug smuggling and spent two years inside for manslaughter when she hit her pimp over the head with a brick. That was enough to convince me that I had better get my men to Merrington Hall – and worry about looking an idiot afterwards. Douglas Merrington doesn't exactly make a secret of his feud with Ted – and Ted was spot on when he said that all complaints about him either come directly from Merrington, or can be traced back to his agents."

"I knew Theo wasn't the violent thug he'd been painted!"

"He's no pussy cat either," said Piper severely.

"Yes, he is," she said with an affectionate smile. He didn't bother to argue. She evidently knew a very different man than most

306

other people.

"Then Professor Norton admitted that the stone circle where Fergus had been murdered was a fake built by Ted's great grandfather," he went on, "As he logically pointed out; if Ted and his druid mates were making human sacrifices to appease their gods, they would do it in the real circle – and be a bit more careful about covering it up afterwards. Ted would hardly have volunteered to take you and little Megan up into the woods and show you the real circle if he had known there was a mutilated body to be found – sun-rise on the stones my eye!" She had the grace to blush at being caught out in her obvious lie, but managed to plough on to find out the rest of the story.

"And that sent you to Merrington Hall, guns blazing?"

"Not just that. The look on John's face when I broke it to him you were with Tanya told me everything I needed to know. He had been harbouring similar doubts, but dismissing them. The moment he realised you were in Douglas's hands convinced him that he no longer wanted to give the man the benefit of the doubt."

"So it was John who made you come and save me?" she asked breathlessly, her eyes aglow.

He smiled at her tone, "Are you asking me something else, Mrs Elmsworth?" She couldn't meet his eyes, "Of course not. I don't know what you mean."

"In my vast experience of the human condition, I'd say he's crazy about you," he said conspiratorially, then added sternly, "Now, shall we get back to official business?"

She smiled happily, "Is he really?"

"Yes. Now it's my turn to ask questions. There is one thing that has been puzzling us all, why did Merrington suddenly throw caution to the winds and attack you? He's been careful to cover his tracks until now."

Fliss looked thoroughly embarrassed, "You wouldn't believe me if I told you," she said at last.

"Try me," he responded succinctly.

"He thought I was going to be able to identify the bog man for you."

"I assume he had a reason?"

"It's a very odd reason. I'm afraid you'll think we are both mad."

"I already think he is so tell me anyway," he advised his tone carefully neutral.

She drew in a deep breath, suddenly aware that she had no choice but to be totally honest with him. Her only defence would be to state the facts in as normal and frank a manner as possible.

"On the night we found the body, I was alone in the parlour of the farmhouse. I fell asleep in the chair and had a graphic dream in which the bog man appeared next to me, still alive, blood pouring from his slashed throat."

He raised an eyebrow but made no comment, so she continued, "Unknown to me, Fergus was creeping around, listening in to conversations, spying, apparently, for Douglas. He heard me describe the man to John. He told Douglas because he thought it was bizarre, but the description must have been close enough for Douglas to imagine that I really had seen the man and could identify him."

"And lead the trail directly to him? You must have been pretty convincing, Mrs Elmsworth."

"I suppose I must."

"Do you believe you could recognise the man if I showed you pictures of missing persons? It would save us a fortune in face reconstruction if you could."

She was astounded, "You would really take my word for it, if I saw his picture?"

"No reason why not. Stranger things have happened."

"Then I'll give it a go. Is his face not recognisable now? I thought he was well-preserved."

"He was – for a three thousand year-old corpse – but not particularly for a modern one. The trouble was, he was left out in the open for about twelve hours, so birds, animals and flies had a bit of a go before he went into the ground."

"Yes, I knew that. Douglas told me. He said he'd left him to be found and frame Theo, but then a sister had turned up and said he'd told her where he had gone to de-tox. Douglas panicked when he realised the body could be traced to him, so he decided to bury it before anyone found it."

"It must have been a god-send that the bog had dried up. He could dig a grave in the certain knowledge that the rain would soon refill the marsh and ensure the body was never found."

"Except that it was."

"Yeah, but until you saw your ghost, he must have thought his secret would be pretty safe."

"I still don't understand why he had to kill Fergus too. The bog man was found on Theo's land, so he would always have been your first suspect."

"Douglas wasn't satisfied with that. He was afraid the forensics wouldn't be strong enough to convict Ted – and apparently Fergus had been hitting the bottle and telling anyone who would listen that he was earning a bit of extra cash on the side by keeping Merrington informed of the goings on at the dig. It was partly a punishment for betrayal, but mostly to keep his mouth shut. Douglas likes to think he is untouchable. Fergus was exposing him for the snide little creep he really is. Funnily enough he harbours an enormous admiration for John Norton. He calls him the only man he's never been able to buy."

"But John allows Douglas to fund his digs."

"Yes, but he doesn't let him control proceedings – and if nothing else, Douglas Merrington is your classic control freak."

"So it was Fergus who leaked the story to the press and told Douglas everything before John had a chance to contact him?"

"Not just Fergus. Douglas had another mole, keeping an eye on Fergus."

"Who?"

"I'm afraid it was your husband, Mrs Elmsworth. I'm sorry."

"How do you know all this?" she asked coldly, and he imagined it was because she wanted to defend her husband's reputation, which he felt was quite understandable.

"Phone records," he said shortly, leaving no possibility of argument.

"I suppose that's why Bryn had a mobile that I didn't know about. No doubt Douglas paid for it," she mused sadly. Why had Bryn done all this? Was he really so short of money that he had thrown in his lot with Merrington and betrayed the man who had tried to help him? Perhaps drugs really were at the base of it all and there were more debts that she didn't know about? Well, it wasn't her problem now, unless he had used her name – and she would cross that bridge when she came to it. Then she would push Bryn Elmsworth off it!

"He did. You must find this hard to believe, I know."

Fliss wrinkled her nose in a slight sneer, "The trouble is, I don't find it hard to believe at all! What I don't understand is how I ever fell for the bloody rat in the first place."

Even Piper didn't have an answer for that one.

She looked suddenly sad, "I wish I knew why Tanya had let me down. She seemed so nice, but Douglas hinted that she would have hurt Megan with one word from him. How could she be so in his power that she would even harm a child for him?"

"I can answer that in one word. Drugs. She's hooked on crack cocaine, amongst other things. There's one creature in this life you can never trust and that's an addict. They'd do anything for their next fix."

Fliss was shocked, "Is that true? Is she really a drug addict? She seemed so elegant and self-assured."

"If you have money you can hide anything beneath a façade of respectability, even drug addiction. She relied on Douglas for everything from the clothes on her back to her regular supply of drugs. She'll have a bad time in prison getting clean."

"But why is she going to prison? She didn't harm Megan, thank God."

"No, but she did lure Fergus up onto the moors with a promise of sex amongst the stones. And the poor sap went like a lamb to the slaughter. Douglas was waiting behind one of the stones to smack him on the head with the ceremonial axe – which he then replaced in the barn, by the way – and the rest, as they say, is history."

He rose to his feet, "Well, I think that's about all I want for now.

310

Can I send some photos over for you to look at? I've narrowed the search down considerably, but there are still quite a few possibilities. Thousands of people go missing every year – most of them because they want to."

"Don't send them here. I'm going home."

"Home being?"

"Theo's, of course."

In Piper's opinion there was no "of course" about it. Living in a crumbling manor house with Ted Armitage wasn't his idea of home, but there was no accounting for taste.

"And your little girl? Do you need Social Services to put her into care for a couple of days, while you recover?"

"No!" A little too emphatic, Felicity, she warned herself silently, "No thank you," she added in a more conciliatory tone, "She's with Emma for tonight, and I'll be fine by tomorrow."

"Well, goodbye, then. Take care. I'll see you in a day or two when you think you might have our man."

"Goodbye Inspector. If you see John, will you ask him to come back in here?"

"I will."

She sat for a long time thinking about everything. There was no doubt in her mind now that her marriage was over. The very thought of being in the same room with Bryn filled her with revulsion, never mind picking up their lives where they had left off. It had been coming for a long time, but this was definitely the end. She might just have been able to forgive the loan-sharks if he had convinced her that he was desperate for money and hadn't meant to put Megan in danger. Even trying to sell the house over their heads was despicable, but understandable if he really believed he would suffer physical harm if he didn't pay off his debts. But this was beyond anything she could forgive. She now believed that he didn't need money – he just wanted it – and that was an entirely different thing. There was very little sadness when she came to this conclusion, rather an overwhelming sense of relief. She hoped he wouldn't request access to Megan, but she knew him well enough to know that he would insist upon it – mostly just to aggravate her. Well, so long as he behaved himself, she had no real objection to his seeing his daughter. He may not have been father of the year, but he had never harmed her either – well, not personally.

This led her to thinking about John and her stomach gave a little somersault at the thought of seeing him again. Was she in love with him? She thought so, but it was too soon after Bryn to make a firm decision. She would not be the same fool she had been when she married Bryn. This time she would take things slowly. If John loved her, he would have to show a degree of patience he had probably never been called upon to display in his life before. If he couldn't accept that, then he would be out of the door. It was ridiculous to imagine she had met the love of her life when the worst mistake of her life had only just been exposed! And she had Megan to think about. The poor little thing had been through enough for the moment.

There was a knock and she jumped slightly, so deeply engrossed in her thoughts had she been, "Come in," she called and John opened the door.

"Are you still adamant you want to leave?" he asked.

"Yes, as soon as possible."

"Good, because Ted is on his way with some clothes for you. I took the liberty of ringing him. Unfortunately I don't have my car. I came here in a police car, following your ambulance."

"Thank you," she said fervently.

"My pleasure. Now, you were about to ask me something, before we were so rudely interrupted."

She looked at him, taking pleasure in examining his features. Yes, she conceded, he had a good face, trustworthy, handsome, full of character, kind.

"It doesn't matter," she said slowly, "It will do another time."

✳

Fliss felt her heart lift with gladness when she spotted the twisted chimneys of Barrow Loe Farm between the branches of the surrounding trees. She had never noticed before that they were fancy brick Tudor affairs. It really was a lovely old house – or it could be if it was fully restored. She glanced at Theo sitting next to her and asked, "Did you ever get your money for the dig, Theo?"

"Most of it. Why?"

"You could afford some repairs on the house now, couldn't you?"

He grinned at her then returned his gaze to the road, "Having second thoughts about living in a derelict hovel? Don't worry, it's all in hand."

"Are you really going to fix it up?" she asked excitedly.

"Yep. The work is due to start next month. I was waiting until the dig was finished, but it looks as though that's over and done with for the time being."

"Well, there's a whole new circle to investigate now, isn't there?" intercepted John from the back seat.

"Come up with the cash and you can dig to your heart's content," promised Theo, with a slightly malicious smile.

"Very funny," growled John.

"Now, now boys, behave. You know you still love each other really," said Fliss, trying not to laugh. Poor John. It really had hit him quite hard, finding out he'd been duped.

"John, I know I owe you something for all I've put you through," said Theo suddenly serious, "so I'm promising that you can investigate the real circle – but on your own. I don't want the place ploughed up by a crowd of students."

Fliss glanced over her shoulder and was delighted to see that this compromise by Theo had cheered John considerably.

"You, my friend, have yourself a deal," he said warmly.

CHAPTER THIRTY THREE

"Vortigern tried to build a grand castle, but the walls kept crumbling. The boy Merlin was consulted and told of two dragons that battled beneath the site every night, destroying the walls"

Fliss had quite a bit of discomfort when she tried to climb out of the Land Rover. It had been bad enough scrambling up into it with cracked ribs, but getting down was worse. In the end Theo lifted her into his arms and carried her indoors.

"You can put me down now," she commented as they went through the kitchen and into the hall.

"You are going to lie on the settee in comfort and I'm going to cook dinner," he said firmly.

"Okay," she meekly replied, "But find me a book or something or I'll die of boredom."

"John can sit and talk to you. I can't help feeling you two have plenty to say to each other."

John, who was following him through the house, frowned slightly at this assumption, but made no protest. Fliss, who was watching him over Theo's shoulder, was not impervious to the implication. He didn't want to talk to her, obviously, so she must be entirely wrong to think he had any intentions towards her. What an old fashioned expression that was, she mused, intentions. What on earth did it mean anyway? Everyone had intentions; they intended to mug you, they intended to ignore you, they intended to make love to you...but apparently he didn't, so that was that.

There was an awkward silence between them after Theo put her on the sofa and went off to the kitchen. At least to Fliss it seemed awkward. John merely examined the book shelves until he found a title that appealed to him.

"What are you going to do, now?" she asked him, unable to bear the lack of conversation any longer.

"Read a book – unless you want to watch television or play cards or something," he answered, absent-mindedly.

"Cards would be good – but actually I meant in life. The dig is suspended for now, so there's nothing for you to do here, is there?"

He picked up a pack of cards that he knew were kept on the shelf and began to shuffle,

"I suppose I ought to go home."

"You don't sound very enthused about the prospect," she told him. This was better. They were almost back to normal, talking as they always had, like friends.

"I'm not." He frowned and dealt seven cards each.

"What are we playing?"

He looked into her eyes, "God knows. It's like no game I've ever played before, Felicity."

He wasn't talking about the cards.

She couldn't breathe. She literally couldn't breathe; it felt as though her heart had swelled into her throat and closed off her trachea. She tried to swallow and managed to force out the words she longed to say to him, "You must know I'm not into playing games, John. It's madness that I'm in love with you. It doesn't make any sense at all – and I have to be sensible. I have a child."

"You also have a husband." He didn't meet her gaze, but flipped the edges of his cards in an extremely annoying manner.

"Thanks for reminding me. I told you it was madness. Well, now I've said it, let's forget it and pretend nothing happened." She was horrified that he had mentioned Bryn, when she had been struggling so hard to forget him. Would the man never stop causing her trouble, even when she had resolved to get him out of her life?

"How can I do that?"

"Try," she said brutally, "I'm going to have to. When are you leaving?"

315

"Tomorrow morning I think. Felicity …"

"Don't say anything else. Please, just don't. It's bad enough that I've made a fool of myself. Don't, for God's sake, compound it by trying to ease the rejection."

He had been sitting on the chair opposite her, in preparation for playing cards, but now he tossed his hand onto the coffee table and went to her, kneeling on the floor beside her, "Felicity, this is not a rejection, I promise. But I don't care to break up a marriage. It's just not me, I'm sorry. I admit I have been at fault. I allowed myself to get close to you when I should have walked away."

"You are not breaking up my marriage," she said coldly.

"I think perhaps I am. And while there is a doubt in my mind …"

"Okay, I get the picture. You are afraid of how you'll be judged by the world. Come back in twelve months when my divorce is through."

He rose to his feet and thrust his fisted hands into his pockets, "Damn it all, I don't know how to deal with this situation. I'm trying to be sensible for us both. How long have we known each other? Something like five days?"

"Exactly five days. Just tell me how you feel about me, John," she said softly, "I just want to know if I've made a complete fool of myself."

He paced the room, fiddling with ornaments, straightening books, doing anything but looking at her, "When I thought I had lost you …"

"What? What did you feel then? A bit sorry, broken-hearted, suicidal?" she demanded passionately.

The smile came back to his face then, "Felicity, I was utterly appalled by what I felt. I wanted to grab Douglas Merrington and break every bone in his body."

"That's a start, I suppose."

"Give me some time, my dear. I need to think."

"If you need to think, then you don't feel the same way as I do. Shall we play?"

She made it quite obvious that the conversation was over by picking up her cards and fanning them out, "How about Rummy?

I have a great hand."

He sat back in his chair and picked up his own cards, "Rummy it is."

When Theo came in with Fliss's supper on a tray, one glance at the two set faces told him that not much had been resolved. He gave a mental shrug. He had done his best, but you could only push so much.

The two men went into the kitchen to eat and left her alone. The tears dripped down her cheeks and plopped into her gravy. Of course he was right; it was crazy to be trying to plan a future when the past was barely finished with. She would just have to learn to be patient.

She hastily wiped her face when the door opened, but it was only Theo to collect the tray.

"Do you want any pudding?" he asked and she shook her head. He glanced down at the barely touched meal, "You're going to have to eat more than that if you want to work on a farm."

"I will, when I get back to normal. Where's John?"

"Gone upstairs to pack."

"He means it then? He really is going?"

"Seems that way. I gather you two didn't come to any conclusions."

"No – well, no pleasant ones, anyway. I was fooling myself, Theo. He doesn't care about me at all."

"Of course he does. But you're not the only one with baggage, you know."

She looked up at him, her eyes full of tears, "What do you mean?"

"He hasn't had a serious relationship since his wife died. He's had a minor fling about every two years, on average."

This she hadn't been expecting. In fact she had not considered for a moment how he had filled his time when he wasn't digging holes. She didn't know if she was more shocked that he had been having affairs, or that he hadn't been in a committed relationship for ten years.

"What was she like?" she asked at last. He met her gaze

squarely, "She was a very attractive woman, funny, clever. John adored her and no other woman has come close – until now."

"Oh, Theo," Fliss covered her face with her hands and sobbed in good earnest, grasping her side as she did so, where her broken rib was giving her considerable pain. He sank to his haunches and hugged her, "It'll all come right in the end, love, you'll see."

✳

Fliss had fallen asleep on the sofa after being fed painkillers and sympathy by Theo, a slight frown on her face. John looked in but seeing she was sleeping, he went into the kitchen to join Theo, who was reading the paper and drinking one of his interminable cups of tea.

"Fancy a cup?" he asked, glancing up. John nodded and took a seat. Theo poured him a mug and added milk, "All packed?" he added conversationally, determined not to give his friend any indication of his feelings. Fliss was on her own with this one.

"Yes. Thanks," he added, as he took the drink, "I'll leave first thing, if that's okay with you."

"Fine. Do you want me to wake you?"

"No, I suspect I'll be up at the crack of dawn. Sleep seems to be eluding me at the present time."

"I wonder why that should be?" mused Theo, "I've been sleeping like a log."

"Lucky old you," said John stiffly.

There was a short silence during which both men drank their tea and Theo noisily turned his paper back on itself.

"Do you have any plans to come back?" he asked after a few minutes.

"Of course. There's the other circle to investigate."

"Any idea when?"

"Does it matter to you?"

"Not to me, no." Theo eyed him and grinned. John put his cup down on the table and rose to his feet, "Stop it, Ted, will you. This is none of your business."

"You're right, it isn't – except that I'm going to be the comforting shoulder for the next couple of months – and I don't know if I can trust myself not to take advantage of your absence."

The only indication he gave that this had hit a nerve was when John's jaw tightened perceptibly. It seemed to Theo that he was on the point of saying something quite acerbic, his expression certainly hinted at it, but then the telephone rang and he went to answer it, casting the farmer a glare as he left the room. Theo merely grinned all the more.

Fliss had woken when the phone rang and had struggled to her feet and out into the hall. She was doubled over with the pain from her rib and John was torn between going to her aid and answering the call. She made the decision for him by waving him away and sitting down on a convenient chair.

It was DI Piper and he was imparting bad news.

"Professor Norton?"

"Yes, is that Matt? What can I do for you?"

"Something rather odd has happened, professor, and though it's not within my jurisdiction, I thought the news would be better coming from me."

"That sounds ominous. What's the trouble?"

Fliss lifted a frightened face and John smiled reassuringly at her, mouthing that there was nothing to concern her.

"We've had a call from some clerk at the Ministry instructing us to close Barrow Loe Farm to the public ASAP. It seems they've had an anonymous tip-off that there's a suspected Foot and Mouth outbreak."

John was astounded, "That's complete rubbish. What the hell is going on?"

"Look, professor, you know it's rubbish and so do I – and in the morning someone will be there to prove it, but in the meantime I'm obliged to warn you that no-one must go in or out. Listen to me, John, I'm serious. You all have to stay there until further notice."

"Just a minute, Matt. I'll have to speak to Mrs Elmsworth and Ted."

He called Ted from the kitchen and briefly explained the

situation. Fliss's face drained of the colour that hadn't been particularly abundant in the first place, "No! I can't stay here. Megan is at the vicarage. I have to collect her in the morning. She'll be frantic if I don't turn up – and anyway, I want her back."

"Alright, Felicity, don't worry, I'll explain that to the Inspector."

He did so, but Piper was adamant, "I'm sorry John, but no one in or out. Megan will have to stay with the vicar until you've been given the all clear."

John shook his head at her, but Fliss limped across and took the handset away from him, "Inspector Piper?"

"Yes, Mrs Elmsworth, I'm still here."

"Good. Please listen to me. I must get to Megan. You know as well as I do that there is no Foot and Mouth on this farm. The accusation will have come from Douglas Merrington as all the others did. He's just trying to cause trouble again."

"Mrs Elmsworth," said Piper patiently, "I'd agree with you except that Merrington is still in custody and has spent the day answering questions with his solicitor. I'm afraid he has more urgent things on his mind that annoying Ted Armitage."

"But he has friends – or employees at any rate – to do it for him."

"I really don't think so, madam. Now please just do as I have asked or there could be serious consequences."

In despair Fliss handed the phone back to John, who listened for a few moments more then replaced it in its cradle.

"Well, that's that."

Fliss limped back into the parlour and John stared after her, his expression one of pure frustration that he could do nothing to help her. Theo went resignedly back to the kitchen. He was used to having Government Ministers ruling his life.

When the telephone shrilled again ten minutes later, Fliss leapt up, giving a groan of pain as she did so, but still she managed to reach the hall before either of the men.

It was Emma and her voice was lowered to a distraught whisper, "Fliss, is that you? Your husband is downstairs. I've managed to sneak up here with my mobile. He's insisting that I wake Megan and hand her over to him. I've told him that she has been asleep for hours and that you left her in my care, but he is threatening to call the police and have me charged with unlawful imprisonment of a minor or abduction or something."

Fliss's legs suddenly refused to hold her up and she groped her way to the nearest seat. She was icy cold and shaking. She knew now who had made the anonymous call. It was Bryn. And this was to be her punishment for leaving him. He meant to steal Megan from her. She thought quickly and spoke frantically down the phone, "Emma, he's bluffing. The police won't take any notice of him. For God's sake, don't let him take my daughter!"

Emma was equally panic-stricken, "Fliss, you must come and fetch her now. I really don't have the right to keep her against his will – he's her father and I'm nothing to her. I can only hold him off if I can tell him you are on your way."

Fliss tried to speak very calmly, but tears were very near, "Inspector Piper has just told me that I'm not allowed to leave the farm. I can't get there before tomorrow. Emma, you must tell him no!"

There was a shocked silence then Emma hissed, "Oh God, he's coming up the stairs. I'll have to go. I'll do my best, but I don't see how I can prevent him for taking his own child."

The line went dead and Fliss turned a ravaged face to John and Theo who both stood in the kitchen doorway, deeply concerned though puzzled as they had only heard one side of the conversation.

"What is it, love?" asked Theo gently.

"Bryn is at the vicarage, trying to take Megan away from Emma and she says she can't stop him. Theo, he has my baby!"

CHAPTER THIRTY FOUR

"Owain, overcome with shame at wronging his wife,
fled into the wilderness and lived as a wild man"

Fliss broke the ensuing silence by holding out her hand to Theo, "Please give me the keys, Theo. I'll have to go and get her," she said calmly.

John took a step forward and spoke briskly, but with a soothing overtone that infuriated her, "You can't do that, Felicity."

"Give me one good reason," she demanded belligerently.

"I'll give you two. We've been told by an official of the Government not to leave the farm – and you can't possibly drive with a broken rib."

"I'll manage – and I'll face the wrath of some jumped up little jobs-worth when I have my child back in my arms."

"I'll drive you," said Theo.

She turned eyes shining with gratitude upon the farmer, "Oh Theo, thank you."

John intercepted hastily, "Ted, you can't do that."

"Save your breath to cool your porridge, John. Fliss needs help and I intend to give it."

Fliss cast John a defiant glance and began to head for the back door, but he caught her arm and said quietly, "Do you have any idea of the consequences if Ted goes ahead with this folly? He'll be fined heavily – he could end up losing his farm." She looked up at him for a few seconds then turned to Theo, "Is that really true?"

Theo shrugged and grinned, "Who cares? Some things are more important than money. Let's go."

That was enough for Fliss and she pulled her arm away from

John and carried on.

"Felicity, you can't ask Ted to risk everything out of affection for you."

She turned on him, "He's a grown man, he can make his own decisions. All I know is that if I don't get to Megan before Bryn, I may never see her again. You don't understand how vindictive my husband can be. He doesn't want our little girl – he never did – but he'll deprive me of her if he can."

John's face was pale in the dim light of the hallway, "Then I'll take you. I won't have Ted risk his livelihood."

She looked scornful, "I'll bet you've never broken a law in your life, and I won't ask you to do it now, when you are so obviously reluctant."

"I'm not going to argue with you. Just get your coat and we'll go. Ted, cover as best you can if we're not back before the man from the Ministry."

Theo had to lift her up into the Range Rover as she couldn't managed to hoist herself and when he stood beside her as she settled herself into the seat, she reached out and touched his cheek softly with her hand, "I'll never forget what you were prepared to do for me, Theo."

"Just fetch that little girl back, safe and sound," he answered, clasping her hand for a moment, before standing aside and slamming the car door. She waved to him as they drew away and thought he looked lonely and rather sad. She wondered why, after all, she was coming back.

"You know he's in love with you, don't you?" asked John quietly. She stared straight ahead and replied in as even a tone as she could manage, "No, he's not. He's just fond of me, as I am of him."

"If you say so," he said cynically. She rounded on him once again, still furiously angry with him, though not really very sure why, "If that was true, he would hardly encourage me to ..." she stopped hastily, aware that she had been about to give herself away.

"Encourage you to what?"

"Never mind. Just drive me to the vicarage then you can go

back to the farm and pretend you never broke the law – or that you ever met me."

Out of the corner of her eye, she saw his hands tighten on the wheel and his teeth clench, but he said nothing.

Emma was waiting at the gate for them, her arms wrapped around her body to try and keep out the cold wind that had suddenly risen. Fliss pressed the button that opened the window and shouted to her, "Has he gone?"

"He's taken her, Fliss, I'm so sorry. I delayed as long as I could. They've only just left, not five minutes ago."

Fliss was about to ask her to get her car out and take her on after them, but John leaned across her and asked tersely, "Which way did they go?"

Emma pointed to the road out of the village where Fliss had travelled on that very first day, which seemed so very long ago now, "I think they were heading for the motorway. He certainly told Megan she had to go to the loo because they wouldn't be able to stop again for a long time."

"Thanks. Ring Ted and tell him, will you?" John slammed the car into reverse, turned with very little space to spare on the narrow road, and roared away.

"What are you doing?" asked Fliss, rewinding the window. John glanced at her, his expression grimly determined, "I believe the term is 'giving chase'," he said.

"But you wanted no part of this. I was going to ask Emma to take me."

"We don't have any time to waste – and I've already been in police custody once this week – what more can they do to my reputation?"

She managed to laugh, "That was for murder too. You can't have much of a reputation left."

He put his foot down, "We could do with catching him before he gets to the motorway."

Bryn evidently thought he was quite safe because they caught up with him within ten minutes. Fliss was the first to see his tail-lights in the distance and alerted John. By now it was after eleven and the roads were deserted except for them, so John had no compunction about speeding up and trying to overtake, but as soon as Bryn recognised the vehicle in his rear-view mirror, he also speeded up and Fliss panicked, "Don't make him go any faster, John. These country lanes are lethal and he'll only have Megan in a seatbelt. I have the car seat at the farm."

John was forced to brake and follow along the interminable, winding roads, not daring to push the other man into reckless speeds.

"What do we do now?"

"We'll be able to overtake on the motorway – and anyway, I know where he is going." She assured him confidently.

"You do? Where?"

"Home. If he is going to do a moonlight flit, he won't leave his precious bloody computer behind."

"I don't think…"

"I'm telling you. I know Bryn. It's his livelihood. He'll hope to shake us off, then dash in and get the damn thing into the car. Where he will go after that is anybody's guess – he has friends all over the country and he'll be able to elude me for years. Megan will be grown up and forgotten I ever existed by the time …" she choked on a sob and he grasped her hand comfortingly, "That won't happen, I promise. Do you want me to try again to over-take?"

She shook her head, despair beginning to overtake her, "It's too dangerous. That's the difference between him and me – he won't care if he does kill Megan, but I can't take that risk."

They followed for what seemed like hours to the fraught Fliss. Her nerves were winding tighter and tighter with every bend. She sat forward, her eyes fixed on the lights ahead, her knuckles white against the dark leather of the car seats. Her rib ached intolerably, but she could not relax and when she started to see the signs for the motorway shining in the reflected headlights, the sickness that had been a vague feeling in the pit of her stomach threatened to make her vomit. She lowered the window by an inch and breathed deeply of the cold night air.

"Are you alright?" he asked with gentle concern and she nodded, too strung out to frame a reply.

All too soon they were on the slip road, but still John stayed behind Bryn. If he overtook him, it would avail them nothing, just give him the opportunity to take a junction off the motorway and then they would lose him completely.

Suddenly the car was filled with a bright light that faded as quickly as it began. John glanced in the mirror as Fliss asked, "What's going on?"

"A lorry behind is flashing me," said John, puzzled.

"Why?"

"I have no idea. I just hope there's nothing wrong with the car."

Bryn suddenly put his foot down and before John could react, the lorry behind swung out past him and cut him up.

"Quickly, get past him, I can't see Bryn," said Fliss in a panic. John started to do as she asked, but with a deafening blast of a horn and a shriek of reluctant acceleration, another lorry shot past them, then held its position right beside them. When John looked in the mirror again he realised that yet another juggernaut had joined the first two and he was effectively blocked into the inside lane, with one in front, one behind, and one right next to them.

"What the bloody hell are these maniacs playing at?" he said hoarsely, seriously shaken by the near miss he had just endured.

Fliss looked over her shoulder and realised what was happening. Her heart sank and the sickness threatened once more, "Oh God."

John blew his horn and flashed his lights, but it had absolutely no effect on the lorries, which maintained their positions with a stoicism that startled him.

"This is deliberate, Felicity, but I can't imagine why."

"It's Bryn," she said quietly.

"What? How can it be?"

"He has a CB radio – and he used to be a biker. He knows hundreds of bikers, truckers – you name it, if they use the roads Bryn has probably spoken to them over the years. He must have gone on the radio and asked for help. They'll shadow us until he's away and clear."

John suddenly realised that shadowing was not all that they intended. The lorry next to him was pulling ever so slightly towards him, forcing him to turn his wheel. Then he realised they had reached a slip road. He was being shepherded off the motorway. Bryn would be off and away, whilst they were led down a maze of dual carriageways.

"Get my phone and call the police," he said tersely, but he knew it was too late. The sound of the wheels on the road changed and a series of slight bumps told him he was crossing over the cat's eyes. They were off the motorway.

For about another five miles the lorries dogged them whilst Fliss spoke to the police and tried to explain where they were. Then as quickly as they had appeared, the truckers flashed their lights and thundered off into the night. John pulled into the first lay-by he saw and stopped, then rested his head on the steering wheel. Fliss could see that he was as white as a sheet and she longed to put comforting arms around him, but instead she tucked her hands securely under her thighs and waited for him to speak.

"Give me a minute, then we'll get under way again," he said quietly, "That was thoroughly unpleasant. What the devil must your husband have told them, to convince them to do that to us?"

"If I know the truckers that Bryn is friendly with, he won't have had to invent much of a story to prompt them to behave like maniacs! I'm so sorry John. You should never have been involved in all this."

"Are you okay?" he asked, ignoring her apology.

"Just about. There was a moment back there when I thought I was going to be sick all over your nice car," she said frankly. He lifted his head and smiled, "Don't do that, for God's sake. You'll stain the leather forever."

"I'll try not."

He drew in a deep breath, "Are you confident that Bryn is heading for your house?"

"Yes,"

"Then you had better direct me to it. We don't have any time to waste."

Fliss didn't think she could be wound any tighter, but the wave of relief that swept over her when she saw that Bryn's car was still in their driveway almost made her faint. Completely forgetting her broken body, she leapt to the ground before John had even stopped the car and she was running up the garden path, with her companion close on her heels. She prayed that Bryn hadn't put the bolt on the front door as she put her key in the lock. She closed her eyes against faintness when the door creaked slowly open.

At first the house seemed empty, then she heard Bryn's voice upstairs, "I'm warning you Megan, if you don't open this bloody door I'm going to break it down and then I'll give you the hiding of your life."

She half laughed and covered her mouth with her hand to smother the sob that broke from her. Megan had locked herself in the bathroom. God bless her, she knew how to manipulate her father perfectly.

She climbed the stairs, "Leave her alone, Bryn. The police are on their way so if I were you, I'd collect the computer and get the hell out of here."

He started violently, obviously so intent on his daughter that he hadn't heard their approach. His face was a mixture of fury and frustration, "You trained the little rat well, I'll grant you that, Fliss. She's driven me nuts all the way home. You are bloody well welcome to her."

He pushed his way past her and walked down the stairs. When he reached the bottom, he found John waiting for him. His sneer was short-lived. John grabbed him by the coat and pushed him crushingly against the hall wall, "God help me, I'd like to kick your head in!" he hissed. Bryn had never seen the laid-back John Norton so much as lose his temper before and it shocked him rigid for a second, but he soon recovered his bravado, "Get over it, John, I have. You're welcome to the bitch and her hell-cat of a kid."

John held him for a second longer, debating whether it was worth his while to plant his fist squarely in the middle of the smug face then he flung him away, so that Bryn fell full length up the hall, "As Felicity says, get your computer and get out! And I'd just like you to know that the cheque I gave you the other day has been cancelled."

Bryn looked as though he was going to get up and take the fight further, but then he suddenly changed his mind. Fliss, watching from the stairs wondered why, then she heard the faint sound of a police siren in the distance and all became clear.

"The computer is already in the car," he said, "I made sure I got that before I sorted the kid out – get your priorities right, I always say. Goodbye Fliss, be seeing you around."

With that he was gone. John slid down the wall and sat on the floor his arms resting on his knees and his head sunk between them. Fliss glanced at him but the pull of her daughter was stronger. She went back upstairs and John could hear her cajoling Megan through the bathroom door, "It's alright, sweetheart. Daddy's gone. You can come out now."

He heard the click of the bolt being shot and Fliss's strangled cry as she grasped her little girl and hugged her tight.

He closed his eyes for a moment then pulled himself together. Bryn's car had screeched off down the road just as the police entered at the other end and he briefly wished he had possessed the foresight to park his car across the drive to block Bryn's escape. On second thoughts, he added to himself, perhaps things are better the way they are.

A policeman appeared at the door, "Bryn Elmsworth?" he asked severely.

"No, John Norton, and Mrs Elmsworth is upstairs with her daughter."

"You got the little girl back then, sir?"

"Yes, thank you officer."

"Excellent, sir. I'm delighted. From what we've been told over the radio, you've had quite a time of it."

"You could say that," said John wearily.

"Well, if you don't mind, sir, I'll just have a word with the lady, then we'll be on our way."

"Be my guest," said John gesturing towards the staircase. He closed his eyes while the police walked past him, giving him a curious glance. No one had really explained what he had to do with all this. The lady had rung the police and given a swift rundown of an average sort of domestic, an angry husband running off with a toddler, but no one had mentioned another fellow – well, that was probably what had made the husband go off on one. It usually was a third party in his experience.

After a moment John rose to his feet and went off to find the kitchen. With any luck he would be able to find the ingredients to make a cup of tea – though it would probably be sans milk. He smiled ruefully to himself as he thought how Ted would mock him now, making tea, when he had spent so long telling the farmer what an old woman he was with his ever-present brew in his hands.

But sometimes you just needed a cup of tea and there was no getting away from it.

CHAPTER THIRTY FIVE

"Rhiannon and Pwyll seemed made for each other but a curse clouded their love and marriage"

When the man from the Ministry arrived, Theo, John and Fliss walked out of the house together to greet him. They all looked weary, he thought, but then who wouldn't have a sleepless night if they thought the curse of Foot and Mouth might rear its ugly head again? He would never know how John drove through the night to get them back, Megan slumbering on the back seat, Fliss silently weeping and alternately fuming in the front. Bryn Elmsworth had been called every bad name under the sun, in a fierce whisper; with many a cautious glance thrown over her shoulder to make sure that her daughter wasn't awake and listening. He had bourn it all stoically. He could have added a few epithets himself, if the truth were told, but all in all he felt it was better if he stayed out of it.

The tour of the farm didn't take long and it was obvious to all that far from being infected, Theo's animals were all healthy and well-cared for. The official took some blood tests, "to be sure" but was happy to assure them that he doubted they had anything to worry about. He asked that John stay until the results were through and then he was gone.

As he drove away, Inspector Piper arrived and they drew up next to each other with their windows lowered. Fliss watched as the policeman showed the official his warrant card and they exchanged a short conversation, then Piper came on into the farm-yard and the other man drove off down the lane.

"Good morning Mrs Elmsworth," said Piper in a bright and friendly voice, "You know the oddest thing happened last night. I had a report from two neighbouring police forces that a woman answering your description was involved in some trouble – but of course I knew it couldn't be you, because I had told you not to stir off this spot."

"Never moved an inch, Inspector," she assured him, equally brightly.

"So the man who was accompanying this woman couldn't possibly have been Professor Norton, then? Even though it was a vehicle which appeared to be registered to his name and it was spotted in the vicinity of your old address?"

John had joined them when he heard the policeman's voice, "What's all this, Matt?" he asked.

"The inspector thought that we had been out and about last night, John," said Fliss, "But I have told him that it must have been a mistake."

"Oh, absolutely," said John, "Can we do something for you, Matt?"

"Yeah, you can drop the BS for a start," answered Piper with a grin, "I've brought some photos and details for Mrs Elmsworth to have a look at, see if we can identify our bog man. Merrington is still holding out on us. He can't deny Fergus's murder is down to him, because his girlfriend is singing like the proverbial canary, in the hopes of getting off with rehab instead of jail, but he's refusing to admit all knowledge of the first man."

"Come inside. Do you want a drink?" asked John, hastily changing the subject, Fliss felt like giving him a swift nudge. He couldn't have looked more guilty if he had tried. It was starting to become a habit with him, losing his cool. She still wished he had punched Bryn last night. She would have liked to see the bully cowed for once in his life.

They went into the parlour and Piper took out a thick file from the briefcase he was carrying, "Take your time, Mrs Elmsworth, I'll understand if you can't find a face to match your memory of the man."

That's because you don't really believe I saw him, thought Fliss cynically. Of course he could be quite right – and she had begun to doubt her own ability to recall the man's face now. It all seemed such a long time ago and it was beginning to seem much less real and like the dream everyone had insisted it had been.

She began to scan the pages, but no-one looked familiar. Out of the thousands he had on file, Piper had pruned the selection as hard as he could. They were all youngish men of approximately the right age and build; they all had dark or auburn hair. They had all gone missing at the same time as the bog body. They all had at least one sister.

As the pile of rejections built, Fliss began to feel depressed. What she couldn't forget was that all these young people were missing from home. She knew now how hard that must be for their parents. Megan had been out of her hands for three or four hours, but every moment had been agony. All of these boys had been missing for years. How much heartache was contained within the covers of this folder?

Suddenly his face was there in front of her. She looked up at Piper, who had been sitting back in his chair, his legs negligently crossed, drinking the cup of coffee that John had made for him. He was having a very relaxing hour out of the office, the only thing missing was a cigarette, but he realised he couldn't light up with a child in the house. Fliss had tried to hide her presence and Ted had been sent to sneak her outside to feed the pigs, but Piper had heard her childish whispering as she had passed the door, "Why have we got to be quiet, Uncle Theo?"

Fliss handed the sheet of paper, with its attached photograph to him, "This is him, Inspector. Kevin Drew. That's the man I saw right in this very room, with his throat slashed."

He said nothing, merely took the document she held out to him. Kevin Drew had been one of the more likely candidates because his sister had reported him missing, saying that they were alone in the world, both parents were dead and they had been raised in care, where they had lost touch for quite a number of years, before being reunited just before his mysterious disappearance.

"You're sure about this, Fliss?" he asked, surprise making him forget formality.

"As sure as I can be."

"Thank you, you've been very helpful. We'll see if we can track down his sister and see if there is anything about the body that will make identification possible. We'll try DNA as a last resort, but I'm not sure if it can be retrieved from his body, due to the tannic acid present. I'll let you know what happens."

"I would like to know, thanks."

She showed him out just as Megan appeared around the side of the pig sty, "Oh, Megan, has Emma been kind enough to bring you home? That was nice of her."

Piper grinned at her, "Don't even go there, Fliss. I'm a detective not a traffic cop!"

She smiled back, but had the grace to look a little shame-faced, "It was an emergency," she pleaded.

"So I heard. Do you want me to do anything about that husband of yours?"

"Oh, I think some minor harassment might be in order," she said, her eyes narrowing as she recalled his behaviour. He laughed, "Madam, I think you have entirely the wrong idea about the police force – but I'll see what I can do."

With that he was gone and Fliss went back in to see what she could find to eat.

Over lunch she told John and Theo that she thought she had identified the bog body and whilst Theo took it as fact, John appeared to be rather shocked.

"And Piper accepted your word?" was his incredulous comment.

"He seemed to. He said he'll let me know the outcome."

"Remarkable," murmured John.

Megan was obviously exhausted by her hectic night and early morning, so Fliss took her upstairs for a nap. John was alone in the kitchen when she returned and she felt suddenly awkward in his presence. Last night now seemed oddly dreamlike – well night-marish would have been a more accurate description – and she had no idea what to say to him.

He smiled when she walked into the room, but it was the polite smile of a stranger and she wondered what on earth he must be thinking of her and Bryn. They had not exactly given the impression that they were ideal parents, or even civilised human beings. She hated to be thought of as common, but what else could one call it when the police were summoned to a classic 'domestic'? She felt like shrivelling with shame at the very notion of becoming a statistic on a police report.

"I suppose you can leave now?" she asked, going to the sink and beginning to fill it with water in preparation for washing the lunch dishes.

"Leave that, I'll do it," he said promptly.

"Are you sure you know how to?" she couldn't stop herself. She hadn't seen him do anything vaguely domestic since she had met him.

"Of course I do," he said, quite insulted, "I'm a single man. I've been looking after myself for years."

"I've noticed you still wear your wedding ring," she tried to sound casual, but the barb was there hidden behind the words. He looked down at his hand then glanced at her.

"So do you," he replied.

Of course she did. But it was only force of habit. She took it off there and then and threw it on to the kitchen table where it spun and rattled loudly in the ensuing silence. She walked out of the room and he did as he had promised and washed the pots.

Fliss climbed the stairs and popped her head around the bedroom door to make sure Megan was still sleeping, which she was, and when she came back John called her to join him in the parlour.

"If you've finished the pots, I'll go and dry them," she said.

"Let them drain," he ordered her and she shrugged, "Okay," She looked around, "Theo not here?"

"No, he's gone to the Weary Sportsman for what he called, 'a well-earned pint'."

"I thought that man told us not to leave the farm," said Fliss innocently.

"And now you want to listen to him?" was the sarcastic reply. Fliss giggled, "I suppose it is a little late in the day for that," she conceded, dropping onto the sofa with a sigh, "I wonder how long it takes for ribs to heal," she added, ruefully gripping her side.

"Does it hurt?" he asked sympathetically.

"Yes, it does."

"As much as a broken heart?" She shot him a surprised look, debating whether to take him seriously or treat the comment light-heartedly. This was territory she had firmly decided she didn't want to explore, but since he had brought it up she refused to be swayed. She lifted her chin defiantly and looked him straight in the eye, "I wouldn't know," she said, "You'd be the expert on that, I suppose. I wanted to lose my husband, but I understand you were very much in love with your wife."

It was evidently not the answer he had been expecting for he looked shocked that she had mentioned it, "Yes," he said at length, as though the words were being wrenched from him, "I was. But it was a long time ago."

"Perhaps not long enough."

He frowned, "What do you mean by that?"

"Nothing. It just seems that maybe you are not ready to move on."

He raised a quizzical brow, "And you are?"

"It's not hard, when you are moving on from a complete arse, is it?" she asked bitterly.

He suddenly threw back his head and began to laugh, a real hearty belly laugh, that made Fliss smile just to hear it, "What?" she asked, "What have I said that's so funny?"

"Stand up, Mrs Elmsworth," he said and in bemused silence she obeyed him, "Where does it hurt?" she pointed to her right side, "So if I were to put my hand here, you'd be able to stand it?" he asked, suiting words for action and she allowed herself to be pulled against him,

"What are you going to do now?" she whispered.

He showed her.

Theo walked in and found them kissing, so he exited hastily. About bloody time, he murmured as he went into the kitchen to make tea, noticing as he did so that there were two wedding bands lying on the old, worn oak table, sparkling in the afternoon sun as it shone through the window.

John and Fliss never knew he had been there and when they finally parted, Fliss sank back down onto the sofa, "You've made my knees go all wobbly," she complained.

"Good," he said, "Now, will you marry me?"

"No."

She had the satisfaction of seeing him looked utterly baffled, "You won't?"

"Not yet," she amended hastily, "I am, of course, madly in love with you, but I have to prove something to myself first."

"And what might that be?"

"That I can manage on my own. I married Bryn because I was afraid of being alone. I won't make that mistake again. I shall stay here with Theo, and I'll find a school for Megan, then I'll get a job – and you can woo me," she added complacently.

"I can what you?"

"Woo me, like in the old days. You can bring me flowers and take me out on dates."

He laughed again, "Thanks," he said, "That's mighty big of you."

"I thought so," she grinned back at him.

"And is Megan still asleep?" he asked.

"Yes, I think so, why?"

"Because I want to share a big double bed with you and reacquaint myself with all those parts of you that Douglas Merrington very kindly made sure I saw in their full glory."

Her mouth dropped open and she blushed deliciously, "A gentleman would never have reminded me of that," she said with mock severity.

"A gentleman would never have looked in the first place."

"Very true. But I'm afraid you are out of luck anyway. I couldn't possibly do anything strenuous whilst I have broken ribs."

He looked deflated, "Dammit, I had forgotten."

"Obviously."

"How long does it take to mend broken ribs?" he sat on the sofa beside her and kissed her gently once again.

"I asked you that," she said, melting into his embrace.